To Cameron!

With Love

Osha

Carter

2023!

MW01532355

Here We Go...

The Grand Finale

O'Shan Waters Books

The Moments Collection

1. *Moments With You*
2. *Making French Chocolate – A prequel love story*
3. *Moments In Time – A Lineage Saga*
4. *Moments Of Reset – A New Beginning*

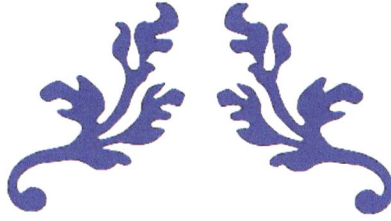

MOMENTS OF RESET

A New Beginning

An O'Shan Waters Novel

Moment Of Reset-A New Beginning © U.S. Copyright 2023

All rights reserved. No part of this book may be reproduced in any form or by any means without the prior written consent of the author.

This work is fiction. References to real places, people, events, organizations, and historical facts are intended only to provide a sense of authenticity and are used fictionally. Artists, groups, and public individuals are credited for their works at the time of reference within the story. All other characters, all events, and dialog are strictly from the imagination of the author, and therefore, not real. Any similarities beyond realism reference for the story are purely coincidental. This book is intended for mature adult readers. It contains adult and intimate situations, trauma, Christian beliefs, mental anguish, and grief that may evoke feelings or be triggering for some.

Nom De Plume is O'Shan Waters
Moment of Reset is published by Primedia eLaunch LLC.
Custom Cover Design by Germancreative – Lesia
Custom Images Designed by Yuri Dikhtyar
Custom Images and Graphic Support by Lai Sun Ip and Kam Wing Lo
Other Images from Canva and CanStock
Edited by Celina Rhoads
Edited by Abusina Salahuddin
Formatting by Shakil Ahmed
Print by Lulu.com in The United States of America
ISBN 979-888895362-4

ISBN 979-888895362-4

9 798888 953624

Acknowledgments

The magnificent circle of remarkable women who carry me through trials and enhance my life joy, love, and encouragement from the true sisterhood bonds we share. Beautiful Diva Dolls: Wendy, Laura, Tamara, Hope, Tiana, and Monti. Agape'!

Dear ladies in Arkansas. The two of you have lifted me higher than I ever thought I could soar. Blessings and love to Shelley K. and Sue K., Gamsahabnida!

Much love and thankfulness to Mom, Virginia, Vonda, Bev'lin, Christina, Sherry, Earl, Derrick, Sheila, B.J., Ms. O, Tavie, Kwam, Rin Rin, Dad, Naya, Rene, Dr. Addie, and others. Arigatō!

Grateful to those authors that shared their experiences to help me shine a bit brighter. Thank you, Shiree, Pepper, Dion, Henery, and Robert.

My complex and beautiful muse, from midnight dreams you inspired me to creatively explore an remarkable story of hidden truth, perfection in imperfection, unbreakable bonds, and true love... Merci beaucoup d'être vous!

.

Dear Reader

Moments Of Reset is the final novel in The Moments Collection. This story will encapsulate the forward path that I had always envisioned for the intricate and beautiful, French, and African American, Sony Music Entertainment International Director, Chantal-Marie Delacroix. The pages within are the next moments following Chapter 61 *Avenir Promis* from *Moments With You*, yet long before its brief *Epilogue-Alors*.

Moments Of Reset is a multi-genre masterpiece with elements of drama, suspense, psychological trauma, emotional and intense situations, interconnecting and complex relationships. There will be descriptions of different cultures, traditional and religious customs, grief, vengeance, fear, hope, sensual love, organizations, and a Christian faith with a speculative viewpoint.

Although this is the continued story from Moments With You, to appreciate the historical significance, and reflection references, it would be important to have read the prequels before this final novel in my collection.

To all who believe in and hope for never-ending true love, Marie and I would like to personally thank you for traveling along this journey with us.

O'Shan Waters

Playlist

This is a list of music to feel the moments within the pages of Moments Of Reset. Some songs are referenced, and others were used for mood inspiration when creating this story. Enjoy. Available on www.oshanwaters.com.

1. Mark Tuan x Sanjoy: One in a Million
2. Maxwell: The Suite Theme
3. Alicia Keys: Butterflyz
4. Lady Gaga: I'll Never Love Again
5. Baekhyun: U
6. Jodeci: My Heart Belongs to U
7. Cloé Mailly: Ici
8. Damien Escobar: Phoenix
9. India Arie: Strength, Courage, and Wisdom
10. Pyotr Ilyich Tchaikovsky: Swan Lake, Op. 20 Enchanted Lake
11. Carpenters: Close To You
12. GOT7: Page
13. Phyllis Hyman: You Know How to Love Me
14. G.Q.: Disco Nights
15. Pasquale Grasso ft. Samara Joy: Solitude
16. Andrea Vanzo: Soulmate
17. Hyolyn: Crazy of You
18. Tony!Toni!Tone!: Anniversary
19. Barry White: Love's Theme
20. Nat King Cole: Fascination
21. Rachelle Ferrell ft. Will Downing: Nothing Has Ever Felt Like This
22. Sabrina Claudio: Orion's Belt
23. Monsieur Nov ft. Tayc: Ma Femme
24. Maxwell: Downdeep Hula
25. Justin Timberlake: Can't Stop The Feeling
26. Michael Bublé: Sway
27. Pamela Williams: The Perfect Love
28. GOT7: Nanana

Table of Contents

Prelude... 15

Collection: Circles and Lines.. 17

1. Moonlight Kiss 19

2. Morning Dew 25

3. Isolated Island 29

4. Ripples in Reality 33

5. Darn Cheng Brothers... 41

6. Bundle of Love 49

7. Korean vs Other People.. 55

8. Uh Oh, Birthday 59

9. Be Wise My Daughter... 65

10. March 12th.. 73

11. Moon and Sun 79

Collection: Close Windows, Open Doors 87

12. Unexpected Kindness 89

13. Black Aunties 93

14. South Koreans 109

15. SME 113

16. Trey Aminbello..119

17. It's June..129

18. New York 135

19. Them Escobar's 141

20. Temptation 149

21. Brooklyn 159

22. Refocus 165

Collection: Change, Conviction, Courage 169

23. Four Fun 171

24. Script Change..175

25. The Best Life 185

26. Adjustments 193

27. Diva Doll Lola..201

28. Breach..209

29. Idol Protocol...213

30. What's Happening 223

31. Busan 235

32. Race 245

33. Beyond..253

34. Win, No Draw 263

Collection: Nuts, Bolts, and Relationships 273

35. Mother - Daughter 275

36. Louis & Tangee..285

37. Music Notes 297

38. Surprise...311

39. Black Love 321

40. Friendship Love...341

Collection: Breathe in Love, Breathe out........................353

41. Jae Lune-Philippe'..355

42. Jin Soleil-Maximillian 359

43. Jolie Arabie Sable 363

44. Kang Cheng...367

45. Shifting Tide...393

46. Ready, Set..401

Collection: Released Trapped Air..................................411

47. Adventure 413

48. London Paris...425

49. Lyon, France...431

50. Unspoken Secrets...439

51. Truth of the Matter.....................................453

52. Unboxed Memories......................................461

53. Grands-parents Géniaux...............................471

54. Au Revoir..477

55. Découverte..483

56. Three Sixty...499

57. Faith & Endurance.......................................517

Collection: Forever and ever and...................535

58. Paradise...537

59. "UWA!"...541

60. Bliss...551

61. Home..563

62. Touch..573

63. Wonderful..583

64. Cosmic..623

65. Rhapsody...627

66. JGGAM..665

67. Euphoria..673

And Then...687

Prelude

Spring 2019

"Is he actually staring at me, right now?"

It looks like I am playing it cool, but deep down I'm melting like butter in a saucepan over high heat. From where he stands, his gaze has me on pause. Our eyes lock. Contact. I am weak. *(What is happening to me?)*

I tell myself, *(Look away, Marie. Look away!)* I can't. I'm doomed. Locked in his invisible clutches, I am trapped in peril yet surrounded by his majesty. Lured into him. As his prisoner, I am securely held. Those eyes have captured me. Silently his eyes of magic fire, call out my name and whisper to my heart.

Yeux Chocolat Noir (Dark Chocolate Eyes)

Stage ready, cameras on
Eyes like carbon atoms under extreme heat and pressure
Captivating they sparkle under artificial lights
Highlighted perfectly with deep definition
You are powerful, sensual, dark and dense
Smoky with a hint of alluring danger
Seductively peering through an intense gaze
Dim the lights, pause, and replay
Natural eyes in their purest form
Almond shaped orbs of the richest decadence
Resting within the color of growing cotton
Its complexity is timeless and unchanged
Quick glances at strangers, lashes flutter
Holding trapped melodies and unwritten masterpieces
A voice speaking without words in an abyss of secrets

Silent sounds giving rise to untold stories shrouded behind
shadows
Through your gaze the language of truth and songs can be heard
And my heart has come alive by your rare and beautiful yeux
chocolat noir.

Once he spoke, I knew I wouldn't be able to resist him. It was his
unmistakable sultry voice that slowly began to break down the
binding fabric of my underwear. Then he gave me that legendary
flirtatious smile of his. *(Oh, my god!)* Quickly, I turned away to
disconnect from his jailer eyes and get control.

Moments later, I stiffened, hearing his voice, "I want to slowly
explore all of you." I gripped my glass as my legs buckled. He braced
me pressing his muscular body firmly up against mine. *(Oh...)*

Inhaling deeply, he mumbled, "kokonattsu." I closed my eyes
and whispered, "Oui noix de coco." He let go of my hair seemingly
surprised that I heard him say, "coconut" in Japanese.

Breaking from our lip collide, at last he shared his secret thought,
"Mmm, you taste sweet and delicious like chocolat chaud français
(French hot chocolate)." I giggled.

My body reacted with a flurry of goosebumps hearing his
command, "Marie, come with me, right now."

With caution thrown to the winds, I will go with him anywhere.

Collection: Circles and Lines

1. Moonlight Kiss

No retreat. No sleep. No escape.

Enrapt eyes dance without movement.

Trapped in the net of gravity pulling us toward each other, yet we are still. Rhythmic successions flow in its transparency triggers between breathless seconds.

Faded consonants and forgotten vowels linger in the air. Forming secret conversations between slightly parted lips, moistened from the unseen drops of heaven's tears. Silent strokes with tastes of liquefied sugarcane, warmed and determined to conquer. Synchronized fingers and palms explore curvature lines slipping through aquatic darkness.

Encased in connectivity with no release. I am his. An enslaved woman held captive by his invisible chains used to bind me. I cannot break away and run. I do not want freedom. Not from those almond-shaped dark chocolate arrows piercing through me with the power of shark teeth on flesh, yet with the tenderness of snowflakes falling. I willingly remain bound to his visual probes that grip my soul and call my name sending me into a responsive shiver.

Touching me I feel, light as air, heavy as earth. My skin melts like marshmallows over a fire, yet your kiss refreshes me as cool water hits the back of my throat on a summer day. Oh, how I delight in the magnificence of you. You, the one loving me. You are absolute in your purposeful existence bringing me to heightened ecstasy with a simple glance. Those airiness tones of coaxing whispers merged with Maxwell's "The Suite Theme" gliding through the atmosphere, seal my skin to yours. As moisten clay maneuvered by your powerful hands, control me to your whim. Don't stop handling me. I am wrapped in love's web. Show me no mercy.

Held delicately within his loving gaze, that it is only now, I can speak the words in my mind. "You're not a firework. Baby, you're my sun and moon, always bright and warm. Lighting my roadway with protection and tender affection. Wonderous. Mystical and comforting to my soul. I was made for you and you for me. A one-of-a-kind cosmic force sharing energy for life and moving the sway of ocean waves. Forever you are... you are my happiness."

"Marie..."

His natural sultry whisper detonates exploding surges all throughout my body. My heart flips as he slid his hands over my arm soothing the goosebumps that had risen from hearing him call my name. His powerful long fingers slid through my loose curls for a few minutes as his mouth continued to slowly collapse over mine. Welcoming his passion, I return the kiss with my own.

(I love him, so much. This is how love is meant to be. I am so grateful for him.)

Seconds away from my thoughts, without warning he gripped the back of my head, pulling his mouth away and breathlessly revealed his message, "Mmm, you taste sweet and delicious like chocolat chaud français. Gimme more, right now."

I giggled because his demand was so ravenous. He plummeted back to my mouth, as if he desperately wanted to confirm the taste again, while simultaneously extracting as much as possible in our connection. Embracing, with entangled lips we delve into the quintessence of one another.

His porcelain skin is firm from his vigorous exercise routine. He's so very meticulous about that; even being thirty pounds or so heavier than when we first met. *(Has it really been over ten years? Doesn't seem like it.)* I recall just about everything that happened in Paris and in Seoul. Down to what his scent was and the designer style of suit he had on. The charcoal grey Giorgio Armani with sapphire pinstripes wearing Acqua Di Gio was one of my favorites. But now I got him Armani Black Code and the scent on his skin makes me weak. *(It must be why I am lightheaded right now.)*

The words, "you intoxicate me." Breaks through my briefly parted lips, just before another firm kiss begins again. To the touch, every muscle feels smooth and warm, strong, and powerful. Inhaling deeply during the kiss I sense sweetness from his breath. *(What's sweet? Oh, it's the pancakes and maple syrup from earlier. Breakfast for dinner. Thanks for the idea, Tangee-girl! It is always yummy, especially getting this kind of aftertaste. Mmm.)*

A brief pause with separated lips and I snapped back into reality. With his thumbs, he began brushing the hair back from my face. Less than a minute later, he was peering into my eyes. Searching through the color of them with such intensity I felt as though he were inside my body tenderly caressing me from within. I dare not blink the sensation away. It was then I heard his sultry whisper, "Sunset on Arabian sand, did you even know, that your eyes energize my body through every cell. You give me power to live each moment. Your sweet coconut fragrance sends me adrift to a place of tranquility. The taste of you ignites the rage of flames inside me. I cannot quench my thirst enough, even if I drink every ounce of you, my sweet love. Beautiful Chantal-Marie, you are my air to breathe."

"Aww … the words you say. Jae-Sung Kim, you always sing to me, even when there is no music playing."

I heard his low slow moan travel briskly behind his airy words tickling my inner ear as we continued our journey of indulgence with long tongue kisses, fingers through hair, wet lips lightly brushing over skin, and interlocking hands.

"Je t'aime beaucoup." (I love you so much.) Echo amongst the airwaves that seem to hold back the hands of time. He groaned lifting himself to search for a deeper meaning from the message within my eyes. My head tilted to the left. Contact.

He smirked before releasing a smug statement of fact, "Awww… I'm your idol king."

Snickering, I nodded in agreement. Running the tip of his tongue along my jawline, he whispered, "Marie, you have to say it." Just before planting sweet kisses down the left side of my neck. Faintly delivering a muffled giggle, I shook my head no, and with sealed lips I confirmed my intentional defiance to not answer. Pausing from his licks and kisses, he rose to face me. I cut my eyes away from him.

"Say it." Firmly he demanded with a wrinkled forehead and squinting eyes. Refusing, I toss my head rapidly and quietly moan no. "Marie, I am your idol king. You better say it, right now." His voice was deep and commanding, but I remained firm in my refusal and pressed my sealed lips harder. Without delay, he lifted his smooth muscular body up from mine several inches and then forcefully fell on top of me. His body bounced on contact. I groaned as the collapse made a splat sound from our nakedness. He elevated himself again this time with more distance between us. He paused, holding himself over me by his hands flat on the bed over my shoulders. He stretched up his left eyebrow in that flirtatious way he does, that melts me like marshmallows over a campfire.

"Say it!" He gave a final warning to comply. I shook my head. He slammed himself on to me again. The impact caused a release from me, "AWW!"

His evil laugh grew louder as I moaned and giggled. When he raised his body off me again to repeat the playful torture. I shouted, "Ne (yes), ne! You're my idol king!"

With a sexy smirk, he froze above me, and said, "I win. Now, tell me... Where ya going, Marie? Where? Say it!"

Weightlessly drifting inside his dark chocolate orbs that seem to slightly shimmer in the moonlight, I reached up swirling my fingers over the butter cream colored skin of his smooth chest. Seconds later, I whispered, "Hong Kong."

He eased his warm body back down over me. Our skin liquefies as one. His lips pressed, my mouth opened, and his tongue crept inside calling its partner to the floor to dance. Deeply his kiss penetrates beyond barrier walls, and I receive all of him with delightful leisure.

(I love the way he kisses me.)

His fingertips send shock waves through my body with each touch to my skin. *(I want more.)*

Clutching for more of him, my hands pull at the thickness as my fingers slip through strands of his soft black hair and synchronize our mouth exchange with deeper dives and passionate moans.

(Oh baby... don't stop...)

While time is on pause and the world no longer turns, my love is about to devour me whole—

2. Morning Dew

As the morning light peeked through two windows of my bedroom, it was then I realized I had forgotten to close them with the ceiling shades the night before. My eyes squinted a moment before gradually adjusting to the increasing brightness of the room. While instinctively recognizing the piano melody of Andrea Vanzo's "Soulmate" being beautifully played and traveling through the air, I take in the sweet scent of the room. Twisting to stretch my naked body, I am nuzzled between soft luxurious bedding and numerous firm pillows covering my king-size bed oasis. Ironically, this expensive Prussian blue mulberry silk bedding set was a wedding present from Madame Angelique Dubois. I'm somewhat enclosed and buried under multiple pillows. Sitting up slowly, I exhale and begin moving all the strategically placed queen-size pillows to the far side of the bed. After moving the last one atop the others, I stop and stare at the pile of them stacked neatly where his body would usually be. For about a year, I had a nighttime routine to feel the pillow pressure snug at my left, just to help me sleep better.

"Was I dreaming? Again? It felt so real, not like a dream. Did that really happen? I think so. When did…?"

Speaking to myself in a low whisper, still reeling from my thoughts of intimate moments with him, I began processing the fragments of my dream to determine when and where it occurred. Then it came to me after several minutes. It was simply a night, years ago in this very room. I gasped holding my bare shoulders imagining him holding me. My cheeks felt a rush of warmth and I pressed my hand flat on my chest imagining his heartbeat next to mine. Hoping not to—nope. The sadness water began to build up like a dammed waterway as my eyes surveyed our bedroom. Our private place of love was so very different now. No longer was there his masculine vibe of black and red with a round pedestal bed and a high cushion headboard on the wall. He changed everything even with colors of cream and a variety of shades of blues to mirror the clear ocean water of our lover's paradise, Cocoa Island, Maldives.

While a few tears rolled down my cheeks, random words just came out, "He changed it for me. I know. I know. But I want to go back to the way it was. I miss… He's not here. Oh baby, I miss you so much."

Wrapping my arms around myself I began rocking back and forth slowly. It was happening again. I couldn't stop reality overtaking my mind. My love was gone. I was without him. My protector, my heart's joy was no more. Unable to bring back happiness from the dream, a burst of anger shot through my grieving tears.

"It's just these damn pillows! You left me here alone! Why did you go? Damn it! No one else… only you! Why?! Why did it have to be you?!"

I began hitting the pile of pillows at my left over and over. Seconds later, while gasping with sobs, I toss several of them down to the floor. When they were all removed, I fell back onto the bed stroking the sheet in search of the outline of his beautiful body. In that moment, it seemed to have faded from my memory and I cried harder. I wept and muddled words within my reality.

We had this incredible, majestic love. Jae-Sung Kim was indeed made for me. How could I not have known that forever was not part of our life together.

"Why were there only brief moments and not many years of being in his arms. Did he know before that he would leave me?"

"Secrets. Another one."

"You cheated me out of being with you. I'm so damn angry with you for doing that. Taking away my time. My right to be with you, every second of every moment until... I know, I know why. You promised but..."

Jae never wanted to see me sad or upset. He worked so hard to make our world special and give me as much love, protection, and joy as I could swallow in one gulp. But knowing why he didn't tell me he was sick, doesn't make me less angry about it. I wanted my time, and I can't have it now.

"I want my time. You punk!" My weeping continued for a long time. I managed to calm myself enough to say a random thought. "Forty-one. Oh, you like it when we are the same age for these two months. Ha-ha. So silly."

I exhaled glancing over to see that the time was 6:10 a.m. Wiping my eyes, I sat up and said a silent prayer of thanks and made a request for guidance and courage, as I did just about every morning before starting my day.

"I am gonna need your help, heavenly father. In just a few days, it will be a year. Three hundred and sixty-five days without him. How do I go on with this constant hole, in my chest, my heart, in my very soul?"

Although I think I handle things better now than I did at first, I tend to dream about him. I can't help it. For some reason around certain dates and with some memories, the dreams become more intense. I feel like I am living inside them, and I don't want to wake up. Jae will always be part of me.

"Marie, get up. You have work to do. It's a new month and a new day."

Prayer given, and mood boosting statement made. I'm off to shower and take on the day. Today is Saturday, March 1, 2031.

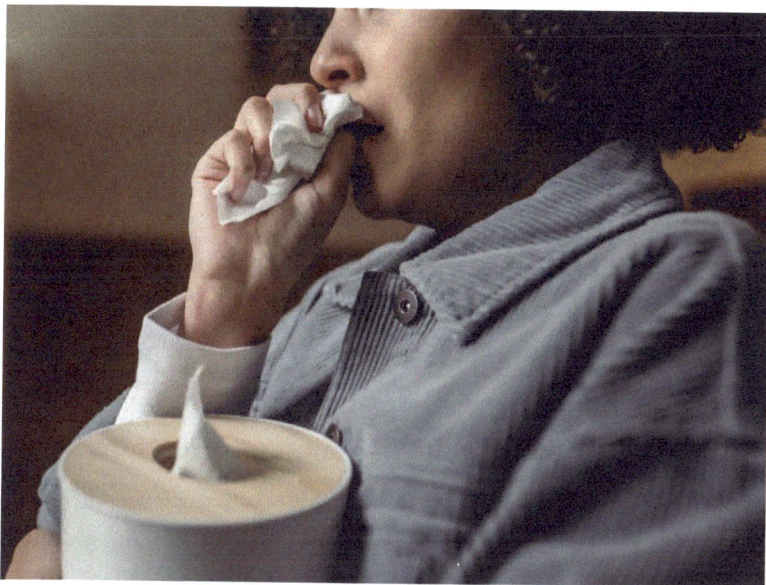

3. Isolated Island

These first months of this year have been more difficult than I thought they could be. I decided to do better by preparing my mind and heart for the feelings coming up from my memories. "How do I even do that? Why is this even happening?"

I reason to myself that maybe it's because I'm now living so far away from everybody. The sting of not having my family and friends around or with closer access like before when I lived in New York is constant. Yeah, I'm sure that's it. I regularly keep up with Renee, Antonio and my little boyfriend, Christopher who isn't so little anymore. "He is my heart, that one. I miss his hugs and kisses."

Now that my hair has grown back out more, Renee has finally stopped yelling at me for chopping it all off after getting settled here. Thinking back on it, some of our conversations were a little funny, especially when she would yell, "I can't believe you cut your hair off like that. I should punch you. No. Lola will! I am calling the Delta Diva

Dolls and telling them what you did! Expect some text messages of cussing out from Lola and Jazz at least! Did your mother see it? I was just there you didn't say anything about— Marie, you ain't getting chemo! This… This is not *Waiting to Exhale!* You for sure ain't Angela Basset playing the abandoned wife, doing the drastic hair chop because of your emotions. He did not leave you for a white woman! Oh, my god! What's wrong with you? You know damn well some sistah's can't do the whole natural hair movement. No matter how much they try, it is still jacked-up! Those who can fund it are keeping the weave hair business going strong just to pretend to have hair down their back that you have naturally. Hell, Lola's peeps would pay good money for it! Oh, you are so stupid, cow! If you are depressed, drink some damn wine! Don't cut your hair off again! Stupid ass!"

She is always so bossy. I liked the pageboy cut. It was easy but I'm glad it is grown back though. Lola did tell me off through an email and a text message, but it wasn't as bad. She has texted me the most out of the divas though. She likes to send silly GIF and Memes to make me laugh, telling me about stupid people in her office and her crazy family. *(She never changes. I love her.)*

Not sure why but we haven't had those Delacroix family calls for some reason. I talk to my parents every week, even chat with tantes (aunts) Gert and Heidi sometimes but it's different than it was before. I assumed my sister, Celeste, had been too busy to write to me or call. Having two growing children, a fireman husband, and a nurse practitioner career at the University of Washington Medical Center is a lot to juggle. I get it but I miss her.

I'm excited to make plans for family and friends to come visit us here in South Korea, maybe in the Summer. I know Renee and Lola are planning a trip. Latrice said she wasn't flying this far, and Tonja said maybe next year because her vacation budget is blown already.

My Delta sister, Tangee and her family connect with me about once a month over a scheduled video chat. My nieces are getting so big. Unfortunately, it's been about six months since I've talked to Jazz. I can't seem to catch her. In those occasional emails she has said her law firm made her partner, so that could be why, but everything is all so very different. In just a year my entire life has completely turned upside down. But I'm not alone. Jae's friends and family have been the best blessing. Especially living here and not having mine so readily available forces me to lean on them and they hold me up. I'm very grateful for them. But it's not the same. I almost feel like I'm surrounded by warm calm water but I'm still like an isolated island.

"I can't wait for mother to get here in a couple of days. I wish Pawpaw could come. But now that he has fully recovered, he said he is working on some things in Lyon with my oncles (uncles) Andreas, Tomas, and Chevalier, and my cousins Kristoff, Henri, and Tomas. I can see him with his musketeer brothers and adult nephews. I bet they are just sampling his homemade wine, watching women, and pretending to fence. *(Ha!)*

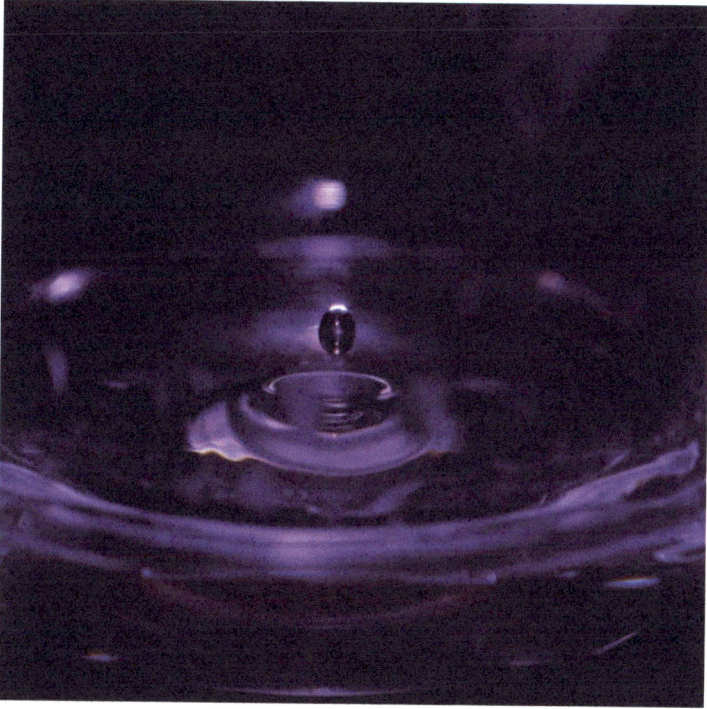

4. Ripples in Reality

Jae-Sung made it his primary duty to manage and control just about everything. He was a serious control freak! It got on my nerves. But it was his way of ensuring I was happy. I learned that early on. I found out much later in our relationship that he even kept life-changing secrets from me, just for that very purpose. So, his heart was in the right place with his mania. *(I love the punk!)*

At first, I didn't understand what he was doing. I mean, since he was sixteen years old, he had been the world-famous model, actor, songwriter, and singer Jin-K. The sultry lead singer of K-Pop boy group DRGN5 for over a decade. He had been this mega star in South Korea, and internationally for that genre of music. Then after that, you add the years of his solo K-Pop and K-R&B stardom; along with being sought-after as a music producer, songwriter, musician, and designer brand model. All that was a lot to carry around in his twenty-nine-year-old, gorgeous 6'1 muscular body, when we met in 2019.

Seems like a lifetime ago. Back then, I had been single and celibate for over four years and laser focused on my international business director career with Sony Music Entertainment. On the rare occasion I dated, it was only Black men, no exceptions. It didn't matter how many different types of men asked me out, it was an absolute no to musicians, actors, singers, or athletes. Everyone close to me knew that after that cheating dog NFL player Marquis R. Bush, my rule was no men with fans.

Celeste had asked me once, what was it about Jae that made me break all my rules that early Spring in 2019. My sister was so curious. Her eyes were huge eating her pizza in my New York condo, eagerly waiting for me to answer. Although I liked a few K-Pop songs from older groups like EXO, and my favorite was GOT7, I didn't really know who he was. Like the mega popular group BTS, I had seen his equally successful group DRGN5 on a South Korean award show. But I listened to all kinds of music from around the world, especially classical, smooth jazz, and old school French and American R&B. There was no way I could single him out. Let me tell ya, Jae-Sung Kim, known as Jin-K was a very popular and wealthy celebrity. However, he loved the fact that I didn't know who he was. He wasn't cocky but charming, mysterious, smart, and crazy fun. Our instant connection intrigued me, especially since there was no reason why I felt that way.

DRGN5's Jin-K was powerful, suave, and sexy, for a hunky South Korean pretty playboy singer of a mega internationally famous K-pop group. Yeah, okay. But I didn't swing that way. He wasn't my type of man, not physically anyway. First, he was Asian with white skin. Renee was right, he was too thin. I didn't admit it, but I weighed more than he did. I dig on tall, thick-chocolate professional men with low fades, chiseled or round pie faces, manicured hands and feet, deep voices that can hold meaningful intelligent conversations. A nonsmoker, educated, goal-oriented, proper English speaking, suit wearing, stylish man with just about everything pressed and oh, yeah, perfect white teeth were required. A giant tree to climb as we used to say. Wow, I sound like my girlfriend Jazz and my auntie Lolli. That's funny. I had a type, you feel me. My close circle knew it well. But I admit it now, my twenty-nine-year-old self just fudged on my rules once I saw his eyes. Those dark diamonds spoke to me in perfect French and English, and I was curious.

Thinking about it now, sometimes when he looked at me from across a room it felt as if I was standing in the middle of a crescendo of ocean water colliding upon rocks. He made me tremble from inside my bone marrow. As an open vessel he filled me to the brim then overflowed me with tantalizing delight. Jae could move me without a single touch. It was the beauty of the forbidden. His intensity when he fixed his eyes on me reminded me of music from Damien Escobar called, "Forbidden Love", Marvin Gaye's "I Want You," Donell Jones' "I Wanna Luv U," Will Downing's "Moods," and October London's "Back to Your Place."

I remember how much he wanted to make love to those songs and so many more. *(Freaky idol man. Hee, hee.)* "Oh, I gotta turn on one right now!" I just fell into having no boundaries. So dangerous! It could've turned out horrible. Fortunately for me, he wasn't some creepy horny guy, looking to hook-up with a plus size foreign Black woman for the night. Renee told me to loosen up and I did. Jae was a gentleman. He wanted to get to know me, not have sex. His K-Pop idol game was so much fun. Well, the parts I remembered, anyway. Then weeks later we met again at the celebrity auction. When he stared at me from across the room, I melted like hot wax from a candle in that designer blue gown Renee picked out for me to wear. That was it. Yep, a seductively thrilling experience for my memory book and late-night fantasy dreams.

Two years later I got a surprise, and I floated right back into him. As we got to know each other, being with him felt like some gravitational pull that I couldn't describe or understand. Being near him just put me in a state of feeling the deepest sense of security and comfort. With him was tranquility at a heightened magnitude. Our unexplainable connection made me trust him right away and do a list of things unlike me to ever do. I fell for him hard. He changed the game, and I did things totally outside of character for me. To be real about it, I was his secret American lover, and I didn't mind either. It's so weird how your heart can make you forget who you are, if you are not careful. My whole life changed, and I tossed my values and self-respect out the window just because of how I felt being with him, what he gave me, what I gave him and the magic we had together. I was so stupid in the beginning! Freely opening my legs and heart to this stranger from another world.

I never believed it was more than it was until he broke my heart. I knew then that I loved him. The brief time helped me evolve as a woman in her thirties and I was grateful for him being in my life. I thought of him as a firework. Something wonderful. A spectacular display of vibrant light that lit my dark lonely sky for a short time and then was gone. He was a famous person, I'm not. Confident and successful in my career, an established bi-racial woman, world traveler but not famous. Who was I kidding? What it was, was a moment, and I was grateful for having the time and the secret love.

As the months past, I... I was over him, right? Yeah, and moving forward. Check. But without warning, I was in a private space with Jin-K, and Jae-Sung refused to let me go. I remember he used to say I was his calming source— a touchstone. I witnessed that to be true.

He loved me and I loved him. It was sensational and deep because we were made for each other. At every moment with my love, I felt I was living the lyrics and floating through the melody of Alicia Keys song, "Butterflyz."

Like I said, over our years together, his meticulously organizing, managing things, and even keeping secrets, protected me. They really did. Jae-Sung cherished me. It was the feeling of being wrapped up tight in a soft warm blanket on an icy cold, rainy night. Don't get me wrong, I did find it irritating sometimes. I'm an independent, educated, commanding and strong woman. I didn't need anyone controlling aspects of my life. But I allowed Jae to handle me that way, simply because it came from an honest place of selfless love. I really miss it, now.

Right before he died, Jae-Sung put specific orders in place regarding our children. So typical. Having the daily help of Nah-Min-Ji's niece Nari as our live-in nanny was one. Twenty-six-year-old Nari Lee is a godsend. I didn't realize how much I would need and value her support and company, living here without him. My man was so smart! Nari speaks Korean, English, Japanese and a little French. Which gave me back up, to team teach our children different languages. She's sweet. Always calling me older female cousin in Korean. Being just twenty-six with looks very close to actress Lee Min-Jung, I curiously asked her, "What made you want to be our nanny? Why not a model? I mean, you're lovely, Nari. Did you want to do this in school?" I had purposefully asked her when we were alone so she would feel comfortable telling me honestly.

She looked up at me holding her teacup, and said, "Eonni (older sister) Marie, I have my nursing degree. But when I was told oppa-sachon (older brother-cousin) was going to have twins, I volunteered to leave the hospital. I wanted to help when kun sam chon Min-Ji (Mother's older brother; her uncle), and oppa Jae-Sung discussed it. There was a list of Korean customs and traditions drafted out to teach each child and provide medical aid. I love children. I saw this as a great honor in our family." She sipped her tea very slowly, waiting for my response.

I hired Nari and she started living with us in August 2030. *(Huh? I interviewed the three girls Min Cha screened for the nanny position. I hired her. Right? He planned this too?)* I was shocked and silent for a while. After processing what she said I wanted clarification.

"Wait… Nari, you mean you were part of the plan all along. I don't believe this!" She smiled and tapped my hand saying, "Eonni, Marie—"

I cut her off, with an elevated voice. "No, don't older sister me all sweet like that! You were in on it the whole time! He planned all this out. Oh, what else am I going to dig up and find out. Oh my god! What a punk!"

Nari looked away trying to conceal her giggling from my outburst. She waited a few minutes before she lowered her head to connect with my 'I'm irritated' rolling eyes. "Eonni, oppa Jae-Sung was one of my favorite sachon (cousin), in our daegajok (large-extended family). I wouldn't have volunteered to help anyone else. Besides I was curious to get to know you at the same time. I hoped to learn French and American things from you. I was given instructions not to say anything earlier."

(Of course, this was all planned. Who was my husband? Dummy.)

Jae outlined what, where, who, when, and how specific things were to be done with his family, especially the Korean culture part. So, on this day in late November last year, I found out instructions were not just for the Cheng brothers, his attorneys, and me but for Nari Lee too. Oh, brother! But I love him for doing it.

5. Darn Cheng Brothers

Jae-Sung delegated his childhood friends and security managers, Kang, and SI Cheng to teach the triplets traditional things. I knew that. He was clear about wanting all three to be culturally balanced little people. We were in sync on that without ever discussing it. Kang, and SI are family. I trust them completely. We had been home for a few months, and it dawned on me that they had been playing an idol brothers game with me. When I would question them about what they were doing with my children, they would grin and say, "Noona (older sister), it's on the list for Korean responsibility."

Yeah, they were lying!

- Giving my babies seaweed to taste.
- Handing them dried squid to help their teeth come in quicker.
- Trying to give them radish kimchi to build good bones.

- Making them crawl around for an hour a day, completely naked for a smooth complexion.
- Wearing edible face masks for special Korean vitamins.
- Teaching them to eat as fast as they can, to honor their Korean ancestors.

And that wasn't all. I grew increasingly suspicious and started to ask their mother if these were customary when raising children. Yeah, aunt Teng shook her head laughing. But before I could confront these idol uncle jokers, it happened…

I had been out with SI's wife and daughter one day. Soo, Hana, and I came in from the market to a scene I never thought I would see. Immediately, I screamed, "What are you doing? Why are they like that?!"

My three eight-month-old babies were surrounded by pillows and colored ropes that created lanes. Each one of my children had a stuffed animal strapped on their back. Kang and SI were on the floor at the far end motioning to them with the bait: a bowl of rice, a few skewers of rice cakes, a bowl of fruit, a chocolate bar, Goldfish bread, and a Hello Kitty cup. The race had already begun, and they didn't stop when we came in. The living room was loud with male chanting in French and Korean.

"Va! Va! Va! Allez Jae, Jolie, Jin! Qui va gagner?"

"Gada! Gada! Gada! Eoseo jae, peuliti, jin! Nuga igilkkayo?"

(Go! Go! Go! Come on! Who will win?)

Shouting, "Stop! Stop this right now!!" I rushed and stood in front of these giant kids that call themselves men. When I looked at the scene, I was really trying not to laugh, as my cute little bundles were giggling and crawling to their uncles luring them with bait. Kang and SI looked at me with sad faces still tilting their heads around me to coax the three to keep coming toward them and the finish line.

"Wait, Noona. Wait. I bet twelve thousand won. I know Jolie will win. Let us finish. Kang won last time; I want to get my money back." SI pleaded with a whiny voice, yet he kept his eyes on the racers. He gave a quick glance over to his wife Soo, before he flashed his fake sad eyes at me, which was code for get out of the way you mean lady!

Before I could answer, in the distance I heard the sniggles and giggles from the drooling three amigos behind me. When I turned around, they had gotten much closer. Jolie was definitely ahead but Jin and Jae were a few inches behind her wiggling diapered booty. I couldn't help but chuckle at the cuteness overload with those happy faces. Once I was distracted watching them for a few seconds, SI and Kang took the opportunity to encourage them with sweet baby talk and food rewards. Soo made a move to pick up Jae from his floor track, marked lane number 2 but as she reached to grab him, there was an echoing thunderous, "Aniyo! Ani, geuleul delileo gajima (No! No don't pick him up)!"

The shouting words came from somewhere and she froze. I turned around confused, looking at her and then the Cheng brothers. *(Who was that?)* I knew it wasn't the five of us in the room. At the same time, Hana got on her knees smiling as Jin started to move toward her out of his racing lane 3.

"Ani (No)! Ani (No)!" Kang shouted. "Soo, if you pick him up, the guys forfeit and lose! They are on the video call. Hana, don't you pick him up. We can still win this. Jae got to win for me!"

Shocked I looked at the projected monitor screen that was linked to an elevated camera, and the connected DRGN5 group members were cheering. "What?! Who is that—BJ, Shane, Ethan . . . You crazy idol brothers—! My children are not— Oh, I... I can't. Whatever. Fine."

Looking over at Soo, she had already backed up from her interference. I sighed and moved out of the way toward the dining room, and just shook my head. As the rowdy chants continued behind us, I nudged her. "Soo, we weren't gone that long. How did they even...?"

She snickered and said, "I think they plan it before we go."

Chuckling, I nodded in agreement. I couldn't believe these men and their idol games. *(I miss being together and games with Jae-Sung. I bet that is on the list to teach them silly made-up K-pop group idol games. They wouldn't tell me, but I bet it was.)* I exhaled. Hana put the bags in the kitchen. We grabbed chairs from the dining room table and watched. As soon as I sat down and faced the living room, all three little amigos were on their way— to me! Laughing, and thinking the game was over, I announced. "Ha, I win!"

But SI shouted, "Okay, now, first one to eomma (mommy) wins!"

Then there were cheers, "Yes! First to mommy!" "Go Jin!" "Get eomma!"

"Noona call Jolie!" "Ani, call Jae! Jae hurry!"

(OMG!)

Those kinds of shenanigans didn't stop. Oh, no, there were too many to write down. Another time, they had all three stacked up on top of each other, timing which one would stay on top the longest. That one I had to stop. After grabbing and securing my infants and making sure no one would fall, Kang tried to look so serious when he explained the so-called tradition. His tone was very diplomatic at first but as he went on, it sounded smug, more like a kid with his toy being taken away, but secretly hiding another one in his pocket.

"Noona! No one was going to get hurt. We would never put them at risk. We are not careless. They are Korean! We needed to see which one stays up the longest. It is a traditional Korean child raising strategy to teach stamina and balance. You have damaged their strengthening exercises now. You should be so ashamed. I am sad for you. Sad for Marie."

SI nodded in full support, I glanced over at Nari and her blushing told me it was another stupid game and not some Korean tradition. After that I created signals on what was customary and what wasn't. Nari would cough a few times. Soo was very quiet but would tap the tip of her nose. Min Cha would just laugh, and aunt Teng would pick up Jolie and say her name three times. We girls had to stick together for real. I love my blended family.

My sweet doll, Hana Cheng

When we are all together, sometimes it feels like Jae-Sung is here. Almost. A few times, we were laughing about some crazy idol brother story, and I looked around expecting Jae-Sung to come into the room and deny it or challenge them to a game of rock, paper, scissors to win the argument.

Just a few weeks ago, I actually said out loud, "Jae, I know Jin-K is not gonna let him get away with that!"

Immediately, Kang, SI, Soo, and Nari stopped laughing and stared at me. I didn't know why they weren't talking for a few seconds. Then it hit me what came out of my mouth. Hana touched my hand calling me auntie and telling me what everyone was thinking, "Mianhae (I'm sorry), samchon (uncle) Jae-Sung is not here anymore."

I suddenly had a feeling of being very cold and gave a fake smile before excusing myself to retreat in the solitude of my bedroom. I remember, as soon as I opened the door, I had a pain in my chest that felt as if it had been ripped open by a crowbar. I fell to my knees before reaching the bed. I cried for a long time.

When I have those kinds of days, I write in my journal. It seems to help me get out what I want to express about him or say to him if he were here. Journaling is still the only consistent way for me to release my feelings during times, I am plagued with memories that are followed by debilitating sadness.

It's amazing how the brain works. An intentional and involuntary receptacle for tangible and non-physical things. Ideas, memories, images, even sounds are recalled back so vividly as if you are right back there in that time and place.

Well, maybe it is just me, but I can see him so clearly on stage performing. Being sexy with his choreographed dance moves in sync with his back up dancers or his idol brothers. I even hear his beautiful voice singing his K-R&B and K-pop songs. The way a crackling fireplace fire can cover a chill on the skin are my memories of him.

Jae was so much more than what he let the public see. My husband was a kind, humble, romantic, and committed man. Even though he told me regularly with positive affirmations of how he felt just when I came in a room. His retelling in detail, what he found beautiful in my curvaceous plus-size sixteen full-figure, the caramel color of my skin that perfectly mixed my French father and African American mother, the scent and wave of my hair, and my eyes. Oh, how he loved to look into my eyes. His lyrics to songs he wrote about me sharing with the world his desire and love for the physical, intellectual, and secret internal parts of me. I had felt a bit astonished how he felt about me and why he would let me inside his protective celebrity cover back then. But I am forever grateful for the true blessing he is. Was— No, he is!

I miss my best friend, my protector, my companion, and my love. Jae-Sung Kim is a one-of-a-kind human being and the other side of my coin, just as my brilliant and amazing father, Jean-Philippe' Henri Delacroix said years ago when he gave his blessing again in Paris.

Jae made me complete, and so very happy. I feel guilty sometimes remembering how magnificent our love story was. Because I get angry that it was so brief. It was, damn it! 2019 to 2030 was not long enough! In there, it was two years I lost because of Covid-19, then the time I wasted leaving him, thinking he would be better off with someone Korean. I want my time back! If I had known our last time would be our last time, I would have said more, done more to show him how much I need him. Love him. Depend on him, adore him. *(Exhale. I need a minute.)*

I need to stop torturing myself this way. There are no do overs or second chances. Time moves forward not backward. I must be stronger than this but keep my memories of our love close living without him, now.

I'm glad I listened to my father and sister and finally put together the story of us in a book. Because it helped me organize my memories and my cherished *Moments With You.*

Saranghae *(I love you)*, Jae-Sung Kim.

6. Bundle of Love

Our bouncing bundle of three are the continuation to our love story. I think so anyway. It's hard to believe my three amigos are going to be one-year olds, tomorrow, March 9, 2031. I remember just about every book I read, music we listened to, movies I watched, and times they kicked me from inside that giant belly. These *Focus Factor* vitamins from Costco, I'm taking must work selectively because sometimes I can't remember if I have eaten or how many glasses of wine I had. But somehow, I remember the details of these miraculous moments in my life. *(Weird.)* It's a good thing I write things down like Pawpaw taught me from a young age.

Without even looking at my journal, the day they were born I remember, it wasn't raining. I couldn't believe it. It always rains in Seattle, Washington. *(Ha!)* Being at Swedish Hospital and going through every breathless minute traveling along this unfamiliar path of amazement, fear, excitement, laughter, and terror shock, looking back, I can say it made me deliriously dizzy with crippling emotions becoming a mother. But I wouldn't trade any second of it. A heavenly blessing leaving me small morsels of Jae I can nibble on as they grow up.

Days after their arrival, Jae-Sung and I purposely chose names we felt would best represent everyone and honor their blended ancestry of South Korean, French, and African American.

Jae Lune-Philippe Delacroix-Kim, our first-born son has his name to honor him. The word for moon in French, as an illuminating force unmovable and constant, strong, balanced, and tranquil, and my father's name to honor him. He is a perfect visual blend of all of us. Jae is a round toddler with curiosity that has him doing many things before his siblings. He loves rice and grapes, together. So weird. Ha!

Jin Soleil-Maximilian Delacroix-Kim, our second son has part of Jae's professional name Jin-K representing his honored parents, J from Jae-Sung's first name, I from his late father's name, N from his mother's name. The word for sun in French, as a bright warming light sustaining life through powerful energy, and my twin brother's middle name to honor him. He looks just like Jae-Sung. Jin is the thinnest but eats the most. He clearly has his father's DNA for that. He is the musical baby, always making noises and investigating sounds around the house. He will stop mid-action and pop his head up with big eyes whenever he hears a chime or bell or music playing. When I see it, I think of "Squirrel" and the pausing dog in the old, animated movie "Up" because he freezes for a couple seconds. It's so cute.

For our daughter I had no vote. He wouldn't even let me suggest. Jolie Arabie-Sable Delacroix-Kim is named the word Pretty and the words Arabian Sand in French. He named her specifically he said, "to represent my deepest love, ultimate joy, and the exquisite beauty I see in you, Marie." She's a blended beauty, yet different from Jae Lune. Little miss is a brown and chubby doll to me. She is smaller than her brothers but is quick. Darting off in stealth mode because she is so quiet. Jolie may very well be part idol brother ninja. She loves reading. When I have a book, she taps on the pages and then tries to talk when I am reading out loud. I think she likes my voice or to debate I haven't determined which.

Being a mother of triplets cannot be accurately described in any blog or book, it's exciting, crazy, scary, and exhausting. One goes one way; the other goes another and the third takes off in a different direction. Often, I'm like a mama octopus trying to grab them once they dart away. "Why did we ever teach them to walk?"

As my Gram-T used to express it when I was young, "Dell, dim babies be a hot mess wit dat quickin' sassiness. I loves 'um ta bits. Dis 'ere be brown pretty babies. Come over here give ya Gram-T sum ya good brown sugar, baby. Yum, yum. Lip smankin'; good! Hee, hee."

My mother's mother was so snuggly, fierce, and kissable. I think that's another reason why I like to kiss! Ha. I can still hear her Louisiana twang in her powerful tone. I miss my grandmothers. Eleanor "Teence" Wilson-Murry was tough as iron, judgmental and opinionated. I saw streaks of it a few times when I was younger, but she taught me a lot about being proud, strong, and Black. I remember she would say "Marie, don't matter, ya be Black. Ya don't crack fur no one. College wit high grades, no exception. Don't let women round ya good Black man. Don't be too trustin'. Be wit a strong Black man but if he cheats or beats, ya be by ya self. After ya beat his ass. Ya prove ya is a Murry by showin' dem how excellent ya be wit ya mind not ya body. No matter what day say, ya is Black and I love ya and ya grandpa Charlie loved ya too."

My grand-mère (grandmother) Marie Celine Delacroix was very different. She was this elegant lady with proper etiquette, gloved hands, and mild speaking voice. She had a prissy laugh and loved dressing up, fine dining and having afternoon tea. I'll never forget when all my French family went to the movies to see, *Titanic* with Leonardo DeCaprio and Kate Winslet. I wasn't even ten, but I loved all of it. Especially on the scene when Rose is on the staircase to meet Jack for their date, my grand-père Jean shouted, "C'est toi, ma chérie. Elle s'appelle Marie et non Rose!" (She is you, my dear. Her name is Marie not Rose.) Everyone laughed so loud in the theater, we were almost kicked out. She just giggled. I had the best of both worlds and am very thankful for my family.

Honestly, my aunt Hellene was more like a grandmother to me, in many ways. I miss her a lot. She is too elderly now to travel but I've got to go see her. She keeps asking to see the triplets in-person, being on video chats isn't the same. I need to figure out something.

We need to visit my mother's older sister in Lafayette, Louisiana somehow.

Each one of my children has this eagerness to learn and a calmness about them like my father, I think. They are planning processers, can see it in their eyes, especially when they show their frustration about something and start fussing in toddler garble and swinging. Reminds me of my mother, with those hand gestures and neck swinging to express their annoyance; it's so funny. Of course, a lot of their musical genius comes from their South Korean K-pop idol daddy and probably a little from his concert pianist father, Ji-Hoon.

My three little amigos won't close their eyes to sleep without his music playing! Any of the songs he wrote or just him playing classics from Chopin, Vivaldi, and others on the piano and they will drift off humming. Often, I imagine him sitting at the keys with them teaching them how to play. His DNA is magically connecting all four of them through his musical talent. They know their father's voice and sounds. It is a little miraculous to observe.

It's not just music, I get excited seeing them in the mountain cabin because they turn into him. Little wilderness boys and girl are so much like their father, inspecting plants and birds, trying to follow where the ants go or examine snowflakes before they melt. So cute. Oh, and when they are so very precise when eating, and sharing things seems to be the manners and properness of their halmani (grandmother), Min Cha, all the way. I see it so vividly as they grow, they are a little splice of everyone. I love being a mom to these beautiful, blended blessings -BBB!

7. Korean vs Other People

Although I had years of experience with Korean and Japanese culture because of my travels, connections, and business partnerships, Asian parenting traditions, I had no clue.

News Flash: Being the super cool and fun taunt/auntie Rhee to all my nieces and nephews is <u>not</u> the same as being the mom. Then you add on raising South Korean babies, oh, that's a serious learning curve. I had no confidence but with my in-laws and friends I picked up quick and did well. I'm learning every day, but I still am getting used to some of the Kim family expectations saying Jolie, Jin, and Jae can do certain things because they are Korean. It does seem they are pretty advanced but in my western brain, they are just twelve months old. I heard:

Min-Cha saying, "Let try, they can do!" "You too soft, daughter. Make them try."

Aunt Teng, "Sit there, you watch. They can do. See." "It's okay, momma."

Kang Cheng, "Ha! Told you. It's because they are South Korean!"

Nari, "It's easy, watch. Now you try. Uh, try again. Good!"

Si, "This is totally normal. Trust me, it wears off in a day or two."

Even Min-Ji and his wife, Eun-Woo would tell me to leave, stand outside the door and let them do it. When I peeked in the doorway my babies were walking at nine months old! Well really Jin was walking much like a drunk baby deer. Yep, like newborn Bambi. Jae was scooting and rocking back and forth as if he is hearing the beat to the song, "Candy" by Cameo, and Jolie. Oh, my sweet Jolie, she was sucking her pinky finger and laying on a blanket. I still cried from excitement and happiness.

With all the nagging, oops, I mean "support" I reevaluate my strict protective 'by the western book' approach to child rearing from six months and beyond expertise. Jin, Jae, and Jolie had proven to me, they can do things their grandma, aunties, and uncles said they can. I recall saying it in amazement.

Everyone here in this country, the few people I get exposed to that is, keep telling me, my triplets are Korean and therefore, they are smarter and quicker to learn than 'other' children. They make a point to add that they are also a little Black too, so they will be physically fit and very strong and athletic. But with the French part, they will love art, cheese, and bread. I wanted to ask, "What is the name of the racial stereotype book you all are reading?" But that would have been rude. I couldn't get offended because they are very serious when they say that kind of stuff. I let them have their opinions and I pick my battles.

As part of our routine, I read to my bundles of adorable chubbiness just about every night like my parents used to do to me. They love it. It makes me melt inside when I hear them say, "Eomma" (mom) and point to something for me to read. It's a special time I treasure with just me and them. But I am not their favorite. Nope, that would be, "Appa" (dad).

The last sounds they hear before closing those little eyes is Jae's voice. Admittedly, sometimes I will stay in their nursery just to hear it too. A few times, Nari must have covered me with a blanket when I'd fallen asleep hearing him reading poems that he wrote, sing ballads, and nursery rhymes he recorded for them in Korean, English, Japanese and French. I drift away every time hearing him. I imagine he is in the room with us, and I am comforted.

8. Uh Oh, Birthday

I never had given much thought to celebrating the triplet's birthday. I suppose because every other month I plan and execute a fantastic theme party for them, like my parents used to do for us growing up. So, I didn't focus on their actual birthday so much. It's probably a little because I don't celebrate mine. The fact is that Jae and I didn't make a big deal over them, or holidays even. We didn't make any of them important in our daily life. We had just committed to loving each other and not so much on some customs. When Min Cha asked me about bringing the triplets to her home on the day for a party, I honestly didn't feel any particular way about it. But I didn't think that their birthday would be a huge ceremony until it was a little too late.

When the gifts started coming two days before, I remembered birthdays could be a big deal for other people that love them. My mother said it first. "My grandbabies are only one. This is crazy. Talk about overkill. They can't possibly use these now." I had no answer and only shrugged with a smile.

Their celebrity uncles sent a few musical instruments for their niece and nephews. Three small keyboards, a koto, a yanggum, and a set of drums, and a few unique international toys and clothes from some recent comeback promotion tours for them to enjoy when they are a bit older. Tayler, SI and Kang had monetary gifts waiting at the elaborate celebration Min Cha and her first husband Ji-Hoon's sister, Hae Won Park set up for them.

Arriving early on Sunday, March 9th at Min Cha and Dong-Hyun's secure compound outside of the luxury district of Seoul, my mother, Nari, and I each had one of my three amigos. Immediately walking inside, all three were snatched away by Jae's father's sister, Hae

Won, Dong-Hyun's sister, Sun hee and Ha-rin, Min Cha's youngest brother, Sung-Ho's wife.

I thought my mother was going to fight Ji-Ho taking Jolie out of her arms without saying anything. "Mother, it's okay, I think they want to change them into those special hanboks they had asked Nari to bring today."

Grunting, she just rolled her eyes at me. *(Good save! Confrontation and potential bodily harm to the petite Korean woman has been successfully diverted. Possessive much? You gotta share them. Ha Ha.)* I knew she was ticked off; she doesn't play when it comes to her time with her grandbabies.

As more guests arrived, I began to feel more disconnected to the goings-on surrounding me. This party wasn't for me, anyway. So, my mother and I were standing around watching the active conversations and movements. I did get tired of being corrected by multiple people when I would speak up and say they were one-year olds. At least five people would shout, "No. No. Korean. They are two years, today. Two years." *(No... Don't roll your eyes!)*

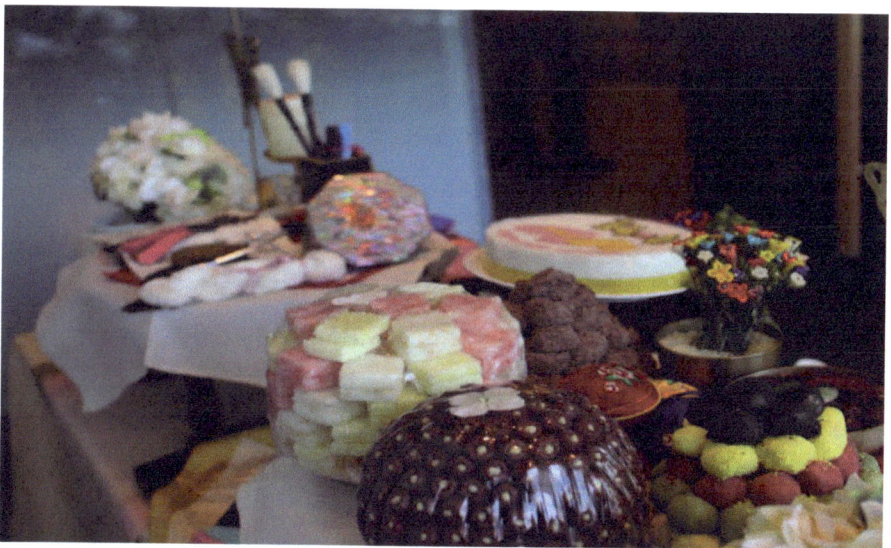

Not only were Min Cha's mother, Kyung-Mi, and aunt Teng helping to put this party on, but they had lots of traditional food and activities that lasted just about all day. I didn't know some of the details until they unfolded much later. The Doljanchi is a big ceremony of future prosperity for a Korean child's first birthday. Jae and Jin wore black hogeon headgear with beautiful prince hanboks and Jolie had on a colorful silk gulle and her princess hanbok. When we arrived from Seattle by way of Busan to our home here, I didn't realize these special handmade princess/prince hanbok gifts were for this ceremony. They were just too big for my six-month-olds. Now I know.

While guest played games. My babies were a tad fussy with all the people, attention, and constant activity. They seemed uncomfortable with all that stuff on. I didn't like the fortune telling or the linked significance of the seaweed soup, rice cakes with rainbow-colored layers, jujube, tteok on the special Dol food table being for some ritual beliefs at all. Neither did my mother but I kept quiet. My mother wanted me to speak up and whispered to me, well she doesn't know how to whisper really but no one heard her.

"Marie, say something! These are your children. Don't let them do whatever they want. Why would you agree to something without researching what it was? I taught you better." She said grinding her teeth.

"Mother, you know I don't believe in fortune telling. Jae didn't either but it's part of this, I guess. I didn't think to ask questions. Min Cha is a Christian. How would I have known this was going to be a spiritual thing? Jae's mother and his late father's sister were doing this, I guess I just assumed."

My mother stood up to stop the activity, but I pulled her arm. "Mother no. All his family, his uncles, their wives and daughters, his older cousins, Nah Min-Ji, and his entire family are here. I don't want to embarrass Min Cha. Please, please sit down. I won't let this happen again. Just please, let's just sit quietly, okay?"

I looked up at her with desperately pleading eyes. Delphine Delacroix gave me that look of "You know what?" right before she pressed her lips together and huffed sitting back down next to me. *(Oh, thank you!)*

She grumbled low but forceful enough for me to hear the unmistakable irritation in her tone. "Marie, you better get it straight. I can't believe you got me sitting here in this with ya. I won't make a scene, but lord have mercy!"

The rest of the event continued without further discussion or interruption. I gave my respectful thankfulness to each person in attendance. I was appreciative for the love shown to my children by my in-laws and Jae-Sung's family and friends. But I didn't feel right about the day at all.

9. Be Wise My Daughter

Later when my exhausted little squirts had been bathed and were fast asleep, my mother came into my bedroom. This was when she was going to talk — no lecture about "the birthday" party.

"Marie, don't let anyone do anything... I mean anything without knowing what's really going on. Look, I know you're working through a lot of grief and changes. But you can't be laxed about these things. Stay woke now. We never celebrated holidays and traditional family things, not your father's or mine, without researching where those things came from. Then your father and I discussed them and made decisions on what we believed and what was right for our family. When you were growing up and you asked why we didn't celebrate Easter, what did we do? We took you to the library and showed you where that holiday comes from. We did the same for Christmas, Halloween, Assumption of Mary, All-Saints, Whit, Fat Tuesday, and so many others. When family and friends asked why we didn't celebrate those holidays, we told them. It's pagan or it's a ritual that is from something bad or what we don't believe in. Either people accepted that, or they didn't. But we stood by our knowledge of right and wrong and didn't just blindly do things. We researched it and didn't just act on emotion. You didn't miss out, we had our own gift giving celebrations for being a blended culture family, we saw a rainbow or because it was snowing. Not celebrating your birthday wasn't something we planned out. Marie being grateful for having life is something we try to do every day not just on the day of birth. It doesn't take away that you are loved and a blessing just because you do something different than others. If you talk to Min Cha, I'm sure she would understand your point of view. She may not agree but you have to tell her how you feel and why. My cute grandbabies are your children. They are not the spirit of their father returned like someone said today. People will only get away with what you let them. You cannot lay down on the job of being their mother."

As I felt my emotions boil up to the surface, I nodded. "I know mother. I wasn't thinking. I'm trying to be upbeat and happy all the time, but my mind gets lost sometimes, when I'm not busy. I've been dreaming about being with Jae... When he died. I'm thinking about it more. I didn't think to ask questions about today. Mother, I can't sleep without pillows smothering me. I'm sorry if I disappointed you, I really am I... I... I miss him. He would've told me what it was. Jae would've explained it to me, so I would know. It is his culture. I... I..."

It was too much happening all at once. Trembling, I began releasing tears, feeling overwhelmed and knowing in a few days more memories would be fresh on my mind again, and I wouldn't be able to shake them. My head was pounding with thoughts of today and quick flashes of being with him on that day. What we talked about, hearing him struggle to breathe. All of it. My brain was mush. Happy and sad.

My mother hugged me without speaking for several minutes to let me get my cry out and refocus. She kissed my cheek, then softly said, "Chantal, my beautiful child. Listen to me. I'm not disappointed. I just want you to be stronger. You can and will be. It comes in waves so don't expect it to be all the time. You need to not let things run away from you while you are grieving. You can't shut down or just function. That doesn't work. You have to put time aside to release your emotions and pour out your heart in sadness, prayer, journaling, boxing, whatever. But then the other times you've got to be on your A-game. Life keeps going and if you are not sharp about your children and what is best for them and you, someone else will take over. You won't know what's really going on because you're stuck in a cloud of grief. Trust me. I know what I'm talking about. You are not broken. Don't let other's think you are and take over your children's lives for you."

I nodded that I understood but didn't say anything. My mother kissed my cheeks again and held me for a long while, humming a soft melody.

Later, as I got myself ready for bed, she made us some tea, while I wrote down in my journal what had happened, how I felt about it, and she gave me the key points again to capture and think about.

Since South Korea is ahead in time, it was still mid-day on the 9th when I called my sister, Celeste, at exactly 5:00 a.m. the next morning. At first, she didn't answer the house phone. *(It's Sunday, why isn't she picking up?)* Then I tried her cellphone. After it rang several times, she finally answered.

"Hi CeCe. How are you? I wanted to call you today and—" she interrupted, "Marie, I don't want to talk right now. I'm not having a good couple of days. It's not you, it's me. I love you but I gotta go." Then she hung up.

(Did this heifer hang up on me? Oh, no, she didn't. Let me call her back right... Wait!)

It took me a couple of seconds to decide not to call her again. However, I heard her say she was having a rough time. *(I should...)* I ordered some flowers and a tea basket to be rush delivered to her later that day. I didn't hear from her at all, but I knew she received it a couple hours later. Perplexed about her lack of empathy, I talked to my mother when the triplets were napping.

"What's wrong with her? Why won't she talk to me?" I didn't know what to think, especially since Celeste had never acted like this before.

"Marie, your sister needs some time and space," my mother said very matter-of-factly while drinking her coffee.

(Huh?) "Did she tell you that? Why? Why the hell does she need space? What 'bout me? My whole world is different! I'm a mother, a widow. I live in a foreign country with none of my family around me. I'm the minority all over again. I'm in a cage where everything is secret for security. I can't just walk outside when I want anymore. Where's my support? Why do I need to tiptoe 'round her? Just because she is the baby?! Jin, Jolie, and Jae are her niece and nephews. I didn't treat the JJ's this way. So, she can't be a support to me as my sister or their tante? You know what... She did this and kept it a damn secret. That's not my fault, it's hers. But now I must give her time? Where's my time? Oh, forget it. I won't call her anymore. I can't deal with this. It's stupid. I don't care. She can have all the time and space she needs; I'm done."

I was angry and I didn't understand. I didn't really care to understand either. In my mind, I was the one with choices being taken away from me. My entire life imploded and exploded with heartbreak and joy at the same time. Flustered, I shoved the fork in my mouth and chewed hard on the spinach, cheese, and egg scramble, as if it would make me feel better. But it didn't, as I continued to wallow in my thoughts. My mother had silently watched me say exactly what was on my mind with no filter. When I glanced at her, I could tell by her slow breathing and equally snail-like blinking that she was counting silently to calm herself down.

I inhaled and blew out heavily. My mother tilted her head to connect with my rolling eyes of annoyance before explaining some things to me. (Crap! It's coming. I'm the mean judgmental one. She's the delicate flower… Blah blah blah.)

"Chantal-Marie…" She paused before continuing. (Uh here we go. Brace yourself.) "Let me remind you, that your sister is not made the way you are. She wears her feelings on the outside; not hidden beneath her armor. Calling her on your children's birthday is like you picking at a scabbed over wound still healing. You're wanting her to be some listening ear to your pain, your sorrow and be ecstatic with joy of your children being born. That is just putting pressure around the wound causing it to bleed."

"Mother, I—" She cut me off. "Let me finish. We all must be sensitive to your needs, Marie. But it won't look the same. I came here knowing this time was going to be very difficult for you. Each day will remind you of things, and it will be a challenge. I understand what you expect from Celeste, but she can't give anymore right now. She may not ever be able to. Your life is not the only one that changed."

"Mother, that isn't fair. I had no choices and I lost…"

She cut me off again, waving her hand at me. "No one is comparing which change is greater. Child, everyone's life is different. I dropped everything to be here with you. In my life, I, too, have experienced tragedy that you don't even know about. But because of those situations, I am more equipped to aid. Sadly, Celeste doesn't have the tools to help you. She can't. She is a giver. You know your sister gave you the best of herself. At no time did she stop and think it through to the end. Celeste didn't plan it out or even consider the cost to herself. She just did it. Now, she is paying the price of that gift emotionally. That is why she needs time and space. When Celeste is ready, she'll reach out to you, and you will know how to communicate with her when she does. But until then, just stop. She is not your girlfriend. She is your baby sister, who has always looked up to you as an example of strength and guidance, confidence, and forward thinking. You can't change the roles now after they've been set that way from the beginning. At least not overnight. You just can't. Do you understand?"

Her daggered words stabbed me all over and I couldn't respond. (*I never thought about anyone else's suffering other than my own. Well, maybe Min Cha's… maybe. It is all these rollercoasters of emotions. It's like I'm reliving it but as spectator on some days versus an active fully engaged participant on others. I hate this!*)

My mother had gotten up from the kitchen table to get herself more coffee, but we heard rustling sounds coming from the dark video on the monitor screen, and she went to the nursery instead.

I exhaled. "I don't know what I'm doing anymore. Alright, don't call her. Don't think about her. She's dealing with her own feelings and can't be here for me. She loves me but doesn't know how to support me or how to be in our sisterhood relationship. She'll come to me when she is ready. I got it."

As soon as I finished summarizing some of what my mother was telling me, a little whimpering boy came around the corner with a blanket in his hand dragging behind him saying, "Ma...ma..."

I gave my son my full attention. I never knew which language each one would speak. It reminded me of my father when he has a little too much wine and switches speaking in English and French and sometimes Japanese without warning.

Inching down to meet this wobbly little bundle, I whispered to him, "Jin, ppoh-po" (kiss) while picking him up. Jin continued rubbing his little sleepy eyes as he gave me a puckered lip smooch with a hug. Feeling his warm body snuggling me, I kissed his cheek and carried him to the refrigerator, asking him in Korean, "Ooo-yoo (milk)? Ju-shu (juice)?" He shook his head, grunting a no. "Mool? (water)" I said, pointing to the water bottles inside. He nodded with a "Eung (yes)." Snickering because my son is just so cute, I got out a water bottle and poured some in a toddler cup and warmed it slightly before letting him refresh himself.

Seconds later, Nari came into the kitchen with Jolie sucking the tip of her pinky finger, and my mother was steps behind carrying a giggling Jae because she was rubbing her face over his round tummy. I put what happened earlier behind me and focused on my full-time job of being a happy and fun mother to my three amigos.

It was known by everyone that my plan was to follow Jae's outline and get as much support early on from his family here in South Korea. We would live in our home here in the district of Hannam and then move to Lyon when the triplets get ready to begin private primary school in France.

At first, I thought it would be in 2036. Jae had this crazy legal written rule that they can't fly until they are six years old. Really? See, here is that control thing again and there was no way around it either. Early on, my attorney, Chris had told me, "Marie, you cannot break this legal stipulation. It is in his will. You cannot take them by plane before age six." I felt stuck.

Then I said to my mother, "During a brief discussion I had with Chris at their party, he gave me a loophole. I can use their Korean age; we can move to France in 2035. I can take them to New York or Louisiana, California, anywhere. They will be five everywhere else in the world but as Korean citizens, they technically would be six. So, there. Jae, I win! Ha! Well, that is a few years away yet, but I have it all planned out, to visit the Jefferies, Lola, and Tangee. Then auntie Hellene and Tamera, maybe Renee, Jazz and…"

I stopped talking as I noticed my mother was snickering and shaking her head.

"What's so funny?"

"Girl, you so excited, shouting I win, like you are playing some kind of game with him."

Confused, I stopped folding the clothes, and said, "I did?" She nodded, smirking and chuckling. "I didn't realize I said that. Oh, that's weird."

My mother added, "Marie, it's not weird. Your husband is always in your heart." The moment she said that I felt a calm come over me. *(He is my heart's dream. I love him.)*

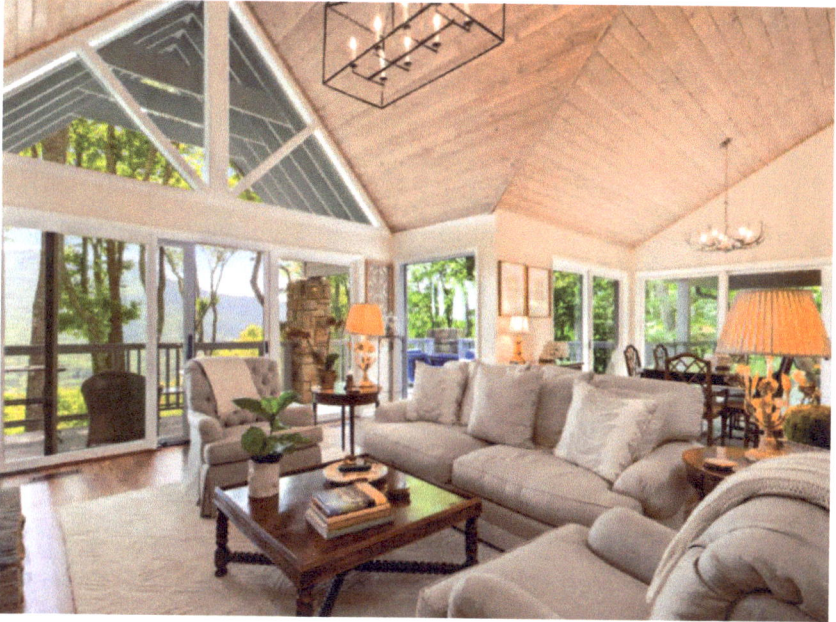

10. March 12th

Some of Jae's family members kept calling, trying to convince me to join them for a ceremony honoring Jae-Sung on the anniversary of his passing. Days before the triplet's party, I had already told Min Cha I wasn't comfortable and wouldn't be participating. I told her again at their party when Hae Won got her to ask me. Min Cha wasn't planning on attending either, especially knowing Jae-Sung specifically stated he didn't want any type of Confucian rite ceremonies after he died. It was not his belief. It wasn't hers either, but his father, Ji-Hoon's family apparently still followed those traditions for her deceased children and husband even without Min Cha's involvement. So, Jae's aunt, Hae Won, kept calling me. She even said I should let her sons, Young-Jae, and Jin-Young bring my children, if I didn't want to come. I tried to be nice when I declined, but she got very angry. I finally let my mother handle it. At the time, I wasn't thinking about other people and trying to please them. Delphine

Delacroix handled everything from my house and my children to shutting down Jae's annoying nagging aunt. I didn't have to worry at all.

Kang pre-arranged everything for me, and on March 13th, he drove me to our mountain cabin home in Ywongwol-gun, Gangwon Province. I wanted to spend the day alone in the last place I was with my love.

I had been inside, talking to myself, drinking soju, and listening to the music he had played that day. I watched a few videos of Jae-Sung and me; and some old ones of him performing with DRGN5. I cried a lot and laughed watching us play cards, catching him cheating and being flirty. I talked to the screen sometimes when some scenes came on, remembering him and how it felt when he touched me. I was emotional seeing memories of when he smiled at me and hearing his laugh. I missed him. I didn't plan to stay overnight but just wanted to have some time by myself.

But when I went to the front door and glanced outside, the black Lexus was there. (*What time is it? Did Kang come back to get me early? Is something happening with my children?*) I turned my cellphone on to check, but there were no messages. It had only been four hours alone on the mountain.

"What's he doing?" I mumbled to myself, walking outside.

I knocked on the front passenger's tinted window. He unlocked the door, and I got in the passenger seat. "Hey, you're a little early Kang. Is something wrong? Are the triplets, okay?"

He didn't say a word; instead, he nodded and smiled.

"Kang, I said maybe I'd stay the night, or just until four or five. It's only noon. Why are you back now?" I looked at him curiously and confused.

His voice was low when he said, "I never left."

"What? You mean you've been sitting out here for hours?"

He nodded without looking at me. Kang just faced forward, almost like a robot.

"Why? I told you I wanted to be alone. You didn't have to stay... I'm fine. Kang, what's going on?"

"Noona, I didn't want to leave. I ... I stayed in the car... I miss ... I miss my brother, phenomenal noona. I miss him." His voice cracked as he spoke. I instantly let out a high pitch gasp and couldn't stop crying. Kang reached over to hold me right across from the driver's seat. He did so for a long time as I just cried. He did too.

Just a bit after three, Kang softly asked, "Do you want to stay the night? I will stay with you."

Without looking at him, I said, "Non. Je veux être à la maison avec nos enfants (No. I want to be home with our children)."

Kang smiled, then went ahead and locked up our cabin home. Then he held my hand as he drove me back to feel the soft lip kisses and squeezes from the little fingers of the three most important people in my world.

The plan was Jolie, Jin, and Jae would bring me back to joy again. However, I remained in bed or my bedroom for eight days straight. Initially, I refused to eat, but commanding and bossy Delphine wasn't having that. By the second day of my isolation, if I was in a full wailing episode when my children came into my room, they would react with sad faces and tears. Nari and my mother would calm them, but they wouldn't take them out and Jae wouldn't stop no matter what they tried.

Because I was forced to get myself together enough to stop crying as they were conveniently placed next to me or under the covers to cuddle, I believed Delphine Murry-Delacroix came up with this plan.

The next day, it seemed as if every few hours, I was never left alone. She brought my little grinning charmer, Jin, in to feed me some of his grapes or read to him. Hours later, she came with the glowing round face Jolie to give me juice, cheese, and light kisses, while she hummed to me. Then not long after that delightful visit, she had Nari bring Mr. bossy pants, Jae. She just dropped him off and left the room. *(What the heck?)*

Jae got under the covers demanding I have some of his shared offerings of vegetable rice. As he said, "Mawmaw mange *(Mama eat)."* Although I repeatedly said no, shaking my head, he still shoved the spoon in my face as the rice tumbled onto the bed in a small pile because I was laying down. Yeah, it worked. I sat up.

"Jae, why are you so bossy?" I mumbled, chewing the food in my mouth, and catching the crumbs falling from my chin.

He just looked at me with those big eyes the color of golden sunrays and said, "Maman voit partager *(Mama see share)!"* I love my babies. I grinned, followed by a light chuckle.

They couldn't possibly know what was going on with me, but these little raindrops of love would tenderly wipe my cheeks, saying sweet words such as "il-eona eomma," "Pas de pleurs," "Amour," "Al-ass-eo," "dangsin-eul wihan kiseu".

Telling me to "wake up mom," "it's okay," "love," "kisses for me" and "no cry," just kept me at the edge of what was happening in the world around me. I didn't completely collapse into darkness like I had when Jae-Sung first passed away, a year ago.

My mother was so smart; she knew exactly what she was doing, and it helped.

That night and everyone thereafter, my children snuggled around me in my bed for me to read to them. I did a little, but I just couldn't make myself get out of bed or stop crying for longer than thirty minutes.

I didn't see anyone. Later, I heard there were flowers, phone calls, and video messages that came for me. My mother mentioned that Kang checked on me daily. As far as Jae-Sung's family, they all were grieving at the same time, and we didn't communicate much right after the triplet's party. But my sweet brother, Kang Cheng, must have given them updates.

It seemed there was a special place where most of my crying fits became uncontrolled, like a full eruption. It was in the tub or shower. But I never could get it all out. It felt so much like a lingering cough with a pressing bolder on my chest, always there with persistent pressure and unmovable.

For the brief times when my mind was momentarily clear, facts came to me. I wrote these random thoughts and ideas in my grieving journal, but mostly, I described all my feelings in words, getting them out into the wind.

11. Moon and Sun

"I am a firework. I whistled and went up and exploded in the sky into something colorful and bright, but now is gone. You have to view me this way to move on. I cannot be but our children are the moon and sun. They are vibrant and powerful never changing their designed purpose to make you happy and carry on with some part of me to be with you always." – Jae Sung Kim

I kept reflecting on our history together and why I wrote the firework poem. "He isn't a firework! I don't wanna forget! Jae is the sun and moon, like I wrote in college. He is!" I cried reading my old journals over and over. Mustering just a smidgen of strength, I pulled out a pad and wrote my feelings in a new one.

"With the absence of you, I wake up cold. I need to feel the passion burn on my skin from your slightest touch. Oh, bright penetrating sun of heavenly warmth, I am lost without you, baby.

Oh, Jae, I can't do this. A moon cannot survive without the balance of its partner, the sun."

About the fourth or fifth day of my solitude, I finally realized exactly why I was drowning in these extreme highs and lows of storming emotions. I felt as though I was on some emotional rocket ship shooting high in the sky and then seconds later, plummeting to the earth and then on repeat.

I laughed, cried, yelled, and smiled with feelings that rushed through me without warning, traveling from zero to three hundred and forty-three meters per second. The speed of sound in the air.

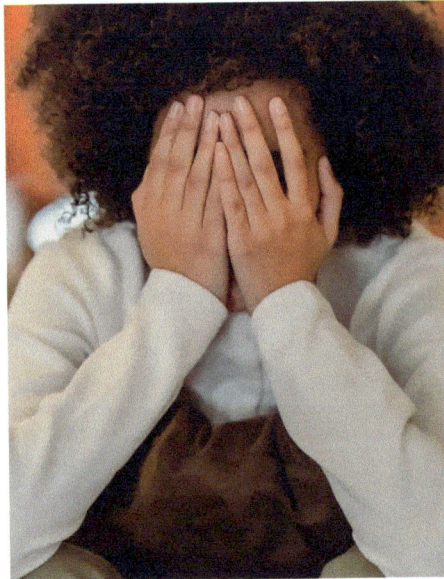

The back-to-back flooding and often overlapping memories collided with joy and pain, pleasure, and grief. Connected to a timeline so close together, my brain had no time to stop, recoup or recharge. It was like an emotional hurricane with no warning resulting in the destruction of my sanity. I looked at the desk calendar and frantically began to list out what was marked as important dates on a journal page.

- February 28th is Jae-Sung's birthday
- March 9th Jae, Jin, Jolie (Triplets) born day 2030
- March 11th Mandarin Oriental NY reconnection after pandemic 2021
- Two days later, I said yes in my NY Condo
- Last day together, my firework — March 13, 2030
- We met, the past, and we broke up all in April.
- May prank surprise. Wedding day in France May 17
- June 1 Wedding Day in South Korea
- Coco Island in July - he proposed
- August our first friends' vacation at Coco Island and the Japan Showcase Tour
- September Seoul w/Idols; Summit and Diamond rings; his first I love you; Mountain Cabin
- December our last

Once I saw it all written out as a list in front of my eyes, it registered just seeing everything so close together. So many wonderful memories smashed with heartbreaking ones. I couldn't compartmentalize them, they were just all there like a maze puzzle in my head, and I collapsed in mental anguish. It was like my mind, and heart exploded at the exact same time. I didn't remember anything after that.

Hours later, I believe my mother must have seen me on the floor of my bedroom, soaked in vomit and tears. I was lethargic but remembered her washing me in the shower. She put me in a clean loose fitting white cotton gown and brushed my hair as I sat in the bathroom weeping. When I got back to bed, everything in my bedroom was now clean, and there was tea and soup on a serving tray. My mother sat on the bed next to me and fed me like she did when I was six years old and had a bad cold.

"Mommy, I'm going crazy. I can feel it."

She paused with the spoon halfway to my mouth. I had not called her that since I was maybe ten years old. At the time, I didn't notice that she had teared up. As the spoon was suspended in the air, I glanced up at her. It startled me to see water collecting in her eyes like a small pool. Adjusting herself, putting the tray to the side and clearing her throat, my mother talked to me like she never had before.

"Chantal, you're not going crazy. How you are feeling is the process of dealing with the pain of death. You will be alright."

"I don't want to do this, but I can't stop. I feel like my skin is on fire and my heart is a block of ice. Why are you so nice to me? I know you don't love me deeply, but you've been so different since the triplets were born. I'm glad you came to help me. I know you're disappointed because I tried to prepare myself for the day he died in my head. I didn't; I'm sorry. I knew this would come… these damn memories again to remind me of each second when he died. I could not get through this if you weren't…"

She cut me off from spewing out random words by putting her hand up in the air. "What?! Wait, let's get something straight here! I am your mother, and it is my duty to fix it or to help you if I can! Girl, did you say that I don't love—" She took a breath, then continued talking but in a lower tone.

"Marie, you are so much like me and so much like your father. You are a strong woman. You could have gone through this time without me being here, but it just would have been more difficult. I'm always in your corner, even if I am not verbal about it or you don't see me. Grief is a process. It doesn't turn on and off like a light switch. You know this already. Dealing with a loss like this doesn't show up on time or like an alarm either. It often is like a sneak attack or quick flash like a mouse darting from behind a cabinet. We cannot prepare our mind and heart in a way to never have grief. It doesn't work like that. We can only prepare for the stages of grief to happen and go through them. When I was younger and read the book *On Death and Dying* by Elisabeth Kubler-Ross in the 70s, it pointed out five stages as being: Denial, Anger, Bargaining, Depression and Acceptance."

I stopped crying and blew my nose. As I sipped the cup of homemade baked potato soup she had placed in my hands, she came closer to me and began giving me her wisdom and sharing a few secrets.

"We've experienced all of them and maybe a few others. First, denial shows up because you are shocked that this loss is actually happening. It seems like our mind tries to hold on to every second right before the very moment you find out things were changing. For me, bargaining came next. I wanted to trade, and I prayed for God to take me instead, but he didn't. God doesn't take people away. That would be cruel, and he is far from that way. But we humans want someone to blame and lash out; reactively blaming God or people, demanding justice for the loved one being gone. It's amazing how this process works because that just drops you smack dab in the hot skillet of anger. It doesn't matter if there is someone accountable or not, anger comes like a flash fire, and it can burn intensely while destroying relationships in its wake in some cases. Marie, I remember each time I went through this, I was enraged for a very long time. It felt as though there was molten rock inside my bones just bubbling and churning like from inside the center of the earth." She paused and I studied her face before she glanced away. I had no thoughts but waited. Then it came.

"Chantal-Marie, I'm not disappointed in you at all. I told you there is no planning how you will travel the path of grieving. You just feel and react to what is happening. Everyone needs something different. When you were in the hospital, I even left to figure myself out."

Being that we had never discussed the past, I was shocked by what she was finally telling me. My brain shifted to my childhood, and then I had questions.

"But you were in Paris when I woke up. You left? I don't remember a lot but... You ... you left?"

"Oui, ma chérie, (Yes, my dearest). Hellene had flown to get me, and she took me back to Louisiana weeks after you woke up. I needed to grieve away from everyone, and I didn't want to impact your recovery."

My mind didn't recall what she was saying, but I didn't think much more about it. Her mild tone and firm embrace over time helped me to not feel as lost as before.

But later when I was alone it came back. "You would be forty-two, baby. If only..." I coughed but held back my tears remembering times with him performing for me, Baekhyun's song "Stay Up" then Maxwell's "Fortunate" and Jay B/Def's "Sunrise" and Honey" I was so shocked having my own private concert. He was so sexy in his black designer tux. I snickered, "He hated singing other K-Pop artist songs, especially the few male singers, I liked. But that day, it was all for me to enjoy." He loved me so much to do that and so many other things.

(Jae's vocal range was so magnificent and unique. Oh, his falsetto was so airy and sultry. He always turned me on.) I thought back to being extremely excited and trying to jump him during the living-room concert. "He was so fun! Then we made music in his studio. Wait... Nasty! Ha… I can't believe he recorded us making love too... I didn't even know he did, until he played the track the next day. Oh, my god, punk! That was strange, hearing what I sounded like. But he made that jazzy music from it. It was amazing. Crazy man." I giggled for a few minutes before tears fell as the sadness returned with my heart and mind acknowledging I wouldn't ever again have moments with him. "Baby, why... why did you leave me? I don't want to do this without you..." After wiping the constant rolling tears, I reached to hit the master control to play the blue disc #40CMK. Floating through the air were the sounds of him playing Chopin's "Spring Waltz" on his Fazioli Liminal piano. The covers were warm, and I had some tea, ready to read his letter. It always made me feel his love and helped me to dream our wonderful moments together. As I started reading, I began to cry, and then I couldn't stop. When I heard Jae's beautiful voice singing Eric Benét's song "Still with you," things changed. It was a song he had recorded specifically for me to play when I was tethered and broken from my grief. As it concluded, I had a jolt to the brain and abruptly sat up. "Stop this, Marie! You can't fall apart. You can't." I mumbled at first, then kept saying the words over and over and got louder each time. I suppose I was trying to shock myself into feeling something other than sadness. Making a conscious effort to get more control of my reality, I prayed more to calm my heart. When my mind wandered into the fog of pain, I started to think about things I had learned and hoped for.

Slowly I got myself together enough to function outside of my bedroom and pajamas. I had been spiraling for almost three weeks. But gradually, I got back to my daily routine and things were better.

Collection: Close Windows, Open Doors

12. Unexpected Kindness

Last year, when we had gotten settled living in South Korea, I restarted my monthly video calls and Bible discussions with my Bronx pen-pal, Joy, and her mother, Stephanie Hamilton. We still chatted but it was usually via email because of the time difference and my new job as a mom. That was why Stephanie introduced me to two older sisters that lived here, in hopes of helping me with questions if she wasn't available. I didn't mind the local contacts especially since the older Korean witnesses were nice ladies. Min Sun Gil lived in Cheongdam and was married to Chul, and her older sister, Haeun Do lived in Hannam with her adult daughter Ami. They attended the English-speaking congregation of Jehovah's Witnesses in Seoul.

But I hadn't spoken to them in weeks. Before my mother got here, I had told them I was going through some things and would contact them when I wanted to study the Bible more. They were very sweet. They didn't pressure me to keep studying, demand to know what was going on in my life or judge me for not relying on God more. They just gave me friendly encouragement and said, "...whenever you need to talk or would like to study, we will come back."

With so much going on in my head and heart, I didn't think any more about it. During my weeks of depression shutdown, I received an anonymous bouquet of beautiful pink, yellow, and white lotus, and orchids with a Get-Well card delivered to my home. Inside it had a scripture, Psalms 41:3 "Jehovah will sustain him on his sickbed; during his sickness, you will completely change his bed." Under the quote were handwritten words, "When you're sick and someone that loves you, comes in and tenderly washes you and replaces your clothes and the bedding with clean ones, even if you are still sick, how do you feel?" When I read it, I said out loud without even thinking, "Refreshed! Comforted." Then I thought about my mother. When she came into my room to bring me her homemade split pea soup, I hugged her and thanked her again for being here and taking care of me so lovingly.

A few days later, I received a card in a basket of fresh fruit delivered with a note that simply had the Bible scripture, Psalms 34:18 "Jehovah is close to the brokenhearted; He saves those who are crushed in spirit." I smiled when my mother brought it to me after washing the fruit. Getting these helped me to remember I wasn't alone in my despair, and I prayed more earnestly for peace and comfort.

When I emailed my good friend, Stephanie Hamilton in Brooklyn, New York to thank her and her young daughter, Joy for their spiritual encouragement, I got her reply saying, "Marie, we have kept you in our prayers, but Joy and I decided to give you some time to adjust, considering you're a new mom, and it's only been a year since your husband died. Being a widow myself, I remembered how hard it was at first. Joy painted something for you, but we hadn't sent it yet."

Right away, I knew it had to be one if not both Korean sisters from the English Congregation of Jehovah's Witnesses, I had met and begun studying with in December. I wasn't really expecting to hear from them because we had only met three months earlier. Stephanie commented once that all witnesses around the world are like a giant family. Everyone learns the same things and tries to apply it daily to their individual lives. They focus on spiritual principles to keep peaceful and care for others, no one does it as masterfully as Jesus Christ, but they try to be impartial and provide kindness to all people. I didn't really buy that, but I heard her. Those women were strangers to me. I mean, I didn't know them like I knew Stephanie and Joy Hamilton. Honestly, they weren't Black, so I was really shocked that these Korean women cared enough about me just to send me something to encourage me. It touched me deeply, much like that random six-year-old's little drawing invitation mailed to me years ago, asking me to meet her in a paradise garden in the future. Joy was such a cute little chocolate drop. Her mother was so kind all those years ago. I'm glad I took a chance and wrote back.

After a long sigh, I made myself a note to personally thank Min Sun Gil and Haeun Do for their unexpected kindness.

Min Sun Gil

Haeun Do

13. Black Aunties

A week before my mother was to fly home to Lyon, two of my aunties came to visit. It was part of the plan to meet their husbands, who had already flown to France. They were off doing guy things for the week with my father and his musketeer brothers, Andreas, Chevalier, and Tomas. I was surprised but a little nervous.

All aunties are great, but there is something special about having Black ones. They are these wild women that are a little bit of your mother, part of a girlfriend, dash of a personal counselor, of course, part cheerleader, a slice of secret agent, and in my world, they include part comedian.

In my family there was no such thing as separating blood relatives from others. We have play cousins with friends and it worked the same with adults. I remember my father telling me he had to have it explained to him a few times after they got married. *(I bet that was an interesting debate.)* But he got it, that my mother's sisters, sisters-in-laws, and close girlfriends were all my aunties, period. He quickly added the practice to his childhood best friends and the musketeer brothers were dubbed my oncles (uncles).

Growing up a bi-racial woman, I had two different types of aunts. I learned the difference early. My father's sisters, tantes (aunts) Nannette, Josephine, and the French-German Gauthier women Gert, Heidi, Elke, and Lylah were not brown and therefore had another way of interacting and expressing their love. Although not the same, they were all gentle and informal, aristocratic, and fun but never did I think of them as extensions of my mother. The only discipline I ever received was from Gert, and that was a stern talking too in both German and French languages.

The aunties with melanin, Lolli, Claudine, Lorelle, Hellene and Marianna had full permission to snatch me up just like I was their own child. It didn't happen. Wait, I remember Renee's mother told me off in Spanish swinging a brush at me after I had tangled up, Renee's freshly done curls while playing beauty shop. I suppose that counts. They all are equal parts of love, support, and gangster that you need tough skin sometimes because if you're in the wrong, they will check mate you without hesitation, even in front of your parents, if need be. Well, it's like a verbal slap and then afterward they'll slip you an ice cream cone or an *I still love you, don't do it again,* hug. They didn't play games or were too soft, is all. Oh, and the title of being an auntie was a badge they wore with pride. Coming to school plays, concerts, track meets, swim tournaments would always require them announcing to other parents "I'm her auntie." Or "That's my niece." It was a requirement to use the title when calling them before saying their name. If you didn't, you could find yourself getting up off the floor from getting slapped in the mouth or popped in the back of the head for being disrespectful. Just sayin'.

I had seen it once with my cousin in Louisiana. As soon as he did it, he tried to fix it, but for over thirty minutes all we heard were statements such as, "What did you say?" "Oh, is ya thinkin' I'm one of ya lil friends?" "Ya think ya grown?" "Boy, them little balls ain't dropped that low yet to be callin' me by my first name." "Uh, little boy, do I sleep with chu?" "Ya bess act like ya got some home training!" "I should beat your ass." "Go pick a switch!" "You know what... look-a-here..." "As long as you are Black, don't you never..."

He got it from all of them at the same time. It was crazy; a real hen clucking free for all. I learned from watching that experience, the stove was always on and hot make sure to say "auntie" first. I think Charlie Ricard was seriously traumatized for the rest of the day. Ha-ha!

Now, growing up, my father's sisters were very special to me. However, my two wonderful French aunts passed away a long time ago. My crazy and beautiful tante (aunt) Josephine died in a car accident with Kristoff's father traveling to their wedding destination in Casablanca when I was very young. Leaving Tomas and Kristoff to be raised by our grandparents. Then a year before the worldwide Covid-19 pandemic hit, my oncle (uncle) Andreas found my sweet bubbly tante (aunt) Nannette unconscious on the floor after she slipped in the shower. He had to make the tearful decision with their children present to turn off the life support. I miss her so much.

Unfortunately, aside from my mother's older sister Hellene who is too elderly to travel, my mother's college girlfriends are the only aunties I have left. My mother's wild and fun identical twin sister, Lorelle, died during Hurricane Katrina with my older cousin, Tamera's husband, Quinton Brown. He had driven down to New Orleans to

95

rescue her, but they drowned after his car was swept off the road. Oh, and, right after college, Renee's feisty, straight-talking Mexican mother Marianna passed away shortly after being diagnosed with ovarian cancer. I miss my aunties that are no longer here. I think of them often and how much my triplets would have been loved by those amazing women I had in my life.

My mother told me she had convinced my auntie Dene and auntie Lolli to come during her last week with us. She said it was easy because neither of them had been to South Korea, and they really wanted to see me. I jumped up excitedly, hearing they were coming. Claudine "Dene" Jefferies and Lolli Toussaint had been my mother and her twin sister Lorelle's best friends since they were in junior high school. It's funny because it's just like Renee and me. Isn't it strange how situations seem to repeat in the same bloodline? (It's kind of weird, right?)

Claudine is a retired state social worker and lives in California, and Lolli is a retired computer engineer from Microsoft and lives in Washington but not close to Celeste. They both have been in the dark like everyone else about the happenings in my real life for several years now, but once Kang cleared them to visit, I was open to share a little bit of my family. (Like duh, they are not the mob.)

I couldn't stop grinning when they arrived in South Korea to spoil my children. Auntie Lolli said she wanted to come sooner, but when she was planning it, her son Marcell and his wife were expecting their first child, and she couldn't get away. Auntie Dene would call me once a month, but she didn't want to come without my mother being here. She said it was because, "…Your mother and I can get dressed up and pick up hot young guys at the club."

I remember squinching my face up when she said it. "Auntie?! Uh, first, no! Second, why… why are you looking for men?" She said,

"Bae. I wanna get those skincare products, and we need a hook up. Gonna open me a side business store sell to the snooty white women and replace Botox. You know like they do with braid and weave hair stores here. Make a fortune! Ha!" I cracked up, laughing.

For security reasons, they couldn't stay with us. They didn't understand why and complained about it until my mother said she would stay with them at the Four Seasons – Seoul. When they got settled, and Kang brought them over, I got so much love and kisses. Well, that lasted for about thirty seconds. As soon as the little wigglers came into the room, I was kicked to the curb.

"Oh... look at these cheeks. Come give auntie some sugar baby, Jolie..." Drooling she giggled in auntie Dene's arms, and they were fast friends.

"Dell, which one is this one here with these wampire eyes like his mama." Lolli said laughing with her favorite joke she used to say when I was a kid. She would say, "Chantal, ya got them wolf-vampire color eyes. Little girl, can you see in the dark too?"

(Oh brother...my poor son is going to get the same corny jokes as we got growing up.)

Fortunately, Delphine got our back protecting us. My mother quickly smacked Lolli's hand and said, "This is my little Jae, and he is the handsomest, smartest little man with beautiful sun-kissed honey-dipped eyes. Ya best shut up talkin' bout my grandson, or we will take out the pictures and discuss those talons your granddaughter, India, has for feet!"

We laughed while Lolli chuckled picking Jae up planting tender kisses on his neck. Nari's face was smashed trying to understand what was true and what wasn't. She looked afraid but was snickering. Her facial expression reminded me of when you have to go to the bathroom, but not sure if it's number one or number two and you're thinking about it. I had to clarify that. "Nari, they are kidding," I said.

"Come on Jin, dearest love, let's find something good to chew on. GiGi got you," my mother said while carrying Jin to the fridge.

"GiGi… Dell, you've been living in France for too long. Girl, you know you are Black right? You are just Nanna like the rest of us. Stop trying to be all extra French. Oh, you so on my nerves with that. Let it go. Ain't no French in you. You ain't no Creole, girl. Ya always trying to copycat," Claudine said, snickering as she rationed out the cheese and grapes Jolie was nibbling on.

Lolli chimed in with her two cents, "That's right, Nanna or Gran…can't be big mama because you lost all that weight and ya not a thick one no more. Ha! Ha!"

My mother put her hand on her hip and made her point clear, "Both of you Dodo birds need to stop hating. GiGi is who I am. It stands for gorgeous, grandma. Thank you very much. I don't need to be Creole to be that. And for the record, I don't have any French in me right now, but when I get home, I betcha I will."

(Oh my god!)

The cackling of these three senior hens echoed throughout my kitchen. Kang had just walked in from the music room and heard the end of what she said. He laughed so loud that it startled Jae and Jin, and they started crying. Jolie laughed with her great auntie Dene playing and singing "Pat a Cake", but Lolli shouted, "Dene, they black! Teach her the Black way. You know it's Patty Cake! Ha, ha!"

(Oh boy. This is going to be crazy fun. They are a mess.)

A few hours later, when my triplets were taking a nap, Nari and Kang went out, and we had ladies' time to chat. I was prepared to get fussed at because I kept so many things secret. I still couldn't tell them many details they wanted to know about my life, but overall, it wasn't too bad.

"Are you doing okay, sweetie? Really?" Lolli asked me before glancing down at her steeping cup of hot lavender earl gray tea she had brought from home in her suitcase. I nodded and said truthfully, "It comes and goes. I'm very blessed that mother has been here during this time. She's really helped me through some of the hard days." When I finished saying it out loud, my mother winked at me from across the dining room table.

While sharing her thoughts, Claudine reached over and squeezed my hand, "Marie, grieving is hard. Babe-ah, it never goes away so take the good days and know they will return when you have those bad ones." Then she said, "This is beautiful—this wall painting; very life-like. It feels almost like we are sitting in the middle of it. Your home is very warm and peaceful. Thank you for having us... uh but how long are you going to stay here? I mean, these babies need to be 'round black folks on the regular. There ain't none here. Looks like an Asian festival." she said it with all seriousness, but she was giggling.

"A few more years, auntie, then we will move to Lyon so they can start private school. There are some Black people here. But for security reasons, we don't engage with many people. When they are older, it will be easier." I grabbed a strawberry sandwich from the display tray we had filled with a variety of sweets and savories. My mother was silent, allowing her girlfriends to work up to the real questions. About ten minutes passed of beating around the bush, and then they relaxed. Their New Orleans twang crept back as they spoke more casually, and they just went for it.

"Marie, I was thinkin' ya lived here for ya damn job. Now, I get here, see these babies, and come ta find out that ain't it at all. It's 'cause ya husband. He wasn't even Black…but an Asian! Lord, have mercy."

"I'm wit Lolli. Babe-ah, we wanna understand dis… we do, babe-ah. A White man… okay, make sense cus' ya mama done opened that door. But he was… from here… a Asian?"

"Yes, auntie, Dene. He was South Korean."

After a few minutes of eye rolling, pressed lips, and sucking teeth without words, they continued to get more information about my life they had no clue about.

"Ya butterin' 'em biscuits long?"

"Huh? What… What do you mean buttering biscuits? Uh, we met in the Spring of 2019. But we didn't… get together seriously until later."

"Babe-ah, don't act up, now. I know, ya know what Lolli means."

"I…I don't…Uh…"

"Hold on. Let me say it in a different way…"

"No, Lolli, let me. I'm much more in the know on how these young folks be talkin'.'"

"Fine, Dene, ya go."

"Marie, when exactly did you open that jar of cookies? Gal, ya tell us now, when did this Asian boy start grindin' da corn? When did this 'ere soul café, start servin' tasty vittles?"

I snorted. The three wise women nodded with grunts. All of them stared at me, waiting for my truthful answer. *(Oh my god!)* My mother lowered her head, smirking while my aunts were snapping their fingers, rolling their necks, and gesturing like Dwain Johnson in "Be Cool" doing that monolog scene. *(Why does she look like when he said, "When you go to nationals, bring it," from that movie? Oh, don't look. Don't laugh!)* I had to turn away for a second. Blinking quickly, I felt their eyes poking at me. Then I buckled and said, "Uh, well that would be in 2019…"

I hadn't finished talking and Claudine blurted out, "You met him that year ya said… wait…"

My mother shook her head and closed her eyes. Gasps and grunts followed with a few piercing sounds accompanied by a wide swing to the back of my head from my mother.

"Ouch!"

"Girl, ya dun gave him some on your first date?" My mother snarled.

"Well, uh, maybe you are really my daughter!" Lolli said laughing, while Dene giggled sipping her tea.

My mother shouted, "Shut up, Lolli!"

Waving my hands, I tried to explain. "No, it wasn't like that. I met him and then… Uhma, we hung out a bit. Then a few weeks later, we saw each other again but by accident. After that we spent time together, but you could say we officially became a couple after the pandemic. Yeah, that's kind of how it was." I said then shifted in my seat.

"If that be so, why didn't we hear nothing 'bout it, gurl? Last we heard was 'bout that football player you were going to marry, and his nasty niggerochi ass had a nappy headed baby with some tramp."

"Auntie Lolli…"

"Yeah! That's right. We ain't no nothing!"

"Auntie Dene, ya see…uh…"

Finally, my mother said something. "Y'all, I told you don't ask. It's in the past."

"Fine…"

"No, it ain't fine, Lolli. Wait, I'm still upset 'bout there being a wedding and I didn't get no invite!"

"Oh, yeah… me too, Dell! Marie, we been knowin' ya all your life! Explain."

"It was quick and private, auntie. With only mother, Pawpaw and Celeste in attendance. Not even my girlfriends knew. Please don't be angry about that. I love you both very much. If it had been different, I would have had a big wedding, but it wasn't something that we wanted at the time."

Deep sighs came from both aunties, but it was Claudine who gave up first. "I suppose I forgive ya. But only because you're my favorite."

I sat up, reaching to hug her and she kissed me. Lolli was sucking air through her teeth, expressing her annoyance. I moved quickly to repeat the loving hug to her. These two always were competing on who was my favorite aunt. I loved them equally. Well, I think they knew Lorelle and Hellene were always my favorites. But they are high ranking with Renee's mom, Marianna, Gert, and Nannette. Honestly, I had the most diverse and fabulous auntie coalition. But then it happened.

"I'm just going to ask. Was he cute? I don't think Jackie Chan looks good but that be me… Can we see a picture of him at least?"

"Yeah, let's see what he looks like... I mean who is this Korean that took my daughter-in-law away and made these cute babies. I'm not understanding how you let my son slip through your fat fingers. He's always had a crush on you."

"Uh, no. Photos are private. I don't have them available for people to see."

"Say what, now? We... we is just people?"

"Oh, excuse me, miss thang. I'm gonna keep my little gift I brought since I be just people."

"Auntie Lolli! Auntie Dene! Mother, help me!"

My mother snickered as she watched me squirm in my seat. "Mom!" I pleaded for help from the scrutiny. She put her cup down and stopped the nonsense.

"Y'all, I told you before that it's security for her safety living here. Don't ask. Ya came to see Marie and my grandbabies. Don't make this your only trip. I just got her calm. Stop harassing my daughter."

Feeling relieved from the pressure they were putting on me, I said, "Yes, that's right. And as far as Toryono and I go, he knows we are homies. But Auntie, I told him we couldn't get married when I was eight and he gave me that pop ring. He got over me. Rachel is the right wife for him, and you have cute grand kids, right?"

Smirking, she winked at me, but Lolli cut her eyes, which my mother and I knew was code for 'they ain't that cute.'

"Security from us? We family! Oh, wait... maybe we ain't family no more... Dene, we been voted off Delacroix Island. It's why we got ta stay in a damn hotel."

"Chantal-Marie, do you even know how many pinches and whoop-ins I saved you from gettin'? Dell is mean! I counted. At least four! All the snacks I slipped you and that fat face girl with the freckles, Renee when I came to visit. Those trips to ya high school and college graduations. Oh, and the gifts. I ain't kicked off. I know better! Now, you ain't tryin' to show us a real person, you say ya been secretly married too. Hmmm…Was it really a sperm-cicle on a stick or in a tube you don used ta get ya babies?"

I sighed, then headed over to a cabinet by the wall aquarium separating the dining room and the kitchen. I pulled out a glass 8x10 frame with a photo of Jae-Sung, and I dressed in white on our first trip to Cocoa Island in the Maldives. Handing it to my mother, Lolli snatched it out of her hand, and she and Claudine immediately huddled up to inspect him. My mother just rolled her eyes snickering and I sat down quietly sipping more tea.

During the silence, my mother winked at me, and after smiling, I thought about the day the picture was taken. For a moment, my mind traveled back to when Jae sang that Jagged Edge song, "Gotta Be" to me, holding my hand and walking over water pier to the place he planned for us. I chuckled to myself, but the memory was abruptly halted when Lolli cleared her throat. I turned to get her verdict on the visual.

"Well, he got some mysterious eyes, now don't he. Your one son does look a lot like him. He's cute." She winked at me. Then Claudine tapped the back of my hand, and I turned to her. As she nodded in agreement, she added, "This is nice. Marie, you look really in love and happy. Your babies show it too. No doubt about it. He's Asian, alright. Girl, did ya weigh more than him?"

They all started laughing while she slid the tray of cookies for me to take one. *(Really? So typical.)* I shook my head in disgust. Claudine kissed my cheek and popped a grape in her mouth and mumbled, "Don't be in ya feelin's. Ya thick like your mama. These people are skinny anyway. It was gonna be a yes, no matter what. But Lolli's right, he ain't no Jackie Chan for sure."

"Jackie Chan is Chinese," my mother chimed in, nibbling on a mango chutney and ham sandwich.

Lolli held up her hand to make a point. "Chinese, Japanese, Taiwanese, Vietnamese, he ain't Nigganeese. Meaning he wasn't packin' a hammer because he was too damn skinny! Body like a teenager who needs to eat. Can't climb no shrubs, girl."

A laugh shot out like a burst before I covered my mouth. The three cackled for a while before handing me back the frame to put away.

After that, my visiting loved ones didn't press me anymore about Jae, or the secrets of my life over the years. We laughed, cooked, and they spoiled us during the seven days we were together. I love having Black aunties. There were tears when they left the following Sunday flying off to France with my mother.

Looking back on those weeks, I believe my mother knew ahead of time this would be how things would go and it must have been why she planned to stay with me so long. "I love you, mom."

Auntie Lolli Toussaint

Auntie Claudine "Dene" Jefferies

14. South Koreans

As soon as my mother left, we went back to having regular relative visits. My children don't get to get out as much as others probably do since everything has to be arranged and secure first. But when we do get in vans for trips or on the rare occasion Kang lets us split up and go out in disguise, it seemed to be when they smiled the brightest, I think. Their eyes are so gigantic, and my three amigos are curious about everything; always trying to investigate something new.

(That is definitely from my parents. Ha!)

The times we've gone to stay at Min Cha and Dong-Hyun's compound outside of Seoul, the triplets get to be loved all over by their great-grandparents Sung-Ho Hak, the head of the family and his wife Kyung-Mi. Their jeungjo-halmeoni (great-grandmother) can't pick them up anymore, but she sits down and kisses those little hands and feet laughing. On every visit she would announce that each one was beautiful and that her heart was happy seeing Jae-Sung in their eyes. Kyung-Mi often makes me cry with joy.

Now, Jae's grandfather was a little different. Sung-Ho Hak would act as if he is too old and has no interest in the triplets at all, but when no one is looking, he plays peak a boo with them. We came up with a plan and will purposely leave the room with them to watch him do it. Then when we come back, he pretends they are on his nerves and starts grumbling from his wheelchair. *(Too funny.)*

Jae-Sung's maternal grandparents
Kyung-Mi & Sung-Ho Hak

We regularly have been enjoying weekend-long stays with their other idol adopted grandparents Nah Min Ji and his sweet wife, Eun-Woo. Staying at their compound was always like being at a tropical resort. When they were younger, Jolie only wanted Min Ji to hold her. She would cry every time Eun-Woo or one of her daughters held her because she wanted him. It's still that way. I told him he had a special touch.

The family secret is that this internationally known tough multi-billion-dollar businessman is a loving baby magnet and teddy bear, who loves to give hugs. I had to swear never to tell that he is a softy! They loved Jae-Sung so deeply and they felt the same about his children. Honestly, I felt they cared about me, just as much. Now when we visit with the triplets, being a little older, they get to play with the other five Nah family grandchildren and blend right in.

We are a happy family. Jae asked me to do it and I'm glad I moved to let his family bond with them and me while we live in South Korea.

15. SME

My one-year personal leave as an international contract director for Sony Music Entertainment was just about to end, when Ayana Fairchild and I met at my home. Taking the leave versus resigning was something I'm glad I did. I was excited to begin my new consultant director position, she had created for me at Sony Music Entertainment. As she had previously explained to me, I would mostly work with the Japanese directors but occasionally with Apryl on Seoul branch projects, if ever needed. Ayana is a good friend, and she gave it to me straight no chaser.

"Japanese directors have been unraveling since you have been away. It has been major roadblocks to getting those men to trust someone new for international support. We lost three directors because of communication breakdowns and culture protocol not clearly understood during project debriefs and contract research request meetings."

"What do you mean, lost directors?"

"Marie, two of them walked out of Sony meetings with Japanese directors and never came back. They couldn't get past the big guards at the gate if you know what I mean. Without having access to data, they couldn't do their job and meetings would be silent. It was crazy." I tried to hold in my growing amusement but failed.

"Yeah, it's funny to you but not to Sony executives or the board. I see your snickering because these men of stone, didn't back down, didn't listen to women, and didn't share secrets. They are untamable tigers. Oh wait, no, dragons. But we knew you had them wrapped around your finger as a fellow dragon. Ha! When I told them you were returning after your mourning period to only work with them as a consultant, they immediately got nicer. One had the nerve to smile. I bet they had a party."

I was curious, so I just asked directly, "Was it, Satoshi-san pulling the strings and acting up?"

She just looked at me with pressed lips for a couple of seconds before she said, "I don't know what you did to him, but he even frustrates me and has gotten Joseph so upset during a meeting that he took two days off to decompress."

I just shook my head and giggled.

After meeting with Ayana, Kang had his own security protocol debriefing in my home office. "Noona, you cannot tell anyone your connections to Jae-Sung or Min Ji. No conducting meetings via video without a security pathway to scramble the location of the home. No one can know where you live, whether you live alone or even have children. Never share your schedule with others outside of Sony partners. Always avoid reporters, social media, and photographers. Traveling to Japan for Sony or anywhere must be pre-arranged by me or SI. No last-minute trips. The privacy contracts remain active, and Mrs. Fairchild is the executive responsible since you will now be working directly for her. I know you trust the Japanese directors, but I don't want them to know any more about your personal life than you are a widow. If they ask redirect them to contact Ayana."

"I got it Kang. It's almost as many rules as before. Like when I was just a secret girlfriend. Ha, ha, ha, ha."

"Noona Marie, I need you to be serious. It can be more dangerous if we're not careful. We loosened the security because you were not working, but now, we have made a few changes to tighten up the process. Ayana and I set up for one of my guys to always be your visible bodyguard. His employment trail has been modified, so it appears that Sony has hired him for you to live and work here. But he has been shadowing you off and on. Marie, you can't go anywhere without him, SI, or me."

Kang waited a few days before telling me a bit more about the visible muscle I was going to have. "He only goes by Trey. He's my computer craftsman; speaks fluent English, Japanese, French, and Korean— some others too, but that's not important. He's in his thirties and a blended man."

"Blended, uh, like a smoothie?" I said laughing but Kang rolled his eyes, and announced, "mixed-race. He is part Māori, Korean, and Black South African. Noona be serious, now."

I didn't like it, but it was my life now, keeping secrets for privacy and safety.

A couple of days later, I met with Ayana Fairchild at the Seoul branch building to officially start my new director consultant position. There were a few new faces but lots of familiar ones. After the official meeting, my colleague Tia Yun, and her former assistant, Andy Soo, who now is a director, were both excited to see me in person after over a year. We made plans to go to dinner soon at our old spot, the Privilege Bar, to catch up.

The next day, we flew to Tokyo so that I could reintroduce myself to the Japanese senior directors. As their senior international consultant, I would work with the same Sony directors I had been with for almost fifteen years. But officially, I was exclusively partnered with senior directors for complex multi-million-dollar international projects requiring my special liaison expertise and assessment review before final contracts could be submitted.

When I entered the boardroom meeting with Mr. Aminbello, my thirty-seven-year-old, six-foot, British bodyguard, I thought there would be more than just the five honorable executives. It was quiet until their official bow and welcome. These older Japanese businessmen did not shake my hand, *(of course not, I am a female,)* nor did I speak first. So, many business rules instantly came back to my mind. I had so many years of perfecting them. I'm sure they were just waiting dormant. Avoid humor and sarcasm and restrain all emotions. Open opportunities for others to save face but show your strength with accurate data, reasoning, and facts. The men are first.

Select the right words for the respect you're giving. Yep, it came back just like riding a bike after being inside during snowy winter months.

To be honest, after being away for a year, I was ready for the facts only and cold business formalities of my international music entertainment contracts career, but as soon as Satoshi Senko saw me his eyes silently smiled. My mind had thoughts, *(Dragon to dragon. Ha, and we're back! Satoshi-san, I missed you too.)* I giggled inside, feeling the welcome home.

Closing the meeting and preparing to leave, Akio-san's assistant, Yuki mentioned to me semi-privately, "we were a kawaii and kakkaii capple *(Cute and good-looking couple),*" after I said the silent man standing behind me was my bodyguard. Ayana and I thought it was funny how they assumed I needed a man close. But this dude didn't flinch. It felt weird, and from that moment, I planned to change things in some way.

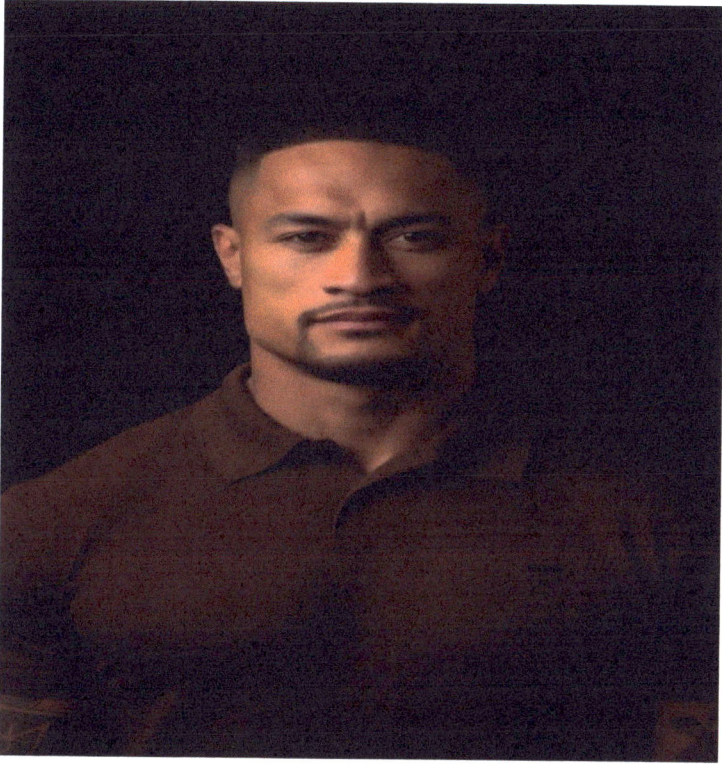

16. Trey Aminbello

Flying back the next day, I was sitting next to my silent islander-looking security, Mr. Trey Aminbello. He never spoke to me the entire time we were together, not even when we met at the airport the day before. When Kang introduced him as 'Trey' I smiled, and he nodded, but his face was stone-cold.

At first, I figured, okay, he is to protect me. This is how it is supposed to be. But I had been so used to my K-Pop idol bodyguards being family. It felt awkward having this giant man follow me around as a pretty hot-looking brown wall of rippling muscles. *(Is he mute?)* I had to admit to myself, I liked SI and Kang being with me. They were fun, like "Donkey" from the movie *Shrek* and less official like a real bodyguard, but I had to get used to this new protocol, I guess.

I had to break the code of silence because it was creepy. Onboard, I told him, "Trey, we have to talk. I mean, you can't just be a statue. It's weird. I know we don't know each other that well but we need to be friends, at least." I smiled at him and continued to extend a friendship branch. "Is Trey really the name your parents gave you or is it code for secret agent, Tyrannosaurus? Oh, wait, no... that's Ty not Trey. Hmmm, I'll think of the code name it's supposed to be. Give me a minute." I grinned and waited for him to react to my joke so we could start a conversation.

He chuckled before his deep voice hit my ear nicely like a low growl. "Alright, let's be friends. I've used the name Trey, since I was young in school in England and South Korea. It was easier to pronounce, and I was already the odd-looking kid around, so it made me stand out as a cooler dude." He smirked while taking a sip of his coffee.

(Oh, he does have a sense of humor. I like that.)

He continued to share, "... and Madame Delacroix, I don't give my full name... unless I'm in an intimate association."

Startled by his comment, I leaned back to study his stone-cold expression for a few seconds before replying with, "What? Well, how intimate do we need to be for me to know it? You follow me everywhere. Here, I'll start, Marie... Just call me Marie. For heaven's sake, I'm not my mother." I snickered. He kept looking around like Kang usually does surveying the perimeter. *(I knew it. He's a ninja too.)*

Moments later, he leaned in slightly to whisper without facing me, "Alright, Marie. Since you asked, it's Treuoloni." *(Yeah, that's better. It fits him for sure.)* I cleared my throat and grinned wider, expressing my appreciation for him trusting me with his secret.

"Merci. I won't tell. Now, we are getting to know each other. See, this is good."

Taking the glass of chilled bubbling champagne mixed with a splash of pineapple juice from the stewardess, I exhaled with ease, knowing I would be making a new friend. I felt confident until he said, "I know a lot about you, Marie Delacroix."

Without thinking, I cut my eyes at him. "Really? Do tell," I said while adjusting in my seat, preparing for his download of information obviously transmitted from the Cheng brothers. *(Alright, what did they tell you?)*

Seconds later, I got a flashback to confronting Jae about having some secret dossier on me. *(That was funny! He was so confused, sayin' what is that. I'm like dude you speak French! Ha! Ha!)* I giggled to myself while Trey began talking.

"You're a very private person. You don't overindulge or live your life being driven by excess or pleasure. In business, you are tough, never weak. You are determined, confident, and professional. I don't recall seeing you react when a Japanese or Korean businessman doesn't shake your hand or doesn't acknowledge your presence in a room. You're cool as ice and gain their respect with your facts, and respect them even when they don't respect you. But they do. You've earned it. It has been pretty amazing to watch from the shadows. You like to write and drink wine. How am I doing?" He paused for me to check in and give a grade.

Nodding with a soft smile, I said, "Basics okay… Anything else?" Gesturing to him to keep going with a raise of my glass, I listened attentively, sipping my delicious mimosa.

"You have a fascination with water, specifically the ocean and tropical places. You love to read, listen to music, and dance, but you do those more privately than in public. You are a strong woman, Afro American, but you don't forget you're French. You seem to enjoy psychology and ethnology." He paused to take a few sips of his lightly sweetened black coffee that he had delivered to him earlier. I noticed the subtle way in which he scanned our first-class stewardess after she brought it and smiled. *(He likes women. Check.)*

Once I cleared my throat, I took the opportunity to speak so it didn't seem like a background check exam. I mean, he already had the job. *(Duh.)* "Well, look at you, making me sound like a stellar main character in a great novel. Ha-ha. I seem rather spectacular. Thanks for that." He chuckled, and the base of his baritone voice rumbled through his throat. I probed if he had any more. "Is that it? I mean, now is your chance to impress me. If you can."

Trey tilted his head and sniffled before rubbing his sharp, smooth chin. He glanced at me with his dark round eyes and long lashes. I stopped my intake of air for a moment before blinking and looking away. The next words from him caused my pause of air to last longer than just a second or two. I actually held my breath for a bit when I heard him say, "I admit I thought you were uniquely attractive when I first saw you in 2019 during Paris Fashion Week. I remember times when your smile lit up the night sky, and your eyes were brighter than the stars."

Shocked, I drew up my fingers to cover my lips. *(Huh? Wait…What did he say? 2019? Has he been around that long watching me? Hold on, was that poetic...Oh, damn.)* He took a breath and continued speaking, even though I knew he heard my reaction and saw me looking off into space. I snapped back and turned my body in to hear what he said next.

"Hmm, off the top of my head, I can say when you were in Egypt in the northern market square. Sneaking off to Niagara Falls with your friends, the Escobar's. That quick fall trip with your cousin to Eric's. The Grammy's in L.A. and all those weeks in Seattle. Yeah, those I can say were times your smile, I mean everything about you glowed with how ecstatic you were. It isn't that way anymore. You have not always been happy, but even that first time on Cocoa Island when you were alone and very upset, I made sure you were safe and didn't hurt yourself or anything. Even then, the light didn't dim from your eyes or smile. I remember thinking it must be because you leave a door open for one more second of possibilities. You seemed to be very optimistic in finding and holding on to love and the happiness it brought you. But things have happened that changed all that. Like I said, things are different now."

My mouth would have hung open if I hadn't been pressing my lips together like I had just sucked on the tartest lemon in the world. I had a thousand questions running through my mind and even more thoughts. I blinked a few times then just said, "Knowing me a bit more than I thought, I see. Alrighty than, you win. I'm impressed."

Trey chuckled and sipped his coffee.

Over the weeks that followed, I learned more about Trey. The two of us were together a lot. We talked about many things including his family, and mine. He is a single heterosexual man with no children. Trey is the only male in his immediate family, since his father and older brother passed away. He has four sisters, two are much older and live in Canada and New Zealand. But he is closer to his younger sisters, Rutalah and Ohanaka, who live in England with their mother, Isla, and their large extended family. Trey shared many of his hobbies, but he laughed because I was more interested in his connection to the security squad that was mega South Korean celebrity idol Jin-K's and now assigned to shadow me.

Unlike the other members of Jin-K's security, operated by NM Entertainment and managed by Kang Cheng, Trey was the only one that had not been with them for over twenty years. He told me that he had met Jae first during his South Korean military duty. Jae and Kang were on a special assignment requiring them to train and sometimes stay on an American military base. Trey was one of the three British soldiers working on an American project with them to protect South Korean boarders. When his duty ended, he wanted to stay in South Korea, and because of his connections with Jae-Sung, he joined NM Entertainment in 2017. Then Kang's idol security team right after my idol boys finished their required military assignment. It was a budding friendship we had going.

Then after a meeting in the Sony Seoul office, a dark-haired tall and handsome Caucasian American executive approached me in an elevator and asked me out. The poor guy didn't realize we were together and made his move. I had to physically stop Trey from jacking him up with some kind of sleeper hold. (That was funny.)

After that incident, we agreed to be more social and casually interact and talk when we were out in public, so it wouldn't happen again. I liked him. It was fun to have a new male friend. However, a bit later, I learned that was sort of a problem.

While in my home office with the door closed, Kang was yelling a little at Trey. "Man, you... you broke silence?!" He got it first. Then Kang turned to me and said, "Noona, what... what are you doing?!"

Apparently, one day, SI saw Trey and I at an executive café in NM Entertainment's building having lunch and chatting after I met with Chris for some legal things. *(Oops. My bad.)* SI reported it to Kang, who was clearly very upset. *(Dang. Need to teach SI that snitches get stitches.)* Trying to explain without fully understanding why Kang was upset, I said, "What did I do wrong? Because we are friendly? Kang it was weird he was like a wall standing around and growling lowly like a bear."

Trey snorted but quickly suppressed his snicker and got serious. Then Kang flung his hands in the air, saying, "He's laughing? Marie, you are killing the idol code. This is serious business. We don't socialize. We are alert, stealth all the time. What you say... we... we are Ninja's. I can't believe you did this. How... How in the hell, did she get you to break silence code, man? I thought you could handle this better than Han, but I was wrong." He walked around my office but stopped to get an explanation.

"Kang, look, it's like this... someone in Japan said something on her first trip and it works better. It's less obvious, more informal. Trust me. It's good," Trey said it with humble eyes. Perhaps he was trying to convince him that he could be closer to me than a silent force or a shadow.

Really watching and listening to the dialog but thinking about things unsaid, I got a feeling it wasn't really a code but a family thing. I wanted to confirm my suspicions.

125

"Trey, can you excuse us for a minute?" Once we were alone in my office, Kang stood across the room still looking disgusted with his eyes rolling around as if he was planning counter moves for security. "Why are you so upset? It was weird, him just standing there like a stone or behind walls watching me. What's going on? Are you… Kang… Brother…Are you jealous?" I asked with a straight face.

His head darted up and he leered at me. "Mwolago Hasyeossnayo? Jiltuhaneun! nongdam-igessjyo (What did you say? Jealous! You have got to be joking, right)?" I shrugged my shoulders and raised my eyebrows simultaneously.

"Ani, igeon sa-eob-iya! Geuneun dangsin jubyeon salamdeul-eul eotteohge yeonguhago, chaleul masigo, malhago, usgeona, geuleohji anh-eun gyeong-u eotteon jochileul chwihaeya haneunji gyeoljeonghalkkayo? (No, this is business! How will he study those around you, and decide what actions need to be taken, if he is having tea, talking, and laughing, and whatnot)?"

Kang's voice was lower and calmer, but still with a twinge of annoyance. Watching him carefully, he seemed to be really upset about it, and I didn't want him to assign someone else now that I had gotten to know Trey better. So, I kept going with where I was leading him to lighten the mood.

"Kang Cheng are you sure? Is it… well, because he's a man, and it looks like I'm on a date? Hmm, which was strictly for Jae-Sung Kim aka Jin-K, the sexy and fabulous leader of legendary successful South Korean Pop and R&B male idol group DRGN5. Or maybe I'm just supposed to talk and eat with you and SI. My handsome and overprotective idol trainee brothers sworn to keep me in a box on a shelf like their best friend told them too."

Kang sat in the chair across the room and let out a long hard breath, which told me he was relaxing his stress.

(Oh, why can I feel that his breath is hot and smells like kimchi all the way over here... Is his face red? Yep, it is. He's so cute!)

"Phenomenal Noona..." Kang swiped his hand over his face before continuing, "Jae-Sung did not tell us to keep you in a box. You can meet people, have friends, more than just us, Marie. But... it is not the same, like when he was..." He caught himself and didn't say what he was thinking, but my brain finished his sentence even if he didn't. *(When Jae was alive.)* "...I need to do background security checks on everyone you are with on a regular basis. It is important. My responsibility is to keep you safe. SI and I... it is our duty, not just to Jae-Sung but you. You're our family, and it could be dangerous living here. We still have to be careful, alright?"

I nodded with a smile but delivered a demand. "I don't want anyone else. Trey stays. He is alert. Trust me. It works this way. You chose the right shadow to come out and play with me. It sounded like you were a little jealous because I like him. But I understand its protocol. I get it."

He nodded, and I knew we were on the same page. When he stood up to leave my office, I stopped him when I said, "Oh, Kang?"

"Ne, ahjumma (Yes, middle-aged lady)."

"Wait, not noona... Why not just older sister? Why did you call me old, like an old lady?"

Chuckling, he said, "You are older than all of us, so you need reminders. Your memory might be going."

I gasped then told him, "Dude, did you have radish kimchi? Your hot breath gave it away, smarty-pants!"

He groaned, throwing a pillow from the chair at my head. "AAH!" I yelped, ducking under my desk, and it flew over me. Then he shouted, leaving my office. "Go back to work, ajhumma!"

Snickering, I yelled back, "Punk-face!"

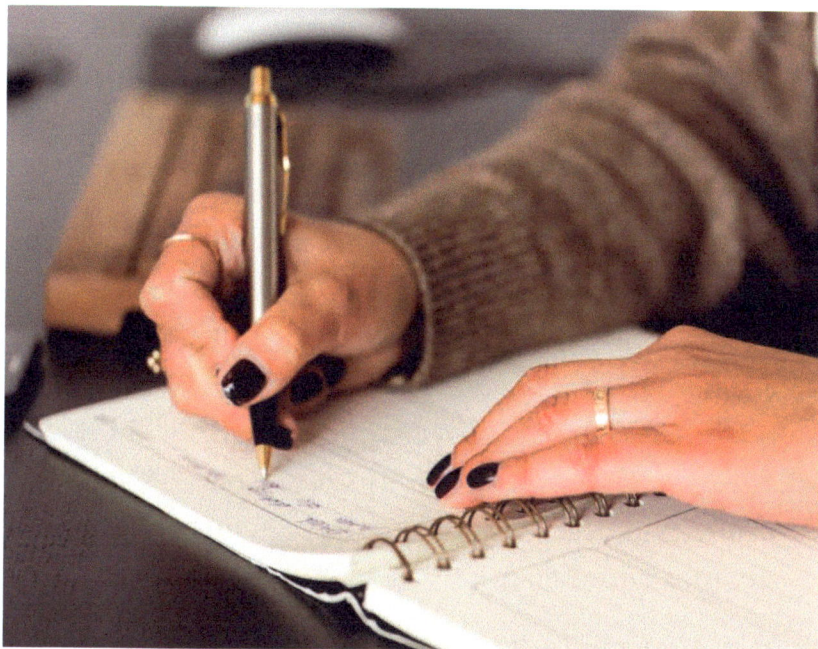

17. It's June...

A letter to my husband.

Happy South Korean Wedding Anniversary, Baby.

I miss you. I love you.

We are staying at your parents' compound for a few days. I am feeling better about it, now. Your mother forced me to come. I wanted to send the triplets and be alone, but she sent Dong-Hyun to get all of us. He waited in a secure van for me to pack something and get to the pickup location.

I wouldn't dare argue with your stepfather.

They had a large dinner planned last night, which was lovely. It was family, and your aunt came with Jin-young. Your cousin Young-Jae is in Australia right now. I didn't cry but Nari made sure to have tissue on stand-by just in case I did.

Your aunt is a real piece of work. She keeps stressing me about having a shrine in the house to honor you. I'm like no! She even had a delivery of some things from your father's family for them to be displayed. Oh, my god! I left them right at your parents' house. I can't put my finger on it but between her and Dong-Hyun's sister, I must control my thoughts and facial expressions when I am around those two.

You told me to be aware they are kind of catty but I'm glad I have more in my corner like your mom and Aunt Tang, Soo, and your uncle's wives. I'm trying not to cuss so our children don't learn that but it's hard. Now that you're not here, it seems like them witches need a verbal beat down every-time I see them.

I love your grandmother! Kyung-Mi is the sweetest. Her health isn't good, but she has really bonded with the triplets. Especially Jolie. Which surprised me since she is the darker of the three. Your mother has a favorite, Jin. I know one reason is because he looks like you. Aunt Teng loves Jae the most. It can be such a hoot learning why people pick their favorites.

I didn't think Min Cha would be up for us to stay after your grandfather passed away last month but she's very strong. I admire her. She's doing better than I would if it were my father. I loved your grandfather. He was very kind. Your grandmother told me this morning, "We are honored and happy you are part of our family. Very proud to have beautiful great-grandchildren from our angelic grandson, Jae-Sung. Thank you for them."

I smiled as she kissed my cheek. That made me feel so good, that I listened to you and moved here. You are so smart, my love.

There have been a few shifts with your grandfather passing away. I don't really understand why your mother's older brother Han-Gyeol or her younger brother, Sung-Ho isn't. But it's your stepfather Dong-Hyun that oversees the family until Kang marries or when he turns fifty whichever comes first. Then he will be in charge until Jae and Jin come of age. If Kang has a son, he will be in line after them. Is it because your uncles only have daughters? Why not SI? I thought it was because Kang is older, but he said it's that but also because of what happened when SI was younger. That's seems wrong to punish him for that.

What about your cousins, Jin-young and Young-Jae. Is that not the same family? You made provisions for them when you died. I don't understand. In a Black family everyone is family. Ha! Maybe, they are not considered to be and cannot be the head because they are your father's *nephews from his sister and not from your mother's side. Is this another noble bloodline rule thing from the secret illegitimate daughter of the Crown Prince? No one will tell me. More Korean family secrets. I'm still an outsider. I hate not knowing what is going on. I wish you were here. I know you would have explained it to me. My life has a giant hole without you, baby. Not just from this but everything. I miss you so much, Jae. I love you, Happy Anniversary.*

After putting the letter in my keepsake box, I watched some of his videos he made for me and drank wine. I cried listening to the love song he wrote, his duets he recorded with Tangee of our wedding song, and I looked closely at the beautiful portrait painting he had made and marked for our Anniversary on June 1, 2030. I remember I was so shocked to discover his gift to me hanging on an easel under a lit frame. The profile images of me gazing up at him while he held my chin with his finger bending down to kiss me was so life-like. I cried more studying the detailed colors, and a moment I wouldn't have again. It was a difficult couple of days.

On June 18th, one of our attorneys, Chris Hwang, came over with Kang regarding a possible legal action against Jin-K's estate.

"What's this about?" I said it offering him a cup of coffee sitting at the kitchen island.

"A former NM Entertainment artist filed a claim, citing unpaid composing credit royalties on three songs written by Jin-K and four songs by two others. The lawsuit is pending, but lawyers are collecting for discovery on the allegations. There is no record of creative rights for Sebastian Khan on any of the songs Jin-K wrote and sold to him. There is a clear bill of sale on them. Jin-K was meticulous about business, but we need to double-check the home music catalog and any notes or draft records here." He took a few sips of his coffee before reaching for the sugar.

Blocking his hand from taking it, I moaned, and he frowned. Kang chuckled.

"Sure. Of course, you can check. But you cannot have any more sugar. The half teaspoon I put in your coffee was enough."

"Noona..." he said it with a sad face and a tilt of the head.

"Nope... Keeping your blood sugar levels low. Chris, don't make me call your wife."

"Okay...fine. It's a conspiracy." Chris sipped the coffee as is but wasn't happy about it. When Nari came in with my babies walking in looking for snacks, Chris shouted, "Wua, these three are getting so big!"

I moaned in agreement, picking up Jolie. Chris and Kang left for the music room to go through Jae's music catalog and business notes that he would have had listed by song, title, date and stored in his library. I wasn't worried. As soon as they left a flash came to me from what Jae wrote in a letter to me before he died.

(*Our attorneys through NM Entertainment, Chris and Eddie will take care of what belongs to me from my music career past and future royalties, which might be the only thing split between you, and some of my idol brothers, Eric, BJ, Kris, Tonee, Shane, Ethan, Vaj, and producer Tayler Styles.)*

About forty minutes later, Chris gave me the update. "Thanks. There is nothing like we thought but we wanted to make sure. I will close this out, and it will go away. The other composers I don't know about but claims against Jin-K's estate will be resolved with no findings."

I confirmed saying, "I wasn't worried. Jin-K was meticulous but could be a little persnickety too. I knew he would have whatever documented, either way."

Kang smirked, "Per what?"

Nari confidently spoke up with a firm tone. "Persnickety...means precise, careful, emphasis on minor details...you know, persnickety."

Kang chuckled before grunting with an, "Ah."

Showing Chris out, I snorted. He said, "Uh... Did you use that word on purpose?" I nodded and whispered, "She has been dying to use it, so yeah. I'm curious to see how she slips in pluviophile and aplomb."

We both snickered because Nari was so proud to finally share a new word she learned. She was grinning so wide; she looked a lot like *The Cat in the Hat* by Dr. Seuss. Priceless.

18. New York

July 30, 2031

I'm in New York for a quick work trip to meet with my direct boss, Ayana Fairchild, on some Sony Music Entertainment APAC business we couldn't discuss virtually. In my senior project consultant role for Sony's Japan and South Korean directors, I have had a lot of flexibility to work part-time or as needed and I loved it. The maneuvering of Ayana creating this position for me to stay on was a blessing. The partnerships I had built up with Sony Japan and South Korea directors took me years to establish. It would have been a major setback in the Asian Pacific market for me to leave, especially in Japan.

I never had any intentions of traveling, let alone leaving my little ones. But it was necessary and seemed to be the normal requirement for occasional travel as a United States citizen working abroad for Sony. Before getting here, I was so busy that I had to be on autopilot when I booked my room at the Mandarin Oriental Hotel here in New York.

It took several conversations to convince Kang that I didn't need security shadowing while in New York. But after reviewing my business plans and talking with Ayana, he agreed and gave Trey some time off to visit his family in England. But only after he flew with me to New York and planned to meet me to return to Soeul together.

Tearfully, I left my growing toddlers at home in the trusted hands of their grandmother Min Cha, aunt Teng, Kang, and their nanny, Nari. The three ladies didn't need me to give strict instructions to keep on the watch because the Cheng brothers are sneaky. I was confident they wouldn't let them do crazy stuff. Especially, their mom, Teng, wouldn't let them slip my babies anything weird to eat, like they constantly try to do when I'm at home, saying it's Korean tradition.

In the New York home office, there were so many new faces but still a few old ones. Eddie Andrews is now married and works as an executive in a new data mining division. Todd, April's former assistant, is now an associate director in the Sony Latin region. Gabriella is the senior director covering France and now leads teams in a few other countries in Europe.

Of course, when I first arrived, I spent quality time with April, and my adorable nieces, Zoe, and Farah, at their home. Chin had gone out of town, and it was just us girls making lunch. The girls are so big, and I loved getting real-time hugs and pinching those Oriental doll-like round cheeks they both have.

When my former international director partner Apryl Nguyen comes to South Korea, we often meet to collaborate on business or just catch up since she still manages the three countries in APAC like before but now with a junior director named Chung-Hee, a young Korean American man that she trains. The three of us work together, and I think he is going to do very well.

Although Ayana Fairchild took over as my direct boss, I got to see my former executive bosses, Mr. Tanaka, and Mr. Perlan, and personally thanked them for the cards and flowers.

(Are they scared or shocked that I am hugging them. Oh, why is he blushing? Yeah, ya like touchin' this thick sista-girl, don't cha. Too funny.)

While on this business trip to New York, my initial plan was to Zoom chat or facetime my children every night while away. But after a few fun hours with April's family, I called them from my Hudson River view suite. Jae, Jin, and Jolie were just a bunch of teary eyed, pouty-faced darlings the entire call.

(Aww, don't cry Marie. Don't let them see you crying. Smile.)

Min Cha texted me right after we hung up that all three were still fussy and maybe I should just check in with her and not talk to them. Honestly, I was wiping away my tears while reading her message and replied in agreement since I would be home in a couple of days.

It had been a long day. Once I completed my review of some documents for the next day's meeting, I took my long hot bubble bath and prepared for my body and mind to shut down. But I couldn't sleep. I just laid in bed thinking about my life in New York before I met Jae-Sung Kim. My restlessness brought back to mind many things I had done each day living in New York. I pondered if I was even happy back then. I reached for my phone and selected to play soft jazz saxophone music from my *Relax* playlist.

As time passed in the night, my mind drifted to several vaulted memories of him that seemed to grow in detail, each time I blinked my eyes. I recalled the details of every moment when I received his singing invitation made from Jay B/Def song, "Come Back To Me," and we met in this hotel after so long. *(Oh, Jae.)* I reached for my phone and changed the music to play the original song. "It's crazy how he and Jae-Sung can sound the same on some songs. Airy, soft, sultry, and sweet. Like feathers on the skin." While the song repeated, I cried remembering his eyes, his long strides coming toward me, his touch as we made love in a romantic suite only a few floors above where I was.

"I miss you so much, baby." Seeped from my lips which began to quiver, and my hands shook tugging at the sheet covering me. Emotions elevated quickly without any emergency break to stop. I turned my face into the firm pillow trying to suffocate my sadness. Constant visions in my mind's eye so clearly outlined the curve of his handsome face, the delicateness of his hairless butter cream skin, the silkiness of his black straight hair, the gentleness of his smile, and his hands caressing me. Mumbling to myself, "I want to remember what he felt like holding me. Jae-Sung, nae salang (my love). I don't want to be here without you."

Then I cried out more in the moment of relived heartbreak. It was the reality of where I was, and what I no longer had, hit me hard again. I hadn't completely grieved. Do we ever stop? I was now in this hotel that held so many memories of us together without any preoccupation or distraction for my brain to cling on to. As each minute passed the quietness brought me back to the abyss I felt in my heart. I was lost and alone. Sobbing with muffled whispers of his name, I curled my body into a tight ball and held myself rocking gently all night long.

After the morning Sony meetings with April, Gabriella, and two directors, my afternoon was free. My next planned stop was New Jersey. I've got to hang out with my Delta diva doll bestie since seventh grade and her family.

19. Them Escobar's

I was in New Jersey with my boyfriend, Christopher Escobar. He still loved me most of all. Well, it just felt that way to me. Especially, when he yelled, "Auntie Rhee" and planted little kisses on my cheek. I adored how he would hold my face still to do it. Christopher was my special little man. I got a great deal of pleasure listening to him tell me stories about his adventures and playmates at school.

Renee, on the other hand, wasn't as lighthearted. She shouted in her kitchen, swinging a spatula with big crocodile tears. "Rhee, you need to move back here. You guys can live with us."

I smiled at her, but before I could speak up, Antonio shouted, "Wait, what the hell are you saying, Suga? The two of you? No! Marie... I love you. You fam, girl, but... No. No. Oh, hell no."

I laughed so loud that it startled Christopher. Renee started swinging the spatula at him as he dodged her hits. "Shut up, Tony! Yes, she can. You wanted more damn kids, so there ya go."

It was that all too familiar Escobar comedy I've been accustomed to witnessing since college. Looking across the table from me, I followed the echoing deep baritone chuckle that I hadn't heard in a long time.

Coincidentally, Adonis Vincent just so happened to be in New York at the same time. We have kept in contact, but mostly through email. My life changed with the birth of my triplets, and, of course, the time difference living in South Korea made it difficult to connect with friends and family without strategic planning.

After quieting his laughter from the Escobar antics, who were now outside running around with Christopher backing up his mother, he just gazed at me with a slight grin.

For the lunchtime gathering, Renee pulled out all the stops for my quick visit. We enjoyed delicious collard greens, jalapeno cornbread, macaroni and cheese *(yeah, it's the way I taught her, with five cheeses, a cream sauce and no gross Velveeta),* fried chicken, smothered pork chops and apple pie with homemade ice cream. It was a large spread, and we even played spades. It was just as if I had never left.

I love the Escobar's but they ain't slick.

Coming up from the man cave, Antonio announced, casually walking into Renee sewing room, "Marie, you should wait a little bit longer before going back to your hotel. I checked, and the traffic is pretty bad. I told Adonis to ride with you so you would be safe. His hotel is right next to Rockefeller Center anyway, and that's close to Mandarin."

Antonio just kept grinning. He looked like the cartoon cat Garfield. Renee's eyes increased in size, and her mouth gapped open. *(He is so obvious!)* I wanted to laugh but it's Tony. He means well. Then I heard a sound from Renee saying, "What the hell are you—" I cut her off quickly before he got cussed out.

"Oh, cool, thanks for that. Antonio, if I was staying longer, I would make you a rum cake, boy!"

Antonio's eyes were huge, and he looked so crazy when he said, "Ooh! Marie, ya almost made a little pee come out. I'm droolin' right now. Can we change your ticket? What do you need to make it for me? Better yet, the sauce. If I had some right now, I'd pour it on French toast. Uh, yeah, and these tasteless vegan cookies my sister made for Chris. Make that for me. You've always been my second kitchen wife. I should've had you make it back in college. Ha! No, for real, make that."

Renee shut that down. "No! She's not making you nothing, Antonio, nothing!" She rushed over and pulled her husband into another room.

I was left standing, wearing the blazer Renee was pinning on me for the fit, and Adonis held his chin smirking. "So, the rum cake is something I never got to taste. He's been saying for years that if he had one last meal, he has a list of what he would want. Renee's enchiladas, his mother's Rellenos de papa, his grandma's Caldo Santo, and your praline cake and hot butter rum sauce— lots of the sauce. He said, it's like a delicious drug. Haa… haa!"

We laughed for a while as I removed the blazer without getting stuck by the pins. Then I checked out a silver slip dress she was making for a client who had a special request. Adonis came into the room but stayed by the door. Then he hinted, "You know what they're talking about, right?"

I rolled my eyes and moaned in acknowledgement of the obvious. Adonis kept talking but he lowered his voice. "We should be overly excited about leaving here together. You know, make them feel like they are doing something noteworthy." He covered his mouth with his fist to hide his wide grin.

I smirked before being serious, "No. Let's not encourage them. They're terrible at it. Stevie Wonder could see their match-making plan." He nodded and I giggled. We crept to several rooms upstairs to see where they were hiding. We found the two plotters giving each other fist pumps before Renee bit her bottom lip and Antonio slammed his face into hers. It looked and sounded like something from a movie with a rating for adults only. Heavy panting and moaning magnified every few seconds. Peeking through the halfway opened door, Adonis and I couldn't stop snickering. Adonis nudged me. I looked, and he mouthed the word, "Wow."

Muffling my snickers, I whispered, "They've always been like this. Even in college."

We watched them go at it, as they frantically sucked, groaned, and kissed until Antonio had his wife smashed up against his office bookshelf freed from her top.

Renee growled, "Bite me! Boy, you better bite me!"

Antonio barked back, "I'm 'bout to mark your ass up, like a daddy Pitbull!"

"Oooo!" she replied pulling his head to her large mounds of newly exposed breast meat. Her bra was just about off, and I couldn't hold in my laughter. I shouted coming into the room, "Ya, always doing stuff! Freaks!" I startled them to stop. Renee snatched her shirt to cover herself.

Adonis added, "Dang, you could've at least waited until we left, or invite us to join!" I turned around to see Adonis with a full grin that turned into a gregarious laugh after he saw my shocked big eyes.

Scurrying, the two laughed while fumbling to put their clothes back on and moved things back in place before their eruption of lust fire started. Grinning, Antonio gave Adonis a head nod. I suppose it was some kind of man signal for bonding as the two chuckled and left the room.

"Embarrassed much?" I said, snorting and helping Renee cover her now slightly red-marked and saliva dampened giant breasts. Snickering with her lips poked out, and her eyebrows raised high, I knew she wasn't. *(Freaks!)*

"Girl, you know Tony can't get enough of me." She said adjusting her clothes.

"Just horney all the time. Just like in college. You guys are so nasty. What…what if it was my poor nephew walking in on this den of hot sex?"

"Our son knows the deal. We got him trained. He got scared one good time and knows better. Chris will just close the door and go play a game or music really loud for a while until we are done. Ha!"

"Oh, Christopher, my baby has been traumatized by his freaky parents!"

"Girl please. I tell you what, he isn't curious, so we know he won't be doing anything until he is older and ready. Tony gave him graphic details of what happens if you play adult games, and you are not ready to be one."

"I will make sure I don't let my children even see you two together." I said laughing as we left the room.

"Oh, don't forget I know a few adult stories that you didn't put in your book, little Miss Hong Kong!" she said cackling and bumping my body with her hip. I glared at her as my body hit the wall from her bump. Then I pinched her elbow, and said, "I hate you, cow!"

Renee laughed even louder, motioning me back into her sewing room to finish the fitting.

Delta Sister-Bestie Renee Escobar

Bestie's Husband Attorney Antonio Escobar

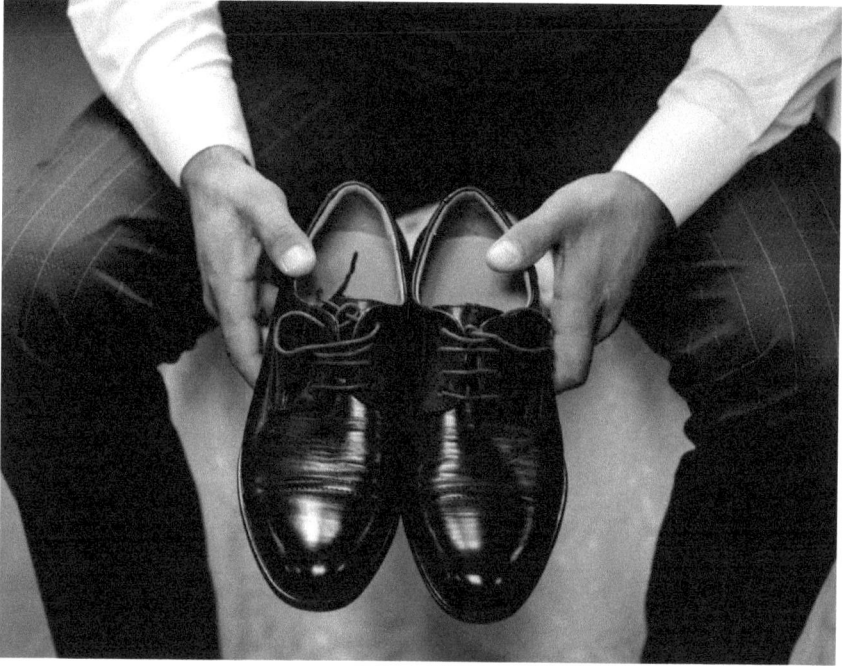

20. Temptation

Around seven in the evening, Adonis and I took my secure transport from Renee and Antonio's house in New Jersey back to the city. Antonio was right, Adonis's hotel was close to Rockefeller Center. It just made logical sense to share when the traffic was a little lighter. In the back of the town car, it was quiet until Adonis said so casually, "You act like you want to say something but you're hesitating. We have been friends for a long time. Why are you nervous?"

Then he took a sip of his tall Starbuck's nonfat peppermint mocha. His 6'4 muscular, 260-pound body stylishly fitted in the thin black mock turtleneck, black belted tan trousers and black leather loafers watched me, waiting for a response. At 53 years old, he was still just as handsome as when we first met with his flawless hazelnut color skin and full head of faded, curly dark hair. But he didn't appear to be any greyer from over the last six years.

(How does he do that? Is there no stress at Boeing? That's hard to believe.)

His neatly trimmed low shadow beard enhanced his plump mocha lips, narrow nose, chiseled wide chin, and jawline. I had always found the slight slant of his dark brown eyes to be a uniquely attractive blend of his African American, Italian, and Japanese ancestry. Adonis was a gentleman, my friend and still very handsome. Looking over at him seated next to me with his thick muscular legs crossed, I grinned and said, "I do? I didn't think I was that bad of an actress."

We chuckled at the same time.

"Marie, we can talk about anything. I had no hesitation telling you about my bunion surgery last year. Now did I?"

I snorted while he grinned playfully at me, periodically sipping his coffee.

"Big A, you did share that, didn't you? I think I would have like to hear the details of your colonoscopy because that would have made me laugh."

He shook his head, "You're so sick." I snickered as he smirked.

Getting closer to his hotel, I started to feel anxiety about being alone. My face must have shown a change because Adonis randomly said, "Marie, would you like some company for a while?" I smiled and nodded that I would.

By passing his hotel, we went to the MO lounge for a night cap. I got a sweet white wine, hoping to calm my nerves, and Adonis ordered a glass of Courvoisier. Although I was still stuffed from the late lunch, Adonis convinced me to order a few appetizers with drinks to accompany our conversation. Like times in the past, being in this space with Adonis was friendly and comfortable. It had been over a year since he left Celeste's house to briefly express his sincere condolences and meet my children with gifts. It felt good catching up with him in person.

After about thirty minutes of work-related information sharing, Adonis picked back up the conversation topic, where I intentionally paused it.

"Marie, we have been updating on everything else, but I can tell there is something you are not saying. Just say it." he said, lifting his glass to his lips.

As my right foot tapped the floor under the table, I exhaled but gave a forced smile. I was reluctant to share certain things. He reached over, covered my hand on the table with his larger one, and slowly tilted his head to find my eyes.

Softly he said, "Whatever it is, you can tell me."

(I'm ashamed to even have the thought. I just want to sit here with him and pretend I don't have to be alone later.)

"Adonis... I..." I felt my throat tighten and stopped talking. Pressing my lips not to release words, I closed my eyes for a few seconds before taking in a final gulp of wine.

Never removing his hand over mine, he squeezed and held it kindly. Then he said, "You miss him, don't you?"

(Oh god, is it obvious?)

I motioned for another glass of wine, catching the waitress's attention as she passed. Then I turned to see his caring eyes and nodded. I grabbed a napkin and dabbed away the forming wetness at the corner of my eye. I couldn't speak to answer so, I just moaned in agreement with a halfway smile. Systematically looking around and away from him, I drank some water as my new glass of wine was placed before me.

Adonis removed his hand but maintained his friendly gaze when he said, "It's normal to grieve for a long time. The feeling will come in waves often when you least expect it, but it passes, and you go on. It means you loved the person that is no longer here. That's a good thing to have a heart that feels. Do you think you feel a little more sadness because you are here in New York?"

I exhaled slowly and sniffled. "Yes. Honestly, I'm so busy at home, I don't have time to stop but being here... in this hotel. We used to... So many things happened in this place... this hotel... and well, memories just hit me all at once last night."

I quickly guzzled the wine down without looking his way. I blew out heavy and ordered another, and said, "I appreciate what you're saying. It'll pass. Thank you for being such a good friend to me, Adonis."

He swallowed his drink and gave me a slow smile but looked away for a moment before reconnecting with my eyes and following up with more encouragement. "Marie, I told you years ago that I consider it an honor to be your friend. A lot has changed since then, but my feelings about our friendship haven't." His words generated a smile with a full display of my top row of teeth. I felt a bit better. I relaxed back in my comfy cushioned seat and started to take a few nibbles of the warm brie wrapped in flaky pastry dough drizzled in raspberry preserves on the table. Adonis seemed to study me but in a calm and casual way as he slowly sipped his Courvoisier over ice. After a couple of minutes of mellow music being the only sounds,

Adonis said the phrase again. "Marie, as your friend, if there is anything you need, just ask me."

In this instance, it made me tremble. I stopped eating and glanced over at his eyes. His face was serious, and his eyes were focused on me.

(What does he mean? I don't need... wait...)

I stared at him, trying to read his eyes. My heart rate instantly increased, and I felt a surge of warmth charge through me as I turned my face away.

"Thanks, I will." I said it in the open air, while biting my lip.

In silence, I felt him probe me with his eyes. I shook my head, gasping and my hand started to shake. I closed my eyes counting to ten in silence. I felt his hand cover mine again and steadied it.

He said softly, "Marie, you shouldn't drink anymore. Let me walk you to your room before I go to my hotel." Without a second thought, I nodded in agreement.

Adonis motioned to the waitress, paid the bill, and silently escorted me to my suite door. Before I opened it, I thanked him, and he smiled at me. As I moved to enter the code, I felt his presence close behind me. He had not moved but I was just more aware of him for some reason. As soon as my suite door clicked open, from behind me, he said, "I'm leaving tomorrow afternoon. So now that you're safe in your room, I'm going to bid you goodnight. Have a safe trip home. Take care of yourself, Marie."

In that moment and without thinking, I turned to face him and wrapped my arms around his broad torso. My face buried deep into his thin sweater as tears fell from my eyes. Silently, I cried and within seconds, I felt his long arms reach around and press me onto him firmly. There were no words spoken for a few minutes. His body moved calmly as he inhaled and exhaled at a rhythm that was slow and soothing. My cheeks felt the softness of his black sweater that lightly smelled of Guy Laroche's Drakkar Noir.

I had a mind full of emotionally triggered thoughts… (*I don't want to be alone. Please don't go… but I can't… I don't want to lose him as my friend… I'm not going to do anything. I… I just miss Jae. I want Jae. I'm ashamed but the way he's holding me feels so… so nice.*)

In silence and embracing at my opened door, I sobbed, squeezing him tighter. Adonis cleared his throat and broke the silence. "Marie… just ask me."

I shook my head no, never letting go of him as more tears fell into the material of his garment. I felt him take in a deeper breath as he backed out of my wrapped arms. I couldn't look up at him. I just tried to focus on his abdomen to avoid looking up.

"Marie, we're in the hallway of a hotel. Sweetheart, let me help you inside and then… I'm gonna go, alright?" I nodded in agreement.

Inside my suite, I stepped to the left into the powder room. I blew my nose, cleaned my face, and washed my hands. Then, I took some deep breaths to calm myself. When I came out and down the hallway, Adonis was in the lounge area, standing by the large window with a hand in his pocket. He smiled at me.

I did a quick glance up to his eyes, then I looked away and far out the window. Embarrassed, I said, "I'm sorry, Adonis. I don't know what came over me. It's strange I am not a crier."

I cleared my throat again and was calm. Calm until he said it once more, "If there is anything… anything… you need from me, Marie, just ask me."

Now I had to look up at him with fear and trembling coming over me again. Tears began to build up in my eyes once more. Within seconds the warm liquid drizzled down my cheeks, but I mustered the courage to say what I had been thinking.

"I can't, Adonis. I... I'm not a woman that... I can't ask you to stay... just because I miss Jae... and I want someone I trust to hold me. It isn't fair. I won't. No, I can't, Adonis. I... I care about you, and I don't want to lose you as my friend... It will pass... you said it will. It will. I only have to be here a couple more days." A few more tears fell as I tried to control my emotional words through gasps and blinking eyes.

Adonis licked his lips as he walked toward me. He held out his arms, stopping and standing just a few feet away and said, "Marie, you won't lose me. I'm always your friend. Whatever you need, just ask me."

His eyes were kind as I walked the few steps into his arms. I exhaled deeply, breathing into the black material covering his upper body and instantly felt a wave of comfort in his strong arms covering me. We stood in the suite lounge for a while, caringly holding each other. I pulled away and looked up at his tender smile and asked, "Adonis, just this once, will you stay with me? Could you?"

He moaned and verbally confirmed, "Yes. I won't go until you want me to."

Quietly and for well over an hour, Adonis Vincent held me from behind in a couple's spoon position. We were on top of the king-size bed, fully clothed but without shoes. My mind calmed, simply by his protective presence, his strong engulfing physique, and his tenderness. He periodically stroked my head, twirled my hair, and whispered my name as he inhaled and exhaled deeply. It was almost like a meditation technique that I subconsciously began to imitate.

Yet, I still had thoughts. I broke the silence with a whisper. "Thank you, for caring for me this way."

He moaned softly. My heart and mind still yearned, and I had flashes of different thoughts that came out of my mouth.

"Adonis, I'm sorry... I couldn't be... with you the way you..." He interrupted my random words. "Marie don't think about things that don't matter now. You know you're special to me. Perhaps we weren't meant to be anything more than what we are now. Just relax. I won't leave until you ask me to."

"Adonis, if I wanted you to do something else, would you think I'm crazy?" He moved his body closer and turned me around to face him. He reached to hold my face with his large soft brown hands, and said, "Marie...you're a woman that thinks and feels a bit too deeply. Caring for you and being your friend doesn't lessen simply because you're lonely and sad. You'll remain in the high place I have you, whether you choose to ask for more or not. That's part of being a friend. To be there and do things that are needed because of the affection shared. Don't overthink it. If I'm free to be available, I'll be and do whatever you need. Wait, except change diapers. That's a negative." He chuckled, and I laughed.

As my laugh faded, my lips trembled. He held my face lovingly and tears fell. Then I asked him, "A, will you treat me... sweet-like?"

He gave me a side smile. Then he leaned forward and gifted me with an innocent, delicate lip kiss that lasted several uncounted seconds. Separating his plump soft lips from mine he said in a whisper, "What else do you want?"

I swallowed and quickly told him, "Nothing. Nothing."

Adonis used his long index finger to lift my face up by my chin. His deep brown eyes, with that slight slant, snatched hold of my pupils, and my body froze. Then he said the words differently, "Beautiful, tell me. What do you need? Baby, whatever it is, I'll do it."

And he did.

21. Brooklyn

Concluding several morning meetings at Sony, I was on my way to Brooklyn. I had my scheduled lunch date with my pen pals, Joy, and Stephanie Hamilton. Finally, I was able to hug my little beautiful dark-skinned bright-eyed friend who was now so tall. I cried with gratefulness embracing them both. Chatting a couple of times, a month isn't the same as being able to touch and enjoy a meal with people you hold dear. I met a few of Stephanie's friends from her local witness congregation, who happened to be over when I was there. It was a wonderful surprise to meet other witnesses she was friends with. I found myself rattling off how we met with joyful tears the entire time I shared the story.

"Joy sent me this letter years ago. I didn't even know her, but I got this card from this little five or six-year-old person, inviting me to meet her in a beautiful garden paradise, where no one gets sick or dies. She said, the animals are friendly, and nothing bad ever happens."

Joy interjected, "I was so little." We chuckled smiling at each other. I added, "She had drawn these pretty little flowers, trees, and I think animals..."

"I'm sure they were animals... I do much better now!" she confessed, pointing at her latest oil painting on an easel, of a clear pond with a few fawns, lambs, and young zebras drinking which I had said should have been in a gallery somewhere.

Everyone giggled. Grinning, I reached over and hugged her. Stephanie's pioneer partner, Amber said, "I remember, that was the time when we focused our preaching work through letter writing because of COVID, right?"

Stephanie shared some of the story from her perspective that I didn't know. "No, it was some years after the world shut down from that. Joy and I helped a few other friends in Manhattan with their letter writing territory, because of safety precautions, some places wouldn't allow us to go door to door. That's how we met. It was a blessing that she wrote Joy back and we talked a lot over the years."

Then I commented with, "Yes. Joy and Stephanie became my pen-pals. I was so giddy having this little doll writing to me and showing me fantastic things that she believed about the future. I told everyone."

Amber's husband, Dyson, spoke after sipping his tea. "In all the years I've been a servant in our congregation, these last twelve have really boosted the different ways Jehovah's message has been able to reach people. Do you study the Bible in South Korea? Have you been to the hall there?"

Feeling a little put on the spot, I nervously adjusted my hips sitting on the chair and pressed my lips. He must have noticed my hesitation and followed up with, "Marie, I was only curious since you said you moved away, and your life is very different for you now. No pressure."

I exhaled and smiled. "Oh, that's a relief. My first thought was you're called an elder and you're supposed to take some kind of recruiting status poll or something."

Everyone laughed. His wife Amber touched my arm, shaking her head. Dyson waved his hand before clarifying, "Ha… Ha… Well, I am glad you don't think that. There is no recruiting. We are all imperfect, perhaps I mistakenly said it incorrectly. Having the responsibility as an elder in the congregation means my role as a volunteer is to support and encourage the brothers and sisters to the best of my ability. There are other brothers, and we work together as a unit to ensure the safety and spiritual well-being of the friends in Jehovah's organization. We are all Jehovah's people; no one is over anyone else. Jesus is the head of the congregation, and we study and try to follow the outline in the Bible from the first-century Christians. Everyone functions the same way in every congregation around the world. I can tell you with all certainty that there is no assignment to check status or recruit people to join. The truth doesn't work that way. A lot of people have a misconception about Jehovah's Witnesses, but our commission regarding preaching is to be the example and share what we know to everyone, until we are told to stop. Everyone decides if they want to serve Jehovah or not. But I look at it this way, it's my job to make sure people are given an opportunity to hear the truth and make the choice for themselves. It's not fair to make a choice without all the facts being presented, right?"

Heads nodded, and soft moans echoed in the room as the seventy something-year-old, round, and white-headed Caucasian man with British ancestry from Connecticut smiled at me before sipping his tea. His wife, Amber, who was originally from Naples and still had a slight Italian accent, tapped my hand softly and grinned.

While Stephanie's friends Chloe and Frank Truman were talking, I thought, (Well, that was new. I didn't get that before. I know what an elder is now. Doesn't mean they are old but a mature spiritual man, who has volunteer assignments based on scriptural qualifications and needs for the group or congregation. They don't get paid for helping. Crazy, some are young with family's and jobs. Okay, and a pioneer is a teacher that volunteers a set number of hours each month. Young people can be one of those if they are baptized like Joy is now. It's the same in every Kingdom Hall all over the world. That's unique. I'm going to check that. They call each other brother and sister because they are a spiritual family. Right. Okay, I got it.)

Instantly, I felt more comfortable with these kind people and told them honestly, "My husband died in 2030, and my whole world turned upside down. I'm still processing everything that is different. I stopped studying just to get my mind right. You know, organizing my life as a mother of three infants and living in a foreign country away from everyone. It's been a struggle. My husband was a popular person there, and for security, my freedom is not like it was before. Before he died, he surprised me by having this beautiful mural painted in our dining room of a garden paradise. It's so life-like with a waterfall— animals, flowers. It looks so peaceful, which was what he was trying to relay for me to remember." I exhaled deeply before stating, "Thank you all for being so welcoming. I'm glad I met you today. Brother Hanover, I... I have not been to the Kingdom Hall in South Korea, but I think I might check on it when I get back."

Stephanie smiled as Joy jumped up, kissed my cheek, and squeezed me with tears in her eyes. After Stephanie showed me a quick two-minute video of what happens at every Kingdom Hall around the world, I was more interested in attending. Excited to share, Joy announced she was taking Korean in school and wanted to visit me soon. We set a date to plan for them both to come visit and meet my babies in person.

Dyson and Amber Hanover

I really liked brother and sister Hanover. This mature older couple were nice people, just like Chloe and Frank Truman. I was so comfortable with them, we exchanged information to keep in contact. They were the cutest couple. The way he affectionately looked at her was so endearing. A few times I thought of my parents and then of Jae-Sung.

(I miss the way he looked at me.)

22. Refocus

On my flights home, I thought about a few things that happened on this quick business trip to New York. I wrote about everything in my journal. All was quiet on my Korean Airlines flight KE5035 from Los Angeles to Seoul. While Trey had on headphones and watched a movie across from me, I relaxed lounging in my first-class cubicle, looking out at the fluffy clouds. It had been only a short time in the air when I came to the realization of what decisions I needed to make for my heart, mind, and soul to be content with a future of complete peace.

"It's like a reset, so to speak." I mumbled to myself before jotting it down.

I thought about when Celeste had told me about her and big Sean Ronan in England before marrying Adam. I pondered on what led her to the affair she had with him. It wasn't something she planned but it happened because of her indecisive heart, lack of knowledge, her confusion and self-reliance. But although it was hard, emotional, and painful to deal with, she had to go through it for herself and with Adam. If she hadn't, she said it herself that she ". . . wouldn't have the good solid marriage they have now. It had to happen to make them better."

It's amazing how things came full circle and touched my life. If none of that had happened, their relationship wouldn't have been a concrete place for Adam to support her carrying my babies. So, if she hadn't had that fling, quite possibly, I wouldn't even have my children.

"How crazy is that." I chuckled as the puzzle pieces of life came together while I sipped chilled sweet wine, and the people around me were sleeping.

(How funny... he works. Making imperfect things perfect and showing those paying attention the open doors of opportunities to become better and acceptable to him. I am humbled by his love and forgiveness.)

Now that I had realized the truth, that no one on earth can fill this bottomless hole, Jae-Sung Kim left in my heart, mind, and soul, I said a silent prayer. I made the promise to myself to freely allow Jehovah God to cover the hole temporarily. I would no longer rely on my own mind to navigate and try to fix what was missing.

Upon returning home, I reached out to those kind sisters, Min Sun Gil from Hannam and Haeun Do from Cheongdam. Then I began my truth research and Bible study again. It wasn't a secret that I had been studying the Bible because I had talked about it for several years. But this time, I will be making some changes. I explained to

Kang and SI how important it was for me to attend meetings at the Kingdom Hall.

"Eh... Why do you want to change things? Noona, if you must go...then... Uh, you should go alone. It's too dangerous with the triplets to be around these strangers a couple times a week." SI said a little grumbly with a facial expression that seemed to scream "I don't get it."

Kang was not better in his annoyance with my plans to meet new people outside of the confines of the K-pop idol and Sony music world. "We already vetted the two ladies a long time ago. But Marie, why can't you do it over video?"

I glared at him with tightly pressed lips. Before I could answer, he blurted out, "Okay, okay. Aish! We will shadow but if you want the amigos to go, we must be armed around you like Special Forces. You said there could be over a hundred people at a hall meeting. All at one time? Just to study? It's not a funeral or holiday. That is too many people. It's just like any other kind of church service, right? Oh, no. You said it's different. We can't do it any other way if you want to go."

Imagining being surrounded like the Mona Lisa would be if it was being transported to another gallery or something, I easily agreed to go without my children and to sometimes attend on video. I witnessed the stress gradually lessen from their faces.

Since I had studied with Jehovah's Witnesses before and talked about Jae-Sung being asleep in God's memory, those closest to me knew I believed God promised to wake him up. At the end of his life, Jae felt that way too. No one seemed surprised that I started again and was taking it more seriously. That is what I thought anyway.

Min Cha occasionally asked me questions, especially when I was regularly out doing new activities and not freely available as much. Nari and Kang observed as I blended what I was learning into my daily routine. I read the Bible and Bible stories to my children at night instead of other books. I also pointed out the details of the mural and what life will be like soon. We discussed playing with the animals and freely running with them. I often scheduled time to show educational videos teaching Jae, Jin, and Jolie about God's kingdom, how to share, have good attitudes, be kind and patient, and to always tell the truth, along with so many other positive things. I found some of the same videos Joy told me about and I had sent to Renee to show Christopher when he was young. I was a little surprised, but it told me the organizational values and lessons were consistent over the years. They didn't change based on the country or social things or laws; they followed principles in the Bible. I liked that even more now that I was paying closer attention to understand who God really was and what his plans were for me personally.

When I started to do more letter writing to share kindness within my community, attending the study sessions at the kingdom hall, and accompany different sisters from the local congregation on outings to encourage others in the hospital or delivering a meal, I looked at the local missionary teaching work as something very exciting to do with my time outside of being a mother and working for Sony.

It was interesting that no one said anything about things I was changing in my life. Unknown to me at the time, I was really under a microscope, and everything I did was being monitored and talked about behind closed doors.

Collection: Change, Conviction, Courage

23. Four Fun

When we moved to South Korea, I started this nightly family tradition. I read to my little ones just about every night and gave them a special kiss. By the time they were eighteen months old, I had added more special kisses because they didn't want me to leave the nursery when it was bedtime. I remember seeing this cute panda dance song in an old movie with Vin Diesel called "The Pacifier" but I didn't want to sing since they listen to their father do that at night. So, it was kisses in specific order.

First was an Eskimo kiss which is rubbing noses together. Next was a French kiss which is a light peck on each cheek. Then came the Butterfly kiss, which is the brushing your eyelashes together like a soft flutter, and finally, they got a Greek kiss, which is a juicy smack on their forehead and a loud "OPAH" at the end. I really loved that saying from the movie, "Big Fat Greek Wedding", so I added it at the end. They loved it! It was just my mommy thing.

If Kang puts them to bed, he does some ninja moves to make them laugh and gets them exhausted. Nari dances with a fan and sings to them. When she does it, they are entranced and start to sway like a snake does with a charmer. The whole thing kind of reminds me of Kah and Mowgli from "The Jungle Book" animated movie. *(Loved that one!)* Aunt Teng sings Korean lullabies. Their halmeoni (grandma) Min Cha tells them dramatic stories of their father, their grandfather and when she was a little girl. Her soothing voice knocks them right out.

Recently, I started to notice an attitude change with my mother-in-law. Previously, Min Cha didn't seem to have an issue with my not celebrating holidays because I didn't when Jae-Sung was alive. But once he was gone, she wanted me to at least come for Chuseok, Korean Thanksgiving. I went to something once when we were first married, but I felt uncomfortable being there without Jae. Now, things are different, and I don't celebrate anything like that. I had told her I didn't want to come during the holidays anymore. I thought she understood because she didn't say much more about it.

It wasn't a big thing, I thought. Because of security, there had been no mention of Children's Day because parks and zoos were always filled with hundreds of families. On holidays, such as Hangual, Pepero, Independence and Black Day, Jae's family didn't traditionally participate, so she didn't press me about those. But it was Christmas and Seollal Lunar New Year that she wouldn't let go of.

"My only one… my son is gone, Marie. This is when we come together as family. It is the least you could do to honor him. It is our heritage. We are Korean. We are proud and have traditions in place that make us who we are. Do you not understand this? Remember who my people are and why this is so important."

I heard her say that a lot. Well, she said it in different ways, but it was the same message. Min Cha made a point to try and argue with me about these holidays and Korean traditions for a few weeks, but then she stopped. It was a great relief.

24. Script Change

In October, Chris called me to meet with him at his office at NM Entertainment regarding a confidential legal matter. When I arrived, I was blown away by what he said it was about.

It was a petition for legal guardianship and management of assets belonging to Jae-Sung's heirs. "Say what?"

Chris gave me the folder out of his briefcase and said, "Read this first. Then I will tell you our next steps."

Fumbling to open the folder and read the documents, the more I read, the angrier I became.

(What the hell is this? Don't swear, Marie. Breathe.)

What stood out was the second page. I had to read it twice.

Legal blood heirs of the late Kim Jae-Sung

- Jae Lune-Philippe' Delacroix-Kim
- Jin Soleil-Maximilian Delacroix-Kim
- Jolie Arabie-Sable Delacroix-Kim

As citizens of South Korea with no legal parent, the rights to oversee their care and assets must be determined. This petition is to legally establish joint-custodial guardianship and financial administration of the three heirs of Kim Jae-Sung to the paternal relatives of the children until their age of eighteen.

My eyes bugged out, and I bit the cap off the pen hanging in my mouth before I shouted, "What!"

Chris removed the pen from my hand before the ink bled onto my lip. Before I could start crying and yelling, he began talking in that calm lawyer way he does. "Marie, I received these documents last Monday from a secure delivery messenger. Before I do anything, I needed to tell you about it."

I started to hyperventilate, and my face felt hot. I blurted out words, "no parent! What... What the hell is this?"

Chris immediately touched my fisted hand on the table and talked a little faster. "Marie, it is a petition for legal custody of the triplets but..."

I sprung from my seat at his conference table, yelling, "They're trying to take my children from me?! Why would they do this? Why? After... after everything. Is it because I'm... I'm Black? Now... it's a problem! Because I'm a French citizen? Or an American one? What the hell is going on!" Tears burst from my eyes as I moved to the window.

Chris darted over to me and put both hands over my shoulders and peered at me to get my attention and refocus on him. "Marie, I need you to calm down. It's being handled. Come, sit down."

Trembling from rage and fear, I let him slowly guide me back to my seat. He handed me some water, and I took a few quick sips before dabbing my cheeks and eyes with tissue from the box on the conference table. Then he kept talking, "As I suspected, no one has hinted anything about this business, right?"

I nodded while staring blankly at the box of tissues. He moved closer to get my attention and I turned to face him. "Alright. No one in Jae's family will say anything. So don't ever mention or discuss it. It's a legal matter, but Eddie and I have it covered. No one knows except the three of us and Min Ji. It is important that it stays that way. The adoption papers we drew, and had you sign in Seattle are privacy sealed, like your identity, marriage, and connections to Jin-K/Jae-Sung. Remember? This means the petitioners obviously don't know about your rights as their legal mother. Jae took care of this ahead of time. So, relax. No one is taking those three Korean, French, Black future K-Pop idols from Jae's phenomenal noona." He winked at me, and I giggled. The stress from my shock and anger evaporated, and I let out a long sigh.

"But Chris, who...who would do this?" I asked, seeking further understanding.

He shook his head saying, "It doesn't list names, but it's a petition to a hearing which would make everything public. It's being shut down before we even get there, but honestly, it could be anyone that knows about the triplets, really. Technically, I can find out, but I'd rather not and just make it disappear after I put a privacy contract, kind of like a gag order on them."

I nodded. "Okay. Yes, just make it go away and silence them. I don't want to know who. But if I had to guess, I bet it's his witch of an aunt, Hae Won Park."

Less than forty-eight hours later, Chris called to confirm the petition had been withdrawn and closed without information about their adoption or any privacy sealed data being divulged. He said things moved quickly with the aid of Min-Ji and Dong-Hyun.

"Thank you, Jehovah! Thank you, Min Ji & Dong-Hyun!"

My attorney Chris Hwang

Although I regularly worked out in the fitness center in our secure building, I had begun doing a more vigorous regimen because I was angry, and I needed to forget about that petition. Swimming alone and boxing with Kang and sometimes Trey helped me just release my anger without talking about any of it. Gradually, for the most part, it had been forgotten. In the back of my mind, I felt very grateful for Jae's stepfather and adopted uncle. As usual, the two men came through to shut down the drama.

However, on November 12, it happened. Min Cha came over to visit, and she began to apply the same pressure again to attend the holidays coming up. It was almost nonstop, with Jae's family creeping in to sidetrack my focused and peaceful life.

Nari had just left to visit her parents, and the triplets were napping when we were having tea, and she said to me, "Are you being brainwashed by these people?"

I took a breath, so I wouldn't be disrespectful to my elder, Jae-Sung's mother. But what she was implying really pissed me off. A thunder flash of thoughts hit me... (*Oh, I'm not smart enough to learn what I need to for myself? I'm just some gullible American, right? Do I not have multiple degrees and run boardrooms with powerful men having them eat out of the palm of my hand? Really? Like... Duh, my father is a scholar... a retired prominent professor. Do you have any idea how many books are in our family library in Lyon? Both my parents drilled into me to research everything. What I'm learning just makes logical sense. Come on. Am I being kind of suckered into believing anything? I know she doesn't believe that. You know who I am. Did you forget? What's happening right now?*)

Finally, I spoke, "Min Cha, my views on these traditions are not new. I was raised to research holidays and practices to find where they got started and why. It's why my parents didn't celebrate many of them. We've discussed this. So, it's not just what I'm learning in the Bible, but it is also my own research on the history of each one. I don't blindly follow anyone or anything. I mean I didn't ask questions before the triplet's party that one time, but that won't happen again. Do you really think I'm being brainwashed? Do you think me that simple?"

I leaned in to study her eyes without glaring at her. She sighed as she rolled them for a few seconds. Then she turned back to look at me and said, "No. No, I don't understand why you are doing these different things. I feel you are not trying to remember my son and raise his children to properly know who he was, where they come from, and who they are to be as his heirs." She said it, all sweet and soft-like, but the next thing out of her mouth sent me closer to *'you know what* and *cuss her out'* mode. "Maybe because you are not their real mother. You—"

Cutting her off, I stood up with an outburst. "What! What did you say?!"

Min Cha cleared her throat, motioning for me to sit down and lower my voice. "Marie, I mean to say that..."

Still standing with my hands on my hips, I peered at her and yelled but not as loud, "No, there is nothing you can mean to say except what you actually did. You think because the triplets came through a contracted legal surrogate, they are not mine?! I'm not their mother?! Is that not what you meant?"

Tapping the table for me to calm down and sit, she answered with, "Marie, you are my son Jae-Sung's widow. You are their mother, but in South Korea the legal mother is who gave birth to them."

I eased back down to my chair. "Yes... yes, I know! Jae knew that too. Which is why I had to legally adopt them the day after they were born!"

She looked at me with surprised eyes, hearing this new and private information. I lowered my voice more, but I kept talking. "Jae-Sung planned everything out for me. Everything. Not only did he have you paint the triplet's nursery to reflect the sun and moon from my poetry, but he also had you paint this..."

I pointed to the dining room wall in front of us. "... as if we are looking from the white terrace into a lush garden with the peacefully resting male and female lions, baby elephants, quakkas, and toucans, along the white stone pathway to the waterfall splashing into the sea. What you hand-painted for me is magnificent, Min-Cha. I have thanked you, numerous times. But did you ever stop to wonder why he even asked you to make it? It's what Jae and I talked about. The earth being reset this way, and I can see my brother again. My twin brother died, and I miss him terribly. I didn't know I would be wishing to see Jae-Sung also in this place, but I do. My learning the truth of the Bible makes it even more real for me. I want our children to have that same faith and hope to see their father awaken one day. What I am learning and teaching my children isn't harming anyone. I have no womb, Min Cha. It was removed from my body after a terrible accident when I was eleven years old. Jae-Sung and my sister lovingly gave me this gift. And trust me, the three of them are every bit, a part of me as if I had conceived and carried them myself."

Sobbing, I stopped talking to catch my breath and wipe my tears. It was quiet for a few minutes. My hand trembled, trying to reach for my teacup. Min Cha touched my hand, and I looked up at her face. Her eyes were glossy from the water that filled them.

"Marie… daughter. I did not know these things. Thank you for telling me. Now that I know they are legally yours, I won't mention how they came to be again. I did not know you lost your brother. I did not know you were unable to have children. My son did not share these things with me. I accepted you as his choice without further thought to your history. My son loved you beyond words and often my understanding. I miss my son, Marie. I cannot lose my connection to him. I will not. I love you as my daughter and my only grandchildren's mother. Let us not argue."

She smiled at me, and I nodded in agreement. But my mind was still going. *(Say it, Marie. Say it!)*

My emotions took over, and I violated privacy with my words, "I can't believe you tried to take them from me."

Min Cha's eyes cut over at me but softened as she prepared to reply. "Daughter, we should not discuss this. But… it is the two of us alone here. I will tell you. I was being asked only to take on the responsibility as my son's mother and their grandmother. Marie, I would never have excluded you. I only seek the best for Jae, Jolie, and Jin. We are Koreans. We have our traditions, and we are proud. Many things you do and say confuse me. I felt I was losing my son's children. I was afraid…I am afraid of not recognizing him in them if you make them different. Do you understand?" I nodded that I did.

In the conversation, Min Cha added that Teng Cheng was not happy about Soo and little Hana's interest in studying the Bible with Jehovah's Witnesses either. I was being blamed for these wild changes in this very formal and traditional South Korean family. It had been the topic for discussion for a long time. *(Oh my…)*

As soon as she said it, I thought, *(This is why she doesn't come over as much. Soo didn't tell me. This is so stupid! Wait… Stop what you're doing. Drop it, Marie before you get angry again.)*

Quickly, I changed the subject. We didn't speak about that guardian petition ever again.

Although their faith was as Christians, I learned from their questions that Min Cha and Teng Cheng had no real knowledge about the Bible and what Jehovah's Witnesses believed until I started studying. They didn't know they are Christians and regularly use God's name. When I showed her Psalms 83:18, she was surprised to see it there. They didn't seem to have any idea what Jesus Christ's sacrifice was for or why he even came to earth in the first place. They didn't know why we grow old, people get sick, die, and how the future hope was clearly demonstrated when Jesus perform miracles on earth and was resurrected. When I showed her in Daniel 2:44 about God's rulership being the only one on earth in the future, she seemed a little confused not ever reading that before. The more I studied the more I shared, but only if they asked, which wasn't that often. Religious beliefs and traditions continued to be a rocky and slippery road we had to travel.

25. The Best Life

After months of study and a lot of prayer, I made a personal commitment to trust in what I had learned and continue to put forth effort to loyally serve God as he requires. I would put faith in his instruction, his son's sacrifice, and live the best life now and wait for his promised future.

On Saturday, December 6, 2031, I symbolized my dedication and was baptized as one of Jehovah's Witnesses. I am not perfect, but I will train my conscience to follow Bible principles and teach my children the same truths about Jehovah and what a loving wonderful heavenly father he truly is.

I was elated to have Joy and Stephanie Hamilton visit from Brooklyn when I got baptized. But what shocked me was when my sister, Celeste and bestie, Renee planned family trips to see us at the same time also. I was glad they came to our English-speaking circuit assembly and had lots of questions about what they heard.

On point to shadow me, SI, Soo, and Hana came too. Joy and Hana had been writing to each other since my July trip. Since Joy was learning Korean, and Hana was learning English, I introduced them. They became fast friends, and Joy was teaching her what she learned in the Bible. Hana was telling her mother, and I think that was why Soo would ask me questions.

Soo wanted to sit in on my study. She did and then quickly started her own with another Korean sister in a different congregation. SI was curious and sat in to listen. After that, he volunteered to be the one to shadow me at the assembly. I think it was to check it out. Nari and Kang stayed home with the triplets because I couldn't get him to budge and let me bring them. "No! Absolutely not!" He seemed a little irritated about my even asking, but I didn't press it further and just let it go.

After the one-day assembly program, Renee, Christopher, Stephanie, Joy, Celeste, Adam, my growing JJ's-Jason and Jacqueline, Min Sun Gil, her husband Chul, Haeun Do SI, her daughter Ami, a witness couple, Ophelia and Stanley Martin, SI, Soo, Hana, and I went to dinner as a giant family. I loved being among friends and family, I couldn't stop grinning.

Jason, Jacqueline, and Christopher are so big, but they loved playing with my three little amigos during this visit. December was such a wonderful month of surprises and gratefulness. I wrote everything down just like my father always tells me to do.

My life became even busier with triplets, consulting for Sony and having the privilege to serve as a volunteer in the Seoul Seobu English congregation. My assignment was to regularly share the good news of God's coming government and the earth's reset to a peaceful paradise earth with others.

Initially, I didn't really consider the inconvenience. But the more involved I became, the more it impacted my security team and protocols. Trey was good at lurking around and being unseen. When I told my pioneer partners, Ophelia, Megan and Min-Youn, they thought it was a little creepy but played along.

Kang had to do background checks and security screenings on each one of them before I could do metro witnessing in public areas as my weekly assignment. For security reasons, I'm not allowed to go door to door, but I write letters, and public witness, sharing with interested one's the comfort and hope from the scriptures.

Kang sarcastically calls us the posse. "You going to meet the posse?" "Who's coming the posse?" "You should be a girl group called J.W. Posse." He would say it and then immediately burst out cackling like Timon from the *Lion King* movies.

"You're so silly!"

"Break it down. Show me your dance moves. Code name, P.H. for Phenomenal Noona! Ha-Ha!"

"Shut up, Kang."

(Him and his jokes. Retard.)

Ophelia and Stanley Martin

Forty-seven-year-old American Ophelia Martin was a lean African American from Oklahoma who moved here to help in the English-speaking congregation four years earlier. She met her forty-year-old husband, Stanley, another American from Kentucky while at a Jehovah's Witness international convention here in Seoul, a year after she had moved. They are special volunteers and assigned to my congregation. The two operate a quaint little soul food café.

Gabriel and Min-Youn Theron

Min-Youn is the youngest of us at thirty and is a native of Jeju. When she met and married Gabriel Theron, who was visiting from South Africa, she quit her high-paying computer job, and volunteered to preach regularly. She worked part-time at Ophelia and Stanley's café. Gabriel and Stanley serve as assistants under the elders in our congregation. Gabriel helps with the building projects and they both support translation efforts.

Megan Chan was from Thailand. She is Chinese and Taiwanese. She's been living here since she was three years old after her father relocated her family because of his job. She's forty and happily single, waiting patiently for mister perfect. She has the liveliest personality of the three, I think. She is adventurous and loves to travel.

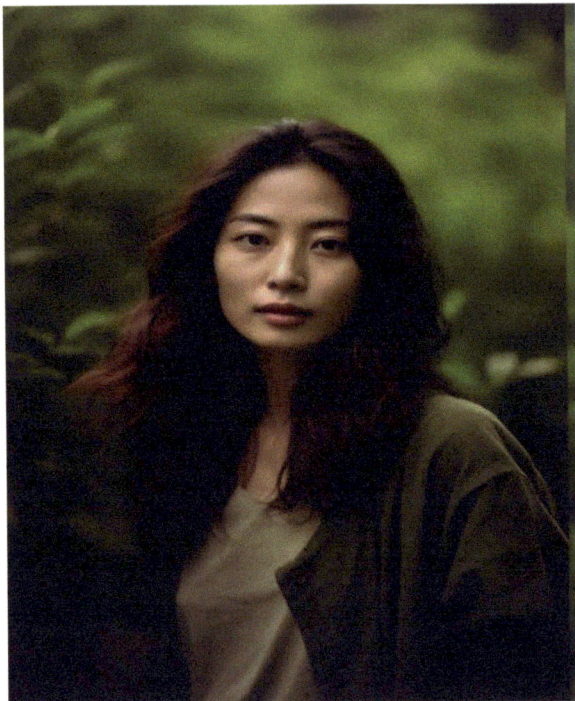

Megan Chan

I mostly gravitated toward Ophelia and Megan outside of our volunteer teaching assignments. Our personalities just clicked. There are several other married and single witnesses I had become friends with that have invited me to do social things, but I usually didn't because of security protocol. Kang is strict about that. The friends are kind. They don't seem deterred by my not joining because they continued extending invitations to have a meal and attend friendly gatherings.

I started to feel annoyed by the restrictions. "This is ridiculous! I'm not in a cage. They work for me; I don't work for them!" I needed some adult time with other people, friends.

Finally, I gave Kang a directive, "The next invitation I am going. You will make it happen!" His face looked shocked, but he didn't make a sound. A few weeks later, Megan and some other friends invited me to a rooftop gathering far in advance. I gave Kang the puppy dog eyes, with droopy and pouty poked out lips, and he huffed but said, "give me the names of every single person that is going to be there. Everyone!"

It was a bit of a hassle, but Peter and Soon Yeun were happy to share their guest list with me to be able to come. After the security clearance was completed, I went. I can't tell you how wonderful it was to be out, laughing and having a good time with other people who loved and served Jehovah. I felt as though I was part of the spiritual family associating with other witnesses. I honestly felt a peacefulness when I was with my spiritual brothers and sisters. I had no fears. I instantly trusted them like I had my Delta sisters and my cousins. It was encouraging and uplifting to my occasional gloominess.

I told myself, "I've been missing all these great opportunities to be upbuilt and supported by friends because of security, well, and me being very cautious. I'm going to do more. I will have to get Kang and SI on board, but I will be doing some things for me. Even if Trey must shadow. This is how normal people live."

(Wait, Trey is laughing at what Lori said. That's why he has a plate of food. Peter was not going to let him just stand there like a statue. Ha!)

Friends from my local Congregation

Everything had fallen into place, I thought. I don't know if it was because I had decided to become a Jehovah's Witness and raise my children with those morals and principles or if it was about culture differences, but a few heat-seeking missiles came over my walls to destroy what I believed to be real.

26. Adjustments

While I was navigating through life with new awareness, close friends, and activities, I didn't give any thought that adjustments in my lifestyle would disrupt the contentment I had. But it did.

After talking to my parents in France, I convinced them they didn't need to make a trip like last year. My father was disappointed because I think he wanted to see us since video isn't nearly as good as in-person. But we agreed it might be better later in the year and for a long stay.

I felt I was in a better place mentally. In addition to my mother and my diva dolls, I had a local network of loving witness friends; I could talk to during the rough times of grief. I was preparing for it to hit me again. I had only a few meetings in Japan to keep me preoccupied, but it was Ophelia and Megan who kept me going with my daily routine.

Since things were a little different, this year, during the time of remembering his death, it wasn't nearly as earth-shattering. My hope for the future really helped every day, I felt depressed and missed him.

Around the anniversary of his death, again, his aunt harassed me for days about a ceremony honoring Jae-Sung. This time she didn't even try to go through Min Cha; she just kept calling my cell phone. Even saying she would just bring my children, and I didn't have to come. Finally, after trying to explain my beliefs and telling her no several times, I stopped answering her calls. She got the hint.

One night, after telling Renee a few things that happened, I felt reassured knowing that although my beliefs are different than hers, she was always in my corner and will even put her hands on folks, if needed. Fortunately, she lived far away. *(She and Lola are so violent. Just like in college. I love her though.)*

"Now, what happened with Jae's family? You said there were legal things, but it got resolved and that was it."

"Renee, they don't like that we don't celebrate holidays and birthdays for one thing. It was more Jae's aunt. She was the one pushing things to the brink of ugliness. Min Cha wasn't as bad. My beliefs and how I raise our children have been the hardest for Jae's family to accept. I don't know why because we talked about things early on. I mean I had always shared what I was learning, and how I felt about the future. When all that was going on, she didn't say much to me, but later Aunt Teng told Soo, she and Min Cha sometimes asked questions at a restaurant they like to go to, which was owned by a witness family in Itaewon. I think that helped her gradually respect my lifestyle decisions more. You know, not hearing it from me but from other Koreans. But girl, Jae-Sung's aunt is a stone-cold mess. She refused to speak to Min Cha because she didn't back her up to do more beyond the legal thing, I guess. Dong-Hyun came through shutting things down. I'm not supposed to discuss it. So that's all I can tell you. I'm glad it's over."

Renee said firmly, "She sounds like she needs to get cut... for real... down to the white meat."

I laughed, watching her grab a large knife from her kitchen counter and swing it around. We shifted to talk about her boutique and Christopher.

The adjustments in my life didn't change others around me and it became frustrating. I had to think about how to tactfully tell people I cared about, to refrain from doing things I didn't participate in. I knew they were their ways of expressing love and support for me and my children but well, it had been awkward. I planned it all out, but it wasn't as easy as I thought. Although I had told everyone we didn't celebrate the triplet's birthday, most didn't hear me.

For several days, the idol brothers; Eric, BJ, Ethan, Seth, Vaj, and Min Ji, my in-laws, Ayana, Lola, and Jazz, still sent gifts, money, and food. I was grateful for the love, but it just made me feel more uncomfortable. I didn't know how to tell them to stop without hurting them. I thought about sending them back. However, I pushed that idea out of my head. "That would be like spitting on them, it would be bad."

I talked to Ophelia and Stanley to get their perspective. Sometime later, I had a few conversations with Min Sun Gil, Haeun Do's daughter Ami and an elder in my congregation on how some of my in-law relatives' traditions were affecting my attitude. I was getting angry that they just didn't stop when I asked them to. I told them the same thing, "I love them, but we don't have the same beliefs. But it's disrespectful they don't listen to me. So how do I tell them to stop sending presents for my children's birthday?"

It was good I had mature friends to talk to because they helped me understand and learn how to be patient in subtle ways and to think about things I didn't consider. They each had given me some direct advice from the Bible, some research articles, and their experiences with non-believing relatives and friends. Some things worked, and some didn't. I was happy to get the full picture from both cultures.

When we met in our small service group, brother Tommy Han told me, "People must see you are serious and need time to process what changes you have made in your life."

During our chat after the Sunday meeting, Min Sun Gil said, "Some may not ever agree with your decision not to celebrate their birthday and join them for holidays. But don't categorize this as a Black or Korean issue. It's a people one."

"Most of my family are not witnesses. They celebrate holidays and family traditions simply to get together and eat. We had to show them other ways to share their love. After a couple of years of standing firm to our repeated, "No, we are not coming for Christmas. But when we have our wedding anniversary party, we would like you to come" statements, they stopped asking about Christmas. Although we had explained that we commemorate Jesus' death on Nisan 14, a couple of my brothers didn't think we celebrated anything. They truly believed we didn't have excitement or gatherings to celebrate weddings, being married, coming babies, or achievements and graduations until we invited them to join us. My older brother and his wife were shocked. Later they told us that they thought we sat around collecting stamps, doing macramé, playing harmonicas, and making unleavened bread." I snorted, as she kept talking. "But we have the coolest parties and real fun. They started studying right after that." Ophelia was laughing telling this story during our break having iced coffee at Starbucks. I perked up. "So, it was how you acted that sparked their interest. Did they become witnesses too?"

Ophelia smiled at me but shook her head. "No. They studied for a while. It provided them with some basics for a better understanding of why my life changed. But they were not interested in changing theirs. Remember, Marie, everyone that studies the Bible with Jehovah's people, unfortunately, won't make the decision you made for their own life, but it may help them respect yours a little more. In any case, we keep trying to be a visual and verbal example, making it possible for anyone to learn about Jehovah and his original purpose for the earth, how to become his friend, and what he will do for his friends now and in the future."

I found it very helpful to be reminded, I am like clay and Jehovah is molding me to fit into his new world. I'll never be completely done being trained by Him. I will make mistakes, but I must keep trying to allow Bible principles to shape me into the best mother, daughter, sister, friend, and person I can be. "Got it!"

Although I had studied for a long time and learned a lot, there was never a point where I knew it all. I was constantly being molded and looking into deeper things of the scriptures. Everyone I closely associated with, knew I was a widow, and my husband had been a South Korean man. But idol protocol forbit them from knowing he was professionally, Jin-K of DRGN5 or his real name. I remember when I asked the much older and wiser couple, Min Sun Gil and Chul questions about my husband after I started to wonder if I was still married. The loving congregation elder, Chul gave me some directions on research to review first. Then when I was at their home for an afternoon meal, he asked me what I thought. It made me sad and a little panicked afterward knowing the bond of marriage ends at death.

My voice crackled a little when I said, "So, does this mean, Jae, and I won't be married? I mean… well, from what I researched in several places, the bond of marriage is broken or ends when a mate dies. But… I don't want anyone else. I want him to wake up, so we can be together. We have children. I can't not be married to him. I love him." I felt tears forming and falling the more I expressed how I felt.

Sun Gil tapped my hand to relax and to perhaps stop dropping tears in my bowl of delicious tteokbokki, she had made for lunch. After taking a few deep breaths and dabbing my wet cheeks I calmed down. Chul and Sun lovingly helped me with words from their forty-years as a couple serving Jehovah.

He told me, "Marie, when you researched marriage in the scriptures and Insight materials did you consider why the prevision was made, and when."

"Huh?" I looked at him confused. He continued, "The scriptures speak about marriage being created by Jehovah in Eden for the first human couple. There was no death at the time, he established the institution of marriage, which is why a mate is for a lifetime of forever. However, the moment Adam and Eve disobeyed, things were different. Sin and death entered the equation. During the time of the Mosaic law, many standards were outlined to keep His people clean and to separate the Israelites as His chosen people from those nations around them doing terrible things. One of which was what would allow for a divorce and for a person to remarry. Death and a couple other things would end the bond of marriage to allow for the mate to remarry if they chose. However, when a mate dies, there isn't anything that says or indicates if the surviving mate remains unmarried, what that will mean."

I listened intently to his reasoning, and it made clear sense as facts easily understandable. Then Sun Gil said, "Marie, I know the resurrection hope to see your brother was what you said, drew you to love the truth and Jehovah, but it was not the only reason you dedicated yourself. I encourage you to think of things this way, Jehovah will do amazing things for his people, his friends. In this system we can only see the hope before us. We will not know exactly what will be until the earth is reset under His rulership but have faith that He will make all things clear to you at the right time."

She poured me more tea and smiled at me. I nodded as Chul added, "Do not focus so much on what is unknown but that His promise is for all to be overjoyed with delight and there will be no pain or sadness. Do you not think He would consider the desires of His friends and make that possible if He chooses? I am sure He will reveal to all those surviving and those returning what is needed for living on earth and forever. Petition to Him in prayer for what you want now and in the future. As our heavenly father, He will give each person what is needed and what is best for us to be truly happy."

I took everything they shared with me that day to heart. Then when I talked to Ophelia and Stanley about something else and the subject came up, they said basically the same thing. Well, kind of.

"Oh, if 'Phee-Phee dies, I am marrying someone else. Right away!" Stanley said, laughing. Ophelia rolled her eyes at him during our metro cart witnessing assignment. Meghan and I snickered as he blew her a kiss.

"Yeah, you will need someone to chop the onions and do your laundry," she said sarcastically. Then she turned to us and said, "It will all work out the way He plans it. We don't need to know every detail of things because all cannot be told to us now. We won't understand it anyway. Remember, the scriptures say other things will be revealed, right? Maybe that is something."

Megan added, "He has given us the basics of what life will be like with Jesus's example on earth. No sickness, death, disabled, all peace and kindness, a clean earth and all in harmony with his father's purpose. I know He will make sure the right mate for me is there and I will meet them, so, I wait. I told you; I have issues from my childhood. I really want to be fair and be a good wife for the great husband He will provide when the time is right. Honestly, I don't think about it much because it will distract me. Knowing I will have what I want later is enough. I try to keep my attention on staying obedient and on the here and now to be there to receive the blessing promised."

I moaned, listening to my good spiritual friends. It was what they all had said and Megan's attitude that helped me not to question or worry about being married to Jae-Sung in the future. I trained my heart to believe that it would be obvious when it happens, and it wasn't important to know right now.

27. Diva Doll Lola

In mid-May, my flirty Delta sorority sister Lola Porter, came to visit South Korea for ten days. Well, it was only seven with us.

"Girl, what are you feeding these giants? Turkey legs filled with steroids." She said trying to pick up Jin.

I snickered while delivering my joking response, "Just a little rice, and ramyun. Ha… Ha!"

She laughed, "You are lying. I know they gettin' some grits, gumbo, corn bread, and fried chicken up in there too. Ha. They are Black." Laughing for a bit, she sat down on the floor with her nephews and niece, and silently admired them before saying, "Diva doll, they are so beautiful. I miss so much living in Sacramento."

When she said it, she seemed a little sad. "Lola, you alright? What's going on?"   She grinned, "Nothing. It's just you're not as close as before. I can't jump on a flight to New York to see you. What is the point of being able to fly for free if your friends are too busy living their own lives."

"Hey, Lola…"

"I mean everyone's life is busy. We don't hang out or see each other, and it sucks. Tangee lives in the same state. She is in L. A. with a husband, kids, and a career. Renee is trying to get her boutique business off the ground after she finally left Sax Fifth Avenue. But her years being a designer buyer for them let her travel all the time but not anymore."

"Lola, wait… You see Jazz, right? Didn't you two just go to Africa. That was supposed to be all of us. Remember, we planned it junior year at Howard, but never went."

"Oh yeah, Ghana was wonderful. Didn't I send you pictures? She's a blast. But you three weren't there, so it wasn't the same. Not like when we went to Japan and came here. That was unforgettable— best of times. Nothing is the same. We are going to be fifty in a few years. Maybe I'm just feeling old."

I slid on the floor to be closer to her and moved a few cushion puzzle pieces around for Jae to put together. Then I asked, "Lola… are you happy? I mean… in your marriage?" She nodded but didn't look at me. Then I just said what I had stored in the back of my mind when she told me she was staying for seven days and not ten.

"Lola, if you're happy, truly happy… Why are you sleeping with him?"

Like a flash of light, Lola's head swung around, and she glared at me, answering with an aggressive voice, "Are you judging me now?!

Now that you're one of them Bible thumpin' witnesses! Marie, don't you dare preach to me!"

"No... No. Girl, come on. It's me. Don't you do that. You know, my asking has nothing to do with my life being a witness. I'm asking because I love you, doll. I felt the same way years ago, when this same thing with him came up in New York, remember? Lola, what's going on?"

She exhaled but ignored me for several minutes while she talked to Jin and Jae on the floor playing with blocks and puzzle pieces. I just waited. *(She'll talk when she's ready. I don't want her hitting me.)* I knew to wait because Lola, the amazon can still get violent.

Nari came in to grab the boys to join their sister for their snack time in the kitchen. Then Lola and I were alone. We didn't move from the floor. Within just a few seconds of silence, Lola turned to me and just blurted out, "Greg had prostate cancer."

"Huh?... What? Oh-no." I slouched back leaning against the couch in shock. Before I could express my concern and show some empathy, she added more details.

"He had two surgeries right after we got married. It's his own damn fault. You know Black men don't get their prostate checked like they should. It's like they are afraid of the doctor or something. Greg's older. He knew better. Big dummy. By the time he did, it was too late to reverse the damage. But with all the needle injections, pumps, pills, and gadgets, it was just too hard for him. Well hell, no it's not hard at all. That's the problem. He can't perform. There has been no real sex life since then. He does other things, but Marie, I haven't had my husband pound on me since 2027. Greg told me he feels he got cheated in life because he can't be with me like normal. It depresses him and he says he feels like a crippled, useless man. I'm drained by it all. I won't leave him. But well... a couple times a year...

I meet BJ Won somewhere. This K-Pop idol dude from Jae's old group is… I mean, that Korean man is magnificent. He makes a sistah's toes curl for real. You know I never broadcast. Only Renee and Jazz know all the Delta secret details of that, but they don't know anything about Greg. I never told anyone that part. Our families don't even know about his diagnosis."

She stopped talking and waited for my reaction. Dumbfounded, I didn't know how to respond without judging her. I pressed my lips together, trying to think of something to say. Then she started chuckling.

"Marie, I was wondering how different you were going to be with all the religious stuff, but you're still my hopeless romantic Delta sister. Always Prissy Penelope. Ha, ha."

I smacked her shoulder, telling her sternly, "I am not prissy."

Greggory L. Porter

I took a breath and then continued, "I just well… you know I never dug on unfaithfulness, not even when we were in college. So, it's hard for me to know what to say. I'm sorry about Greg and these challenges with his health have brought to your life and his. Uh, and, about BJ… well, uh… there were sparks between you before you even met Greg Porter. It strange you didn't travel outside of Black man town, before our Delta Sister vacation trip that one year. Then you went kind of crazy, even in France. Maybe it's my fault for introducing you to Jae's close friend and K-Pop group mate back then."

"Yep… it is and thank you!" she said laughing. I gasped.

Lola continued to share. "Girl, please. It's not a secret from my husband. Greg knows what I'm doing. He actually has said to me a few times, 'your attitude is stank. Do you need that *Karate Kid* to wax on and wax off or something? Book a damn flight soon, so I can get my wife back. You are being an evil witch.' After that, I quickly made contact to schedule an appointment for my Korean treatments. If you know what I mean. Ha-Ha-Ha!"

""Oh my, goodness. Did he really say wax-on wax-off like…like the movie. Ha-ha-ha!" covered my mouth, trying not to snort while I laughed.

"Girl, I just don't want you to judge me, okay? I wanna enjoy you, my Delta sister, and these cuties. I don't want to talk about BJ or feel pressure from you on that situation. I love Greg, and we are good. So don't worry about it. Just be my friend. Deal?"

Nodding, I agreed with a smile. "Deal. No judging. Your life. I love you, Lola. If you ever need to talk or want to learn something new to consider a different perspective on life and the future, tag I'm it. Alright?"

"Bet! Now, where are we eatin'? Is your cute bodyguard coming to protect us? I bet he can lift me up, dang. Let's get Kang too if we can. Either way, I need to change into my free drink shirt. We need to play their game of rock, paper, scissors but make them boys take the Soju shots, this time!"

We laughed and hugged each other before making plans for dinner and drinks.

HR Director & Delta Sister
Lola Mathews-Porter

It has been said, there is calm before a storm. I was feeling secure and safe in my daily routine. I had spiritual and mental peacefulness, the love and happiness of my beautiful growing children, and my close circle of friends and family. I wasn't paying attention. It was only the calm.

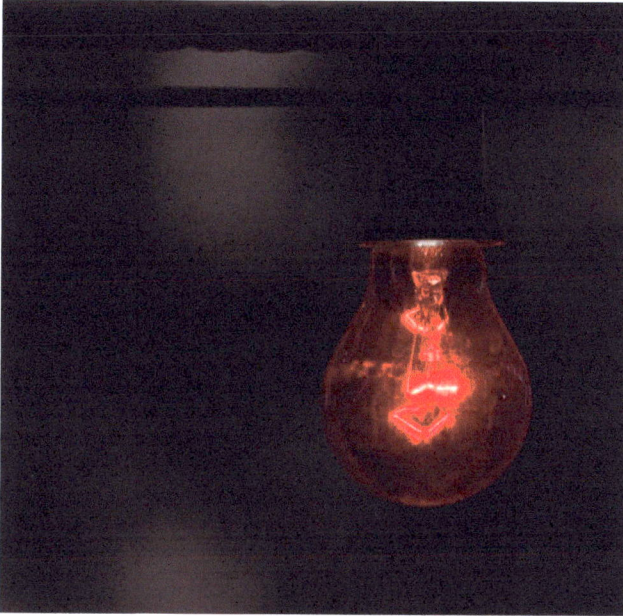

28. Breach

Thursday, June 29, 2032

Since the weather was nice for my quarterly revenue finance meeting at NM Entertainment, Nari and my babies came with me. They had done so once a few months ago, when Nari was to meet with her uncle Nah Min-Ji before going to lunch with Eun-Woo and her mother, Minah, on the same day. It was just easier to ride together and have SI drive the triplets and I home.

So, when Nari got a secure message delivery to meet her uncle at the same time to discuss an upcoming family celebration, we bundled up my two-year-olds and joined her in the security van Nah Min-Ji sent for her.

When we arrived at the NM Entertainment building, our security van driver pulled up for Nari to get out in-front of the northern underground security elevators. Her meeting was in a large media conference room on the second floor, but I was heading to the legal department, which was closer to the southern security elevators on the other side.

"The three of them is going to be a lot. Do you want me to take one with me?" Nari said, gathering up her things, as he opened the sliding door. Before I answered, our driver said, "Naega doum-i doel su issseubnida. Gwaenchanh-ayo. (I can help. No problem)."

I glanced at my three little ones, and they were already asleep. "Aww, they're sleep." I slouched and frowned a little. It was obvious I didn't want to wake them.

Sitting in the front passenger's seat, SI turned around and said, "Maybe, just leave them with me. We are just waiting here. Eh, your meeting is only about forty to sixty minutes, right? How long will you be, Nari?"

Nodding, I moaned yes. Picking up my purse and briefcase I prepared to be dropped off in the elevators closer to my meeting.

Stepping out the door, Nari said, "I'm not sure. But SI, if I'm not back when you are ready to go, just use this van. I can get my own way back, don't worry."

She smiled and swiped her security access card, and the gate and elevator opened. The driver closed the door, and we were on the move to the legal department's security elevators. Then I felt a bump, as though we ran over something.

"What was that?" I said while checking if the movement woke my children. They were still fast asleep. Then the driver stopped.

"We hit something?" SI asked as he removed his seatbelt.

"I did not see anything," our driver said, unbuckling his seatbelt seconds after SI.

The underground car garage and entrance were bright with lights and lots of cameras. I was thinking, *(Must have been something black or a flat tire?)*

Suddenly, I heard gasping and choking. SI reached over to the driver. "Gwaenchanh-a (Are you alright)?"

"Mwoga munje ya?" I asked what was wrong since I couldn't tell sitting behind a row of three car seats in the back of the van.

"Simjang mabiga issneun geos gat-ayo (I think he is having a heart attack)!"

"What?!" I started to panic and grab my phone but there was no signal underground. "I can't use my phone. I'll get help. Unlock the door, SI."

The gasping driver, who had now fallen forward and was hunched over the steering wheel, appeared to stop breathing. I stood up to squeeze between the seats that were securing my sleeping children as SI got out of the van. While he began punching in the code to unlock the side door for me to exit, the van suddenly jolted with a screech. I fell back partway onto my seat and the floor.

I could see SI holding onto the door when the van bolted forward and took off abruptly, turning a corner. Milliseconds later, I grabbed my purse to get my phone. There was a spark of light, a rapidly growing mist, or fog. Suddenly, I began coughing, and then there was complete darkness.

Fatigued and groggy, I slowly began to realize my head hurt like I had a migraine, and my eyes burned, even though they were covered with something over them. It was tied too tight around my eyes with a knot behind my head, and probably the reason I had a headache. I coughed and someone said, "ib-eul yeol (Open your mouth)!"

Not fully awake and confused, I didn't. A strong gloved hand snatched my face and shoved a bottled water in my mouth and tipped it. It was way too much, and I began choking as water overflowed soaking my blouse. Seconds later, it stopped being poured down my throat. I shook my head to wake up and catch air to breathe.

Then a spark came to my brain, *(Oh, my babies. What happened? Why can't I see?... Marie, breathe.)*

Immediately, I began shouting, "Where are my children?! Where?! Who are you? What do you want? My triplets! Are they alright? I don't hear them. Are they next to me? Take this off my face! I want to see my children! Right now! SI! SI!"

No one answered. I felt the sting of a powerful hand striking my cheek. Surprised by the slap, I paused to absorb the pain and think. When I tried to move, I couldn't. My hands were tied together in front of me, and my legs were tied to what seemed like the legs of the chair I was sitting on. I started to hyperventilate as my thoughts became clear.

(No! This isn't happening...Breathe. Don't panic. Breathe slowly. Everything will be alright if you stay calm. Oh, Jehovah, please help my children be alright... Wait... Think... People wouldn't hurt little sleeping babies. Relax. Find out where they are. Find out what these people want... Breathe... Where's SI? Where's SI?)

29. Idol Protocol

Nari made it to the second-floor media conference room to meet her uncle, but it was empty. Confused, she went to the twenty-second floor to Min-Ji's office, and his assistant told her, "He had flown to Japan a few hours before."

Rushing back down to the security elevators to wait in the van, she tried calling SI's cellphone. However, each time it connected, an out of service recorded message came on. Nari started to worry since it's security protocol never to turn off the phones when in public.

"Something is wrong." she mumbled a couple of times to herself.

With her panic growing, Nari called Kang. "Mwonga jalmosdoeeossda! SIga eungdabhaji anhseubnida. hoeuie wassneunde hoeuiga eobs-seubnida. naneun malina se ssangdung-iwa hamkkehaji anhseubnida. mwonga jalmosdoeeossda (Something's wrong! SI is not answering. I came for a meeting, and

213

there is no meeting. I am not with Marie or the triplets. Something is wrong)!"

When she got to the legal security elevators and went down to the basement parking garage level, she noticed several security personnel clustered together and an ambulance driving away. Under her breath, she expressed her feelings out loud, "Oh, please let them be here." Nari looked around to locate the security service van, SI, or the driver, but there was no such vehicle in the area.

Terrified, Nari broke down crying. She covered a hand over her mouth, so she wouldn't scream. Two security staff approached her and asked if she was alright. She told them she couldn't find her transport or her waiting friends. That was the moment she learned a man was injured and unconscious in the ambulance that had just pulled away for the hospital.

She said, "A man? Who? What happened?"

A second guard took her to another area adjacent to the closest elevators to view the security footage. Immediately, she recognized the van in the surveillance video.

"That... that's my friends," she squealed, wiping her tears from her flush cheeks. As she continued to watch the silent footage, showing a flustered SI getting out of the vehicle, it appeared he was holding onto the side door when the van drove away.

The security guards said, "...must have been some heated dispute between the driver and passenger."

The video then showed SI being dragged, and moments later, his body flew and crashed into a parked car. It wasn't clear if he was holding onto the door latch or if he was somehow caught on it. However, everyone around speculated he must have been caught because the driver didn't stop, perhaps not realizing it. Police from inside the building were called. They followed the ambulance to the hospital to question SI when he woke up. The extent of his injuries was unknown. Nari sobbed hearing the information from the guard. Seconds later she fell back in her chair, visibly shaken.

After about seven minutes, Kang, Trey and two of the off-duty shadowing security from the fourth floor of the building arrived. Idol security protocol was to contain any breach situation within the K-Pop idol management and security team. Never involve local or international authorities unless absolutely necessary and only as a last resort. However, this was not a South Korean celebrity. It was Marie Delacroix-Kim and her two-year old triplets.

Kang commanded things to be treated as if they were Jin-K, and everyone was on board. He sent one of his team to the hospital with Chris to legally block police from talking to SI. Simultaneously, he had Trey tried to locate Marie with the tracker hidden in her cellphone but there was nothing. Next, he took charge of the situation and instructed the building security to let him, and his team take over. He did so by stating that they had gotten a tip that there had been an unmarked vehicle of fans or media paparazzi in the underground security garage. The head of the building security staff quickly allowed them to do whatever they wanted; since they knew they would definitely lose their jobs if fans or media were in the garage on their watch. Kang and his team extracted the previous two hours of surveillance recordings and stored them on a portable drive. Then they removed them from the database.

Kang and a few from his team took a hysterical Nari to a hidden secure location inside the NM Entertainment building and viewed the recording again. As one team member began scanning the footage on his laptop, the others had the video connected to the large media screens and computer system in the soundproof breach room. Quickly, Trey hacked into the public videos on the street.

Unfortunately, the scan of those recordings only gave them enough of a visual to see the security van had traveled southbound into a residential area. The van wasn't seen leaving on any public surveillance. Kang sent Jusan, a member of his team, to go check out the residential area where the van was last spotted. After which, he questioned Nari.

"Have you seen this driver before?" Kang asked her, sliding her a box of tissues.

"I think so."

"Where?"

"Here... at NM... I wouldn't have gotten into the van if he didn't have the right badge and looked familiar. SI was with us. It all seemed so normal."

"Let me see the letter for your fake meeting."

Still wiping her continuous tears, Nari pulled out the typed letter on official NM Entertainment letterhead. While he looked it over carefully, Nari said, "We've got to find the triplets. Marie, we need to find her! Oh my god!" Nari sobbed with worry.

A few more members of Jin-K's former security team arrived. Kang's team was small, loyal, and highly skilled. After a debrief of the situation, Kang tried to have one of them escort her home. "Nari, Han will take you—" She cut him off, "No. I'm not leaving. Don't try to make me. When my uncle gets here, if he won't let me stay, then I'll go. But not before!"

Her being there with her emotions was going to be a constant distraction, but he let it slide. Although he didn't show it, Kang was worried. It had been too long without any real breakthrough clues. He wanted SI to be alright and wake up to tell him more details, he knew Nari wouldn't have thought to pick up on. But time was ticking away.

It had been about sixty minutes, and the tension could be felt in the air. Everyone involved was getting increasingly more nervous with each passing minute. Chris called saying, "SI never regained consciousness and was now in emergency surgery."

Breached security protocol made everything secret. Only Kang and his team, Chris, Eddie, Nari, and Min-Ji knew what was going on. No one could be notified at all. Everything was locked down until Kang had answers.

Lee, a member of the team, asked, "Do we need to tell Soo about SI? What if he doesn't make it?"

The words instantly hit Kang like a blade slicing through the tissue of his heart. Exhaling deeply, Kang had to decide. He had two choices; one was to break protocol and tell them, and the other was not. And if his younger brother died, he would have to carry the guilt of not telling his wife, child, and their mother ahead of time. Kang cleared his throat, and firmly gave a clear order, "Don't ask questions, you already know the answers too. Follow the damn code, Lee."

Not allowing others to distract him, Kang took a chance, hoping maybe he would get a hit this time.

"Trey, try the location tracker on her phone again. See if we get a hit, now."

"No. I don't even get a signal." Trey's tone was low, and flat. He was clearly deflated by the lack of a result.

"Damn it. I hope they are, but maybe... Wait, we have been assuming their together. What about the ones hidden in the car seats? They are set to activate if she isn't with them. Marie's phone and the sensor in her purse triggers them if they are not within ten feet for more than ten minutes."

"I didn't know...I don't have access. What is the frequency code?"

"KDrgn3^^...Hurry!"

"I got something!"

"Where?"

"South... Traveling fast..."

Lee spoke up, "Freeway...maybe by car?"

Trey was monitoring the computer and calculating the signal. Then he said, "No. Seems faster."

Han shouted, "Faster? Eh, train!"

"Hold on...let me check them. Tapping into trains going South at this speed..."

Everyone was anxiously waiting for some clues to locate Marie and her children. Trey was sweating and feeling the pressure. His fingers were flying so quickly typing that he didn't even feel them touching the keys. Han came closer to better scan the videos that Trey dropped onto the four monitors. The access was illegal. Trey could only tap into a particular surveillance video for around seventeen seconds without being detected by authorities. His hacking controls jumped from train to train and car to car. The quick flashes on the monitors had peering eyes scanning every area of the frame with heightened intensity.

Moments later, Jusan called. Kang put the incoming call on speaker and said, "Go."

Jusan reported, "I found the van in an empty warehouse here in Goyang."

Lee mumbled, "Goyang is just 16km away from Seoul. They moved quick."

Jusan continued talking, "It's wiped clean, but the camera shows two other unidentifiable security vans were here before it came, then the recording stops. Seems like a grab and swap. No tracking on this van either. It looks like it was painted to look like the security company NM uses, but its registered and reported stolen from a bakery in Busan and—"

Out of nowhere, Trey shouted, "Busan train! Got 'em! We're an hour behind but this train car mid-way middle on the left. Here... see... backs of two... looks like a man and maybe a woman, baseball hats, tall, lean and medium build with shades, pants and dark jackets. They have three car seats converted back into a stroller. Can't see in the stroller. It's covered with a screen or something. Here is the still photo!"

"Let's go!" Kang shouted.

The evidence proved what he feared from the start, that Marie wasn't with little Jae, Jin, and Jolie anymore. In any case, he had to get them all back safely. Kang remained levelheaded as the leader and the one to get them back as soon as possible. But inside the calm, calculating demeanor, Kang Cheng was anxious, afraid, and very angry.

On the way, Kang called Chris, and he informed Min-Ji, who had immediately left his meeting and was on a flight back to Seoul. Min-Ji made a few calls to Kang and another trusted person. He called

Dong-Hyun over at Samsung and casually asked to meet with him at NM Entertainment as soon as possible.

"I have some meetings that I cannot reschedule. Can we meet around 5:30 p.m.?" Dong-Hyun said while gathering files from his desk to rush off to a technology meeting.

"I'll be in my office." These were the last words spoken by Min-Ji before he hung up.

Arriving a few hours later, Min-Ji met with his niece privately, who had remained in the breach room at NM Entertainment. He downplayed what was happening to calm her emotions. Once she could speak slowly without crying, he had her break down everything that had happened.

Afterward, Min-Ji directed Nari to return home and wait quietly. "Do not contact anyone," he said firmly, holding her shoulders and peering into her watery eyes. Still sobbing, she nodded in agreement. Min-Ji's driver took her back to Marie's home while he waited for an update from Chris or Kang.

And he waited.

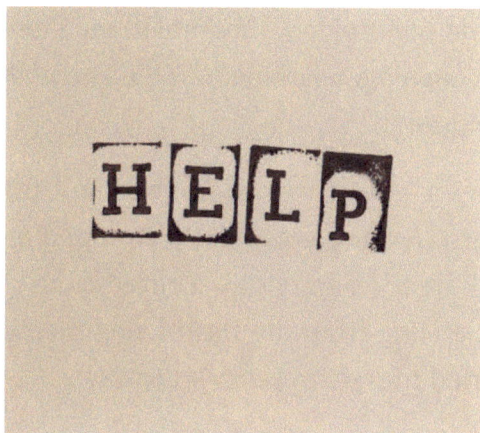

30. What's Happening

"I'll have all the money I need when you sign these papers. Sign them!" The husky voice said, shoving a pen between my fingers. His words were understandable, but English was not his primary language. His accent was too thick.

(He's Korean or Chinese...) I dropped the pen on the table that I felt was in front of me.

Another voice that sounded a bit higher and nasally said, "We know you are Jin-K's widow, and those are his children. The public would be thrilled to learn of your existence and theirs. I can get a lot of money just to report it to the media. Your life will never be private again. I can expose you to the world. But that isn't what I want to do unless you force me. Sign them!" A gloved hand grabbed my right hand and smashed it over a pen and some papers on the table.

(There are two of them. Men...This one is different. English sounds clearer, less of an accent. English is distinct but more European not American...)

Still gagged and blindfolded, I mumbled my demand, "I want my children! I'm not signing anything until I know they are alright! Where are my children?!"

Seconds later, a gloved hand grabbed my bound hands and yanked me forward. A band was tightly wrapped around my arm. I struggled to break free. As an oddly, scented cloth covered my nose and mouth, I felt a sting from my flesh being pierced on the top of my right hand. I tried to scream but felt drowsy.

In moments, it was dark and quiet.

***

An unconscious SI Cheng was in recovery from the emergency surgeries he underwent to stop the bleeding from severed branches of his femoral artery, and stabilize his right hip, right leg and left shoulder with traction, bolts, wires, and plates. He was heavily sedated, and the next few hours would determine his rate of survival. Doctors were also monitoring any other injuries or complications initially undetected from the accident.

Chris contacted Kang and Min-Ji with the news. A NM Entertainment high security staff had been stationed outside of SI's room. No one was to enter without authority. Chris was to be contacted immediately when he woke up, but doctors warned; it would probably be a couple of days if he did.

***

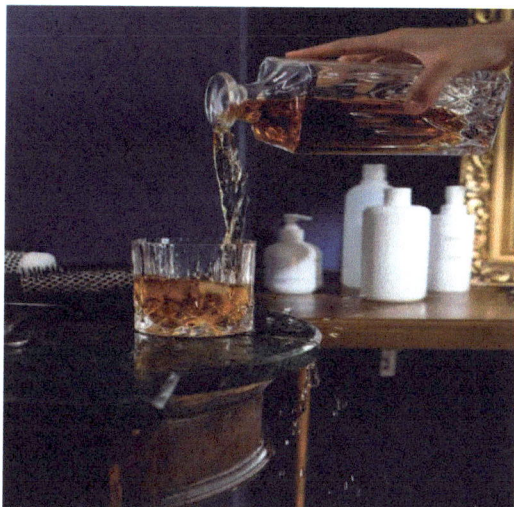

NM Entertainment's owner billionaire businessman, Nah Min-Ji, sat in his large modern office, surrounded by one-way windows, alone. He began pouring up another glass of Chivas Regal 25-year-old scotch, when a buzz from his secretary came through, notifying him that Dong-Hyun Kim was on his way. Min-Ji relieved her for the evening. Then he chugged down the expensive alcohol; he kept tucked away in a desk-side bar that looked like a bookshelf. He reached into the bar and pulled out a bottle of Gowoon Dar Soju and a glass for Dong-Hyun Kim.

Min-Ji exhaled, trying to relieve some of the stress he had built up, knowing he had to tell his long-time friend something he never thought he would have to say. Jae-Sung Kim was Min-Ji's adopted nephew, just like all his DRGN5 group members. They were very special to him. A great deal of NM Entertainment's multi-billion-dollar portfolio as an international music company had been built on Jae-Sung and his former K-Pop idol group's success.

He handpicked Jae-Sung when he was fourteen years old after he saw something special in him out of all the talented young people in the competition. Then when Jae sang, Min-Ji knew that was what it was. He was already a musical prodigy mastering the piano. But at such a young age, his airy baritone sound was a rare diamond-mine. Min-Ji nurtured it into a magnificent, sultry 4-octave range that made women and girl's panties melt away. He taught the young Jae-Sung the business side of the music industry, and he grew to be successful in everything. The media even tagged him with the title NM's golden boy, long before DRGN5 disbanded when he was twenty-seven, and launched his solo Korean R&B and Pop career. Back then, Min-Ji had no sons, and these young men, especially Jae-Sung, were the closest he got. He loved them and protected them from anything toxic, harmful, or damaging, not only to their career but their lives. A trajectory of successful businessmen was his plan for the five of them.

In all the years, Jae-Sung had been the wealthy and handsome Jin-K, leader of K-Pop idol group DRGN-5, singer, dancer, model, actor, composer, and musician, traveling the world with millions of fans, and being ranked the ninth top K-Pop group of all time, there had not once been an incident like this one. It wasn't Jae-Sung, but his wife and heirs that were caught up in a safety breach. Min-Ji had a heavy heart preparing for the conversation.

As Dong-Hyun Kim entered the office, Min-Ji didn't stand or speak, he simply pointed to the bottle and glass that he had poured for him. Dong-Hyun was older, and this was not behavior customary for showing respect to one's elder. However, the two businessmen were alone. They had been good friends for many decades, and it was acceptable to be informal with Jae-Sung's stepfather in this instance.

"Ah..." Dong-Hyun said, before sitting down. He sighed before chugging the alcohol. Without a word, Min Ji honored him by pouring another for him and he drank it quickly. Moments later, Min-Ji told his old friend the situation.

Dong-Hyun Kim

Still in hot pursuit, the worry had reduced because locating the triplets looked more promising with the clues they had gotten. Now only an hour away from Busan, Kang, Han, Lee, and Trey were getting warmer. The tracking signals were stronger, moving slower, and much easier to hone-in on. The visual detection through their computer made navigating through locations also easier than hacking public surveillance tracking. But there was a lot of ground to cover. The signals led them to one of the largest markets in South Korea, Nampodong Market. But by the time they got there, it was crowded and difficult to get through. Scanning the area for about seventy minutes, they shifted gears because the signals again were on the move on a highway. Marie's security teams gathered and in their two customized black Lexus sedans quickly followed. Trey concentrated on the computer tracking road with Kang who had been on point driving the entire time. Han and Lee were behind them in the second car. When the signal stopped moving, Trey got anxious. Motionless for over an hour and a half, Trey had Kang pull over.

"What?" Kang said, anxious to know since it was growing dark.

"Wait...it's..."

"What, Trey?!"

"This is weird."

"Huh?"

"Kang, maybe they found the trackers... Uh, and dumped them."

"Not possible. Untraceable. Where are they?"

"It…it says, Gamcheon Village. I even have an address," Trey said, almost in a whisper.

Kang didn't pause but turned the car around and zipped back onto the freeway headed to Gamcheon Village with its steep streets, twisting alleys, and vibrantly painted houses that looked a lot like Santorini.

Trey's thought just came out of his mouth, "Tourist area? This…this seems too easy."

Kang mumbled, "Let's hope so."

After Dong-Hyun called his wife, Min Cha to inform her he wouldn't be home due to a long meeting, the blood seemed to rush from his face. His ghostly appearance was all the reaction he had for thirty minutes. Then he got another drink before asking questions.

"Is...is SI...is he alright?" His hand shook, bringing the glass to his mouth.

"The surgeries were successful, but he has to recover and wake up."

After swallowing the alcohol, Dong-Hyun's voice elevated with anger, "We need to call the police, Min-Ji! This isn't music fans! These are my grandchildren. Jae's children—Min-Ji...his wife!" Dong-Hyung sprung from his seat, tossed his suit jacket in the chair and began to pace around the room, rubbing his hands over his face.

Calmly, from his desk chair, Min-Ji confessed, "Dong-Hyun, it's the same. We can't involve the authorities yet. We need three days...three. Then if we can't resolve it, we alert them. Too early will increase the danger and the risks. You know how this works."

He turned and shouted, "My son's children, Min-Ji...my son! Give them whatever they want! I don't care!" Dong-Hyun collapsed onto the lounge couch and began to softly sob. He covered his face from shame but didn't stop weeping.

Security Ninja Jusan Park

Still in Goyang, just sixteen kilometers away from Seoul, Jusan moved swiftly to hide inside the warehouse when he heard the lock and door being opened from the outside. A man entered while talking in Korean on a cellphone. His head was covered with a low cap, and he wore a dark painter's all-in-one jumper. Although the man made the conscious effort to hide his face, he was unknown to Jusan who remained still, but attentive to make out what was being said. The man got off the phone, got into the van and drove southbound.

Jusan followed the van but didn't rush because he had already put trackers on it. While driving, he called Kang and relayed what he heard and where he was headed.

"Say again," Kang demanded.

"He said, change of plan. Ask for ransom. Dump body."

Trey's heart sank as he bit the corner of his bottom lip. Kang blew out heavy before giving instructions. "Jusan, man, you're the only one close enough...don't lose him, man. Don't get caught."

"Copy that!" Jusan said before hanging up.

Jusan felt the weight of his responsibility even more after the call. Knowing that Marie's life was at stake, he was the closest person to finding her, dead or alive. He quickly mumbled a low prayer not to fail as he concentrated on merging between cars on the highway.

***

At 8:07 p.m., Min-Ji's desk phone rang. Line number two's light flashed with the ringing. He answered by putting the call on the phone's speaker. Dong-Hyun, Chris, Eddie and Jet, Min-Ji's personal security, were anxiously waiting. A computer-generated voice recording began making demands.

"Ten million. Electronic transfer in US dollars to an international bank within twelve hours. If there is no transfer by the deadline, one child will disappear, and then there will be two. If there is no transfer within twelve hours and fifteen minutes, then there will only be one child. If there is no transfer within twelve hours and sixteen minutes, DRGN5's Jin-K will have no heirs."

The caller hung up. Min-Ji spoke, "So, it is, money they want."

Dong-Hyun fumbled with his phone to move assets and get the ransom. He knew he didn't have it on his own, but he would gather what he could.

"I... I have almost half... Use Jae's accounts to get the rest. Pay them! Pay them now!" Dong-Hyun was flustered and wanted to resolve things quickly. He made his feeling known that it was just money and not worth the lives of his grandchildren.

But Chris paused him with his words, "We can't pay." All eyes were on him as he continued, "What about Marie? It said nothing about her."

"Pay them, damn it!" Dong-Hyun shouted. "Maybe…maybe they don't have her or maybe they know Jae's children are the key to the money. I don't care, pay them! Get my grandchildren back completely intact and right now! Damn it, pay them!"

Eddie darted to a computer to access Jae and Marie's accounts. The South Korean accounts didn't have enough to convert over to the ransom amount, but the American and French accounts were available with funds to transfer. Eddie announced, "The BNP in France will take too long to get and move. Chase or Bank of America accounts would be the fastest to transfer to the numbered bank account. But we need to do it in a branch. It's too much money to move electronically without flagging suspicion."

Min-Ji finally spoke again, "I'll pay it," while motioning to Jet to open his safe for some code keys to his personal account and continued, "Let's make this easy and not involve banks. That would lead to tracking and questions. Jet will move it for you to transfer Eddie. Dong-Hyun, you need that to live. I'm concerned about Mrs. Kim. They didn't mention her. That worries me."

31. Busan

After several street and alley turns, they were right on the signal. It hadn't moved in over three hours and was strong. Lee and Han scouted around the modest home. It was bright inside but with all the window shades closed. There were no cars or people in sight. When they came back to inform Kang and Trey, the two were already out of the car and in the trunk assessing the situation for the needed equipment.

Kang had a thought... *(Babies.)* Returning his automatic weapon to the hidden side compartment, he announced to his team, "No, we can't risk it inside. Han, you, and Lee cover out here. Use silencers. Light them up if they so much as peek around the corner. Trey, we will get our hands dirty. No mistakes... Triplets can't be hurt."

Simultaneously, the team gave a "Copy that!"

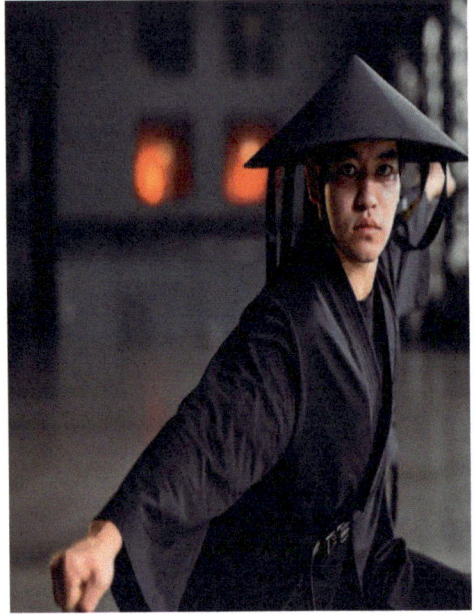

Ready for war, all four men were armed with thin leather straps, nine-inch metal blades, and covered in black. Kang and Trey silently scaled up and over a side wall of the enclosed property.

There was no movement, but classical music was playing from inside the house. No alarms went off. No animals came rushing to protect the property. The two crept to different side windows to get a visual. Trey motioned with a hand signal, confirming he had none. Kang returned the same motion. The two moved around, surveying the house; they checked all around, but all window shades were closed. The two men arrived at the halfway point of the home.

One side small window was open. The breeze moved the screen just a little for a visual to a larger room with the empty converted stroller. Trey got there first. When he saw the empty stroller, he instantly felt anger and disappointment. They had been duped. (*This was too damn easy.*) He thought.

But when he looked again, he saw part of a large crate or something with beams or bars. He couldn't make out anymore, waiting for the breeze to aid. He wanted to blow it to move and see more, but it would make noises that could alert the kidnappers.

Fueled by his rising anger, Kang was tired of waiting. Feeling himself lose patience, he tried to control himself, *(Triplets…they are in there…Be calm. Think. Don't rush.)*

After ten minutes of surveillance and no adult figures or movement, Kang signaled to Trey to break from monitoring and move in quietly. Trey slipped his hand between the frames and pushed the windows an inch at a time wide open.

When Kang checked the front door, it was unlocked. Ducking low, he eased it open. Silently, the two entered the home from opposite sides and checked rooms along the way. Every room they covered had no furniture or people. Kang reached the larger room first. Moments later, he then let out a sharp inhale of air before covering his mouth with his hand. The sound made Trey rush to the area. When he got there, he froze. Inside a large wooden crate and on top of a fluffy mat, Jolie was laying between her brothers, sucking the tip of her pinky finger while Jin, and Jae were asleep.

Swiftly Trey completed the external safety check for booby-traps triggers or tracking bugs connected to the kennel-like crate and their bodies. "Clear" softly was his first word. Before Trey got the words all out, Kang was reaching over to pick up Jolie. Colliding with emotions of surprise, joy, anger and relief, his heart raced, and his tears fell as he smiled at little Jolie Kim. As she focused her large green iris and pupils on seeing him, a sweet cheerful familiar word came from her lips, "Samchon (uncle)."

He nodded releasing, "Eh" as he panted with slow-falling liquid. Seconds after seeing her smile, Kang's words escaped from his mouth as a breathy sigh, "Jolie Sable Arabe (Pretty Arabian Sand)."

Jolie wrapped her little light-brown fingers around his neck and squeezed while rubbing the tips of their noses together. Feeling amused, he snickered by her innocence and her giving him an Eskimo kiss. He said, "Je t'aime petit (I love you little one)."

She nodded with "Eung. Gomawo (Yes. Thank you)."

Trey wanted to shout, but the boys were cuddled up sleeping. He hit Kang on the shoulder, then stepped away to notify Han and Lee to come in. The team performed another security sweep of the location and all the items left inside the empty home. There were no additional clues.

Kang messaged Min-Ji, "Drgn3 located-safe. Need to speak privately."

Min-Ji motioned to Jet to wait. Then he picked up his cellphone and dialed Kang. Only listening, Min-Ji did not speak at all as he got the update from Kang. "No one knew we were on the trail. We were two hours behind from tracking. The house was abandoned. Han checked public records; it belongs to a modeling agency for photo shoots. No one around. Triplets were safe. Scanned them, no trackers, or injuries. Backpack not here, but they appear to have been fed, bathed, and changed to nightwear that had not been packed for them. Whoever took them, had no intention of harming or mistreating them."

Min-Jin exhaled then spoke, "Take them home. I will call Nari. By the time you get there, she'll know what to do. Good work!" Min-Ji continued grinning, but it faded when he commanded. "Now, find her."

Kang replied, "Copy that."

Jusan had followed the man in the van for several miles outside of town to a secluded hilly area. He stopped in an abandoned lot. Jusan watched the man pull up to a second car, grab gasoline cans from the car trunk, and douse the van inside with what appeared to be an accelerant before setting it on fire.

Before the man could rush to the car to speed away, five-foot-ten muscular and combat-trained Jusan pounced onto the six-foot lean man. Once the two tussled and Jusan beat him to unconsciousness, he tied him up for transport.

In Min-Ji's office, elation and sighs of relief filled the air as Dong-Hyun cheered taking another drink. Chris and Eddie grabbed a glass of soju and toasted with Min-Ji and Jet. Several minutes later, the office became soundless. Then out of nowhere, Dong-Hyun mumbled to himself what everyone possibly still had on their mind, "But where is she?"

On the road, Kang wasn't separating from them again. All three were in the back seat of his car fast asleep. It was quiet for most of the ride until Trey spoke what was on his mind. "This is weird. Why grab and ask for ransom but leave them. If you didn't have those trackers on the car seats, we would have never found them. No one knew about those being there, you said. Right? Did Marie know, and maybe she told someone? The door was unlocked, but...every house around is empty. They got rid of their backpack. That makes sense; it had trackers, but they kept the car seats that converted into the triplet stroller. It was less obvious than carrying three kids around, but they didn't think of the possibility of it having something on it. That's odd. Not pro's as I would expect. We would have dumped everything. Maybe that's really what they were expecting; no one to find them at all."

Kang nodded but said nothing. His mind was processing several things at once.

NM Entertainment Mogul

Nah Min-Ji

Since no money had been transferred by the deadline given by the kidnappers, a follow-up phone call was expected, but one never came. The four men waited in Min-Ji's office until nine the next morning, with Kang and Han joining.

Dong-Hyun, Chris, and Eddie agreed to return at 3:00 p.m., only if an update or change occurred. No one was to communicate details over the phone. Kang had already reassured everyone that there was no concern of a home invasion since the building was secured because the pick-up point is always at another location. However, Lee was stationed at Marie's home with Nari.

By 9:30, Chris, Eddie and Dong-Hyun disbursed to their respective homes. Now alone, Min-Ji, Han, Jet, and Kang could speak more freely. Kang reported one kidnapper was "being held and questioned by Trey and Jusan."

"Good. Where they live is still secure. We don't have to relocate them," Min-Ji said while checking it off a notebook list on the conference table of his office. The three men nodded as they continued to review the details, evidence and data obtained from hack searches on the property, van service, bank, computer call and bakery theft records.

Han said, "Maybe we should have stuck around the house in Busan to see if they came back. Not calling about the ransom means they know we have them."

Jet spoke up giving his opinion. "Why call and ask for more when you don't have them. But not asking for ransom for her...she's the widow. Worth more it would seem if money was the prize."

Kang chimed in, "It's not. Marie… She must be the prize."

All eyes darted over to him. Min-Ji gave him a look to go on with his theory, and he did. "Separate them was first. We go for children, right? Easy to track on public transportation. Trey said it…too easy. Especially for us. They must know what we are capable of… Ransom call, only for triplets. Decoy…it's not money. She…she's the prize."

Nodding, Min-Ji said, "Yes. She is. Removing her is the endgame. Which means it's someone with a connection to gain from her being out of the way."

Kang stood up, "I need to find her. Let's keep this between us. I'll feel safer until I know more. I can't lose her too. I won't."

"Question him well. Just as I trained you, Kang." Jet said to his former assistant.

"Copy that." Kang said it as he and Han left his office.

⁂

When Jusan brought the van driver to an underground soundproof room in an undisclosed area outside of Seoul, he had no identification, and his face was distorted and swollen from the previous beating.

However, after hours of being targeted with repeated questions by the security team, the man was exhausted, swollen, and bleeding. When Kang arrived, the man began hysterically laughing before Trey's fist forcefully made contact with his gut. Pulling his head back by his bloody and sweat-soaked hair, Kang wanted to see the face of the assailant. Startled when he saw his eyes, Kang immediately let go of his hair and grabbed his phone. He fumbled to dial. It rang twice. Then a voice from the other line came through clearly.

Min Ji answered, "Neh (Yes)."

Kang shouted, "It's…Sabastian Khan!"

32. Race

Former South Korean singer Sabastian Khan debuted as a solo artist with NM Entertainment, after the mediocre success of his K-Pop idol group, Splice, was not picked up by its management company.

The male and female quartette disbanded, and its lead male singer, Sabastian, was signed to NM Entertainment after winning an audition competition. His first and only album, Sensational, was released in November 2027 and was produced by megastar producers Jin-K, former lead singer of DRGN5 and Tayler Styles. It even featured chart top-ten duets with American soloist Tangee Arnold and a charted dance collaboration with British rapper Chrix Kool. His popularity skyrocketed and he continued to tour until a drug scandal in 2029 halted his career, and he was dropped from NM Entertainment.

Sabastian Khan

Although the scandal trial resulted in acquittal in Singapore, he had been found guilty of lesser charges filed in Japan. After serving his confinement sentence of fourteen months, Sabastian attempted to collect past unpaid royalties from NM Entertainment productions for his songwriting credit. However, his lawsuit against Juan Park, Coral Yun, Shawn Tinkle, Min-Ji, and the estate of Jin-K were all dismissed or withdrawn.

Kang took over the 'questioning' process with a vengeance. After several strikes, and questions about Marie's whereabouts, their prisoner still refused to answer. Sabastian's taunting laughter ignited Kang and he lost control. He unleashed a cyclone of fury on

Sebastian Khan. Several times Kang had to be physically wrestled away by his men so he wouldn't torture and beat the man to death. In less than forty-five minutes, Sabastian Khan had broken his silence.

"Bukhansan… bl…blocked… cave… no…no water…" were Sebastian's last words before unconsciousness. They were also the ones that rang repeatedly in Kang's ear.

By 1:45 p.m. Kang and Trey were speeding to rescue her. His heart raced as he mumbled to himself. Trey was equally nervous, but the car didn't go any faster around the sharp turns and twisting roads to get up to the mountain. Bukhansanseong was a walled mountain fortress built by connecting the peaks of Mt. Bukhan in the second century by the kingdom of Baekje. It was a popular place for locals and tourists to visit inside a National Park. However, after a small earthquake a few years earlier, one of the remaining ancient fortress sections of the mountain had partially collapsed and been blocked due to fallen rocks. Areas around that section had been known to have rockslides and a few caves, but due to safety concerns, the entire section had been restricted to tourists.

Trey conducted research through computer hacking and was able to narrow down two possible caves to the south of the restricted area. The larger cave had a creek of water running through it. Based on Sabastian's confession of no water, Marie would have been dumped in the smaller cave on the four-mile Uldong-Baegundae-Wonhyobong trail. According to park photos and records that he extracted mapping out their approach, the cave was high up to access the entrance but descended once inside. (Dangerous. They didn't want her to ever be found.) He thought, nervously nibbling on his lip, and glancing at the time.

247

It was a treacherous hike on the over four-mile difficult trail through the forest, over rocks, steep hills, and up the south side of a mountain. Falling from the slippery rocks, the two men helped each other over the treacherous terrain. At the halfway point, the trail was covered from an earlier avalanche close to the seventh gate of the historical landmark.

Although prepared to encounter animals, after a couple of close call run-ins with a wild boar, a Mongolian wolf, and two water deer, there was a greater heightened sense of urgency. The facts flashed in Kang's mind, as they climbed, *(Marie is out here in the wilderness, completely defenseless.)*

They were running out of time. Kang kept his mind focused on the time because Sabastian whimpered that his partner dumped her body earlier the day before. He thought of nothing else, but his heart lowly murmured that Marie could already be dead. It triggered him to action. He picked up the pace, deviating from the suspected pathway. Kang made noises like some wild animal, grunting, and growling as he aggressively climbed, moving over rocks that tumbled over cliffs at the left of them. *(Faster…Go faster!)* His emotional actions created small rockslides as he waivered even further away from the hiking trail and into the trees and cliffs.

Without warning, Trey lunged forward grabbing Kang's foot in front of him and yanked him to the ground. The action avoided an opening covered by trees, that dropped several feet onto jagged rocks below.

"Kang! Man, ya gotta focus! Look! We can die out here if we aren't careful. It's just us. She's waiting, alright? Waiting."

Kang looked at the escaped calamity and exhaled. Some of the fury eased but he was sweating profusely. Kang nodded, and the two kept moving through fallen trees and scaling a small drop off to a landing where the trail started again. Following the old hiking trail more carefully, the two avoided more unnecessary dangers. If they had notified rangers, they could have gotten there quicker by helicopter or been guided by skilled hikers who would have known an easier pathway, but it was a security breach. No one could be notified. They were on their own to get to her.

It had taken them almost two and a half hours just to get to the point of the off-trail cave entrance. The cave had been partially covered by boulders and a *'do not enter'* warning sign. However, their adrenaline kept them moving forward. Now visually able to see exactly where they were, Trey located a safer and wider road west of them that led back down the mountain. Although they had brought with them food, first aid and other supplies, the two men only drank water.

"I need to find her, Trey!" Kang shouted before they climbed over the boulders to enter the dark cave-like opening as wide and seemingly as deep as an adult Bowhead whale.

Out of breath, Trey nodded and followed. Kang tried to slow his breathing and pulled out his sidearm. Trey had turned on the high-definition hand-lantern lights to see around and in the cavern darkness.

Kang mumbled, "Noona, just wait. I'm coming... I'm coming..."

After about ten minutes of scanning and walking cautiously around rocks and debris, a long object was spotted next to a pile of rocks and under several tree branches. It was difficult to make out.

(Animal?) Kang aimed his pistol, ready to hit whatever it was if it moved.

Moments later, as Trey moved the light further ahead, it became clear. It was a human leg in suit pants.

"MARIE!"

Kang shouted, darting toward what he hoped, and prayed would be his sister, friend, the other half of his family. With tears of desperation, he cried out, "Marie, please… Oh, please…" spewed from his chapped lips as he lifted her body into his arms.

Marie wasn't moving. Her skin was very cold. Her body was limp and unresponsive to stimulation through her senses. The two men fumbled with the aid bag. She was barely breathing. But at this moment, Chantal-Marie Delacroix-Kim was still alive.

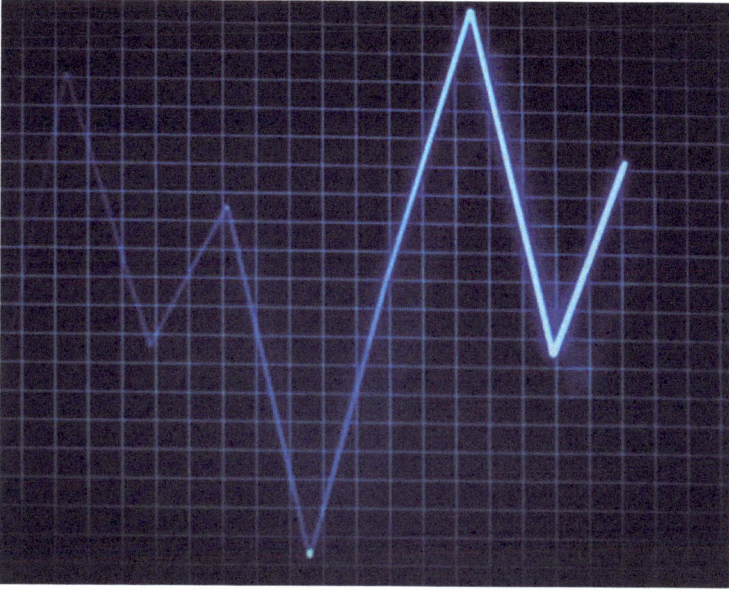

33. Beyond

I didn't remember anything after I refused to sign papers. After I had been found, I had been unresponsive and asleep for nearly three days, due to hypothermia and a toxic mixture of illegal narcotics in my bloodstream. When I slowly opened my eyes, I was in a hospital bed and connected to several tubes. There were small ones in my nose taped to my cheeks, but I could lick my lips that seemed to already be moisten with something fruity flavored. As the area I was in came into focus, I could tell it was Min-Ji's house. I knew because the room looked like the same secluded cottage we stayed in after we got married.

There were multiple vases all around with a variety of colorful orchids and roses clusters and bouquets. Focusing my eyes, I noticed a middle-aged Asian woman in white with a stethoscope around her neck and clipboard in her hand, smile at me. Turning my head to the left, away from the window, I saw Kang Cheng smiling. My lips parted. Before I could moisten them again and speak, Kang firmly pressed his mouth on mine. I felt my eyelids rise a little higher as I became more aware that Kang Cheng was kissing me. His eyes were closed, and his intake of oxygen was forceful from his nostrils onto my skin. Touching me, he felt almost as if he was trembling. I heard him whisper a soft moan, then I reached up while his mouth moved over mine and brushed the dark skin of his smooth jaw with my fingertips. He relaxed and eased from his lip kiss. Locking eyes, he then leaned forward and kissed my forehead and then my cheek. I grinned.

Leaning over me, he whispered, "Gyeong-iloun eonni, aideul-eun anjeonhabnida. god dangsin-eul bangmunhal geos-ibnida."

I frowned and squinted my eyes. Kang paused a moment. Then he said it again in English. "Phenomenal Noona, children are safe. Will be here to visit you soon."

Slightly, I shook my head and squinted my eyes more at him. Kang had a confused expression, perhaps thinking I didn't understand him. He repeated what he said but this time in French. "Sœur aînée phénoménale, les enfants sont en sécurité. Sera là pour vous rendre visite, bientôt. (Phenomenal Noona, children are safe. Will be here to visit you soon)."

Raising my eyebrows rapidly up and down the same way Jae used to do, Kang chuckled with tightly pressed lips. He rolled his eyes and made a smacking sound from sucking air between his teeth. I heard him mumble a curse word, "Ssi-bal" while pinching my right cheek. Giggling, my eyes released tears from the happiness those words gave me. In my mind, I thanked my heavenly father and everyone that helped find me and kept my children safe. I knew everything would be alright.

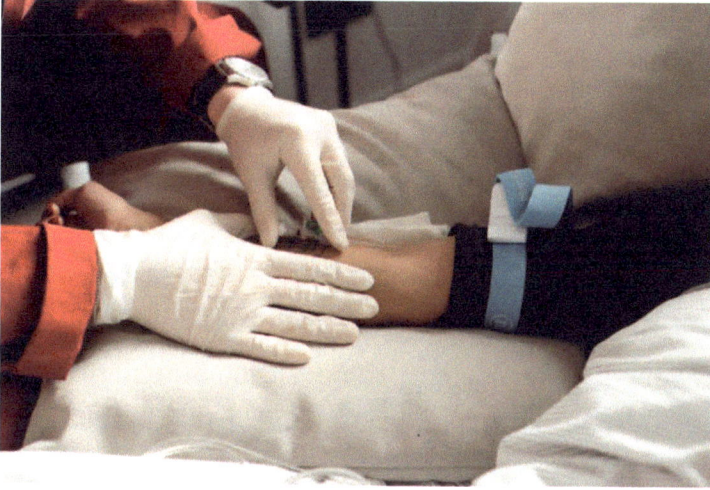

Days after waking up, but still at a private hospital in a body cast, SI was demanding to see me. He had been worried I blamed him, and he was desperate to explain. When I was able to visit him, all I did was tearfully hug and kiss him. I repeatedly told him, "Nothing to explain. I love you, SI. Jehovah took care of us. Nothing to forgive. I am glad you are alright, little brother. Don't worry. I love you more than ever. Jehovah blessed me with you. Recover well, and let's make cookies soon." He just cried. Then Soo started to cry, which, of course, made me and Hana cry more. It was a blubber fest until playfully annoyed Kang snarled with, "Aish (Ah-shit)!"

After that, we laughed wiping tears away.

Over the next several weeks, it was made clear to me that the code was never to speak about the ordeal. Not to anyone. I was informed by Min-Ji, "The security breach had been resolved. There is no future risk or danger." He said it wasn't anyone I knew, so it was closed.

In February 2033, my babies were growing bigger and bigger and remembered nothing. I finished the required trauma therapy Min Ji arranged and was cleared because I hadn't had any more nightmares since December. I was feeling good.

My sweet brother, SI had some permanent nerve damage and sometimes must use a cane. As a result of his disability, he lost his government license to carry a weapon and was reassigned by NM Entertainment for security support from an office rather than in the field. He was very busy and no longer was on Kang's shadow team, so we only saw him and his family occasionally on social family visits.

Never was there any mention of what happened, and that was how these things worked. I was to pretend it never occurred. It seemed to be much easier to do than I thought. But by this time, my mind wouldn't let it go and I was nervous about leaving the house still. Right after my rescue I had privately pressed Kang to tell me more. He wouldn't. But one afternoon, I asked him again more like pleaded because I was scared, thinking maybe they would come back or there were others out there trying to hurt me.

"Kang, you know, I don't like secrets. There must be more to this. What harm would it be to tell me who these people were? What did they want? Or... How did they know me?"

"Marie, everything is as it should be. There is no risk, I promise. Just need you to trust me, the code. It's over."

"I trust you, but you don't trust me. Tell me. Don't do this idol code stuff to me. Kang...it's not right. Not for something like this. They tried to kill me. I need to know."

"Noona…"

I paced around my home office before closing the door to ensure Nari, Lee, or my children wouldn't hear what I was hoping Kang would tell me.

"I won't tell anyone. I won't change how I am. I won't. I promise. Tell me. Please?"

"Never…not even your parents. No one…ever. Swear."

Sitting back at my desk, holding up three fingers like I saw in a movie with girl scouts for three seconds, I nodded in agreement. Kang exhaled and then told me, "Sabastian Khan— a K-Pop singer. Not long ago, he had attempted to back Min-Ji into a legal corner over songwriting royalties. He had been released from NM Entertainment after a drug scandal. He had collaborated early on with Jae, Tayler, and your friend Tangee too, I believe. The guy worked with some other people. That's who was behind it. But they are gone. Don't worry."

"Wait a minute. What other people? What do you mean gone? Min-Ji said it was a breach that is resolved by idol protocol, which means… uh, no authorities. If that's right, then how can they be in jail?"

Kang sat in a wide chair across from my desk and reached for my hands. I gave them over to him. He held them and smiled at me.

"Kang… Tell me, Kang."

He was hesitating, perhaps nervous. But I didn't know why. I tugged at his hand coaxing him to speak up.

"Marie…" he looked away and sighed.

Seconds later he turned to me and said, "Sabastian Khan and his older brother Vincenzo. His brother was your driver that day. He is not in the music industry but has been seen at the NM building in recent years as a security delivery driver. This was why Nari recognized him as being familiar and safe. It was Sabastian who drugged you, but his brother was the one that left you on the mountain. They executed their plan with their friends."

"Friends?"

"Eung (yes), Vincenzo and Sabastian worked with… Jin-Young, Young-Jae, and their mother, Hae Won."

My body felt a chill, and I immediately tried to snatch my hands out of his, but he held on to them firmly, and I couldn't break free. Stuttered words came as I confirmed what he said, "Jae's…Jae's aunt and…and…his…his cousins tried to…?"

Nodding and looking away for a few seconds as shock and fear fell over me, I wanted to flee. I started to panic, "I…I…can't live here… I… need to get out of this place… I… Oh…I…"

Holding a tighter grip of my hands, Kang's tone was forceful, and he peered at me with frightening intensity. I stopped fidgeting from nervousness when he said, "Marie, they are gone. No danger, no more. Everyone is safe."

Calmer, I whispered, "Gone?"

He nodded.

"Gone? Gone, where?"

"You don't need to know anymore. You are always safe. Marie, no one can ever hurt you. I won't let anything happen to you. I swear. We made sure. I made sure they are gone."

"Kang, what did you…"

Quickly he released my hands saying words with a now ominous tone, "Don't ask me. Drop it."

I nodded with thoughts, *(Keep your secret. You made sure there is no more risk. It's over.)*

He swallowed hard, looking away from me and by his expression of coldness and guilt, I knew for certain I didn't want to know anymore.

Once I had answers, I felt confident that the threats were gone, and I listened to Min-Ji and SI getting back to my volunteering activities. Security was adjusted, a little tighter, but more from behind the scenes and screening beforehand was done without my knowledge. Life went back to normal, and I didn't worry about the past.

On August 19, during an overnight Sony business trip to Japan, I was alone in my hotel room, and I couldn't sleep. For some reason, it came to my mind, and I started to become more curious and wanted to find out where these criminals were.

Using my computer, I did a little digging through social records and news archives available, searching for names of Jae's family members. It only took me twenty minutes to find out that former Kaleidoscope Entertainment singers, Young-Jae and his younger brother, Jin-Young and two members of their private security team were presumed dead after they leased a small yacht for a two-day trip and disappeared. The report stated the brothers insisted on taking the island trip without more of their personal security staff.

When they did not return a search was conducted. A day later, the small luxury yacht was in the opposite direction of their trip plan, adrift with small amounts of blood splatter on the outside stern. Authorities confirmed through forensic testing that the blood belonged to both brothers. There was no evidence of any crime. However, that same day the bodies of their two-security team members were recovered by fishermen. According to the medical examiner the cause of death was accidental drowning. No other bodies were ever recovered.

My husband's cousins

Jin-Young & Young-Jae

That report came days after local news reported a fire in a Gangnam-gu home had killed an elderly woman named Hae Won Park. Another news article had more details that stated, after an investigation, it was determined some frayed electrical wiring in the kitchen caused the tragedy. Hae Won Park's body had been discovered trapped in her bedroom that was locked from the inside. A medical examiner speculated that she possibly had been asleep when the fire broke out and unable to escape as her home burned to the ground.

Hae Won Park

My mind wandered and thoughts escaped my lips. "He didn't… did he? Stop, Marie. Don't think about it. Let it go. Read something." I reached over and opened a book of poems my husband had written to me to relax my mind, and I gradually dozed off.

Hours later, onboard our Japan Airlines flight home, Trey leisurely sipped his black coffee with a splash of coconut milk while cutting his eyes and smirking over at me. Irritated by his silence, I said, "What Trey? You say nothing for like twenty-four hours and now you're looking like a cat with a canary in your mouth. What's with the goofy eye rolls?"

He sniffled before saying, "Marie... you know, I can see everything you do, right?"

"Huh?" I paused. Within seconds, my face felt warm, and I wanted to throw up my morning omelet. "What are you talking about? Like when I'm getting dressed... You...You watch me?"

Snickering, he whispered, "Mmmm, that would be fun..."

I elbowed him in his left-side ribs. Chuckling, he spoke up, "No...no, but your computer, your phone..."

(Shoot, I'm busted.) I exhaled. Then I tried to explain, "I was only..."

He stopped me from babbling by raising his hand. Then my handsome bodyguard, who helped save my life and the lives of my children, said to me, "Give me your phone and computer, I'll erase. Don't do it again. Never ask. Forget."

I humbly nodded and did what I was told.

"Thank you, Trey. Thank you." I said as he winked at me. I continued to express my relief. "I'm glad we're friends. Kang would be so upset with me. I don't know what he would do if he found out that I didn't follow the—"

He nodded in agreement before cutting me off, "I got you, Marie. I always got you." I felt like crying a little hearing his words that sounded vaguely familiar, but I didn't. I only smiled. *(But how am I supposed to feel about them being... Relieved? Happy? Sad? Their dead... someone killed them... I don't know.)* I was numb on the topic and didn't think about it.

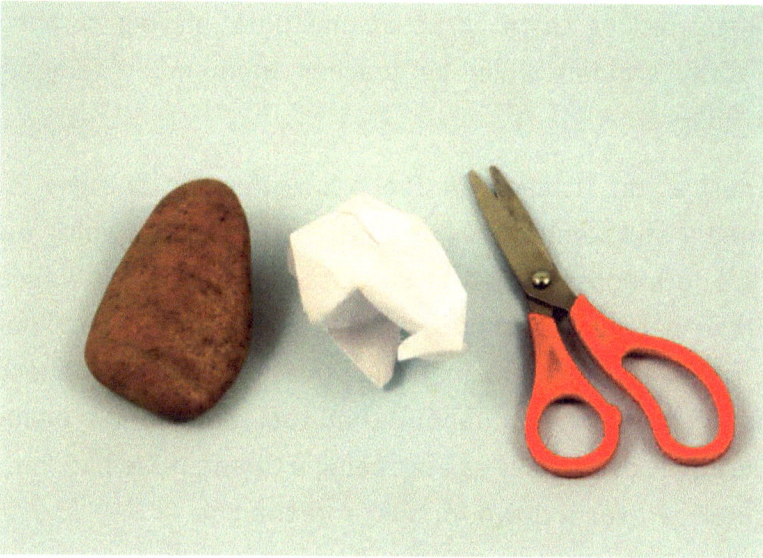

34. Win, No Draw

Just shortly after the breach and kidnapping last year, I couldn't stop Kang from moving in. No matter what I said or how I reasoned, he wasn't listening. I even tried to challenge him to resolve things their old K-Pop idol way, with a game of gawi, bowi, bo (rock, paper, scissors). Yeah, nope. Kang just got mad and stormed off cussing under his breath. *(Wow! He is serious about this.)*

He looked like his head was going to blow off his body during our last argument. When he firmly said the words in French, "Je m'en fous! Fais juste ce que je dis, femme (I don't care! Just do what I say, woman)!" His face was red, and I just gave in with a respectful bow and silence.

At first, it was a little odd having a man living with us, but honestly, life flowed much easier. The ninja and Trey shadowed me, anyway. Having Nari and Kang here really has been a blessing. At this critical age, my children get to have such joy with their super strong uncle Kang picking them all up at one time, playing on the floor, being softly scolded while he teaches them many things about Korean culture.

I must admit, it made me feel a lot safer. But because of what happened, I still sometimes got a little fearful about going out and living in South Korea. I tried to be extra cautious, but it worried me more than before. I learned from my husband and the K-pop idol codes, rules, and protocol that our privacy is directly connected to our safety. He was right about that too, but I don't believe he considered his own family as ever being a threat. If Jae had, he would have surely written it down for our protection.

Time seemed to fly with all the activities going on and the visitors coming through. I don't believe I had any debilitating moments of sadness that I can recall. My family took our seasonal trips to the mountain cabin for nature exploration and appreciating Jehovah's creations.

Although we haven't been invited to stay over at my in-law's or the Nam's compounds socially this year, we had several day visits with all the loving women of the family. I heard that my father-in-law and Min Ji had been extremely busy, which made it pretty much impossible to see them.

I talked to Renee every couple of weeks and was happy she was thinking about a visit soon. She had finally decided to sell her designs to a manufacturer online, rather than bother with her own brick and mortar store. *(Good move.)*

Megan, Ophelia, Ami, and I continued our partnering in the public metro volunteer work and letter writing to neighbors. And there were a few social gatherings I attended with some brothers and sisters; both old and young, from my congregation and a couple of others.

I kept up my monthly correspondence with Celeste, my aunt Hellene, my cousins, Joy, and Stephanie, and the Hanovers, which helped me stay connected to them and what was happening, on their side of the world.

My French cousin, Odette, and Jae's idol hyeong, Eric Choi married the year before in a private ceremony in Bali. I wanted to go but didn't have the band width to take that one on at the time. It was too soon after… well, anyway. While Eric was on tour, Odette visited me from France and stayed for two weeks. I screamed when she came because when Trey snuck her into my home, I didn't recognize her, at all. She was disguised as a middle-aged overweight woman with a jacked-up nose. I didn't tell her but for a split second, I thought she was a bag lady or the old woman with the apple from *Snow White and the Seven Dwarfs* animated movie. *(Why does she look like Robin Williams as Mrs. Doubtfire? What's with that prosthetic nose and fat suit? Ha! Wow, Eric's fans must be seriously trying to get pictures of her now. Oh, the idol wife life. I'm glad I didn't have that problem. I was a French chocolate secret, Jae used to say. Ha!)* Honestly, those two weeks were the best I had in a very long time. I really missed my family.

Just days after Odette left, Joy and Stephanie Hamilton came again and stayed for ten days. During their visit, they hung out with Megan and Ophelia this time. My three amigos and I had the most amazing vacation time at our mountain cabin with Min Cha, Hana, Soo, and aunt Teng. Soo and I even took a pottery class with Min Cha, and I made a tall flower vase that I put Jae, Jolie, and Jin's handprints on before it was finished. It is filled with fresh flowers every week and sits on my bookshelf in my home office.

Life was busy and I settled back into a new normal.

These days I have been repeatedly told that I am mean. "Let them play it!" At every turn, the idol brothers shout those words. Over the years, only the idol brothers played Jae's exquisite piano when they secretly came over. It was probably for sentimental reasons, but they coaxed my children to hit a few keys as they told stories of making music with their father. I can see in their big shiny eyes of excitement, that the triplets couldn't wait to grow old enough to play their daddy's piano. But I wouldn't let them touch it if the idol brothers were not around. *(Nope! It's a $700,000 piano!)* Obviously, either Kang or Nari had been ratting me out to the others about it.

One day, after hanging up with Seth's call from California, who fussed at me about not letting them play the piano again, with my hands on my hips I confronted Nari. "Ms. Lee, when a Black woman says, snitches get stitches or you 'bout ta get cut, do you know what that means?" Her eyes widened like large bowls of rice. She shook her head no. Waving her hands franticly she blurted out, "It's Kang. Not me! Not me!"

(Dang, she gave him up with the quickness. Yeah, she knows what it means! Ha!)

My inner tranquility came back rather quickly, but I was really missing my relatives and being in France. I had an increasing feeling of being confined as though I was now losing touch with parts of myself and both cultures that made me who I am. I tried not to think about it too often, but sometimes I couldn't help the feeling of disconnection.

To date, Lola had visited us in South Korea about four times. Just as she had done in the past, her plans included spending time elsewhere after hanging out with us. After her first visit, we never had any further conversations about her relationship with BJ Won. I made a conscious effort not to pry. Lola knew how I felt about it and didn't hint or divulge so the topic didn't come up when we spoke, or when she was with us.

My little growing joys had started learning how to play the piano, after BJ arranged through Kang for a music instructor to provide home lessons. *(Huh? Lessons?)* It didn't matter that they were very young, he bought each of them a keyboard and spinets to have the lessons.

"Who makes mini pianos?" I asked when Kang had them delivered. *(These idol musicians can be cuckoos. This is nuts.)* My talented three-year olds play by ear what they hear or mimic BJ or the teacher, Keyah. I think it was spectacular watching them play. It reminded me of their father. *(He would be so proud.)*

It was an established secret pattern that BJ crept over in disguise to play music before running around chasing my children. BJ Won was the sweetest of Jae's K-pop group mates. I loved them all, but BJ had always been my favorite. He and Jae were very close, and I spent the most time with him. Kang told me that BJ kept up on the best times to sneak over and knew whatever was going on as I found out later, he got private updates from his cousin Jusan. The first time I had even met security-ninja Jusan was after I recovered from the breach. I made Kang's team a huge Louisiana fixin's *thank you* meal for them. That was when he told me they were related. I remember thinking, *(They do look alike. Handsome. Uh, they are definitely related, how many salmon croquets, beignets, and oyster-shrimp mini-po' boys have they had? That...that is their third bowl of gumbo. Just like Kang, SI, and Trey, they are so gonna get the 'nigga-ites'. HA!)*

I hadn't ever hinted or said anything to BJ about Lola. It wasn't my business, but when Kang told me he said, "Hyeong (older brother), I feel Phenomenal Noona's eyes of disappointment when she looks at me. It is starting to creep me out. Do you think she is going to tell me to stop coming over?" I made the decision to say something about his relationship with Lola the next time he popped up again unexpectedly.

"BJ, you know I adore you. Kang told me what you said. We love you. I suppose I can sometimes have those judgmental eyes like my mother. I don't mean to be. I really need to work on that. When I didn't know about your thing with her. I mean, you know before, it was much easier to mind my own business. But I do know about it. I want what is best for both of you. I love you. But this affair between you and Lola isn't a wise choice. It's dangerous. It's wrong. She's married, BJ. Is sex really all that important?"

He smirked at me while sipping his beer at my kitchen island. I blurted out, "Don't you look at me like that. That is a performing Jin-K K-Pop smirk! Stop it!"

BJ started laughing. Then he said, "It's been a long time since you have had it. You are older than me. Maybe you forgot."

I smacked his hand. "Stop it! I'm being serious. You two have been doing this for a while. It's bad. Someone is going to get hurt, BJ. Can you just stop? I mean, if she wanted to end it, would you?"

"Noona, I know you care, and I love you too. But it's not your business to care about that part of my life. I will tell you; Lola won't stop. That's how good I am. But in a year or two, I will end it because I'm going to get serious about someone else and probably marry them."

"Marriage? Someone else? You...you aren't waiting for Lola to...leave him or... Wait? BJ, you can have sex with anyone. Why would you keep sleeping with her if you don't want to be with her for the long haul. I don't get it. Wait, is this like the Kang and Jazz, thing? Just for fun. Is that what you're saying?"

He confirmed my suspicions, "I like her. I have since we first met. There was something magnetic about her. We felt it then and it was still there in New York. It's not just sex, Lola is an amazing woman. We have fun together. But it doesn't matter if her circumstances change or not. It wouldn't be anything more than this. I do like her. But...but I am not like hyeong, Marie. I'm not even close. Jae-Sung was a unique person, and you... Well, you're phenomenal. It made perfect sense that the two of you would work out to be more and get married. But I'm not that special."

(Hold on. Not Jae? Special?)

I wanted him to tell it to me straight. "So, you wouldn't let yourself love her? I mean if she wasn't married or became free, you wouldn't go beyond just meeting her places for a few days just to dip your wick in her pond. Is that right? I guess, I thought maybe you were in-love with her or something, but then I realized you didn't pursue her after New York. Then I remembered, you didn't tell her you wanted her before she even married Greg, either. I asked. So, what you're telling me is Lola is another international booty call for you. She can keep a secret so there is no risk for you. You can have a smart, sexy, thick Black woman to have sex with and enjoy but you can't be serious about her, and it's not because she's married. Am I wrong?" My voice had gotten a little louder as I kept telling him the things I was concluding from the conversation.

Without waiting for more questions from me, BJ said plainly, "Marie, my wife is going to be a Korean girl, no exception."

My heart kind of sunk a little. I gave a low, "Ah." In that moment, I saw him differently from all the years of knowing him before. There were several minutes of awkward silence before I reached and hugged him. We didn't speak about this topic again. *(She's Black. Wow, some things haven't changed. Racism.)*

Later when I had some time alone, the conversation with BJ drifted back into my mind. I had to analyze the facts. I loved them, but things are different for me and not them. BJ and Lola were doing exactly what they want and there was no deception for either of them. Not even for Greg. Everybody knew what they were doing and are content with it. It's not me. I had to stop trying to fix it in my mind to be okay with some hope of something beautiful at the end. It's not. It's wrong to me not them. How do I show them from the Bible that they are cheating themselves in many ways. My heart felt a bit sad because I didn't know exactly how to get them to see the wonderful future that I see.

Idol Brother Ben-Jin "BJ" Won

It was obvious, there had been a gradual shift in some of my close relationships. I was evolving and having deeper connections with those that had the same goals in life as I did. Honestly, it made me miss talking to Jae-Sung even more. We were always in sync, even if we didn't agree. I remembered something my brilliant father told me, 'It is best to love and be loved by the person of your heart, the companion that complements the mind and completes the soul.'

"Pawpaw was right. Everything about him I miss. I have to wait. I know but I miss my lover and best friend." Feeling the start of an incoming wave of sadness, I quickly grabbed a few love letters he had written. As I read a couple, I could feel his love through his poetic words. It soothed me and I didn't emotionally breakdown that time.

Collection: Nuts, Bolts, and Relationships

35. Mother - Daughter

January 2034

Being in my forties, for some reason it seemed each time my mother and I got together, I learned and appreciated her just a bit more. I feel as if I grow inside a little taller from being around her and studying the intricate parts I had never seen before.

When my mother came to help me, downsize, and pack for our move to France, a few things happened that changed our relationship. The triplets were with Kang and Nari with their grandmother, Min Cha for a few days, allowing my mother and I to concentrate on packing a room or two quickly. However, after a heated discussion the night before, she opened a history book and exposed me to a world of the past I didn't know about.

Before she gave me her 1999 journal to read, I had no idea about parts of my own ancestry. I got a brief introduction to stories about three African sisters, my great-grandmother, and my mother's older sister. There were these warnings of mixing with non-Black men, and women circles of sisterhood storytelling and support. It was fascinating to read about their close relationship with Renee's parents, while we were young and oblivious to the adult happenings around us.

After reading the journal she handed me from her suitcase, my mind was filled with questions and thoughts. My mother even asked me random questions attempting to bond more. *(OMG! First times? Idol sex levels? Jae's package? Me and... No! No!)* I was shocked and embarrassed. Never would I tell her anything about those private things. She thought my reaction was funny, laughing like creepy Alexa.

A bit later, when she left me alone to replenish the tea pot and cookies, I breezed through a few pages of the other notebook she had left on the table next to me.

May 12, 2004

Philippe' planned for us to be in France for a summer with his family. He purposefully did so after the holidays because we don't celebrate them but respect that Jean-Pierre, Marie, Andreas, and Nannette get together for those traditions.

Celeste and Chantal had returned to visit numerous times, but this was going to be my first time back since the accident. I wasn't nervous. I was excited to see my in-laws and all my nieces and nephews.

During the second week of our visit, everyone came together for a special dinner party organized solely by all the Delacroix grandkids for Jean-Pierre.

Tomas, Kristoff, and Henri were in charge since they were the oldest and on leave from the military. It was a treat to have Ava, Lylah, Gert, and Elke helping the kids with cooking and planning for the party. It took them two days to prepare and decorate.

Early on the day of the dinner party, with all the children preoccupied with each other or the party plans, Philippe' wanted to talk to me. He took me to the beautiful grand ballroom with its shiny wood floor, over twenty-foot ceilings and chandeliers sparkling from the midday sun. He adjusted some things behind a hidden wall and turned-on music to begin a waltz.

"Philippe', what are we doing in here?"

He didn't say anything before strutting out to the middle of the room, holding his arms out for me to position myself to dance looking like a tall, gorgeous statue of a deity at a museum. "Look up, Dell…" and the music began as soon as my hands landed inside his. In sync with the melody, I stared up at him and sang along with the Carpenter's "Close to You" as we began our glide across the floor. *(He loves this song!)* Five minutes later, he started humming Nat King Cole's "Fascination" as it played. *(Oh, another favorite. He's in a mood.)* We didn't stop waltzing. Philippe' looked so gallant with his elegant strong posture and tilted head. When I relaxed my body melted into his arms, he cut his eyes at me smirking. I immediately straightened before he swirled me around like a spinning top in slow motion. *(I love to dance with him.)* As the song faded to end, Philippe' slowed, pulled me closer, and ever so tenderly kissed my lips while my dashing blonde Frenchman dipped me backward, gazed into my eyes and said, "I love you deeply, my cherished black diamond. As the sun and moon, we were meant to be in constant movement channeling energy to and from one another for all eternity." I smiled wide, anticipating another kiss was coming. *(We are so going to do it!)*

277

But minutes later, I found out exactly what he had on his mind. Holding me in the middle of the Delacroix grand ballroom, Philippe' had this far away gaze, and I nudged him. He pulled me into him and kissed me passionately.

When he pulled away, and said, "Nous n'avons pas de secrets et vous me faites confiance comme je vous fais confiance de tout mon cœur, mon corps et mon âme. Nous sommes un, toujours. Convenu (We have no secrets, and you trust me as I trust you with my whole heart, body, and soul. We are one, always. Agreed)?"

I nodded peering at him, not fully understanding what he was setting up but curiously excited.

"Come with me, my dearest."

Philippe' kissed the back of my hand before folding my arm over his and silently led me to the enormous two-story family library for an exploration game I would never forget.

There was no more on the page or in the rest of the journal.

"Wait. What happened? Uh, I remember that party. I was sixteen and it was when..." I refocused on the incomplete story from the book. "What happened?" My face twisted a little wondering, but I quickly put the book down when my mother returned. As we sat sipping tea, the two of us analyzed the past, and the blessings of having true love, I wanted to ask something more but hesitated.

"I have one more but..."

My mother watched me stalling and gave me a verbal boost. "Child, ask me."

"Uh, since you and Pawpaw don't have secrets. I mean... I've been wondering what happened. Well, I mean... how ever did Pawpaw get you to accept him for me."

I was nervous but eagerly waited for her response to a sensitive subject we never talked about in our family. My mother put down her teacup and pressed her lips together for a moment before speaking, "Hmmm. That's a little more complicated. Philippe' is very strategic and calm, so, it took him a while before he told me. Not because he was keeping it from me, but he had to really search his own heart first before including me on the emotional journey. We both discussed it several times reliving the past and we researched more on what forgiveness really meant to us. Then when Philippe' took me to meet Jae-Sung in Paris, I really listened to what he said, about what he had been through in life, growing up with his family, his loss and guilt and some things he experienced in loving you. He reminded me of things I learned and read about hearts being trapped or weighed down from tragedy and suffering from a true love you can't have because of things you can't change. I thought about the stories of my grandmother, Lurell and John-Robert Dixon or Ayasha the African and the slave owner, Doyle MacGregor. I even remembered things Marianna had told me about her love for Henry right before he re-married. Marie, I honestly didn't want that life for you. A heart that yearns for something pure and true but is restricted by circumstances that are beyond changing. No, it wasn't fair to either of you for me to hold you back from being the right pieces for each other to mold together and make something beautiful." She stopped talking and watched me nibbling on a cookie. "Does that make sense?" My mother said tapping my knee and breaking my trance.

"Yes…so you're saying you forced yourself to not care."

"No. Marie, of course I care. But I focused on the person and not the circumstances."

Nodding I sipped some tea. She smiled at me as her eyes seemed to dance, watching me understand her words. "Mom, it's kind of like the way I love him. I mean, I didn't think about what brought us together but that we were, and he overfilled my cup with wonderful."

"That is how I felt about your father and still do. It's why we gave you that same scripture to live by and know what true love is from God's perspective and to be clear about what it's not."

"Mom, do you think Celeste has true love?"

"Your sister is different than the two of us. She has a love that she is content with, and she is happy. It is not close to what your father and I have nor what I believe you and Jae had. But I hope in the new world, we'll all come to a better state of being. Yes, I'm sure after a reset of things, they'll know, understand, give, and receive true love and happiness as intended."

Surprised, I sat up. "Wait a minute. Mom, did you just ...did you say a... a new world...like ... a ... a reset..."

As my mother witnessed my mouth hanging open and my eyes triple in size, she just giggled and winked at me.

"Mom?!"

Then she raised her eyebrows like the Dr. Suess character in *The Cat in The Hat* book. I snorted because she looked crazy. She grabbed a cookie, smirking.

I wiggled a bit in my seat and asked the obvious, "Mom... are ... are you studying the Bible? I mean not on your own but with ... with Jehovah's Witnesses?"

She playfully smacked my hand on the table. "Don't make it a big deal. You know your father, and I like to research and debate lots of things to find out what's true. When you were doing all that talking about when people die, they are just asleep in God's memory, and it is He that reads hearts and can wake them up like Jesus if he wants too, it was an interesting concept. Your father and I felt it was a very comforting thought for when we lose a loved one. But we wanted to know where it came from, and how it was reasoned to be a theory of belief for a hope of a better life to come. Your father and I are retired. So, we don't have all the distractions young folks have with making a living, raising a family, getting out of debt and whatnot. We read, dance, discover, and travel to enjoy the beauty of nature and really think about what God intended. We have philosophical discussions and study how intricate and wonderfully our bodies are made and operate. Like when you cut the skin and new skin grows because the cell restores and replaces the dead ones. We asked ourselves, now why would our body be made to rejuvenate itself but still grow old and die? Or take the design of our circulatory system. It's connected to the heart and pumping blood that moves through us like on a fast freeway, nourishing cells and tossing out the waste, using these winding vessels, capillaries, and veins. Oh, or conception that whole process is magnificent when you take the time to research how it all works. It's marvelous to learn about these remarkable things, especially with your father. He is so fun to explore with. It logically didn't make sense to give us this magnificent work of His hand to have us flying around in the heavens. At least not to us. So, yes, we've been doing some research with a few Jehovah Witnesses."

"Oh… Who? Who?"

"Are you an owl? Ha. Philippe' met Clause at his pre-op appointment for his heart procedure a few years ago, when you went to stay with Celeste when she was pregnant. They were seeing different doctors for the same operation. He asked Philippe' a question and they just started talking. After you got settled in South Korea, your father introduced me to his wife, Sarahphina. We have known them for a while and had been going to the local Kingdom

Hall to study. Philippe' has shared things with his musketeer brothers. I have added some encouraging points of reference to others from time to time."

Speechless, I stared at her. A few drops of salty water slid down my cheeks as my heart flipped inside my body from happiness.

"Girl, don't you dare start crying! You know, your sister said that Adam has been a bit curious too, especially after she went to the Kingdom Hall in Bellevue to check it out one Sunday morning. She said she started asking questions of these two ladies that were outside of the hospital with a witness cart of books. She said she was going to learn more on how to be a better Christian wife and mother. It's no big deal. You were raised that knowledge is power. Marie, stop it! No crying."

I wiped my eyes nodding as I giggled. *(Thank you, Jehovah, you opened their ears, and mind to hear what I've been saying, praying about Jae-Sung. I believe you'll wake him up one day. I just know it. I hope my friends and family choose to serve you too and we can all be in your new world together. Oh, I hope so.)*

My mother's face got serious, and she said, "I'm serious now, don't you be getting all excited, I just want to clearly understand what you're teaching my grandbabies and make sure it's right!"

Trying not to snicker, I nodded with a moan of "ah". *(Yeah right.)*

She smacked my hand and grinned.

The last three weeks of my mother's visit went too fast, but we got a lot packed and shipped to France. During this time, we talked a lot more, laughed at the same time, and hugged several times more than I think we ever had before. I could be wrong. She said I was, but it felt that way to me. It was wonderful discussing aspects of myself and my mother, our ancestors, and the future. I felt more like a better version of myself, knowing the truth of things I didn't understand about her.

At the airport I gave her a wrapped gift of her organic chocolate lavender tea and a book of poems I wrote when thinking of Jae and our children inside the mural in our dining room. Before she went through international security, I held her hand and locked onto her warm dark eyes and with a smile on my face, I told her, "Mom, I'm very blessed to have you in my life. As my friend you balance my heart sometimes. Mommy, you are truly a remarkable woman. I know more about who you are, and I am thankful for that privilege. You are strong and courageous, knowledgeable, fun, complex, reasonable, and caring, proud but humble at the same time. I admire your resilience and your radiant Black excellence. I love you so very much. Thank you for being my mom."

"Oh, Chantal..." was all she could say as she wept holding me in her arms like a mama bear. *(I'm her cub. I love you.)*

Ninety-minutes later, my mother was on her way back to France. Although I had tears parting from her this time, in my home that light scent of lavender lingered for days reminding me of her, and I smiled.

36. Louis & Tangee

On April 4, 2034, late at night Louis Edward Kanden shocked me.

"Wait, what do you mean? Mr. Kanden, clarify please?"

I was taken back by what he just said and wanted to confirm what I thought I heard. The fair-skinned light-brown haired, glasses-wearing, medium-built introverted man, who looked like a not so fun middle or high school teacher, had the nerve to be snickering on our Zoom call.

"Ha-ha. Marie, you heard me. The girls and I are coming during the last weeks of the tour. My plan is we will be able to kick it, get on down, even bust a move on tour and then later with you guys. I know you don't believe that after all this time, I'm finally flying to South Korea, Japan, and Thailand. But it's going to be a vacation trip for all of us. My princesses are all very excited. Stop looking at me like I just laid an egg or something. What I said, it's not all that startling." He laughed before taking another sip of whatever he was drinking from his A-list real-estate office in the Hollywood Hills.

"Louis, I'm totally shocked! You never fly! That… That's one, but did you actually say, you were going to kick it, get on down and bust a move? Who are you right now? I think I need to see your driver's license to confirm you are really Louis Edward Kanden III. Pop quiz, do you still love cheese?"

He laughed even louder with his mouth so wide. I could pretty much see his tonsils. That made me laugh. *(What is happening right now?)* Then I told him, "Louis, I am super excited about the family coming. I can't believe you're going to fly out of the country … and … and you're speaking in slang. I'm just astonished by this new Louis. You've been that introverted, small-town older brother from "A River Runs Through It" movie, conservative White man from Montana. The world as we know it, it's over. Ha, ha, ha."

Waving his hands, he confessed, "You know who my wife be don't cha'? I can't be talking out the side of my neck. I know the deal-lee-o sista. Don't trip chocolate chip, I'm down wit the brown. You—"

Coughing from laughter, I cut him off. "Oh my god… Stop it!! You're killing me. I can't! My head is gonna explode, ARRTI aka Louis Kandin is hip, and cool, sort of."

"Marie, you are so funny. I have always been cool. My wife is half Black, you know that right? I am in like Flynn!"

Nodding with efforts to control my coughing fit from laughter and wiping my tears, I agreed. "My Tangee girl done put it on ya. I see you, Louis. Here, we, Delta Divas thought it was the other way around."

"Okay, Marie, look to be honest, the girls were saying things they were learning from school and their cousins. I felt like I needed to up my vocabulary to be in the know. Ya feel me, girlfriend?"

(Why is he bobbing his head. He looks like a proud rooster. Oh, I can't with him. Don't tell him…let him live out his Blackness. Is he biting his lip? Ha! Ha! Wait 'till I tell Renee.)

He kept telling me the backstory, *"Marie, even* though her parents moved to Palm Springs a few years ago, Tangee's brothers, Tyriq and Telvin still live in Inglewood with their families. They hookin' me up, with the vocabeezie, when I don't know what I am saying. Anyway, since it will be the end of her tour, I will get you the exact dates, we'll be in South Korea. Tangee and I've talked about staying two weeks. Hey, that should be enough time for me to teach your kids all the things I know. Ha Ha."

Louis was chuckling at his own coolness. *(He's too funny. I always liked him.)*

My hip friend Louis Edward Kanden

Delta Doll Tangee Arnold-Kanden

aka Tangee Girl

My Delta Sorority sister, Tangee Arnold-Kanden's music career continued to soar. I was so proud of her. Winning a Grammy, an Asian Music, and a Billboard music award were great accomplishments. Because of her love of all types of music and foreign languages, she expanded her catalog and exposed her beautiful voice to larger audiences around the world. I've learned her love of music was in some ways similar to Jae's. She has the most magnificent voice, but Tangee had more enjoyment from blending her voice with others. I think Jae was that way. It's probably another reason he liked her so much. A few times he seemed to be overjoyed with collaborating and concerts where he shared the stage with his idol brothers or other artists. The Connectivity Tour, Tangee was going to be ending before her visit was another international artist collaboration event.

Tangee and my friend, SK Songbird are contracted with Universal Music Entertainment and have worked together a lot over the years. They make the most amazing music together. *(Maybe I can see SK Songbird too after their tour.)* Two days after talking to her husband Louis, we spoke, and I got more details. I wanted to set things up to go to the concert long before she made my heart stop beating from what she said.

"Marie, it will be one of the largest summer music festival concerts of the year. It's going to be at the Seoul Olympic Stadium. I'm going to be singing where Michael Jackson performed back in the 90s. Ha...I'm bad... You know it! Ha-Ha."

"Tangee..." She didn't take a breath to stop.

"Do you think Kang will set up security for you to come? It's a couple months away, but it's already sold out with 68,000 tickets gone. Uh, but we have guest passes and two private tents next to the stage. Marie, I... I know you don't go out much, being so busy and everything... Uh, but it's going to be a very different type of concert."

Curious, I said, "I haven't been to a concert in so long. What do you mean different?" I could see the smile in her eyes as she explained, "We were invited to join the event by the collaboration teams and promoter. See, the one-night event is a kind of tribute concert to some K-Pop groups of the past. They told us they wanted it to be as diverse as possible for international fans. My label mate, SK Songbird and me are the Americans. British singer/rapper, Tristian Blak, Italian singer, Gabriella, and Australian tenor, Symoni Inga are the other international artists coming to sing with some of the members for the one night. It's after my tour, so it worked out great. It's not to showcase anyone's solo career, only the groups, but we were asked to come as special guests for the international broadcast ratings, I think. Try please? I really think...uh it would be so much fun you... and me...SK will be excited too. She and I can serenade you as our special guest in the audience. Ha! I'm sure Eric would want to do it, but I know idol brother code won't let that happen."

Snickering, I nodded, and said, "Married to my cousin Odette, Eric Choi? I haven't physically seen him in a while. He always sends gifts, but you know the idol security code. He couldn't come here anyway. Okay, it's one night. Who else is going to be with this tribute showcase concert?" I started to feel a little more excited and curious.

"Maybe I shouldn't tell you. Never mind." She said it mumbling and then turned away from the camera.

"Huh? Cow, you better tell me. Look at me Tangee Shanice!"

Giggling, she said words that made me flutter inside for many different reasons.

"The concert will feature a few old K-pop idol group soloists. Like uh, Hyolyn from Sistar, Jackson Wang from GOT7, BJ from DRGN5, of course, and Baekhyun from EXO will perform duets... Uh, yeah..."

I started to tingle. It sounded like an amazing concert. A memory flashed in my mind... *(I haven't been to a concert since Jin-K and Eric's collaboration tour in New York years ago. When he sang... Arabian Sand the last time... Oh, Jae-Sung... I miss...)* I pushed back the emotional sadness and stayed in the conversation. Tangee kept looking away, so I couldn't see her grin and silly expressions. She knows I loved listening to some of these old school K-Pop groups and singers. She continued to speak slowly, "I know SK and Jackson Wang are doing two songs from the OST they recorded last year. Eric and Hyolyn, I'm not sure which songs. But Baekhyun will perform two songs with me from his old ep and an OST, and one with SK from his newer one. BJ is going to perform with Tristian and Eric their Hip Hop hit, and I think BJ and Eric are going to do one from an older tour. Jin Young will perform with me one song and one with Gabriella..."

I interrupted hearing another name from GOT7. "Wait, Jin Young? Jin Young from GOT7 too? You didn't tell me two members were going to be there." Tangee grunted. I started pacing around the room with a wider smile, "Wow, he's such a popular actor, but his voice is really nice. This concert is sounding better and better."

She added while giggling, "Yeah... Eric's old group is going to be performing but probably not doing those old dance moves."

"Ha! Ha! I bet the bend and snap moves are seriously over for most of those old groups. It's the music, we old folks like anyway." I said still laughing.

Tangee gave me a thumbs up, and said, "That's why I don't dance! Marie, actually...ugh, some executives put together... Uh... Gabriella I think ...uh, is gonna sing a song with Jae Beom—."

I stopped breathing for three whole seconds. *(Clarify. Jae who? Ask!)* I sat down. A strange growl released from my throat before asking, "Wait, who is singing with Gabriella? Jae, who? Jay Park?"

She purposefully was looking up in the air and scratching her head at the base of her neck, like she used to do in college when she was stalling to answer.

"Tangee!" I screamed to get her to spill the tea. Her eyes eased back in the camera, and she nibbled on the corner of her mouth before confirming. "Uh, it's GOT7's Jae-Boem. Your man girl... Performing Jay B. I know how much you liked his voice."

My eyes widened. I stopped breathing again for a few seconds. *(Oh... Oh... I can't feel my body.)*

"Marie, breathe! Lordy...I didn't want to tell you. I remember, he was your favorite before you met Jin-K. They do sound similar sometimes when he sings. But Jae-Sung had a crazy range and...Uh. Well... I wanted you to come and have a good time with us. So, I'm telling you the surprise. Eric said I 'shouldn't mention it at all and just invite you.' But Odette and I told him we wouldn't know how you would react once he started singing, especially a ballad. Eric got a little annoyed saying, 'hoobae (younger male) doesn't sound like Jin-K, not really.' But I think he was trying to defuse the situation. I told him Jay B's voice would be a trigger because to you, he sounds like Jin-K more than anyone else and it might bring back memories of him. If that happened, you'd be depressed or upset, which is the opposite of what we all want. Eric got it, and I had to warn you. I told Odette even knowing in advance might make you emotional or break down or something. Maybe overheated with no way to have sex afterward. Either way, it could be very bad. I can't do that to you."

My eyes were watering, and I thought... *(I love those guys' voices— their old music. I haven't listened to anyone else since Jae passed away… I don't know if I can do that. His voice does always remind me of Jae, but it wasn't exact… it didn't matter, Jae-Sung was so jealous, when I listened to other K-Pop or KR&B male groups, or artists, especially him… Best penalties was making him sing Jay B songs like on Cocoa Island… So funny. Wait, what did she say? Sex? Oh, please, I am dead down there!)*

Tangee kept talking, "Eric said he would get you something to rub on like a vibrating pillow. He is so crazy. I'm just gonna tell you even though it's not public yet. It's already confirmed that Bam-Bam, Yugyeom, Young Jae, and Mark Tuan are coming because GOT7 is one of the groups they are honoring. Eric's old group 887S, EXO, and Super Junior will be honored as well. Marie, are you alright? Oh lord, are you… hyperventilating?"

Taking in a few deep breaths, I just nodded without saying a word and grinned. My mind was going a mile a minute, thinking of old songs I liked from the groups performing. I had a few time-leaps recalling drinking Soju with Apryl at a karaoke bar or being in our Sony office singing all the words to some of them. *(Seems like a lifetime ago. Such great times, we had.)*

Tangee quickly changed the subject to her family visit afterward. I refocused on her coming visit to South Korea and getting to hug my pretty nieces, Emelia Rose, and Emma Azalea.

During a video chat with Odette a couple of days later, Eric just happened to be home and popped into the conversation acting crazy as usual, speaking nonstop.

"Idol uncle in the hiz-ouse! What's up in Soeul? Where's those little mini-Jae-Sung Kims? They need to write some songs for me. I need better material to work with some lyrics I had locked away. I know BJ and Min Ji have them almost experts now, right? Task masters. The three of those little idols have the DNA to write

write amazing songs. I need to tap into it before someone else finds out the secret gold mind of Jin-K's offspring. I already bet BJ, Ethan, and Seth, and I won so, they must wait for me to get a crack at them. But if Nah Min-Ji figures out, they have skills, we are all on the back burner and he will mold them just like he did Jin-K. Marie, they will be the next Peter, Paul, and Mary but Jae, Jin, Jolie. Ha, ha! Ya gotta let them play that piano more! Damn, stop holding out. Oh, yeah, did you get the electric cars we sent? The red Mustang is for Jin. The black Porshe is for Jae, and that pink Corvette is for Jolie of course. SI can take them somewhere secluded to drive them. I want photos!"

"Babe, stop. We are talking about the concert." Odette chimed in pushing his face out of the camera lens. She giggled with his playful licking of her fingers.

(Oh brother.) "Uh, I can call you back Dette." I said shaking my head and pretending to close my eyes.

Eric stopped and got louder, "Oh, so you are coming? We wanna see you have fun. You can't come see us. I know it's hard with our fans, and we can't come to you, but this is how we can get to see you in person without any issues. You will love it! It's going to be amazing. I already talked to Kang and his team. It will happen. Phenomenal Noona has to be there to make it all worth wild. We miss you, Marie. Alright, I had nachos earlier. I gotta take a big dump. Love you!" Then he dashed away.

"Ewww! He's joking right?" I asked with my nose turned up in disgust.

With a slightly red face of embarrassment, Odette answered with a simple, "Nope." We laughed for a while about that.

(He's still so crazy!)

Jae-Sung's older idol brother Eric Choi

My cousin Odette Moreau-Choi

37. Music Notes

Around the middle of June when my parents came to visit, they picked up my cousins, Tamera Brown, and Tonja Murry, on the way. I was speechless and had a lot of emotions seeing and touching them at the airport. I had no idea they had planned to stay seven days during my parents' month-long trip. I found out later that Kang knew because he had to clear them first.

While my parents spent time spoiling my children, I got to play tour guide for five days, taking my cousins all around to hot spots for shopping, history, spa time, and food.

"I see, there are a few Black folks." Tonja said after Trey, and I picked them up at their hotel in Seoul.

"Tee, act like you have some home training now… come on." Tamera mumbled.

"Why are you always Debbie Downer...I just said I see color."

(Oh, here they go, sisters that bicker...I missed them.)

"Y'all ain't gonna be fighting the whole time, are you?" I asked, amused at my Black family love antics.

Tanja spoke up, "Rhee, it's her. You know how Tamera is. Bossy Betty! She's always trying to tell somebody what to do. Flexing that she was born long before we were. We know, cow. We know!"

"I'm older and wiser, ya wild cat!" Tamera mumbled it loud enough for anyone within thirty feet to hear.

Snickering, I announced, "I've missed you two. I'm so glad you're here."

We laughed on our way to Gyeongbokgung Palace and Namdaemun Market. While walking in the market I faintly heard, Tonja's voice saying, "Are you married?"

I looked at Tamera. She raised her eyebrow and whispered, "She's on the hunt."

Leaning in I asked, "What happened with... Oh, what's his name? Wasn't that serious?"

"Girl no. He didn't want to get married, so she dropped him, with the quickness. I didn't like him anyway. Kevin said I was judging him based on nothing. But there was something creepy about his beady eyes. I still think he was one of them Hot-Lanta down-low brothers. He was too pretty."

I wanted to confirm, "Was there evidence of that?" I said leaning in closer to hear the gossip.

"Nothing outright but Rhee, you know our Murry sense start tingling. Those of us that got 'em anyway."

(Yes, cuz, ya do like to judge folks, girl. Glad you never saw my beautiful skin pretty eye model husband. Ha!)

We snickered pretending to shop while ease-dropping on the flirty conversation as Tonja made her move on Trey, who wasn't trying to deflect or run away from it either. *(Chemistry alert!)*

<hr />

Leaving my parents with my children I dressed up in dark jade wide leg pants with a pirate sleeved jade and black corset top. Tamera wanted to play in my hair, so I got dressed at their hotel and she gave me all these long ringlets. My Mac styled face was flawless with emerald smoky eyes and mocha lips with a pop of red.

Feeling a bit strange that Jae wouldn't be seeing me from across a room and licking his lips, I questioned what I was doing. "Why am I getting dressed up like this?"

Tamera squeezed me and said, "Cousin, you lookin' beautiful because you are sexy, free, relaxed, and happy. We are gonna have a good time and we need to look the part. That's what momma used to say, remember? We are pulling back out that New Yorker Sony director Chantal Delacroix."

"What?" I started laughing.

"Yes, honey. You are not this over forty sista wit three kids. Nope, not tonight. Don't let the memories or the past set you back, alright? I've been in this same emotional place before, and it sucked the spark of life right out of me for over twenty years. You are not depressed or unhappy like I was. Cousin, you have done so much better than I did during those first years as a widow. But life goes on when you let it. I found Kevin and love happened again. We never know what will happen, so don't close the door. Tonight, Tangee and Odette said you are in for a treat, and we are going to have a good time. Got it?"

I nodded with a grin. Then Tanja shouted, "Ya need some tequila girl! Here!"

Waving my hands and shaking my head, I firmly said, "No. No... I don't!"

"Yes, cow. You do. Here! Take it!" She handed me the shot of Milagro Anjeo and a lime wedge. I drank it. Without a break, she shoved another in my hand. I drank it and squeezed the lime between my teeth and lips.

"Rhee, get all that lime juice out. Yep, suck it! Suck it like you mean it!"

I snorted and smacked her high round booty, that she had fitting snug in her green leather shorts. We cackled for several minutes and then I let Trey know we were ready to go.

Arriving at the stadium in secure vans and with police escorts through backways and tunnels, it was kind of crazy. (*Dang, we aren't performers.*) We had VIP seats in one closed off tent section at the right of the stage.

Honestly, I felt young and started to get goosebumps from all the excitement. It was spectacular, with the backdrops, video images, the lights and sounds of the artists. I couldn't believe I was at a Korean music festival honoring my husband and some K-Pop and K-R&B boy groups from the 2000s. Being here with Odette, Tamera, Tanja, Kang, Nari, Soo, SI, Trey, Jusan, and Han made it even more special, I think. I continued to have these memory flashes in my mind of the concerts in Japan and New York. Automatically my brain would identify similarities and compare the experiences. But after a few minutes I realized, my Jin-K of DRGN5 wouldn't be singing to me like before. *(It's supposed to be fun, Marie. Don't be weird!)* I quickly got a glass of wine from the VIP bar to relax my nerves.

Tangee and I never followed up after Kang talked to Eric and BJ and told me he was "making it happen as an idol fun night out." I got busy in my life routine and didn't think any more about it. Once I saw the line-up, I actually began fanning myself due to some internal waves of warmth from scanning the program and recognizing boy groups names. *(I shouldn't have had that tequila.)*

While EXO performed, I fell right into dancing and singing with their songs, "Monster," "Cream Soda," "The Eve," "Cinderella," and "Touch It" and I thought, *(A great group! I love their harmonies and Baekhyun is my favorite crooner of these guys, and Kai makes me wanna dance.)* Then when, "Private Party" started, I couldn't stop dancing. Super Junior and Big Bang were next. *(I don't know them, but I remember SK telling me how much she loved listening to them.)* They were a little older, but I liked them. Then when 887S came on and I cheered. *(I only know this as Eric's old group. But I enjoy Jae's crazy idol brother's sound but apparently not as much as his wife. Why is Odette screaming? Ha ha!)* It was awesome to see 2DZ1 with all their members. They performed twenty minutes after another group. *(I haven't seen Jae's idol brother Kris, KIZZL in forever. He looks so good. Married life and fatherhood suit him.)*

I had already been in full hyperactive mode enjoying myself when DRGN5 came out. Jae's old boy group performed second to the last of the groups. My mind and heart raced like on a speed track at the Indy 500. *(BJ, Seth, and Ethan sounded really good with Eric and KIZZL standing in for Jin-K and Joon Nam. I have the originals at home, but this is very nice. They are representing well.)* I sang along because I knew all the words to every song they sang. "My children would love this!" I shouted. Everyone in our private tent laughed.

(Ha!) When I glanced over and saw SI singing, and Kang was but with his eyes closed, I thought, *(I bet they are remembering being behind the scenes at their concerts and tours. Oh, how fun.)* The idol brothers from Jae's group didn't jump around like in those old videos he left us, but they still had some moves. Unexpectedly, Odette kissed my cheek. I sang and clapped the loudest in our tent.

I got another shot of tequila and a Corona, just before I screamed in my hand covering my mouth. GOT7 were the last group to come onto the stage and perform several of their old songs. *(OMG! All-time favorite group of young men in K-Pop. Wait…I love my husband's group too. Their harmony and ballads are out of this world, but I didn't know them back when they were a group like these guys…I'm allowed a secret right? I can listen to these fellas all day. Why are Kang and SI eyeing me right now? They are funny. Jealous much! Yeah, not going to say it out loud but Jay B sounds so much like Jae-Sung I…I… just love his breathy tenor but my husband's vocal range could never be mirrored or matched. Oh, I love JinYoung. His voice is a little higher, airy, and soft. He sounds wonderful and so delicate, with an easy listening tone. Jackson Wang that Chinese man and his sound of distinct huskiness makes me want to dance. Love his rap voice. Mark has this youthful sound that is nice on the ears. YoungJae has that powerful voice and holds you in suspense. Bam Bam with his free spirit and fun sound I like his playful soft songs and raps. Yugyeom with his slight nasal-like tenor blends so well with Jay B and JinYoung but alone is solid with great songs to dance to. Used to love listening to these guys… Whyever did I stop? Oh, I know this song too…)*

I was not at all carrying how I looked or sounded, I sang every song they performed during their set. *(I can't believe I know all the words still!)* I swayed and sang along when GOT7 sang their songs "Just Right" "Breath" "Aura" "Page" "Calling My Name" "Poison"

"Angel" "I Like you" "Nanana" and my mind flashed back to a time I was much younger.

After their standing ovations, each group received presidential honorable achievement trophy awards. In the program an image of a golden crane swirled around music symbols was one type of award, and another was a long crystal microphone that seemed to be as large as the palm of my hand. The duets were next, and I was ready to see and hear my friends from Los Angeles Tangee and SK Songbird join the stage. I don't know why I screeched every time the announcer said their names.

We spent time together the day before, just the three of us at lunch, but there was something about seeing Tangee and SK dressed up and taking center stage to sing. I smiled so hard my jaws started to hurt. SK Songbird was decked out in a white crystal jumper with wide leg pants and long flowy sleeves that sparkled when she walked in her white pumps.

Suzette, who professionally goes by her initials, is a one-of-a-kind statuesque, blonde bombshell with an angelic voice. Knowing her for all these years, she really had been a friend. Not many can say that in this industry, but she has been doing this for decades. As a four-time Grammy award winning song writer, she is serious about her craft. But the private SK is a fun diva that makes everyone feel at home. Just like her adorable mother, Sheila. *(I need to visit them when I'm in L.A.)* The way she harmonizes with Taeyang on "Eyes of Light" she wrote is just beautiful. *(Oh, another one?)* The crowd of close to sixty thousand fans was still cheering from the duet ending when Jackson Wang came out to join SK. Everyone went crazy. I couldn't even hear Tanja talking to me.

Turning to her I asked, "Girl what?"

She moved closer and said it again, "That's Jackson Wang— had that "Slow" song with Ciara years back. I played that out. Jackson is down with brown."

I shook my head, "You are stupid! It's music." She turned her nose up and began snapping her fingers to the beat. Walking out to meet her on stage, Jackson hugged SK. They sang two songs that were chart hits from 2024 and 2027. One she wrote for that film called, "Snow Fall" and another love song he wrote called, "Shelly's Sunrise" *(Oh, these ballads are amazing. He really can sing, not just rap. They need to make another album.)*

"Go 'head Mr. Jackson Wang!" Tanja shouted. Tamera rolled her eyes. Soo and I laughed at them. Again, they received standing ovations. *(I'm going to not have a voice tomorrow.)*

Seconds later, my Delta doll sister, Tangee Arnold came out in her pretty hot pink and black shiny pant suit with her hair in a twisty bun. *(I bet she has on something Disney.)* Her soprano voice floated through the air as she sang with JinYoung on "Be With You", Beakyum song's "U" and then when Jay B came back out singing his song, "Dream Knight Special" from the OST, Tangee and SK joined him it was like something I had never heard. "Just beautiful." *(I love all these old songs.)* There were more standing ovations.

BJ Won walked out onto the stage and joined Jay B, YoungJae and Jackson. They sang a song they wrote and produced for a collaboration tour a couple years ago, called "Dance Tonight." Everyone was dancing and singing. It was lively and fun. But after the cheers, everyone left the stage except for BJ. He spoke directly to the crowd in Korean and then in English.

"Thank you for tonight. Coming together as our old groups and singing some of our hits was a blast. We are humbled by your love and support over the decades. Although we came together and made magic, I wanted to end my set with a tribute to my lost DRGN5 brothers, Joon Nam and Jin-K."

While he was talking men from all the groups came out with the five international special guests and filled the stage. I knew they would probably sing the song the idol brothers had written for the Joon Nam's Children of Trauma Foundation concert. So, I smiled and sat down. "Time in the Sky is a really pretty song." I said to Soo, who came and sat next to me. She gave a low "eh". Tanja was talking to Trey. Tamera was refreshing her drink. Kang was talking to Nari about something across the area and SI was on his cell phone in the corner. I heard BJ say, "this is for you brothers. We love and miss you."

It was quiet. But a few minutes later, DRGN5's fans Yong, Yo and Kyo started screaming. I stopped sipping my water and grabbed my chest. My heart sank while salty liquid formed. Soo grabbed my hand and held it with firmness. I closed my eyes and swallowed hard. Tears flowed with my eyes sealed closed. From the first few notes I knew it was Jae-Sung's song, the one he wrote about me. It wasn't as if I hadn't heard it since he had passed away; it's on a platinum album, he recorded it several different ways, and left it for me to remember but...but... GOT7's Jay B was singing... He was singing my love song, "Arabian Sand." *(Oh, my.)*

Slouching in my chair, I began melting like butter plopped on hot corn on the cob. In my mind's eye with my eyes closed, I could see Jae-Sung singing to me: playing the piano in our living room, at Madison Square Garden, on the beach on Cocoa Island, and in our bathtub watching the sunset. My breathing became irregular, and my heart was beating like I had been running in a sprint race. *(Jae... He sounds so much like Jae... Breathe... Soon... Jae will sing to me again... Soon. Right?)* I exhaled slowly and quickly wiped my cheeks. When I opened my eyes to find Soo's face inches away from me with a look of worry. Kang and SI were right next to me with a hand on each shoulder. I tapped them and smiled. Continuing to listen to the beautiful song my husband wrote about me being sung by his private nemesis, gave me a wave of emotions. When the thought came back to my mind, I gasped before covering my mouth with my hand.

"Noona?!" SI's tone was of concern. I glanced over all the loving eyes of worry now peering back at me. I removed my hand and basically announced what we all knew was true, "GOT7's Jay B is ... is singing *Arabian Sand*."

Kang nodded. Tamera had her face twisted from confusion shoving popcorn in her mouth. SI moaned, "eung (yeah)" and Soo squeezed my hand. A moment later, what I was thinking came out, almost like an echo, "Jin-K would be... So...so mad right now." Immediately, I started laughing and couldn't stop. Kang shook his head smashing his lips together, trying unsuccessfully to hold in his laughter. SI lowly chuckled. Soo's dark moon lid eyes were huge as she kept blinking, staring at me in silence.

Finally, Soo said, "Noona Marie, you are too much." I leaned over to whisper to her, but I was still laughing, when I said, "Oh, I can't wait to tell him when he wakes up. He's gonna be so pissed. Oh, I can't wait. Hee-hee! I win!"

Kang and SI gave each other a fist pump and released full gregarious laughter, understanding my twisted idol pranking mind.

Now snickering, Soo gave me her truth, "Marie, you are still just as idol crazy as they are. I want to be there when you tell him."

"Deal!" I shouted. She hugged me.

Tamera said, "I don't get it. Who is Jin-K?"

I played it off real cool with, "Oh, someone they know."

She didn't ask anymore, and we continued to listen to the last song performed by all of the artists called, "Time in the Sky". It was a lovely tribute, especially with the lights and rainbow color fireworks show.

⎯⎯⎯⎯⎯⎯⎯⎯⎯⎯

It was a magnificent night. I'm glad I went, but after a long hot shower and kissing my sleeping children goodnight, I made a single pot of hot lemon lavender tea, grabbed a frozen Fuji water bottle, and settled my tired body into bed. While I sipped my tea, for some strange reason, the words from 'My Firework' that I had written about Jae many years ago, simply popped into my head:

(Jae-Sung Kim is like a firework. It got lit and then sizzled, whistled while it traveled fast and high, then exploded, showering the sky with brilliant colors of light. Then, in mere moments, its beautifully illuminated design was gone but remembered with joy and a smile.) Then I started to talk myself.

"No, he isn't, a firework. I wrote that when he broke my heart breaking up with me. He isn't like that, he isn't. He's the sun and moon. Like our children. I told him." I remembered exactly when. We were in New York after he saw the journal that said Firework and he wanted to know what it meant. Right, I said, "You're not a firework, but you are the sun and the moon. A heavenly creation that is everlasting with divine beauty from natural light, not like an artificial wonder. But truly vibrant with powerful heat and cooling energy, supporting all life as it shines upon the earth. Never changing your designed purpose as an element precisely positioned to rise and fall at the predictable majesty of God's rhythmic eternal clock." I touched him, studied his eyes, and said, "Jae to me, you are like the sun and moon, always bright and warm lighting the roadway to my life and the force moving ocean waves beyond my dreams, forever you are my truest happiness for eternity.

"I remember his face at that moment. He was overflowing with his love for me. Then Jae read to me right then in my guest bedroom. He is always in my heart, in my memories. I will always love him. Always. I'm going to make one of his favorite dishes, Sundubu Jjigae. Yes, tomorrow. I will. Oh…" Now trembling, I began feeling a brewing tsunami wave of emotions quickly building.

Instinctively I began to arrange the pillows on the bed to surround me. Then without any thoughts, I grabbed the control system and dimmed the lights to the candle flicker mode in the ceiling and pushed play on the blue disc #40CMK. The soft sound of his perfect piano strokes over ocean waves filled the room, and I exhaled. "I miss you, baby. I need you so badly to be with me. Oh Jae… I miss you."

Slowly pebble-sized tears slid down my face as I adjusted the reading light and pulled out his last letter. To imagine him near me again, I began to read it out loud:

"Thursday Morning, February 28, 2030, 09:27 KST

A letter for my wife Chantal-Marie Delacroix-Kim.

Marie my love, read this after the private family service but before you return to Seattle, Washington. Be alone, open the shades to see the sky, and softly play the blue disc #40CMK. Be warm under the blankets with a cup of your favorite, lavender lemon tea. Not wine, nae sarang, tea.

To my magnificent sunset in Dubai. Beautiful and sweet Arabian sand, my love, you are my soulmate until the end of time. We began in 2019…"

The next morning when I woke up, I still had the preserved letter in my hand.

❧

Tamera and Tanja left the following Monday. While my parents went to Japan, the Kangden family and mine got to spend long overdue quality time together. Although Tangee and Louis did some touristy things with their girls, we spent four days together in our secluded mountain home. It was the best time. Good food, fun, nature, music, dancing, and lots of laughter. The best thing to hear beside my husband's voice is our children's laughter. There was a lot of that.

While the fellas were outside, we girls were inside dancing to old GOT7's "My Home," "Thursday," EXO's "Call Me Baby," and KAI's "Reasons," "Domino," and Jay Park's "All I Wanna Do" dance songs. I was taking a drink from my water bottle when my daughter stopped dancing and turned to me with all seriousness and said, "Mawmaw, why are you singing these songs by other men? You know Appa (father)doesn't like it. He told us to watch you."

Tangee screamed, "Oh, my god! He told you to...to what?" Right before she burst into loud high-pitch laughter. Her daughters laughed at their mother's reaction because of the sound she made. Water shot out of my nose, and I wet my pants a little laughing so hard.

(Was this in some of those private messages he recorded for them? He told my children to spy on me. Punk! Oh, I can't wait to tell him about Jay B singing his song!)

❧

38. Surprise

A great surprise came a few days after my parents left in late July. Soo Cheng called asking me to meet her for lunch. We went to Soul Food Café and chatted with Ophelia for a bit, before she went to help Stanley make smothered pork chops, rice and gravy, collard greens and corn bread for us. *(This is so good! Reminds me of Gram T and auntie Hellenes cookin'. I miss them. I miss home.)*

Halfway through the meal, Soo randomly said, "Noona Marie, I wanted to tell you something important."

I stopped chewing. "Are you pregnant?" I asked, cheesing with all my teeth showing.

She snickered, "Noona, no. Why do you always ask me this? Hana is enough for us. No more children."

I waved my hand at an invisible fly and rolled my eyes. *(Aww man.)*

She decided to tell me more details, "After SI's accident, I prayed a lot. I was an orphan. I don't have my own family, only the Cheng & Kim family. It has been hard for me to be close to strangers. It has always been just SI, Kang, and Jae-Sung. Marie, you were my real friend— that helped me try harder. But being different, doing different things than expected, it takes courage. I didn't think I had courage until I saw you go on without Jae-Sung. Once my mother-in-law listened in on some of my Bible learning with Ami and Suzie, she wasn't upset about my studies anymore. When I asked her why she wasn't, she said she saw how happy Hana had gotten from her friendship with Joy and a few young girls from our Korean congregation. Then she wanted to see what we did at the Kingdom Hall and came with Min Cha. They met several people, even a couple that Min Cha had known from her youth at university. Since then, everything has been much better. I'm sorry I didn't talk to you about everything before. I had to keep going for myself and not let others control what I wanted for my life and future."

"What? Min Cha, went to a Kingdom Hall? Why didn't she tell me? Why must everything be such a secret?"

"Pride. It's their pride, Noona. We Koreans are tied to our customs and ancestors. Going a different path isn't normal, honored, or encouraged."

"Hyeong (older brother) Jae-Sung changed everything first. He deeply loved you, and he wouldn't let go of that love. Not for his family, his friends, or his career and fans. I wasn't supposed to tell you, but it has been a long time now, and I don't think he would mind."

Swallowing my tea, I put my cup down and glanced at her with peering eyes, "Tell me what?"

"Jae-Sung told and wrote many things to my husband and Kang... Uh, it was to them, so I wasn't to share but he told them to listen to you. Your heart was good, and you were very wise. He believed he would wake up and wanted to see them, his family. Jae-Sung asked them to respect you and your decisions no matter what happens because it was what the two of you hoped for. Maybe a year or so after Jae-Sung died, SI mentioned it to his mother. I'm sure she told Min Cha I'm sure of it."

Watching her with a blank look on my face, everything she said was brand new information. I wasn't quite sure how to take it, except as another secret. I didn't have anything in my brain to muster a response. I just listened carefully.

"Over the last couple of years, Min Cha has been traveling outside of her compound. She has been visiting friends she used to have and making new ones. She had been secretly meeting my mother-in-law and talking to some that are Jehovah's Witnesses. Like me, they were curious about what you were saying about being asleep when you die and that there is a clear earthly hope for the future in the Bible. They asked questions but didn't want you to know about it. Dong-Hyun has been very upset about how she is changing. He has not been very kind to her. But she said she now felt free from the guilt she carried about her first husband and their children dying. What they showed her made her feel good about a lot of things, she said. You have helped us all in different ways. Hana and I have been so happy you are our family and live here."

"We are sisters, Soo. I love you too."

"Marie, you are in the English congregation. We have different assembly and convention times each year, but do you think you could come to ours on baptism day?"

My eyes bugged out at her in surprise. "Really? Oh, Soo… you are, really? Oh, yes, of course, I wouldn't miss it! My sweet friend, I am happy." Shy Soo Cheng lowered her head and nodded with a grin and a slow flow of tears. I reached over to hug her as tight as possible without breaking her. We started laughing, and Ophelia came out from the kitchen saying, "What's going on?"

Soo told her, and the congratulation hugs now increased to all three of us for a few minutes before Ophelia went to tell Stanley. Soo, still wiping happy tears, said, "Noona, when you come, you will see what a gift Jehovah and his people have been. It's a family among friends, and I'm so happy to know and serve him."

My eyes squinted to analyze what she said. But I was too excited to probe more into her statement meaning if there was one. We embraced again, giggling.

(Oh, how wonderful. In his own time, Jah makes things grow. Thank you, heavenly father!)

Although my congregation already had our three-day English-Speaking convention the month before, it was good to hear the same program of spiritual instruction and encouragement being delivered to the Korean speaking brothers and sisters in other ones. I left the streaming information for Kang and Nari to connect to the program for my children to watch this special dedication moment for their auntie Soo Cheng. I went with my security muscle Trey, who looked fabulous by the way, wearing his navy-blue tailored suit, and polished leather navy wingtip oxfords during Saturday's program.

My heart was so full of happiness. I felt like shouting from the joy of seeing not only Soo but Hana walking to the changing room to change before being submerged in the warm pool of water. There were so many people observing the ninety-three male and female baptismal candidates walking in single file to the changing rooms. Moments later, individuals came to the pool entrance. I only got a glimpse of the two of them in their long shorts and loose shirts over their bathing suits. From that alone, I had a plastered grin and felt my eyes trickle with the flowing wetness. When we moved from our seats closer to the pool area was when I could see Soo clearly speaking to two of the assisting brothers inside the pool of waist-high water. Steps behind her my sweet niece, Hana, carefully followed her mother. Glancing up, I gasped, seeing SI behind his daughter. "Oh!" I was louder than expected.

Trey asked me, "Didn't you know he was studying too?"

I shook my head, holding my fingers over my lips and smiling wide as tears fell. After they had left the pool, I turned to sit down in the empty seat behind me, but then it happened...

Trey nudged me saying, "Noona, wait."

I glanced up at him. Trey gestured by rolling his eyes to look back over at the neatly dressed crowd of onlookers around the large pool. My head followed his eyes. Seconds later, my mouth dropped. I clasped both hands over my mouth in shock. *(What?!)* My eyes instantly re-filled with salty water that released between blinking. My body tingled all over seeing my dear aunt, Teng Cheng stepping into the baptism pool in her long covering jumper over her one-piece bathing suit. Trey smiled watching my reaction, finally knowing the tightly held secret.

Other newly baptized ones entered and exited the pool, and I remained speechless, dabbing my cheeks. Roughly ten minutes later, I looked up at the projection screens, and stood up from the seat. Without a word I dashed to be closer. My heart was racing while making my way to the pool. "Sillyehabnida (Pardon me please/excuse me)." Kind friends moved to the left and the right

315

letting me pass in front of them. Holding on to the edge of the pool, I stood stunned with eyes streaming with tears as I witnessed my mother-in-law enter the pool in her cotton pants and long loose shirt covering her bathing suit.

(Jehovah God, what is happening right now? Min Cha...she... she is getting baptized to be a servant of yours...like me... like Soo, SI, Teng and Hana. Someone pinch me. No catch me, I may pass out. I'm so happy, I can't stand it!)

"Min Cha!"

She found me in the crowd of bright, grinning faces and smiled back at me; before taking the brothers' arms. When she came up from the water, she walked a few steps toward me and tenderly kissed my wet cheeks. Then she allowed two brothers to assist her out of the pool.

Thirty minutes later, the group of us were still hugging, and laughing while enjoying our packed lunches. "Trey, you knew too?"

He smirked and said, "Code, Noona."

Later that day, I found out it had been challenging to keep it from me but there were things happening behind the scenes that made it necessary not to share with me that they were studying and drawing closer to Jehovah. But in that moment, I attempted to pinch his bicep, but there was just muscle so as an alternative, I pulled his pinky finger and he laughed. SI shook his hand and said to him, "Thanks for keeping it quiet. Hana wanted it to be a surprise."

"Hana this was you? You didn't want me to know?" I hugged her lovingly as she giggled and nodded. I kissed her cheeks several times and said, "It was a glorious surprise."

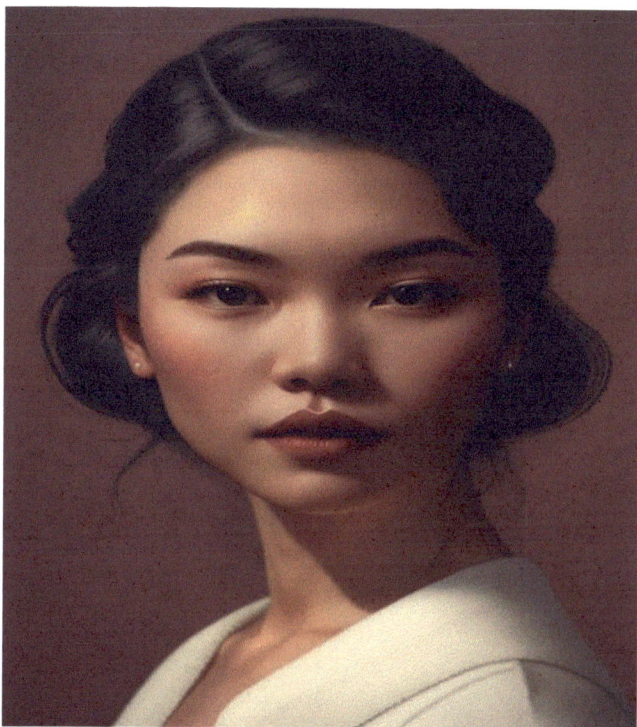

My beautiful sister Soo Cheng

Sweet Hana Cheng

Aunt Teng Cheng

My mother-in-law, Min Cha Kim

39. Black Love

"So how was the couples' trip?"

"It was nice. You remember how pretty Jamaica is don't you?"

"Yes. How could I forget, the girls trip. Lola had that man chasing her. What was his name? It was an herb, spice, or something. Thyme, Cumin, Paprika… Hmm… Renee, help me."

"Girl, his name was Basil! I can't believe I remembered that!"

"That's right! Oh, and Jazz had Ron the ice cream man with his nasty tongue."

"Ha-ha-ha. Girl, he was so weird, but he bought us all kinds of drinks. Why was Tangee pullin' the old white men and got that diamond/gold bracelet."

"Tangee-girl had it goin' on. She straight pawned that to buy her meal card and books for the year. That was fun. Did you go to that family-owned rum factory again? Is it even there, been so long ago. I wonder where Tracey and Jsa'Tay are these days. After they moved to Chicago and Denver, we lost track of them. You need to find them, Nay-Nay."

"I'll get on that. It wasn't a small group but nothing like we've had before. No, we didn't tour a liquor factory this time. We planned to be more relaxed with only a few couple courses. It was just four: Intimacy Reboot, Talk No Touch, Battle of the Sexes, and Truth, Dare, Debate. Smaller groups usually work out more fun for me anyway. Like when we went to Maldives with you guys. But this was amazing. Adonis and Yvonne came. She had never been to an adult couple's retreat trip before. Girl, she thought the learning stuff was going to be corny like that one movie. I told her, uh no, do you see Vince Vaughn around here? Adonis's brother Alphonso and his wife joined. Hey, did I tell you, Tamera's son came this time."

"Really? Quinton Jr. was there? He is all grown up."

She confirmed, "Yeah, I had to pause a second before jacking him up for pee'ing on me when he was a baby, and we were trying to change his stupid diaper." I choked a little laughing thinking about it.

"Marie, that little knucklehead is fine. I thought it was going to be weird but nope. It was no drama folks. You know I don't play 'round with silly nonsense. It was Jazz, Derrick, Lola, Gregg, Antonio's brother and sis... Hold on, let me send you these pictures."

A few minutes later, I opened the message and scrolled through several photo images of couples and groups from her trip. Still inspecting a few I commented, "Oh, wow. You all look so drunk. No, I'm kidding... relaxed is the right word." I tried to control my snickering. "Is that Adonis's brother? They look alike. Looks like you had a good time."

Nodding, she added more information, "Marie, it was so much fun girl. You should've seen us climbing Dunn's River Falls. We were all linked together, but Lola slipped, and Tonja tried to catch her. You know me, I let go and the silly cows fell. I got pictures! It was so funny. Lola was trying to be cute in her two-piece and just a sarong, the dummy should've had on shorts. When she flipped over the rocks and landed, her bottoms ripped away and she was on her back spread-eagle for a few minutes."

"Oh, my god!" I shouted before muffling my hysterical laughter imagining the scene. Renee continued telling the story, "Go on and laugh. It was funny as hell. Lola was cracking up, especially after Jazz said, "chick your monkey all out lookin' like two mini-muffin tops." Greg was defending his woman, though. He shouted at us to stop makin' fun of his sexy wife because he loves eating fluffy muffins. We howled. The comedy. Antonio and I bought them dinner and drinks because we laughed the most." I laughed harder and shook my head to turn away from seeing her story telling hand-puppet gestures. She continued, "Jazz got her flirt on and had our bartender make our special drink and they were bomb."

I calmed my cackling and sat up, "Wait, what special drink? Not the one from college. How? You're in Jamaica."

She snickered, "Yep. It worked with jerk chicken and coco bread. Them Nigger-ita's were the hit! Oh, Rhee, Kevin was scared to say it. We were like go on man, it's just a drink. He was like nah, I'm just gonna point and say one of those. But girl, after he had two, Kevin was tossing up East-coast hand signs, crip walking, and shouting, Nigger-ita! Nigger-ita!"

"Aaahhhhaaa! Drunk much!" We laughed about that.

"Marie, it was black love couples all around and in full effect! Except for your cousin and Kevin. He's an old school Stanley Tucci kinda Calabrian man that is darker than me. But it was all good."

"Renee, everyone is darker than you! Ha-ha!"

"Shut up, cow."

"I can just imagine them jokers in their man huddle with Cuban cigars." I said shaking my head.

"Oh yeah, you already know that was what Tony, Ulrick, Kevin and Alphonso were doin' with the *I'm old and cool* look, posing with a drink in their hands. Some of the fella's don't do the *I'm gonna smoke a cigar on special occasions* thing, but they tried it. So, we girls left them chimneys and got massages. Except for Jazz and Lola had to do a quick cigar puff-puff with them for a little while first. I told them sometimes I think they wanna be dudes. So gross. Tangee and Louis passed on this couple's trip like always. At first, I kind of told her off because they act like they can't ever hang with us brown folks. But I took it back when she told me she had a tour and their whole family was going. Whatever, it's because I said it was a Black Love Retreat! I know it is. Shoot, ain't nobody told her to marry the whitest man in the world! Ha! Ha! No, seriously, I heard their baby is due at the end of the year. Tangee gonna have a litter of kittens. Crazy chick."

"Yeah, she thinks it will be a boy this time. You know now that they are vegan, she feels like she can sense these things. Hee. Hee. When she finds out in a couple of weeks, she is going to let me know. I hope she is because, they are going to let me name him."

"Oh lord. I hope not. Marie, you got all of them crazy names for your kids. Now, you are the damn naming convention for us, Delta Diva Dolls. Who voted for that? Ha. I'm glad I ain't having no more. Christopher is enough. See that was a nice normal name."

"Hater! I gave you Christopher, remember!"

"Oops yeah, my bad. So, what is it going to be... Elfinstien? Theodorious? Cleitusefo?" She said it sarcastically under her snickering.

"You stupid! His name is going to be Edwin Lucian Kanden. You cow!"

"Oh, it's... it's normal...Ha Ha...Louis let you give it some swagger. That's good."

"The nerdy man from Montana is now very hip. He says he has been more urbanized in his older age being married to Tangee all this time. Uh, he likes to announce that his wife is Black, which makes him automatically cooler than most. Louis is fun. We had a good time when they were here."

"Well, she done put it on ARRTI. Didn't she? Took her long enough. You half-White women are so damn slow with the sexiness. It was painful, like watching salmon swim upstream to spawn. No... no...it was like trying to get a rhythmless person on the beat. Like that White guy from school, Joe. Oh, yeah like that!"

I shouted at her, "Shut up! Whore!"

Chuckling, she continued her comments, "But I will admit, you both tapped into your sistah super sexiness later in life. Lola, Jazz, and I knew you had it in you. Just didn't come out when we were tossing it at Howard U. Ha Ha."

"You three did enough tossing for the two of us. Y'all were giving out samples like you were working for Costco! Nasties. Black love? No...if we look at the facts, you must mean Blexican or Blarican love. Hee Hee...You're only half. You Mexican Black girl, with your Puerto Rican and Black husband."

"Shut up! It's Black love if there is one ounce in there somewhere, stupid!"

"Oh, are we doing that one-drop of Black makes you Black, thing? Okay, that means, my love was Black love too."

"You wish. Nope! Sorry Sis, but...that was so just *Kimchi and Croissant Love* all the way." We laughed, wiping a few tears from the humor of it all.

"Sounds like you had a real good time."

"We did. We did." Renee agreed before taking several gulps of her giant glass of white wine that she continued to refill during the conversation.

"Anyway so, I got ta tell ya something. We never talk about Adonis but girl, I told you he was dating this judge, Yvonne from Seattle, right?"

"Yeah, you told me. He brought her to New York. You met her a while ago. Good for him."

Renee appeared to be hesitating a little, nibbling on olives, cheese, and asparagus wrapped in prosciutto. *(What is up with her? Did something happen on the trip?)* I was curious but not wanting to rush her to divulge, I changed the subject.

"Well, you said the couple's activities turned out good. We didn't get to do any with you guys, but we had different fun on Cocoa Island, remember?" I said smiling. She nodded while drinking more wine.

"True, nothing will ever be like that trip. Or Seoul and Niagara Falls! I miss K-Pop slanted eyes and those wild stupid games. So much fun. Maybe I need to drink some Soju? Nah, it's not the same.

It wasn't like our Black love trips, but they were great times." I grinned, nodding in agreement.

Derrick Ramsey

Delta Sister JazzEtta "Jazz" Henderson

Alphonso & Nedra Vincent

UlRick Escobar

Nadene Rhoads

Quinton Jr. & wife Michelle Brown

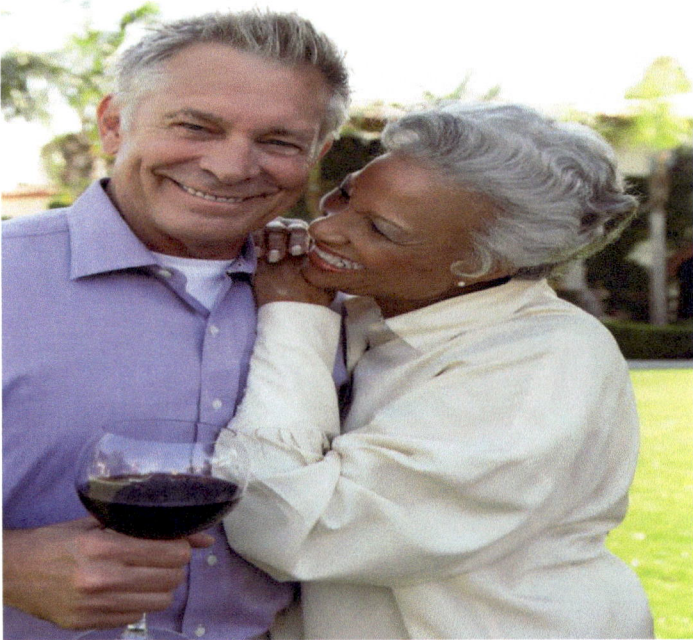

Cousin Tamera Brown & Kevin Marino

Alana Escobar

Domonic Lenox

Cousin Tonja Murry

Reggie Dubois

King County Judge Yvonne Judkins

Strategically, Renee did a segway back into scoop she wanted to tell me. "Anyway, it was a blast. Ten days of magnificent sun and fun. I wish you could have been with us girl. I miss you. Anyway, Adonis and Yvonne are serious. As serious as Adonis can be. You know there will be no marriage for him, but they have been together for over a year. You would like her. She's good people. Yvonne went to the University of Washington. She's from South of Seattle, Tacoma, I think. I told you how they met, right? Well, they met after she hit the back of his new car on the freeway during stop and go traffic. Thought that was funny. On this trip, I learned she's good friends with your aunt Lolli's daughter, Michelle Toussaint. She said, they actually grew up together. Small world, right? Uh, Marie… He asked me privately about you."

"He did?"

"Adonis told me he misses the friendship that you guys had. He thinks of you often; he wonders how you are. I told him you were good and a Jehovah's Witness now. He was shocked at first, but then he said that made sense. Marie, did you know his youngest brother, Achilles, and his wife, Melonie, are witnesses too? I met them once when we went to Scottsdale. They are nice. Anyway, I didn't get what he meant, and he didn't elaborate when I inquired. Why don't you talk anymore? You just ghosted him. Did something happen between you? Tell me. I asked him. He said nothing happened. But I don't believe that. It's weird. A few years ago, you two were cool friends but now it's like you don't know the man. Does the brotha owe you money? Did he do something I need to cut his ass for? Don't lie to me, Rhee, did you guys have a falling out?"

"No. I just have other things going on and he has his own life. I'm glad he has someone special. You can tell him I said that. But I won't be contacting him. How do you think his lady would feel about me doing that. Naw, I'm good with you relaying that message. Yeah, and you can tell him the triplet's Seahawks jerseys still don't fit! Ha. Crazy man getting newborn babies a kids size medium 10-12."

"Alright, I will. Hey, Lola told us she has been to visit you five damn times. I hate that heifer flies for free. She was so smug announcing to us girls that she had been in South Korea with you for two weeks before we all went to Jamaica."

"Uh, yeah... Lola is really attached to the boys."

(She isn't always with me when she is here.... And she is attached to...stop it! Ha!)

"That's way more than me. I was just there when my little munchkin loves were younger. I need to come visit and bring Chris with me again. He had so much fun with his three cousins. You know he loves Jolie already got her a teddy bear to send and some trucks for Jin and Jae. This boy tried to wrap them up in paper towels because he couldn't find any wrapping paper. He's so his daddy."

I snickered, and then she added, "Uh, so you know about Dick Tracey."

Peering at her confused I said, "What? Who… who is Dick Tracey?"

"Marie why are you acting brand new? She told me you two talked about it. You know that's your stalker Delta Sister. She finds BJ anywhere in the world and will fly to meet him just to get that boy's Korean di—"

I howled with laughter, cutting her off mid-sentence. Tears trickled down my cheeks from the comic reference. Renee took a few sips of wine and said, "That's what Jazz and I have been calling her when she told us she had gotten some more of that Korean wand after that one-time in New York. Remember, years ago when everyone was having sex, you and Jae, Jazz, and Kang, well, poor Antonio ain't get none that night because I was trippin' being fully engrossed in the *Ripley's Believe It or Not* sex edition going on in your Plaza Suite bedroom! Hot damn! Ha!-Ha!"

"Shut up, you perv!"

"Anyway, during this trip to Jamaica when she pulled us aside to tell us some recent details, I enjoyed the play by play but… Marie, I swear, when I hugged her, she smelled like fermented cabbage and MSG. I'm just sayin'. Damn, the girl needs to pace herself. Geez!"

Coughing from continuous laughter, I waved my hands for her to stop talking. "Ahhhhaaa! Stop! You gonna make me pee! Woo!" I said between coughs and yelps.

"Lola told me you didn't discuss details, but you know about it, now. I won't say any more. I know how you are. But let me just say this… I know he ain't really a brotha in disguise like Jae-Sung Kim, but BJ must have some real serious negro tendencies for Lola to be so latched on to him like a hungry baby on a damn breast nipple!" She demonstrated the wild motion with her mouth open, tongue hanging out, and growling. I lost it again, dropping the phone.

We both cracked up about that for a long time. Finally, I cleared my throat with a few more coughs before intentionally shifting to a different conversation.

"Renee, tell me about Jazz and the Federal Marshal. I thought after Lola's wedding she broke it off. I am surprised she went back to that. A while back, she had that side fling with Kang again for like a minute. Then a short stint with a stuntman friend of Tonja's. What's up with that? I thought the Delta rule was never go backward."

"Girl, JazzEtta is so cool whipped over Derrick. She ain't going nowhere. Sista-girl is singing "All My Life" like in the movie *Glitter,* but she don't sound like no Mariah Carey, more like the chick who thought she was cute that couldn't sing!"

I snorted then laughed out loud. Renee added, "She told me he has her toes curling. They go to the gun range and after he blows holes in the fake man, she gets so turned on they make out right there. Ha! Can you imagine her little 5'4 round behind trying to jump this 5'11 tree in a gun range. Dang bet its comedy for real. This younger chocolate man likes that they have their own homes. He doesn't need to get married, just got her on his arm, and that's good enough. Oh, she said he likes it when she takes charge. I was like okay go 'head, Ms. Officer-Tie-Him-Up! She laughed but gave me the nod. You know that's just what she likes."

Chuckling, I said, "Yes, she does. Well, tell her I said Hi next time you talk to her. I can't ever seem to get her. It's been a really long time, since we have actually spoken. Emailing doesn't count. She sends presents but uh, do you think she's upset with me? Did I do something?"

"I will. She didn't act like it in Jamaica. She did say, she didn't know what to say to you. Everything felt a little weird."

"Weird?"

"You know, different. You live way over there. You are a mom with three toddlers, your beliefs, you don't go anywhere, things are not the same as when you lived in New York, and we used to go on diva doll vacations together. That was all she said. She loves you doll, but she's afraid she might say the wrong thing. I think she doesn't feel like you have much in common anymore. At least that was what she had told Lola. Girl, please, don't sweat it. You know she is probably on a plastic pony saying ya can't catch me cop'er like an escaped con with the Marshal in hot pursuit ready to stick her with a real hot warrant. Ha-ha. Oh, I kill me!"

"You stupid, Renee!"

"Marie, are you doing okay really? I mean you sound happy. Is something going on?"

"I'm good. Really busy, of course."

"Uh, does Kang and Nari still live with you?"

"Yes. They have their own places but spend about four or five days here. I'm probably going to tell them soon they don't have to stay as much anymore. It's fun for the triplets and me to have them. But we are getting ready to move, so maybe you can come and help us."

"Well, that was a given, I was going to ask you when. I won't bring Chris if it's during school. Marie, are you still getting drama from Jae's family? Or did they chill on that nonsense about you not celebrating holidays and having a shrine in your house thing? It was his aunt who really wanted it and said you weren't honoring him and their traditions, wasn't it?"

"Yeah. No, it's all over."

"That was crazy how she tripped. I remember you said she tried to get all of Jae's family to take the triplets from you, saying you were unfit because you were raising her great nephews and niece to believe a different way than their traditions. I'm glad they accepted things."

"Renee, Jae's aunt, died in a fire a while back."

"Well, problem solved. Bye Felicia!"

"Don't say that. But yeah, it got resolved."

"What about your in-laws?"

"Didn't I tell you? Everything was quiet at that end for a long time. I didn't see my in-laws at all, really. Everyone is so busy. Min Cha goes through Kang to see the triplets because our schedules constantly conflict. I only saw Soo and Hana maybe once a month too. It was kind of weird. But when my parents were here, we got to hang out at a concert in July. Tamera and Tanja were here, so it made it even more special just like old times. I told you that, right? Oh, I must have spaced on that sorry. Let me tell you, Min Cha, SI, Soo, Teng and Hana all got baptized at their convention. I had no idea they were studying, not like that. I was so frazzled with excitement from the secret surprise. Renee, sometimes if you wait long enough, you might get a glimpse of a person you had never realized was there. Oh like my mom. We 've gotten very close. I mean, she isn't what I thought at all... But more like Pawpaw. It's so strange. Uh, I'll tell you later. I will email you our travel plans. Maybe you can meet us on the way or something. But it's late, girl. I gotta go to bed."

"Okay, doll, love you!"

"Love you, too, Nay-Nay."

Seconds after hanging up, my phone chimed with a text message from Renee. I tapped it to open it and saw a picture of Adonis.

(Why is she sending...) "What is she doing?"

I texted her back, "Heifer, you're so not funny!"

She sent a smiley face emoji around the words, "He looks the same a little grey on top but the same. I know you, Rhee. You can't lie to me. Something happened between you and him. I feel it but you are just not sayin'. Must not be bad enough for us to beat his ass like we did Bryce, so, I'm gonna leave it alone. But this is for some Black is beautiful dreams, Sis. Stop sayin' you're dead down there! It all works. Need to start it up every once in a while, when it's in the garage! Self-love is exercise which is good for the heart. Definitely will help you sleep. Ha! Ha! Now close them golden eyes of yours. Night."

"She makes me sick!" I said smirking from reading her message. But instead of closing my phone, I stared at his picture again. *(Dang!)* Then without much effort to stop, my mind took me back.

Boeing Executive
Adonis H. Vincent

40. Friendship Love

Back in 2031, once I landed back in South Korea from that first New York business trip, I honestly didn't give any more thought about what had happened in my Mandarin Oriental Hotel suite.

But tonight, after getting more comfortable in bed, my mind replayed parts of the conversation with Renee, and I smiled. Within a few seconds her questions, "What happened with you and Adonis?" and "Why don't you talk?" flashed through my mind, and I started to recall the details of my last moments with Adonis Vincent.

It was August 1, 2031, and sometime around 4:30 a.m., we were awakened by the quick ringing from the hotel phone. My wake-up call had been pre-set from the day before. Adonis brushed my hair with the palm of his hand while I laid wrapped in his arms, slightly on top of his firm bare chest. Feeling the light sensation of his skin on my cheek, as he moved each time he took a breath, I visually inspected the details of his tattoos.

My eyes traced the Japanese characters over his heart, which I recognized as his mother's name, *Akiko*. It was right above the handle of a detailed Katana with characters inside its blade that read, *First Born King.* The blade seemed to end somewhere below the waistline of his belted jeans.

After clearing my throat, I broke the silence, "Thank you, Adonis. Thank you for staying."

He grunted, coughed, and then said, "I'm laying here touching you. I should probably be thanking you, instead."

I giggled, not moving my head from his naked torso that vibrated as he chuckled. He whispered gliding his fingertips up and down my right arm. "See, nothing is different. We are just as before. Friends."

I moaned in agreement. My thoughts of sadness, loss and desperate longing paused momentarily, and I fell asleep with his strong arms securely around me and my face simply touching his skin. I had floated away to a dreamland as if I was experiencing a past intimate time with my heart's joy, the man I love most of all. My mind thought only of Jae, as I imagined him as the one holding me, and that was what I needed.

However, just like driving down a dark road and a sudden flash of light appears from oncoming traffic, reality hit me much sooner than I expected. Adonis spoke again while moving and lifting me to sit up to face him. "Marie, I have a few requests."

Unsure of what he was going to say, my mind went blank, but I just replied, "Okay." I waited to hear what he had to say. It seemed like I was watching a movie but half-asleep. Honestly, I was disconnected, with no feelings or thoughts at all about what was happening in the present. It was yet another mistake I had made. His expression was like it usually had been, serious and professional. Not like the man who whispered my name in tones of sweetness like a lullaby, as I drifted to sleep hours earlier.

"I know you and I are very confidential, but I need to say not even Renee can know about tonight. That is one."

(Wait…What is he thinking? I had no intention of ever mentioning this to anyone. I was thinking you were Jae… I'm ashamed - I wished you were Jae the entire time you were here. I'm sure I said his name at least once as I dreamed of him. No, Adonis, I won't be telling Renee or anyone.) I didn't respond with words, but simply nodded.

"Second, if you need to be held, to be kissed or if one day you want a man to do anything, I'll be the one…the only one. But don't make this more than it is."

(Huh? Why would I?)

I spoke up, "I don't think I'll need this again. It's just been so soon after he died, being in this hotel… I didn't think about what being here could mean. I had no plan, and then all these feelings came. You know… kind of like what you said."

He unexpectedly gave a quick peck to my lips, then said, "We're friends. If you need more, I'm here, but no one can know about it, and we can't talk about it afterward. We don't want emotions to distort our friendship. Let's keep things simple. No guilt or judgment. We need to remain as we are, friends."

After hearing what he said, I was a little confused. *(What is he talking about? More… I don't want any more. Something isn't right here. He doesn't make sense…He is a man that's offering to… What the heck is going on?)*

Since I was silent and thinking, I noticed his breathing got heavier. He cleared his throat more frequently as I watched him. Adonis wasn't as calm as I had known him to be. He bit his lip and looked up at the ceiling, blowing out from his nostrils with slightly more force than before. I observed him closely.

"Adonis, I don't understand."

He looked at me before confirming his commitment and intentions, "Marie, I'm just saying, if you want me to help you, I will. Grieving a loss from the heart takes time and sometimes you may need comfort. I just want it agreed that it will be me. That's all."

What he said made sense, kind of. But it was in that instant that the situation became clearer to me. What I was doing was all very dangerous; being alone with him and asking him to stay to hold me was simply leading him on and giving him the notion that I could want more physical things. *(What did I do? Why did I let him come in? Why did I ask him to stay? He isn't Jae. He'll never be Jae-Sung. I used him. He didn't deserve to be treated this way. What's wrong with me?)*

Desperate women can do and say things they wouldn't normally do. I knew that and slowly began to wake my brain back up from its hibernation. But his explanation wasn't clear enough for me to understand him. So, I asked questions to get answers. I sat up and adjusted my body more to face him. As I moved, I felt electricity sparks from my nylon-covered legs rubbing against my skirt and the comforter.

"Why are you saying this? Do you think I'm some... promiscuous woman because I asked you to stay, take your shirt off and lay on top of the bed, holding me while I slept? Do you think I want to have sex with you just because I did that?"

"Marie…"

"No, Adonis, is that what you think? Do you?"

"You might. I just want to be prepared if you do. Set the ground rules now. Being transparent here, you know I've wanted you for a very long time. But I need you to understand that I won't marry you now. I can't…I can't do that. I wanted to. I would have before, but you have this man's children, and… I can't."

I just stared at him for a few seconds, then I said it. "Marry me? Uh, I shouldn't have had you stay. I'm sorry. I should've been stronger. Maybe it was all the alcohol, or maybe I was just subconsciously counting on the way you felt to give me what I wanted. In any case, it was wrong. I used you, and I'm sorry. It's complicated but now you think I want something that I don't. I won't ever want to have sex with you or anyone else, Adonis. Not ever. I'm sorry I've hurt you by asking you to… Uh… pretending that you were Jae holding me…"

When I slid my legs around to leave the bed, he pulled my arm back toward him. Adonis held my face with both hands and moved his body closer to mine. His eyes were slightly glossy, and his reply was vulnerable and heartfelt, and now that I was more alert, it showed me another side of Adonis Vincent. Upon hearing all that he had said to me next, I deeply regretted asking him to touch me.

"Marie, I'm going to say this now… Stop, stop talking. Don't analyze the situation. Just let it be what it is, alright?" He let go of my face and moved his body back but remained focused on my eyes.

"Adonis, I'm sorry… I…I can't. I wasn't a friend to you hours ago, but I'm going to be one right now and tell you the truth. I used you. I know I did. I didn't plan to, at least not consciously anyway. And I'm sorry that I did. I was so caught up in my sorrow that I just wanted to be held. But Adonis, I'm… I'm…not your ex-wife. I'm not going to pretend you are someone else and then send you on your way. I am going to be accountable for what I did. I hurt you and I'm sorry."

"Marie, stop please. I really don't want to care about you more than I already do. Don't say this stuff. You're making what I said way more than it is. I just don't want you to hope for something I can't give you. I don't want you to feel lonely or want to be held, and some good for nothing opportunist is in the right place at the right time. Slipping something in your drink or worse. I don't even want to think about it. Women use men just like men use women. But you're not my ex-wife. Don't put yourself there because, Marie, you are not even remotely close to the lying, conniving, unfaithful bitch she turned out to be. But don't think I am a saint either. Because I am not. Do you know you mumbled your dead husband's name the entire time you slept? You did. Do you think I gave a damn? No… No because if you had asked me, I would've given you every inch of my heat knowing full-well that you'd be thinkin' about your damn dead husband. Do you know how I can let you touch my skin with your sweet fingers, be so close to you like this, and not ease myself inside you? Baby, it isn't because I'm a eunuch. I have control, and I don't manipulate or force women. But trust me while you slept, if you had hinted …I mean just a word… that you wanted just a little more, I would've gladly given you every inch of me and in all the different ways I've dreamed about." (Oh, crap. I… I….) My body started to tingle, and goosebumps quickly covered my arms. I swallowed hard and slowly began to count to ten. *(One… Two… Three…)*

"Marie, I am an intentional and self-controlled man. You are the only woman I've felt this way about in a very long time. I know what's real. I'm a man that wants a woman who doesn't want him. But even though she doesn't, I won't hurt her just to have a few hours of pleasure being inside her. No, some of her in my life is better than no her. Does that make sense?"

I briefly turned away to get my words sorted in my head before studying his eyes, and replying with, "So, let me get this straight, you would do whatever I want; whenever I want; how many times I want, as a way to have some of me?"

"Oh, baby, I'd travel anywhere, anytime, just to break you off. Mmmh, I'd enjoy every time I was deep in that thick black jungle of yours."

(Damn, he's a nigga.) I wanted him to stop killing my image of him, but he kept on going after clearing his throat. "We have friendship love, and it is a powerful thing. I've been where you are before. I recognized it in your face and body language when we got into the city. The closer we came to my hotel, the more your energy shrunk, and you were covered all over with sadness. I felt it without a word from you. I made myself available because we are friends and for no other reason. You asked me to stay and hold you. Well, that was me being your friend. I did whatever you asked, no more. So don't feel guilty about me or the fact that you had a need to physically connect with someone you trusted. That's what I'm saying."

I nodded, then I needed to know more, "If I hadn't asked you to stay then...you...you wouldn't have?"

Affectionately cupping the left side of my face, he shook his head saying, "No. I told you... I don't take advantage of women, not even the smart, pretty ones I desire. It was odd at first because I prefer a dark skin sista, but you are this intelligent and sophisticated woman that I was immediately drawn to from the very beginning. So, trust me, baby, I do desire you, very much. But you asked me, so, I obliged." He cleared his throat and said, "Look at it this way, Marie, you imagined being with your late husband. Touching me relieved you of your sadness and pain from him not being here. That's it –

nothing more. Focus on that because it's the only reason you asked me to stay. I knew that. What I imagined lying here isn't important. So don't think about it. I helped you, which is what a friend is supposed to do."

I just stared at him blankly, truly amazed at his cavalier attitude. He was so straightforward with the situation. I was a bit mesmerized by his emotionlessness. But then he got my attention with his next words. There was no way to misunderstand because they came like a bolt of lightning across the sky, "Marie... I'm... I'm going to say it. I love you. You know that don't you? I've wanted you for so long. You and I are a good match. We fit perfectly. You've felt it. Because of you, I thought I might marry again. I waited for you, to be ready. I had no one else. I just waited. But I came just a few minutes too late to be in your heart. If only you had come to your sister's that summer when it was planned for us to meet. If only you loved me, I would've given you my everything, Marie. Everything."

His words were profound verbal expressions that confirmed without a doubt what the time with me meant to him. I was speechless, wrapped up in this moment of my selfishness and his confession.

Adonis Vincent was a gentleman and my friend. He was educated, wealthy, charming, kind, and very handsome. This was the only time he showed me his hidden self. He revealed the secret of his heart, something that he had kept concealed for protection. Adonis felt he was in love with me and tortured himself a little because of it. Something I believe he must have taken away from his experience with his ex-wife, who I don't think he had completely healed from. He practiced being emotionally detached to survive but he loved the thought of me as a match, even though I was unattainable.

I didn't figure this out on my own. In addition to everything that had happened, it was more of his honest declarations that Adonis whispered to me that early morning. "I don't trust women. Not after she did that to me. I didn't allow myself to trust another woman after she did it again and got pregnant. At first, she tried to say it was mine but there was no way it could've been because I had been in Japan for four months. Before I figured that out, she left with him, her boss. I trusted no woman not for years. Marie, then you…you made me weaken. I saw us going through life together. I have not felt this way in a long, long time. Vulnerable. It's not me. But with you… Why? Why on earth did you marry him? He couldn't compare to me. Then… He left…left you alone. I am a strong man, Marie. I can walk with you, carry you. Willingly I would, but you have his children. I…I… can't and won't compete with some ghost or raise another man's child, not like that. I…I'm just not made that way."

I said nothing, only watched him sitting up on the bed with my legs curled underneath me. Adonis leaned back on the headboard, loosely holding the fingers of my left hand. Then he said what he had been building up to say. "I'm going to say it just once. Marie, we can be this way, but only the two of us can know. I can commit to being with only you. Only loving you in any way you need me. Will you think about it? It will be the best way for both of us. No one can be included in our relationship. Marie, it will be how I can love you and you can let me." I adjusted my body to study the sincerity in his eyes as he moved his head to face me. He was honest about what he wanted. It wasn't just sex, and I knew that. His manicured hands and silky fingers slid slowly over my jaw and down my neck. I felt the lure of temptation just staring up at him. My breathing got choppy, and my skin began to tingle all over my body just from his trusted, loving touch. But just moments later, my eyes lost focus from a growing cloudy haze, and Adonis seemed to disappear.

Then it happened…

In my mind's eye, a vision came from my subconscious. Clear and unmistakable was Jae-Sung's face as he struggled to breathe. I was in a past moment of clarity while Jae's eyes delved deeply into mine, seemingly swimming in the pool of tears within them. In my head, I could hear the precise tone of his sultry voice while catching sight of the leisure movements of his lips, telling me, "Baby, I'm asleep in God's memory. Just asleep. Don't forget, one day, I will wake up for you."

My body shuttered from my subconscious memory and imagination overtaking my mind. Instantly, I remembered my promise, and what I hoped for. Lost in the silence and stillness of my thoughts, I didn't realize Adonis had his lips firmly pressed on mine. I didn't even feel it until his tongue grazed to enter a place not meant for him. My body jerked away from him, but I said nothing, I only slightly shook my head, and covered my mouth with a few fingers.

Adonis grinned before easing forward to kiss my cheek. I flinched. He paused and said, "Sweetheart, I am patient. I will wait because you are worth it," a split second before withdrawing his touch and putting space between us.

I gave no answers while I watched him put back on his sweater and slip on his shoes to leave. I did not move or speak. Not even as he eased down to tenderly kiss my cheek, and said in Japanese and English, "Aisa sete kudasai, kawaii Marī. (Let me love you, sweet Marie). I love you. Take some time and think about it."

Paralyzed within the moment, I replied with only a partial smile from my seated position on top of the bed. Minutes later, Adonis left my New York Mandarin Oriental Hotel suite. Exhaling and inhaling deeply, I felt the warm air escape between my lips. I glanced around the semi-dark room, and my mind quickly began to connect many events to formulate a precise picture of everything.

Over the years, our friendship helped me in many ways. I knew I could be loved by a good Black man because he was one. He didn't see me as a trophy, or as a competitor. He was honest, strong, and he really cared for me, deeply like a mature man seeing the value of me as a strong Black woman. I believe he was a man I could lean on, and he would protect me. Adonis confirmed that positive, united Black love as they say, is possible and we could have it. If only we had met earlier, that is.

The grieving brain fog had lifted away. I saw beyond the here and now. Miles passed my sorrow, the narrow pathway back toward Jae-Sung became much wider and clearer. Just hours after Adonis Hiro Vincent left that early morning, and I was in a secure car on my way to the Sony building, I decided I no longer needed him as my friend. Honestly, I cared about him deeply, too. But our relationship was a temptation. The more I thought about it, the situation reminded me of when I was younger and in France. Because of that history, it came to me rather quickly that it wasn't going to be healthy or safe for me to stay connected with him. So, I never reached out or saw him again. I knew quite well that Adonis was a very strong gold and green personality type; purposeful and strategic. He was well-aware and even prepared for our relationship to end. I'm sure of it, especially since he never tried to contact me either. Leaving it to me to decide was going to go one of two ways. I truly believe he hoped I would've said yes but he knew deep down, I wouldn't have agreed to that kind of life.

Finally, recalling Renee saying Adonis had found love again, "I'm glad. We do have friendship love, Adonis. Be happy, my friend," came out from my heart's truest wish for him. Then I turned over, prayed, and drifted off to sleep. I never thought of him again.

Collection: Breathe in Love, Breathe out...

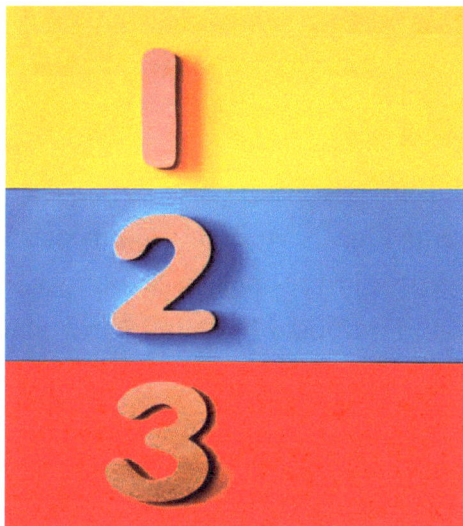

41. Jae Lune-Philippe'

My Jae Lune-Philippe is a tall and handsome boy, long and fit. Jae had distinctive physical features beautifully blending his Korean, French, and African American ancestry. Specifically, his strong jawline, that narrow nose that seemed slightly wider at his nostrils, and the shape of his eyes being almond with a very pronounced slant on the outside. His eyes are fiery amber like mine and his skin is this creamy beige tone, his face is round, and he has plump peachy tan lips.

Because I have been homeschooling them from infancy, Jae Lune is a studious boy, so far in a fifth-grade level of reading, writing, and speaking in Korean, English, and French, and learning the basics of Japanese. My introvert child is a charming little protector, a natural leader, and an analytical perfectionist. In just about everything he is organized, responsible, and meticulous. It amazes me how much I see myself in him. Jae is my learning machine always asking questions to find out the why of something. He loves nature and inspecting God's creations from animals to plant life is one of his greatest passions. He can be outside for hours drawing or writing about the grass, snowflakes, ants, birds, or something. He is so cute.

One of his favorite things so far is to read and write stories much like me and my father. The difference is he likes to make some stories into plays and then have us act them out sometimes as he directs. My screenwriter in-the-making, I suppose. However, he can be a little controlling and bossy like, you know who. Of course, his father and grandma Delphine, but I think a little of Renee Escobar is somehow up in there. It seems to come out when he is frustrated with his brother and sister not following the rules of something. It's funny to me and annoying at the same time. Occasionally, I will scold him for being overly controlling over his younger siblings, who were only minutes younger.

"Jae, you need to be a little more flexible. Your brother and sister are not like you. They have their own way of doing things."

Once this boy gave me this stoic stare with all seriousness, and said, "Mommy, they don't get to do it their way because I'm the oldest. I'm in charge. They need to do it my way, or it'll be anarchy."

(What?) "Jae, who told you that word?"

"G-G... Grandma." *(Of course, my mother!)*

Before I could get my words out, he said. "Yes, I know what it means. It means a state of disorder. No rules. Like running around screaming with no clothes on."

(This boy...) All I could do was giggle.

Jae loves music and likes to sing but prefers to play the piano and guitar, which he does with ease. I would say he is not a musical prodigy like Jae-Sung, or his father had been but more of a perfectionist. At this age he practices constantly until he does it correctly, especially complex sheet music must be played very close to perfectly for him to stop.

Sometimes Jae can sit at the window for hours watching the sky. He is very keen on nature and the details of living things. Jae writes down what he thinks and what he imagines. I see a great deal of my father and my mother in him. He is a remarkable young person.

42. Jin Soleil-Maximillian

My Jin Soleil-Maximilian is very different than his brother. He looks older and is tall with slick black hair that can have a waviness to it when it gets wet. He likes it long with a slight part and sometimes falling just below his ears. It has this natural shine to it. Jin has this porcelain-looking buttery skin tone that is just like their halmani, Min Cha. He is just about a carbon copy of Jae-Sung with his amazing almond-shaped dark deep chocolate eyes, thin light pink lips, sharp jaw, narrow nose that has a slight point when he smiles wide, and two flat dark moles above his left eye.

When we watched videos that Jae-Sung recorded for us and some older ones from his K-pop group and KR&B solo career, Jin used to get a mirror and look at himself and be a little confused for a few minutes before he would dance. Now that they are older, when his hair is too long and covers one eye sometimes it reminds me so much of his father on stage. If I'm not expecting it, I will take a double take or feel a bit startled.

A few times, Jin would notice me shocked and say so sweetly, "What's the matter mommy? Oh, I know. I look like my dad, don't I?" I would nod. Sometimes he would smile with a wink with those long lashes then say, "You can kiss me, now." I would crack up and give him a giant kiss on the cheek. *(My adorable Jin.)* Other times he would proudly announce to everyone in the room, "Yeah, I look like my dad. No, sorry, no autographs." We would roll our eyes as he came in waiving as if he was in a parade. He's a natural clown for sure. *(He makes me giggle. Silly boy.)*

Jin Soleil quickly mastered the piano, and his vocal teacher says he has an impressive two octave range at this young age. Fluent in Korean, English, and French at a fourth-grade level, he is very creative and loves picking things apart and putting them back together, as well as playing games. Jin is a fun and gregarious young man when he is not concentrating on music. He has this delightful larger-than-life laugh that fills the air and makes any around smile, especially when we are playing a game he made up. He likes to step back and let his brother play protector, but they debate and can be playfully competitive not only with each other but also with their sister. Jin usually doesn't let her win just because she is a girl. Sometimes if she does, he acts overly animated or dramatic when he loses to her. With a lot of breathing heavy and pretending to faint while saying, "she won only because she has a bigger butt, and her fingers are like huge suction cups." *(HA!)*

Jin is a true musical prodigy like his father and grandfather. At this age it really is magnificent to listen and watch him play and write music. My parents like to connect just to hear him play the piano. My son is a gifted little sparkle of joy.

Once every couple of months on a Saturday, he or his brother will lead their siblings to perform a mini musical concert in our living room, where we dress up and invite some of the family over for lunch and a show.

Jin usually wrote the music by himself or with Jolie and if there are lyrics to the piece, Jae created them from his poetry.

I always tear up when he plays something his father wrote but I'm not the only one. When Jae-Sung's good friend producer Tayler Styles, his wife, Binna and their son, Duran are here he also sheds a few tears. We don't see them as much but if their idol brother uncles, Ethan, Eric, Kris, Tonee, Vaj or Shane were in town or able at the time, they would video in and be very emotional if he played those songs too. BJ makes a point to sneak over in disguise and teach them different types of music on their father's Fazioli M Liminal piano. However, BJ spends the most time playing music with Jin.

43. Jolie Arabie Sable

Jolie Arabie Sable is my beautiful daughter. She prefers to be called Jolie (pronounced Szj-ho lee) which means pretty during the week, Arabie (pronounced Are ah bee) which means Arabian on the weekends, and then Sable (pronounced Sahb-lay) on special occasions. However, when I call her entire name, unlike her brothers, she instinctively knows she's in trouble.

Jolie is my little darling. She has this pretty creamy walnut color skin with these unique shaped eyes the color of jade green. She has these long lashes that curl naturally. So jealous! They really do make her look like a doll complementing her plump round face, deep dimples and thick, mid-back length, brown maple color hair that ripples with wavy curls. As she got older, her hair changed from straight to curly and got darker, but it still gets these radiant golden highlights after she's been in the sun for a while.

Jolie seems to be a rare balance of Jae-Sung and I and our parents. She is very creative, loves nature, and is like my father in her calmness and sense of humor. She's an ambivert like Jin and loves stories about nature and history, especially Bible stories. She can't get enough of the Caleb and Sophia series. Being fluent in English, French, and Korean, she watches the video lessons and sings along to the melodies in all three languages. Sometimes, she'll make her brothers do it and quiz them. If they get a word or lesson wrong, they owe her a coin. She has a jar halfway filled with Korean, US and French coins. *(I have no idea who taught her this.)*

My daughter really has a fascination with butterflies, whales, jungle cats and quokkas. Jolie is more of an artist and likes to draw, paint, and even sculpt with clay. She is drawn in by nature and vibrant colors as well. She can play the piano but prefers her small cello to which she plays complex musical pieces very well. When I asked her why she wanted to play it at age three she told me, "Mawmaw, it sounds like butterflies if they could sing, or we could hear them when they fly." It took me a while to find a child's cello, but Nah Min Ji got one and arranged for a music teacher just for her. At the time, I didn't notice, but now I believe she also wanted her own teacher to do something by herself. She is very independent and doesn't always like being lumped in with her brothers. I remember telling her once when I was doing her hair, "Jolie, the three of you shared food and grew together, born only minutes apart on the same day, and have the same mommy and daddy, you can't be annoyed that you are a triplet." She said, just matter of fact, "Mawmaw, I'm special. I'm the Nubian queen."

"You're a what?"

"A Nubian queen, Mawmaw. But I need to beat them up. Can uncle Kang or uncle SI teach me to fight?"

"Jolie, we don't fight. Jesus didn't beat up people. Why would you want to beat up your brothers? Who told you that you were a queen? Where did you get this?" I stopped brushing her hair into a ponytail and turned her around to look at me. Without flinching she said, "If they need a beating, I got to give it to them because I'm special. Auntie Nay-Nay said, "My body is different than theirs. I have a monkey and they just have wiener-schnitzels, so that means, I'm the queen. I know what my parts are called but after I told her Hana got a funny look on her face when we were having girl teatime and she said she had cramps. When I asked her if it was her period time, she said, "What do you know about that little one?" I said, you bleed from your uterus and vagina as part of your menstrual cycle. It is how a female body prepares for motherhood. She looked strange and didn't talk for a while. Anyway, auntie Nay-Nay said to use monkey and wiener-schnitzels from now on 'cause some people can't take knowledge from small people. Then, auntie Lola says they are supposed to protect me. It's why they are bigger. But I have to learn to beat them up, so they don't take advantage of me. Auntie Jazz has it engraved on my leather briefcase she sent me. It says, *'Nubian Queen, do your thang.'*

Listening, I kept thinking, *(I gotta stop them from having private conversations with my sorority sisters!)*

44. Kang Cheng

November 2034

When my children and I returned from our seasonal two-week trip to our home in the mountains, Nari went on her well-deserved six-week long vacation. It was just me, Kang, and the triplets. Kang volunteered to cook more so I didn't have to, and everything had been as usual when it was the five of us. After their dinner, Kang gets them all tuckered out from running round playing "Canimals" or "Pinkfong" reenactments and laughing. While I give them a bath, Kang was often on Naver checking on things. He would get the boys ready for bed while I take care of Jolie. I read to them every night, they all like to be on my giant bed, but it wouldn't be long before the three would start yawning. Usually, Jin will pull on his ear and Jolie will start sucking on the tip of her pinky finger.

Jae will just flop his head right down on a pillow. These four-year-old are so cute. That would be the sign for bedtime. I'd call Kang to come and grab two of the squirts while I took one to their room and put them down for the night. Next, I set the music system to play one of their father's recorded nighttime melody files for them. Then, I adjust to dim the star lights on the ceiling, and they drift off to sleep. After it was all quiet, sometimes Kang would go out, but he doesn't leave when Nari wasn't here.

But tonight, everything changed. After they were tucked in and sleeping and we were picking up the living room, I had a notion to get into my friend's personal life. Yeah, be a little nosy. "Kang, you're going to be fifty in a few years. When are you going to settle down?"

Picking up some blocks and putting them in a basket, he chuckled and said, "Are you saying I'm old? Technically, you will be that age before me. Hmm, maybe I should go back to calling you, ajumma."

I tossed a stuffed animal at his head, which made him get a little louder with his chuckle.

"Shut up! I'm serious. Are you seeing someone? What happened to you and Nari? You both seemed to...well. I know you didn't sleep with her. I figured you were in love, and I could be in your wedding party, just like you were in mine."

Smiling, he exhaled, handing me the end of a large blanket to begin folding it. He said very casually, "We're friends. I told you. She's a sweet girl but young. Besides, she's Nah Min-Ji's niece, which makes us family. Hey, I don't sleep with everybody, Noona." He took the blanket from my hand to put away with the basket of toys, chuckling.

I was still curious. Honestly, I was worried he didn't seem to have much of a life now that Jae was gone. I didn't know why it never hit me before now. Kang went everywhere with Jae; he was his right hand. They were Batman and Robin. He knew things I didn't get to know, even when we were together. Jae, Kang, and SI had been brothers for a long time, since they were young teenagers. I was not the only one whose life had completely changed and was now totally different. But it has been four years. *(Hmmm…)*

"Do you want some wine?" He came back with a bottle of sweet blush and two glasses.

"Uh, you know I do. That's my favorite, and who said you could have any. There is beer in there, or are you going to be sophisticated with me?"

He chuckled while pulling out the beer from under his arm for himself.

I shouted, "I knew it!" We both laughed.

I adjusted the television from the ceiling and turned to stream Netflix. I searched for an old movie to watch. After selecting the 2016 film with Park Chan-Wook called, "The Handmaiden," I sat back and took a few sips of wine. Kang sat on another couch, and said, "Oh, it's going to be a *who done it*, this time. Okay, but when it's my turn to choose— it will be an action movie."

The film had been playing for about twenty minutes, and when Kang got up to get us snacks, and then mumbled, "He said it would be like this."

(Huh?) I heard him but didn't say anything. Kang came back with a plate of fruit for me and a bag of Takis for himself and sat down.

"Thanks. What would be like what?" I said pausing the movie and glancing over at him as he was about to drop a hot chili pepper lime flavored chip in his mouth.

"What?" He said while crunching.

"I heard you say he said it would be like this. Who and what did they say?"

Flipping his hand, he tried to blow me off, "Oh nothing. Play."

I scooted to the edge of my couch and glared at him. "Kang, was it Jae? Tell me."

"Nothing really, he said married life was like this. Relaxed. He said I'd like it one day. That's all." He popped a few more chips in his mouth before sucking the red powder off his fingers.

"You aren't dating anyone are you? I mean, you don't say anything. Are you going to get married?"

"I'm private. You know that is how we were taught. K-Pop idol rules. One day, when she's ready." He motioned toward the television projection screen.

I got a little excited, and it came out in my slightly elevated voice. "Oh, this is why nothing happened with Nari. Your mother must not have met her yet then, because she would've said something to me. Yep, I'm sure she would have told me. Does she know you live here? How old is she? How long have you been seeing her? This is so exciting. Wait, wait, it's not Jazz, is it?"

"Who? Your friend, Jazz? Wow. No. That was a long time ago. I told you before, that was just for fun. Stop asking. Forget about it. Marie, start the movie." He grumbled, trying to change the subject.

"No, now, just a second. Is she Korean?"

He didn't move or look my way. *(Clue!)* "Okay, I'm gonna take that as a maybe not."

I started to bounce a little on the couch, then said, "Oh, is it uh, that model from London, what was her name? Hmmm, Shar. Yes. She was cute, Kang. Darker than me. Wasn't she African or West Indian mixed with something else? Dang, I don't remember. Yeah, she was very nice and smart. Is it her?"

He shook his head popping more chips in his mouth.

"I liked her. Shoot. Hmmm." I was still thinking, knowing I had no idea who he had dated, it could be anyone, but it was fun to guess.

He gestured for me to play the movie, but I was too busy thinking of what women I have seen him with. Not many.

"Marie... forget—"

I cut him off, "Is it the Puerto Rican and Black model in Miami?"

His head darted over at me, and he started coughing a little before he said, "How and the hell do you know about her?"

Giggling, I said, "Oops, Odette told me. She saw you with her a few times when you had gone to Eric's."

Kang rolled his eyes as he shook his head. Then he turned the bag up to his mouth to devour the chip crumbs.

(I didn't know he was dating. Seriously, he must be waiting for her to get older or something. He couldn't have seen this other girl for long. Hmmm. Why won't he tell me? This is weird.)

Kang had always been private, but something didn't seem right. My Delphine Murry Delacroix radar was pinging my brain, and I couldn't let it go.

Since his chips were gone, he got up and headed toward the kitchen. Still very curious, I asked, "Why won't you tell me?"

Passing in front of me, he said softly, "I'm hungry. How about you?"

"Kang, I thought we were close. You don't trust me?" I said as I began to feel a little hurt, that he didn't confide in me. He came back and stood right in front of me, then held me by my shoulders and exhaled.

Locked on my eyes, he said firmly, "We are very close. I trust you. I don't want to talk about it. I'm here to take care of you; you, my nephews and niece. SI has a family. There is just me. It's my job to be whatever you need. Now, what do you want me to cook? Anything in particular?"

When he said it, he didn't blink. Kang smiled, released me, and then started to walk toward the kitchen through the dining room. In that instant, it reminded me of Jae when he was telling me a secret plan. Then it hit me. *(Wait a minute.)*

"Hold it!" I shouted, pointing my finger at him.

I got his ass to stop right after taking five steps closer to the dining room. He didn't turn around to face me. He was tilting his head, pretending to look at the fish in the wall aquarium. I got off the couch and walked in front of him. He had his eyes closed not to look at me.

(You're so busted. Dude, you are not invisible. I see you!)

"Kang, look at me. You said you would be whatever I need. What exactly does that mean in the world of K-pop idol brothers secret codes and crap?"

He exhaled, opening his eyes but stared up at the ceiling. I snatched him by his black T-Shirt and pulled his body to look at me. *(Okay, I must've caught him off guard because this ninja doesn't move unless he wants to even when he is pushed. Dang, all these muscles.)*

Kang was avoiding my glare and chewing his bottom lip for a few seconds before he eventually looked at me and said, "Nothing special. Just if anything came up, I needed to be around for you." He looked so guilty. My gut was telling me he was not coming clean.

"No that's not it! Tell me right now or...or you...you will be banned and can only shadow! You'll have to move out! Never to return. Not even to visit. I mean it!"

Grumbling, he started to whine, "Aisshh (Ah-shit). Come on, Marie. It's the idol brother code."

I squinted my eyes at him, and he broke like a twig.

"Jen-jang (Damn it). Jae wanted me to step in for him if I felt you got too lonely."

"Huh?" I let go of his shirt while still looking at him in confusion. *(Did he just say what I think he said?)*

I took a couple of steps away from him, moving my head from side to side as if what he said needed to get settled in my brain first. Kang just stood there looking off into space, trying to disguise his embarrassment.

(Don't yell, the triplets are asleep. Don't yell!)

Walking into the dining room, I sat down at the table with my hand covering my mouth. Then I huffed, and said, "Let me get this straight. My husband... Jae-Sung Kim, asked you, Kang Cheng...to...to do what? To...to have sex with me?!"

"No!" He rushed over waving his hands and sat in a chair next to me at the dining room table. "No. Marie, no. Look, he asked me to step in for him when you missed him too much. You know, over time be his stand-in to give you contentment, companionship, peace… enjoyment."

I was stunned. "He what?! I don't believe this! You guys and your idol secrets!"

(What the hell was going on in that damn cabin, when I was in Seattle with Celeste.)

I couldn't move. Only my eyes followed his hands loosely holding mine on the table. I had a flashback memory and realized; Kang looked so gentlemanly like he did on my wedding day in France.

He smiled softly. Then he explained, sort of. "Marie, we discussed it. We did for over a month… a whole month before you came on the day, he..."

Kang cleared his throat and kept speaking, "Jae didn't want you to grieve forever. He was very worried about you feeling lonely. He didn't know how you would feel about his request, so he didn't tell you."

My heart was racing, I felt so many things. The strongest emotion that was ready, front, and center was unmistakably clear. I was instantly pissed off.

(How dare he arrange for me to be with someone else. Bâtard! How dare you make decisions for me without my input or even asking me, again! Punk! How dare you dictate how I am supposed to feel and what I am to do about it! I will never be done grieving, you…you…A-hole!)

"Controlling, presumptuous son of a—!" were the words that came out of my mouth as my mind was reeling. I caught myself before I finished my sentence because I love my mother-in-law and was trying not to swear these days.

Kang let go of my hands and sat back in the chair, watching me process what he was saying. Without a word, I went and grabbed the bottle of wine and turned it up for several large gulps. I continued to take it to the head, walking back into the dining room. *(I need to calmly talk; he looks a little startled.)* Finally, I sat down and placed the bottle on the table. I stared at him and then said exactly what I was thinking.

"K-pop idol brother secrets. Okay, is this the idol code to let your childhood friend pimp you out? I don't believe you would throw your life away for a code. I'm really pissed right now…for a whole lot of reasons." I said before grabbing the bottle to drink more. Kang stopped it from touching my mouth and placed it back on the table.

"Marie, you know I told him you were not my type."

I burst out laughing, but quickly covered my mouth to muffle the sound. Kang just grinned as he waved his long black eyelashes at me. Then he bit his bottom lip. It made a sucking sound when he released it, and said, "But I didn't hesitate to agree."

Within seconds, there was a distinctly different feeling in the atmosphere around us. "Quoi (What)?" I swallowed slowly and my body lightly quivered. He was serious as his dark brown eyes seemed to call to me very softly. There was no way to misunderstand the way he was gazing at me and how my insides started to warm a little.

Kang Cheng was a nice-looking man. Over the years he had bragged about being taller than an average Korean Chinese man, standing at 5'11 and a half. His face was defined and chiseled, and his eyes were round but mysterious; not in a sultry way like Jae's were but intense with power. His skin was of a darker complexion. He wore his black hair short now, but I had seen pictures of it longer. He had a large tattoo of a phoenix on one side of his chest and shoulder. Although I didn't really care for tattoos, and Jae was picture perfect with none, I admit it was rather cool looking when Kang worked out with no shirt on. Kang was a solid wall of muscles and fierce, almost terrifying, but he was gentle and kind, especially with me and my children. Yes, to me he was very handsome. Probably even more so because I didn't just look at the outside of a person. He was beautiful inside. I loved him.

While analyzing his body language, I sharply inhaled. Then exhaled slowly before speaking from my heart to my friend and dear brother. "Why would you agree to such a thing?"

He smiled, before sharing more. "Why wouldn't I? The four of you are my family. Jae-Sung and I . . . We had a friendship no one could understand. There were things that only he and I have seen and done. He was more than my best friend; he was a part of me, in a way. We were fourteen; it had been close to thirty years as brothers, always looking out for each other, supporting, protecting, pushing to be better, and enjoying the ride. He even saved my life a few times. One time, he literally took the gun out of my hand, pointed it at his chest and told me 'If you want to go, I'll go first.' Being a K-pop idol is not what people think. It is hard, very hard on a person. You know, inside. There is a level of dysfunction that almost everyone has in some form being in this industry. And the more popular you are, the more it can eat away at you. Jae-Sung and DRGN5 were ranked 9 out of the most popular K-Pop groups of all time, not just in South Korea but internationally. Marie, Jae was very close to being a shell of a man because he poured everything into his music and for his fans. But when he met you, he was determined.

Kinda obsessed to find out if you were the one meant to change his life, filling it with what was missing. And you were, Marie. You did. Do you know that I knew how he felt about you before he did? I knew why he loved you and how much. What he was willing to sacrifice for you and that love. It amazed me to see him that way; happy and at peace being with you. I was fortunate to see it all happen right in front of me. When we were on the mountain, I begged God to let me trade with him. Over and over, I asked and pleaded with Him to let me be the one dying, and not my brother. I am no one special, but Jae, he is and has a beautiful family waiting for him, three little babies and a phenomenal woman as his wife. But God didn't hear me, and every day for those few months, I had to watch my brother suffer and die. I was angry with God about it. I admit that. But all he talked about was waking up and seeing you. I didn't know what he was talking about, but he showed me things you learned from the Bible, and that was his hopeful dream. He said everything he was doing was to prepare you for when he was gone and to be happy. Why wouldn't I do whatever he asked for his family, for my family?"

Stunned, I was motionless with no words for a long time. He leaned forward, touching my hand, and confessed, "I…I won't lose both of you. I won't."

Although he had no tears, I felt his emotions as he spoke to me. In all the years I've known him, I had only seen Kang Cheng emotional with tears a few times. The first time was when I met him outside the door of our cabin rushing to see Jae-Sung. I remember another was after he passed away, and I stayed the night here alone. When Kang came to pick me up for the airport that day, he… (Uh?) I started to wonder, (We never talked that day. No, we hadn't discussed when… Wait… Is this because of that?)

After exhaling I just asked, "Kang, is this why you don't date? Why you are just here all the time? It...it's not just because of that breach either, is it? Is it because of what happened before... When you found me. That's it. Isn't it? Oh, Kang. Don't you think I'm okay? It was right after Jae died. That's been so long ago. I am alright, honestly. You don't have to worry."

He said with conviction, "I'm not taking any chances."

"Kang, my studies; my hope for the future gives me the right mindset for me and my children to serve Jehovah to the best of my ability. I'm better. Can't you see that? I won't hurt myself. I'm okay." I reached out and held his cheek for a moment, locking eyes and smiling at him before I slowly sat back across from him.

Kang nodded before sharing his thoughts and feelings about the time right after Jae passed away and I stayed in our home here alone. "I didn't listen to my instinct. Something told me not to leave you alone. But you were so calm and insisted you were alright. When I came in to take you to the airport to fly back to Seattle the next morning, and saw you sprawled over the bed in only a robe, not moving; and there were empty bottles of wine and all those pills on the floor. I shook you... You didn't move... I thought..." He paused a few seconds with eyes closed, and seemingly taking himself back in time.

Then he looked back at me and said, "Standing in the cold shower trying to wake you up, again I was begging God, but this time not to let you die. I would have no one... left. A person can harm themselves or others especially when they are not thinking clearly, deeply depressed or in anguish. I knew that it only takes a split-second to do something that could end a life or change it forever. I've been in many dangerous and life-threatening situations, but nothing made me afraid. Not like that. Before the breach... At the time, I don't think I had ever been so terrified. But then it happened again, after we finally found you in the cave, and you wouldn't wake up." Kang nervously rubbed his hands together before leaning his head back and blowing out hard from his nose.

I watched him and when his eyes opened to find me, I said, "Kang, I'm sorry, you thought I had taken those sleeping pills; I must have knocked the bottle over. I didn't take any. I drank all that wine though."

Chuckling, "Yeah, I got that after you threw up everywhere in the shower. I probably shouldn't have been bouncing you up and down under the water."

We both snickered as we remembered that part. Then I got a thought, *(Wait? Did he?)*

"Wait, did you see me naked?" I said, looking at him suspiciously.

His face stretched up, his eyes grew wider, and his voice was slightly higher than normal. "Marie, I can disassemble and reassemble several types of automatic weapons with my eyes closed. Uh, who do you think dressed you?"

"Oh my god! That's right!" Gasping, I hit him as he snickered while covering his mouth with his fist.

A few minutes later, Kang added more, "The breach, Marie. I mean… You and the triplets were gone. I had to find you, all four of you, and make sure everyone was safe. I won't let anything happen to my family, not ever. Do you understand what I mean? That is how important you are to me. I need to be here always. Protecting you. You need me too and it's what I must do. Just let me do it."

Taking a few deep breaths, I thought of what words I should say. When they came to me, I told him, truthfully, "Kang, I'm deeply touched that you would want to be Jae's stand in. But even if you tried, no one could replace him. I'll miss him until the very second, I see him again. I won't ever stop loving him. I want you to be happy and be my brother. Oh, and keep being the triplet's Chinese Korean sensei. Ha, ha." He laughed when I said that. But his smile quickly faded, and he stared at me with an intensity and seriousness I had never seen before. Then he said, "I want to marry you, Marie. Not just because he asked me. I'm not him, I can't be him, but I do love you. You guys are my family. I can't lose you and the triplets. I can't."

(Oh, my heart...this man is so...but he's afraid we will leave him...this must be why.)

I stood and kissed his cheeks, then said, "Oh, Kang, I love you. I do. You are my rock. I couldn't do any of this without you. I need you in my life, always. You don't have to marry me just for me to stay close to you. I'm never going to abandon you, Kang. You are my family too. The triplets adore their big uncle. You deserve real love in your life, just like Jae and I had. You don't feel that way about me."

Kang lowered his eyes, then licked his lips slowly. When he looked at me again, his stare was so magnetic. I got a chill from the intense vibes he was sending. *(Uh, oh.)* Kang's voice got significantly lower when he said, "Marie, I've known you for many years now. I've watched you for a long time. You're a very strong woman. I care about you not like any other woman. Honestly, I don't know what that kind of love feels like. I only watched it between the two of you. Marie, I didn't think of you for myself, but always the best piece for Jae-Sung. But he isn't here anymore. We both miss him. But don't misunderstand, my feelings for you are not because of that. Jae must have thought I could make you happy in his absence. Why would he make me swear to love you the way he did? Why would he tell me his private thoughts about you? How deeply you feel, give and love. Why would he tell me the things that excite you and what to avoid because they make you sad? Jae wanted me to do this, Marie. I want to do this not just for him or you but for me. I've learned how to love you the way you need. I want to be the triplet's stepfather, raise them with you. If you're not comfortable with me making love to you right now, we can just be married on paper. In time, I will take you beyond ecstasy in ways you've never imagined. But until then, I'll protect you and this family like always. Alright?"

(Marry him? What's he saying to me? Fix this! Why... Why am I so hot right now?)

Goosebumps rippled over the skin of my arms. My eyes filled with tears, while my heart was beating so fast. Small droplets of perspiration formed underneath my breasts and glued me to my bra. I had never heard him speak this way, not ever. He was vulnerable and it moved me to tears.

(Oh, what do I do? What do I do? Alright... I know. Reason with him. Tell the truth.)

Scooting to the edge of my chair, my body moved closer between his parted legs as he sat leaning back facing me. Kang was breathing so deeply; I could feel his breath on my skin as his eyes carefully watched me. Easing my hands over his, we instantly locked eyes. My chest rose and fell as I felt something creep up inside me. It had been years since I had felt any lure of temptation, but I recognized it growing at rapid speed at that very moment. I swallowed, and whispered, "Kang..."

His voice was low and airy. Almost sultry. "Yes..."

"Could you be with a woman that you knew truly loved someone else? Could you live your life knowing she was only thinking of him every minute of every day? When she is lying next to you at night, she's dreaming only of him... Honestly, Kang could you be in a

381

marriage and never touch your wife, or be touched intimately by her? Is that really what you want?"

"Yes, if she is you. Marie, I want..."

I leaned forward to seal his lips with my fingers as tears began gathering in my eyes. *(Why is this happening? Oh, father help me!)* I felt my body weaken a little, thinking about the physical comfort he was offering me. But I shook my head and spoke reality's truth.

"Wait... But don't you want to have a woman to see you the way I see Jae? To share her inner self with you and you with her. Don't you want to know she is all yours? Your very own treasure to protect, adore, surprise, love and grow with? I don't want to hurt you. Really, I don't, but I can't marry you. I love you. You're my brother, my family, but there is no room for anyone else, not like he was. I'm full of love for my children, Jehovah God, his son Jesus, the brothers and sisters around the world, family, and friends. My hope for the future keeps me solid. My faith is strictly focused on the new world and not right now. I won't let you be a sacrificial martyr because of a crazy idol code promise you made with my dying husband. No matter how good his intentions. You don't love me like that. You can't! Please understand. I care about you deeply, but not the way you truly deserve in a partner. I..."

I took a breath and stopped talking. Then I smiled at him. Kang stood up, guiding me to rise. Affectionately his left hand cupped my face and held it. Kang brushed the tear tracks from my cheek with his fingers. Looking down at me, his eyes seemed to search through mine, and I felt increasingly nervous when he said, "I wanted to wait until you were ready for me, but I can't pretend anymore. Marie..."

My lips parted to speak, but before I could, he whispered, "...I love and want all of you. The way you are, right now." Kang reached for my waist and pulled me toward him. I seemed to float as if I was no longer in control of my body. I felt warm all over, and I didn't know why. Soft bells were going off in my head every time I blinked. I started to pant a little when he slid the back of his index finger over the outline of my lips and along the side of my jaw. Kang's dark and mysterious eyes grabbed me and pulled me into him. I gasped as he kept talking. "We don't have that same kind of love, but we have love. I think of holding you in my arms and feeling the silkiness of your skin against mine. He told me how to please you, and I want to, Marie. I want to."

(He feels so...) I couldn't escape his magnetic stare. I trembled as he inched his mouth closer to my lips. *(No...don't kiss me.)* Blinking quickly, I paused my intake of air, when he said, "As my wife, I will make love to you... and only you will have all of me. I'll be gentle, just the way you like. I know the parts of your inner thigh that you want me to nibble on." *(Oh...)* "Marie I know where to lick your neck, your back, and when to squeeze the firm cushions on your body. I know which queues you give to go deeper, and which levels will make you scream the loudest." *(Oh, shit.)* "I think about being with you in every way. Making you happy. Marie, that is what I want for my life. I want you. You are the woman I want."

(Oh, my god.) I was getting weaker by the second, and very soggy with each word he spoke and each stroke of his fingers on my skin, much like a graham cracker being constantly dipped in milk. I was soaked. It had been such a long time. I wasn't dead down there. I wanted to be, but I wasn't. When his thumb traced along my bottom lip the tip of his tongue simultaneously wet his lips in slow motion. It made me quiver and pant. I was crumbling like an old sandcastle on the beach when the tide came in. Kang was the tide. A crash of complex emotions took over me. My tears were constant like raindrops, but I said nothing. What could I say? I was conflicted. Underneath my T-shirt, the darkest points of my breasts hardened as his body came closer. Subconsciously, my head shook, and I moaned

no, while the smoothness of his lips breezed across mine, only to tilt his head and firmly pressed them onto my cheek for several seconds. Trembling, I just stood there. Kang broke our eye connection and turned slightly to glance behind me. He seemed to be admiring the beautiful paradise mural Jae had painted in front of him. Cascades of tears drizzled down my face, I whimpered as my mind went blank. Held securely within his arm wrapped around me, my body gradually softened like room temperature butter. As his other hand caressed the small of my back it caused a tingling sensation up my spine for the few seconds of silence.

Suddenly, Kang reconnected with my eyes, and seconds later he said, "Paradise…" but then he paused with no expression hovering over my mouth with his. Instantly, I tensed up feeling his kiss was coming, and I couldn't stop it. Did I even want to stop it? I didn't know. My mind was empty. He began inching to my lips, he stroked my chin whispering, "Oh, sweet Marie…" I gasped. Then seconds later, he licked his lips right before he said, "You do realize you could have just told me no."

Startled, my eyes rapidly blinked to clear the glossiness of tears that still fell and the sound of "Huh" escaped from my throat. He began lowly chuckling and shook his head. Kang loosened his hold from around me. Confused, I stepped back from his arms and sat back down on a dining room chair.

"What? What?" This one word was all I could get out. Not understanding why, he found the situation humorous.

"Marie, you really are an amazing, phenomenal woman. I love you very much."

I grabbed my head and tried to make myself come back to my senses, I said, "Kang, please I —"

Smirking, he waved his hand to cut me off, and kept talking, "My brother gave me explicit instructions. I have completed my task. The words I am supposed to say next are, 'Chantal-Marie Delacroix-Kim, you have been successfully pranked by your loving husband Jae-Sung Kim, your idol king, as payback for what you did to him in Paris."

My mouth flew open as he slid the bottle of wine over to me. I stared at him dumbfounded. Kang snickered and closed one of his eyes, waiting for me to swing at him. I was still in shock and had questions to clarify what was actually happening.

"You mean… You…you don't love me? He… He didn't tell you to marry me?"

After letting out a grunt, he said, "Are you kidding? Jae said I'm to chase anyone away and make sure you wait for him to wake up." He leaned back wiping his mouth with his hand and chuckling.

Trying to compute everything, I asked, "Pranked me? Wait, what was true and what wasn't? I'm so confused."

Kang positioned himself tilting his torso forward, and said, "Everything was true." He paused only a second and continued, "Except the part about me lusting for you, knowing the intimate things you like, and him asking me to marry you. See pranked."

What he said took a few minutes to register in my brain, then I shouted, "No!" and slugged him a few times in his iron hard chest as he chuckled like an evil villain.

"I… I don't believe you pranked me! You, damn K-Pop idol brothers. What a punk! He's a punk too! I was really upset thinking you were not going to take no for an answer. I hate you, Kang Cheng! How long was this supposed to go on?" I said huffing in disgust with an undertone of giggles that increased into full laughter while he answered.

"Well, he asked me to wait a few years but to deliver it when you were in a more settled routine of life. To be truthful, the breach set me back emotionally for a bit, but after a while, I remembered what I was supposed to do. I would have held out longer, but Nari is getting anxious, so I had to do it now."

Taking a large swig of wine from the bottle, I swallowed, then asked, "Nari? What does she have to do with this?"

"Our marriage date is in a few weeks, and she has been bugging me to do it so she can talk to you about it. I almost took it a bit further, you know, grabbing you and pleading all this hot lust and desire to be inside you, but you started crying and feeling sad. Honestly, you looked a little afraid, so I had to show my joker card."

"I…I hate you. I hate you so much right now! But he got me… Oh, you both got me good!" I admitted defeat, exhaling in relief and rubbing my eyes.

"Not my plan. It was all his. He said I had to do it and be convincing because I helped you in Paris. My original plan was a little bondage, but I dismissed that thought quick. I couldn't scare you with my equipment, especially after what happened. Jae said I could do whatever I wanted to get you to believe me as long as I didn't kiss you on the mouth or touch you… you know inappropriately. He was adamant about that part. Hey, yeah… he can't ever know about the shower thing or the breach and kissing you when you woke up…not ever!"

"You…you did kiss me. Didn't you?"

"It wasn't a real kiss. I was just so… I mean, you woke up. I was… excited. But it doesn't matter. Jae-Sung won't make an exception. He…he can't know. I'm serious. Yeah, I'm not a pluviophile. I like the sunshine. I don't want it to ever be like that with my brother. No matter what, I'll be aplomb but still, he can't ever know about any of it."

"Deal! I bet he didn't want you to kiss me. Controlling much, Jae-Sung! I'm going to write this in my journal. I can't believe this. Hold on, did you just use Nari's flashcard words in a sentence? Ha! She's seriously rubbed off on you. She knew the entire time! Oh, she's so gonna get it! Wait…did you say, marriage date? Oh, you do love her. I knew it! A wedding when…when?!"

"Awww, you did hear that. Ha! I'll let her tell you. We had to cool it so the prank could work. I'm going to call her tonight and tell her to come back tomorrow. She has been waiting at her parents' house."

"Wait… So, she didn't go to Thailand with her friends for vacation? What a little stinker!"

I jumped up and hugged him. Kang didn't let go as he stood up. We squeezed each other for several minutes with an undertone of continued snickering.

Kissing his cheeks repeatedly, then I told him, "I love you, you ninja-punk!"

Grinning, he whispered, "I know. I love you too, phenomenal noona. I love you, too."

A portrait of Kang at 34
Painted by Min Cha

Days before his wedding ceremony, Kang Cheng was directed to meet Jet in Min Ji's office. A short time later, an angered Kang asked, "Seonsaengnim, jeongmal hwag-indoen geongayo (Teacher, is it really confirmed)?" Pointing to an encrypted document and several sheets of paperwork he had read and laid on the conference table.

At the very moment, Min Ji arrived in his office, Kang had already consumed a glass of whiskey and paced the room several times shouting obscenities. While seated next to a window, Jet was applying pressure to nerve points on Kang's neck to lower his rising blood pressure and calm his fury.

"Kang you must know your duty. Once you marry, you will be the head of a family with royal blood ties. Traditional honor codes outlined by our ancestors are strict. You cannot deviate from the responsibility given to you by Sung-Ho Hak as the replacement for his grandson. He knew all and chose you. For reasons you do not know, why Jae-Sung was chosen and not his sons, Han-Gyeol and Shung-Ho. I will tell you, neither have sons, and that is what is known. But long-ago Han behaved dishonorably. He forced relations with a young girl who was not yet fourteen. He was twenty. Although the criminal charges and his punishment are privacy sealed, he was ineligible because of it. In his youth, Shung was involved with an older married woman. The politician's wife became pregnant from the affair. Upon finding out her condition, the politician killed his wife and himself after driving off a cliff. Being the cause of this tragedy, Shung too was ineligible to lead the family."

As Kang slouched in the chair listening to facts that he had never known about Jae-Sung Kim's uncles, his mind became clearer as to why his best friend and idol brother had been under so much pressure since they were fourteen. While Jet slowly removed his fingers from the veins in Kang's neck, Min Ji reclined taking quick sips of his freshly poured whiskey from his secret bar. Then he continued to give facts and instructions.

"Jae-Sung was the last of his pure bloodline. Kang, you are older than your brother. However, if you did not exist, SI would never have been chosen due to his unclean past. You know this to be true. You cannot fail. Tradition requires different handling in this instance. You or your people cannot hold guilt, dishonor our ancestors, or the path set before you. The sacrifice is made and therefore necessary for safety."

"Honorable uncles... How do I... lead such a family as this? I am not pure nor am I honorable as was my brother, Jae-Sung. I cannot take back things I have done." Kang said with sincere yet water-filled eyes.

Jet, his master teacher spoke first, "Before you were my highest pupil. I have been proud. But now your path is no longer as I have taught you, Kang Cheng."

Min-Ji nodded and said to him clearly, "As I said, it was all known before you were chosen. Refocus your skills as a leader of these men, women, and children and not of an elite group of specialists. There is no one that can take this role if you fail to fulfill it or fall short, while his sons are not of age. Kang, you cannot allow your vengeance to invalidate what has been put in place. It is an honor for you and your mother as a Chinese Korean man. Do not destroy Jae-Sung's family because of your pride. Control your feelings and channel them toward your responsibilities."

Humbled and no longer filled with anger, Kang bowed to Nah Min-Ji and Jet, showing his understanding of how things were to be and that his ancestral responsibilities were his top priority.

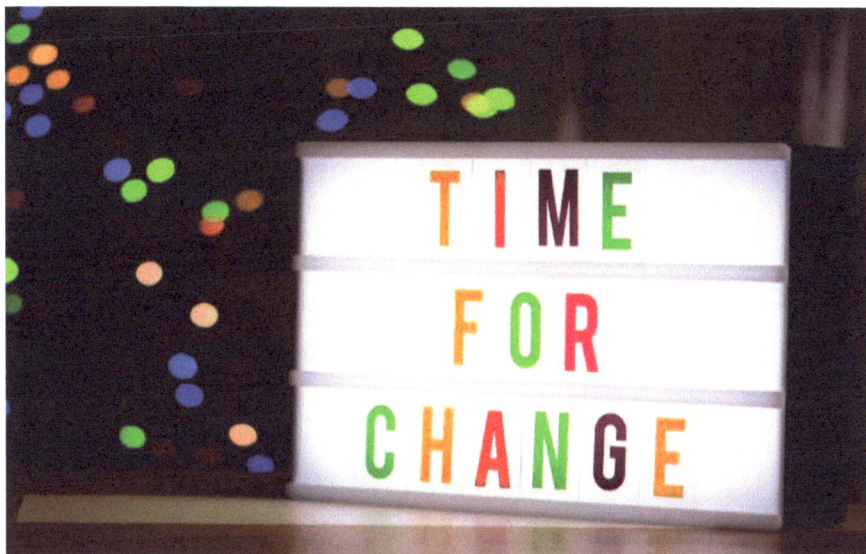

45. Shifting Tide

After a couple of one-day Sony business trips to Japan, conference calls, and another weeklong trip to New York, I began to feel a growing sense of disconnection from my international director career. My priorities had shifted. It didn't have the same fulfillment I felt raising my children. It was odd. I kept asking myself, "Why don't I love doing this? What's wrong with me?"

I was older, and I believe the experience being kidnapped taught me some things it took a while to settle on my heart. Life was not promised, and anything could happen at any time. I started to ask myself:

"Do I want to be on some plane missing this great moment with my babies?"

"What happens after we move to France?"

"How much time is reviewing data for these multi-million-dollar music and entertainment projects taking?"

"Could I be doing something else with this time?"

"Why am I even doing this? I don't need the income…"

Then it came to me. It was what I had been trained to do. Routine. Tradition. My circumstances are different now. I was holding a spot for someone else to be in and do well. I can just retire. Wow under fifty and retired, but not slowing down. Just not working for Sony Music Entertainment. I made the decision.

"When Ayanna comes for the quarterly debrief, I will talk to her. In person is better than phone or email. Sony has been good to me all these years. I want to let them know how much I loved working for them." I planned out what I would say and wrote it down right then.

"I need to do something special for… Something a dragon would do for another dragon as a farewell for Sony Japan Senior Director Satoshi Senko and his wife, Yukiko. Yes, and his board members need gifts. But Satoshi-san was privately very kind and generous to me. If not for him, I wouldn't have ever seen Jae-Sung again after we first met. That's funny… it was his tickets to the auction in Seoul that he gave me for trimming half a billion yen from that music arena project. I owe him, and he doesn't even know it."

I needed to plan something very nice for him before my departure and reached out to my father to get ideas and perhaps get his help. A few days later, I had the perfect gift for them.

"Pawpaw, were you able to see if you still had those rare bottles of 1996 Dom Perignon Rose Gold Champagne from Grand-père Delacroix's private collection?"

"Oui, I checked. There were two left, but he privately gave those expensive bottles along with many others in his collection to your cousin, Kristoff. I asked and he said of course, you could have them and anything in the collection that you wanted."

"Oh, he's so sweet. I only need one. I will have the Olivia Reigel Dogwood flute sets ready for you to pick up and combined with it to security ship directly to them in Japan. Merci, Pawpaw."

During my last business trip to Japan, I met privately with Satoshi-san and Yukiko at their compound outside of Tokyo for a lunch farewell. Trey did not come as requested. They were surprised and very grateful for the beautiful gifts from France, they had received three weeks prior. We were to speak informally. I was happily surprised to see his mother again, Mayumi's smiling face and warm welcome. She had always been a sweetheart on the two occasions I had met her, informally.

Bowing I spoke in Japanese, "Kisha no o yakunitatete kōeidesu." (It has been my honor to be at your service.)

"No, dear girl, it has been my honor." Satoshi Sanko spoke in English. Something he never does. "We are informal today. Please sit."

Engaging in a friendly tea before lunch was the highlight I wasn't expecting. After which we enjoyed an array of fresh seafood and traditional dishes. Over the afternoon, we casually discussed memories from our years of working together, and he expressed his delight that I returned for a time.

Satoshi had his favorite green tea cakes served up and several packed away for me to take home. *(My children will love these!)*

It happened while enjoing dessert and fruit, the connfession period. Satoshi-san and his wife shared with me very candidly that they both had several discussions about me after the first time I corrected him with facts during a private meeting with Sony International Directors.

"He was very angry but also amused." Mayumi said smiling at her son. "I told my son, you must hear and see without ears or eyes. This girl sounds very rare but very familiar."

Satoshi-san followed up with, "I felt strange. You are a young woman. American and African but you spoke with such honor and showed me the most respect. I liked that. I was curious about what you would do next, so I intentionally did things to test you. You never failed to do as I would have done in each situation. I said to my wife, she must be our child from another life source because she acts so much like me."

We giggled about that. I bowed to respect him and show aprecation for his kind words. *(I figured early on you were testing me. Ha!)*

More was disclosed to me after that conversation that blew my mind. I sat stunned as he told me more things from years ago that I had no knowledge of.

It turned out that after a few years partnering, Satoshi-san knew more about me than I knew about him. When he told me, "Over the years, Nah Min Ji and I have exchanged many things." I think I wet my pants a little when I hiccupped and choked at the same time. *(Huh?)*

"You talked about me? I did not know you... you had a connection to NM Entertainment Company's owner." My eyes must have been wide as saucers because Yukiko tapped my hand. He smiled in an almost devious looking way, and I felt warm all over. Minutes later, he said, "Our association is private. As with many things, we cannot always communicate parts of ourselves to others. But I will say, we have exchanged much about you long before your wedding day to his adopted nephew."

I gasped and held my breath for several seconds from the shock. When I spoke, it came out garbled. "You... you... have.... married... his..." I took a breath then expressed clearly, "I do not understand."

He bowed before telling me more, "It is not known to others, young dragon, but I often informed him when you would be in Japan. Years ago, it had been privately arranged for me to obtain tickets for you to attend an exclusive event during the end of a showcase tour of former K-Pop idols."

My heart felt as though it had burst open, and I screamed, "Satoshi-san!"

Simultaneously, my mind flooded with flashes of when the diva dolls came with me to Japan. Renee was pregnant with Christopher. Tangee and Lola weren't even married… and Jazz got her first whiff of Kang Cheng. *(Oh, my god!)* I didn't even know in advance he was performing. Then a flip to a memory of hearing his voice sing Arabian Sand in public came to me, while small tears slid from the corners of my eyes. *(Oh, the afterparty… and we…)* Giggling commenced after the minutes of purposeful quiet, to allow me the time to process what was said, I'm sure.

Over the lunchtime meal, a few more details of the behind-the-scenes maneuvering between these powerful businessmen and their wives was revealed. The two had crafted a plan that if there was an opportunity to put Jae and I in the same room they would, just to see what would happen. Min Ji confessed to him that Jae was happier and more balanced when he had been involved with me in some way. Satoshi-san admitted to him that he and his wife had grown accustomed to having a personal interest in me having a joyful life, and he often gave me gifts of appreciation for my work and dragon spirit.

With tears and laughter, my farewell lunch with Senior Sony Director Satoshi Sanko and his wife, gave me comfort and peace in ways I never could have imagined before this day. "Shin'ainaru doragon-sama, hontōniarigatōgozaimashita, (Thank you very much, dear dragon) Satoshi-san." Oh, I will miss you.

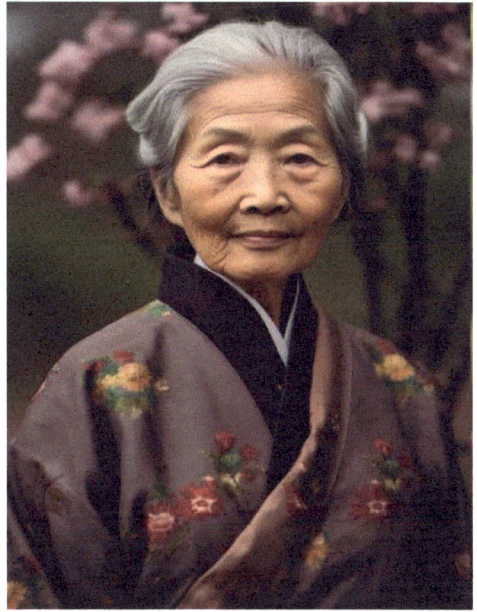

Yukiko Sanko & her mother-in-law Mayumi

Sony Japan's Senior Director
Satoshi Sanko aka "Dragon"

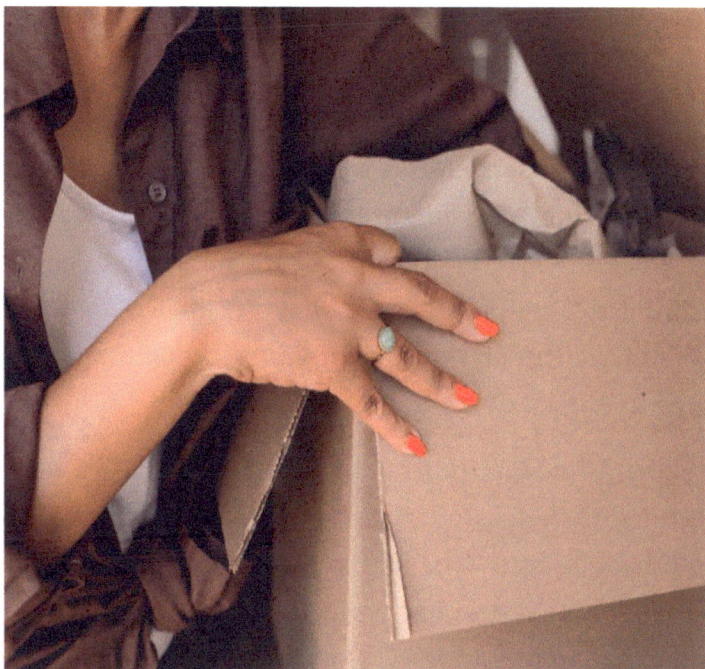

46. Ready, Set

The way I was raised, it seemed totally normal to spend a bunch of money and make the move from living in Hannam, South Korea to Lyon, France an amazing over the top once in a life-time adventure. Time was flying by so quickly now, it seemed. This year I'd been so busy, I couldn't remember the last time I saw Dong Hyun. Min Cha and I talked regularly, but when she arranged to see her grandchildren, it still had been through Kang not me. I've been pretty much out of the transaction altogether. I assumed because after he got married, he was the head of the family, and it was easier. Kang and Nari would take the triplets to our mountain home, and she met them there, staying for days.

(She loves being outdoors camping with them... just like her son. Well, it's not really roughing it, Jae did say I remodeled it to be a hotel. Ha!)

Aunt Teng, Soo and Hana have come over about twice a month to help me pack for our trip. I love their company. SI had more responsibilities, so I hadn't seen him a lot, either. Come to think of it, Min Ji I had not seen since Nari's wedding day. I do pass along photo gifts for him and his wife when I'm at my quarterly legal meetings with Chris and Eddie. Nari tells me they are so happy to get photos of Jae, Jin, and Jolie. But I personally haven't talked to them. Times were definitely different than when I first brought my children to South Korea in August of 2030.

Our flights, the ship, hotels, and connecting plans were all set. Travel documents, funds and security were in place, and we were on the countdown for our trip in the summer. Since my handsome boyfriend, Christopher Escobar was in school and wanted to see us, Renee and I worked it out for a Delta Sorority Sisters meet-up on our way to Europe. "I'm so excited." I called to chat with her, but she wasn't home.

"I'm glad you changed it so we can come in the summer. I want to see you, auntie." Christopher said as his voice cracked from low to high and back down to low again. *(Oh, someone is growing up...)*

"Sure, you do. I think you want to see Jolie and Hana more...maybe Emelia. Ha!"

"No, no... I mean, I do but they don't hold a candle to my beautiful god mother."

"Oh, you are so fresh, boy. Do you want to marry me?"

"Yes ma'am. Is that allowed?"

"Nope. But you can get extra kisses from me. I love you, Christopher. You're my favorite boyfriend."

"Aww auntie Rhee, you make me feel so weird. No one calls me Christopher but you."

"I named you, so I can say it. What do your friends call you?"

"I'm C-note or just Chris."

"C-Note… like in music?"

"Not really, more like Carlton from The Fresh Prince."

We laughed.

"You are not like that character, except for being very studious. You know how to dance. Ha!"

Chuckling, he said, "I'm a little both Carlton and Will, dad says. Uh, auntie, can you tell Hana I got her email, but I've been kinda busy. Tell her I'll write back soon, I didn't forget, okay? Yeah, uh, I'll tell mom you called."

"Oh, so, you've been writing to her but not me. I see." I snickered seeing him start to blush. "Sure, I will tell her. Thanks sweetie, love you. Be good. See you soon."

My boyfriend-nephew
Christopher Escobar

On Thursday, June 14, 2035, it was less than a week before my family was to board a flight to Los Angeles and meet up with the group for a few days. I was summoned to NM Entertainment in the late afternoon. I expected a car to be sent for me, but I heard, "I'll drive you," from Kang, who had just brought in some more toiletries for Nari to squeeze in one of their suitcases.

Min Cha, and aunt Teng Cheng were there and stayed with Nari, and Jusan and my children. We were living like visitors since our home in Hannam-dong was pretty much sealed up like our mountain cabin until we returned to South Korea. I had not planned on when that would be. Maybe during a long school break or next summer. We camped out in the living room and got takeout for meals because it was just easier.

When we arrived, Chris was the only attorney in Min-Ji's office. I knew that Eddie had been on vacation with his wife and assumed they weren't yet back from New Zealand. Trey was already seated when Kang and I entered and sat down. I was a little surprised to see him there. However, I smiled, and he grinned a little.

Exchanging greetings and a smile, I sat and waited. When I looked over at Min-Ji, the powerful and successful businessman, owner of the multi-billion-dollar music company, NM Entertainment, the idol uncle of my late husband, and the witness to our wedding in Korea he had glossy watery eyes. He dabbed them with his monogrammed handkerchief. "Samchon (uncle)" slipped past my lips from the surprise of seeing his emotions. The room was still. I glanced around the table and noticed Kang, Trey, Jet, and Chris had lowered heads. It was unusual that none of them would look at me. My gut started to bubble, and I suddenly felt a little queasy.

Finally, Nah Min Ji cleared his throat and spoke. His voice was low as he delivered his message in English. "Daughter-in-law, I am honored to be your family. You have been a colorful rainbow. I have felt your brightness in the sky of Jae-Sung. Thank you for bringing love and happiness to him... and to us."

Automatically my mouth grinned wide, and I giggled. He took a pause from speaking. No one else moved or made a sound. Instinctively, the mood told me there was going to be a word coming like But or And from him. *(There's more...)*

Min Ji stood motioning for me to come and sit next to him. I moved to the closest chair at the conference table. He had my full attention. Unsuccessfully, I attempted to read his mind waiting for his next statement. *(What is it? This can't be just because we're moving…)*

In an informal and fatherly way, Min Ji reached for my hand and held it as he said, "I am telling you these things only because you and your children will be leaving to live in France. Everything will be different once you go. We will no longer have close contact, as we had these years… and… I am sad for that. But it is necessary for safety protocol." I nodded. Having a full understanding of the South Korean idol world, codes, protocols, and security, I was not surprised. *(I'm sad too.)*

He continued, "Kang Cheng is the head of Kim Jae-Sung's family, and all things must go through him or your attorney Chris Hwang. There is no need for two attorneys to oversee your legal matters and financial accounts connected to NM Entertainment. Eddie Yun has been reassigned. Chris volunteered first to stay with you, but he also won the three rounds of rock, paper, scissors."

I snorted and heard several faint low chuckles from the men across the table on my left. "Chantal-Marie, I decided to tell you something that is not to be repeated outside of this room. The situation is resolved, and you need not fear anything more."

(Huh?) My body tensed and my heart started to pound with heavy thuds. He kept talking, "We uncovered important information after your mother-in-law brought concerns to me. It was a private matter to be discussed between life-long friends. Dong-Hyun's abusive behavior increased to a point that Min Cha came to me privately. We discussed some past matters and set protocols in place for her protection."

"What? I had no idea. She never said anything to me…" *(What is going on? Wait Marie, don't panic, wait.)* I closed my mouth quickly.

Min Ji continued speaking and holding my hand, "When I spoke to Dong-Hyun, he shared a secret past rivalry with Ji Hoon, and his winning away Min Cha after he died. He made a few comments about his distrust and growing anger feeling unappreciated by his sacrifices, that alerted me to have Jet investigate further. We discovered through anonymous money transfers, archived surveillance video, and other evidence that the kidnapping and plot to murder you had been orchestrated and funded by Dong Hyun."

I froze hearing what he said. All the blood felt as though it had rushed out of my body by way of my feet. It was instantly cold, and I had a slight ringing in my ear. Min Ji stopped speaking and tugged at my hand. For several minutes, my body felt as though I had been locked inside an Artic glacier with no sunlight or escape.

"Marie…" Trembling my head turned to him. Nervously my eyes blinked without focusing on anything. But within seconds, Min Ji's dark eyes fastened onto mine and held on to me so I wouldn't panic. This powerful man stared at me with great tenderness while softly stroking my hand with his thumb.

"Marie…" Hearing my name again, my mind came back into the room. I took a deep breath, and he continued to reassure me. "No need to fear. It has been resolved."

(Resolved like… gone?) From the past, I had a feeling I already knew what he meant, and my heart sank a little. *(Don't ask Marie…it's not something you could control. Don't feel and don't ask.)* I nodded and kept my mouth sealed shut.

"You have questions, I am sure. But the answers we cannot tell you. Know the fact that we in this room have secured Jae-Sung's family's safety."

Without thinking it through, the words just creeped out like a whisper, "Min Cha... Alright?"

"All is as it should be." He said it nodding and with a slight smile while patting the top of my hand. He gestured for Jet to bring me some tea. Then he instructed me to drink while papers were brought and sorted into a few piles on the table for me to sign.

Shortly thereafter, we were on our ride home. I felt strange thinking about things Min Ji had said about Jae's stepfather. The man was my father-in-law. My mind thought back to the last time I had seen him, and it had been well-over a year. Things were going on, and I didn't even know it. More secrets. I started to fidget sitting next to Kang as he silently drove. *(Did he... kill someone? I didn't do it, but I can't be around people like this... It's wrong... a crime... a sin... no matter how wicked they are... you can't kill people. Heavenly father, what do I do?)*

Just ten minutes of silence, and as if Kang could read my thoughts, he reached over to touch my hand. I pulled away. Not once did I look at him, but I heard him sigh. Then out of nowhere he said, "Ask me... only this once. Ask me. I'll tell you the truth."

I hesitated, but it came out fast and slurred, "Dead. Did you kill him? Did you? Murder Don—"

He cut me off, "No." I took a breath as he reached to hold my hand. Then he said it again. "No. Marie. I did not."

"But he... he's dead though. Isn't he?" He moaned, and I gasped, covering my mouth with my free hand. Kang volunteered facts he wasn't to ever speak about, but I was glad he broke this code for me to know.

"Marie, he is gone. Don't ask questions you don't really want to know the answer to. Reassure your mind and heart that I committed no crime or violated any law of heaven. But I will tell you, if we had known the truth at the time, I would not be speaking on the matter. No one could have stopped me from taking him out. No one. But now, I'm the head of this family. I cannot be as I was. My priority is to protect and honor my family, so for you, the triplets, and Min Cha, he no longer exists. But I had to change myself. After hearing what you believe and teaching the amigos, having talks with my brother and my mother. They have shown me things about God, that we didn't learn growing up. I could not be the one to take a life now having this responsibility and knowing these things."

I glanced at him as he spoke very calmly while squeezing my hand. "Oh, not you." I said it with a long sigh of relief. *(…but…)*

"But… Did…did Trey? Jusan? Or…"

He shook his head before I could name them all. Then replied, "The ancestral code is to resolve the matter at a level beyond those around you."

My mind flashed with who it could be. *(Jet? Min Ji. It must be through Min Ji. He said no contact anymore. Ask Marie. Ask.)*

"Is this why he said we won't have contact ever again?"

Kang's silence told me the answer. Turning away from my constant stare to face the road, I told him, "I understand. Thank you for telling me without telling me." He squeezed my hand and securely held it until we arrived in the guarded parking garage of my building. I had lots of feelings about what happened, anger, fear, guilt, sadness but not joy. Someone was dead. Quietly I only thought of the facts. Like Jae-Sung's aunt and cousins, it wasn't my fault he died. They killed him not me. It wasn't anything I could have known about or prevented even. It was a protection not to know. I prayed for guidance on how to feel and forgiveness if in some way it was my fault. Then once we left the car, it was forgotten. My heart was even more relieved that we were moving away.

Collection: Released Trapped Air

47. Adventure

"Girl, this is crazy!"

"I'm so excited!"

"Of course, you are, cow. You're a weirdo."

"Don't be mean to my Tangee girl."

"No, I am not putting that on."

"SI you and Kang have to wear the mouse ears. See everybody is doing it!"

"You lost the bet. All males must wear them."

"Hey, if you don't, we will add more to the penalty! Let's make them hold Tinkerbelle's wand, it lights up!"

"Yeah!"

"No! Alright I will wear them. But only for the photo. I am not walking around with this on my head."

"I never thought I would be doing this… I'm kind of scared."

"I'm here. Don't be afraid. We will take it slow."

"Mmmm, is that you tryin' to flirt?"

"Shut up!"

"Consider me open to explore."

"Well, alrighty then…"

"Shhhh, Marie got her holiness armor on. We can't expose her to thoughts of sex…"

"Oh, please, you are all horny cows. But you three are the worst."

"Yeah, I might be giving him a little something later."

"I don't want to know, freak!"

"Hater. I do stuff."

"I can't help it if I'm lick-able."

"Tonja, watch your mouth! Children are near."

"Too bad someone isn't here. I should have called him to meet me."

"Oh, don't start. You know Rhee can't handle you smelling like Korean Fried Chicken."

"I'm walking away."

"Marie, come back…"

"Ready everybody…let's go!! DISNEY WE'RE HERE!"

"Oh, brother…"

"Auntie, you're so funny."

"Uh, who is she talking to?

"Eomma, why is she hugging that person dressed like a cartoon character?"

"Jin, that is Minnie Mouse. She's married to Mickey here in Disneyland. Jae, your auntie Tangee is talking to Disney air. Ha… Ha."

"My mom loves Disneyland; we told you guys."

"Yeah, but why… why is she skipping?"

"She's happy. This is why dad stayed home with Edwin. He can't skip."

Like my triplets, Kang, Jusan, Trey, Nari, SI, Soo, and Hana had never been to Disneyland. So, Saturday, June 23, 2035, was an adventure for all. We laughed so much because Tangee wanted them to go on every ride and try just about everything they had to eat. Renee, Tanja, Celeste, Lola, and I had been to Tangee's home away from home with her before. Tangee loved everything Disney. We knew what to expect, from her hysteria and excited screams to her frolicking from adventure to adventure. *(Ha! She is a nut!)* The men were stuck all day with a bunch of cackling women and laughing children, while walking for miles, riding rides and being guinea pigs to sample different foods throughout the overpriced, amazing, and fun theme park.

"Taste this…"

"Don't be chicken, all men do it…"

"It's not hot! Dude, you eat nasty kimchi."

"Try it. It will make you Black."

"What do you mean it's not a real corndog?"

"Just a little nibble."

"Dole whip is not cool whip from Hawaii!"

"That is so lame. Take a man bite."

"You need Tums?"

We had a wonderful time with Tangee's family. It was a blast staying all together in the huge beachfront mansion in Malibu. *(Thanks for that Louis!)* Barbecues, late night chatter, play dates, drinks, and outdoor sand and water fun was all the rave. Celeste and Adam brought the JJs for the weekend adventure trip. Renee brought Christopher and Lola, Tanja, and Tamera flew to meet us. SI, Soo, and Hana only stayed a few days before returning to South Korea, but it truly was a fantastic diva doll family meet-up adventure that everyone couldn't stop talking about.

My brother-in-law Adam Williamson

My pretty niece Jacqueline

My handsome nephew Jason

My amazing younger sister
Celeste (CeCe) aka Glee/Joy Williamson

After the escapades with the divas, Celeste and I took our families for a day trip to see auntie Claudine, uncle Tony and their family that lived close. I hadn't seen my handsome corporate attorney cousin Toryono, in ages. It was nice to meet his wife. His sisters, Rhilynn, Rayna, and Roshonda live in Brookdale, Fort Lauderdale, and Raleigh. But I got a chance to chat with two of them over a video call. That was fun. Before we continued with our travels, I had a day outing by myself to a beautiful ranch style estate outside of the city. It was a wonderful lunchtime affair with SK Songbird and her sweet mother, Sheila. I had not been there in years, but they are always so hospitable and kind. I adore them.

When we flew to New York for a few days, we met up with April, Chin and their daughters, Zoe, and Farah. I had this burning desire to visit some of the places I loved with their father. I planned it that way. Telling them some fun things about how wonderful Jae was and some of the places we had gone was a different experience than watching videos of him from his career or messages he left them.

On this trip, I had a different feeling when I purposefully booked us to stay in the Mandarin Hotel's New York Skyline suites, to have easier access to Central Park, the Met Museum, and the Russian Tearoom. I wasn't sad at all this time, not once.

Later we connected with my old Sony boss, Ayana Fairchild, and spent time with Joy and her mother, Stephanie, who prepared a wonderful meal for us at their home in Brooklyn. While there, I got to introduce Jae, Jin, and Jolie to brother and sister Hanover from their congregation, who joined us.

The next day, we had planned a day trip. But something unexpected happened. "Hey, how much does it cost? I mean, we can drive up ourselves, but Antonio and I were talking and want to go too?" When Renee said it, I stopped my intake of air for at least four whole seconds. I know I did because she smacked my arm to answer her. "Oh, I think there is room on the giant coach bus Kang has. It is free to tour the branch. You... you want to come?"

"Yeah, it's a nice day. We don't have plans. Antonio's three-week vacation started yesterday. Never been to Wallkill, NY. I hear, it's pretty. So, yeah."

"Oh great. This will be fun. I've never been before either. We can discover together."

The Escobar's joined us on the day trip to tour the Headquarters of Jehovah's Witnesses in Wallkill and the educational operations in Patterson. It was where we met brothers and sisters, married and single from around the globe, who worked there as volunteers on assignments sharing their talents for us to enjoy. I noticed brother Hanover got to have deep conversations with Antonio and Kang, who were asking questions about where we were going and what went on at the branch and in other subbranches around the world. They seemed a little fascinated that they are all connected and in sync with the same processes, goals, and information no matter what country because Jesus is the leader. I heard Trey chime in and say, "like in a band or symphony." I thought, *(Is everyone curious? Oh goodie. No one has an attitude feeling they are being forced to explore with us. It's going to be fun.)*

Although they didn't say much while on tour, I could tell a few were observing everything and very impressed by the beauty of the land, the organization and cleanliness of each building, and the genuine kindness of the friends working there, when we had lunch with them. Jolie was mesmerized by the artwork, and she recognized ones she had seen in her Bible story book, and in a few study magazines. Jin was more fascinated with the music studio, the orchestra, and the drama video production process. Jae focused his attention on the translations department and the spiritual artifacts. Christopher and Renee recognized the video series characters before my children did.

(Why are they so giddy... They look like Tangee at Disney. Funny.)

I'm glad I took lots of photos from the tour and lunch. The group ones with the replica of Caleb and Sophia characters from *Become Jehovah's Friend* video series are kind of my favorites.

The next day, Kang, Nari, Trey, Antonio, Renee, Christopher, my children, and I boarded the all-inclusive Ritz-Carlton Yacht Evrima and set sail for London. By the second day in our two-story suites, my children were less rambunctious and much more relaxed with spa treatments, reading, music lessons, games, and pool time. I told them this was their second time sailing on an ocean.

"Really? We have? When?" Jae said with a squinched face as if he was trying to recall it.

"Oui, from Seattle to Busan with your grandparents and your auntie Renee. You were only around six months old, but you did. I'm sure you don't remember. It was a different kind of ship— a very large cruise ship. But your uncle Kang said we couldn't do that again. So, I chose this more exclusive way. Are you enjoying it?"

"Oh, yes, very much. I feel like I'm floating."

"I do too. I kind of drool when I sleep." Jin said proudly. *(Just like your grandpa.)*

48. London Paris

Three days after arriving in London, we had tearful hugs parting from Renee, Antonio, and Christopher. The Escobar's left for home by way of Puerto Rico while we spent several days in London with Elke and Kurt. I introduced my children to them and their play cousins Piper and Penelope Rana when my play-uncle Oliver-Pierre and his pretty dark-skin African wife Banyata came with their grandkids to meet us. Kang seemed surprised that I didn't know they were also Jehovah's Witnesses. I found out about it this trip that their daughter, Navya, and her husband, Demetri started studying with them many years ago. That was an exciting new discovery. We gave and received many more hugs after that happy reveal.

It was unfortunate that we were not able to see others like my college girlfriend, Nicolette, and her husband Raja Abdullah Zahad.

The two were in Dubai with their four boys visiting his family when we were in London. I missed connecting with them. But I relayed a message through Navya, who worked with Nicolette at the national museum.

Next on our travel adventure took us on the Venice Simplon-Orient Express train from London to Paris. This was Jolie's favorite part next to our voyage, she said. It was a little obvious because she hummed while inspecting the details of the ornate train and the decadent food she ate. *(She's so adorable and so much like me.)*

My parents just couldn't wait any longer to see us, because in Paris, they surprised us waiting at the station. We stayed in our penthouse flat my parents had owned since before I was born. The two of them had been waiting to show off Paris to their grandchildren. First were my father's old stomping grounds, Bibliothèque nationale de France, and Sorbonne' University. Next was a trip to the Arc de Triomphe de l'Étoile, the Eiffel Tower, and the Louvre. My son Jae wanted to eat the delicacies of Ladurée, mostly the chocolates and patisseries every day. He was a little obsessed with kouign-amann, croissants, and cream puffs *(This boy loves pastries...what is that about? Why is mother giggling?)* I had to stop him, but his siblings were just as bad. Jin devoured every macaron and berry filled crepes with crème. Jolie was inhaling any kind of soufflés, but her favorite seemed to be chocolate-raspberry. *(Must be something about berries. She is tapping her feet and moaning. Wait, so is Nari. Ha!)* She loved joconde cake and eggs benedict too. But once the three had a real authentic croque monsieur and a croque madame, that was all they wanted every day for lunch for a week. My father was so pleased. *(We are all his mini-him. Ha!)*

I just gave up trying to space things out and let them enjoy it. We met a couple of witnesses with carts near a metro station, and I asked when their meeting was held. It happened to be that night. Kang didn't hesitate to let me take my children to the Kingdom Hall in Paris. Probably because my father, mother, and Trey were going with me. *(He seems to be easing up on the security. Maybe.)* Nope, he had already sent Jusan to meet us there. Jusan, who I didn't know, had actually been traveling ahead of us to conduct security scans and clearance before we would arrive. *(Wow... Ninja Kang.)*

There was no plan to visit family while in Paris because this was my parents' special time with their grandchildren. They were so excited to explore and so was Nari who was thrilled with her first trip to France and learning so many wonderful things with them. Everyone enjoyed the two afternoon tea services we had at Hôtel de Crillon and at the Four Seasons Hotel George V. However, some folks were annoyed because they didn't get the humor of being at the Hôtel de Crillon. Kang and I kept glancing at one another, snickering recalling memories of the idol game we played when we met. My mind began to drift. Soon there were these constant flashbacks of wild intimate moments in the same hotel after we had gotten pranked. Lost in those memories for a while, I giggled to myself.

(Damn, I really miss Jae-Sung.)

Finally, we boarded an express train to Lyon. Home.

My Beautiful Mommy

Delphine Murry-Delacroix

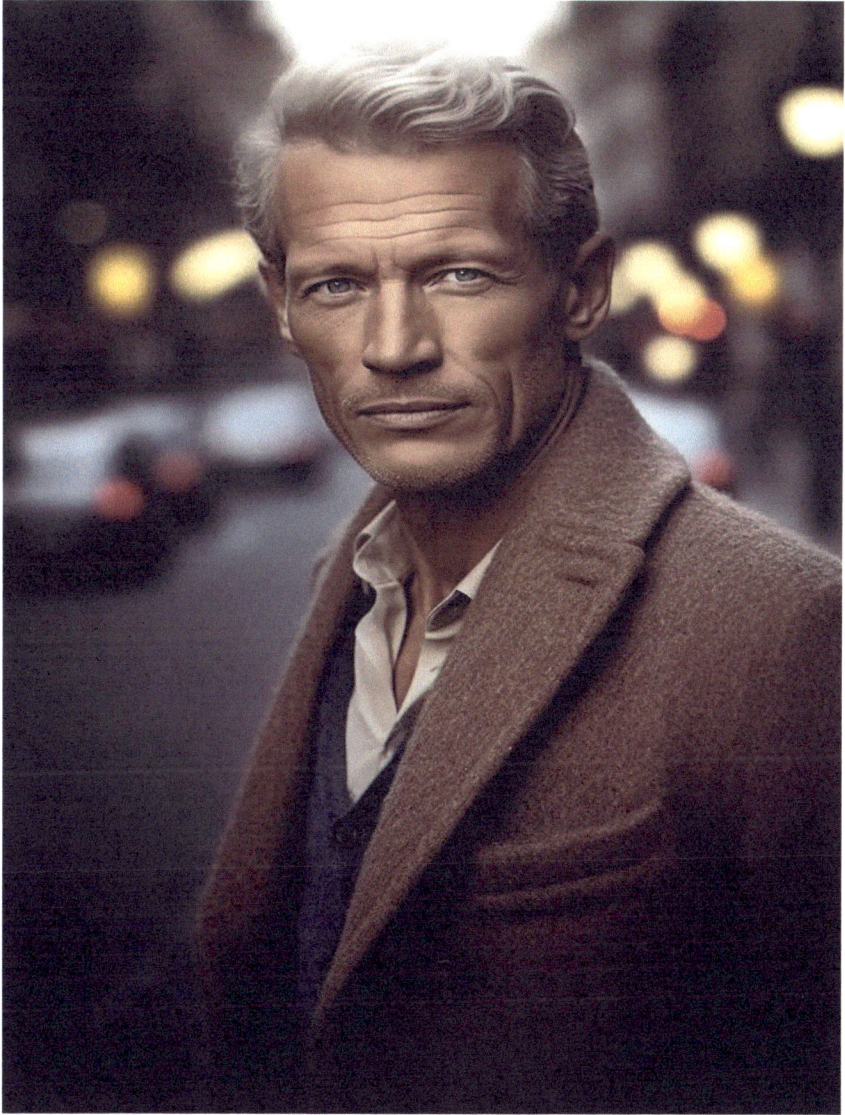

My Dashing Handsome Father

Jean-Philippe' Henri Delacroix

49. Lyon, France

When the vast acreage and pristine 17th Century, three-story Delacroix Chateau came into view, my children gasped, and their little eyes lit up. *(I knew they would love it.)*

It had only been about twenty-minutes from getting home, when it was whispered to me that my super sweet tante Gert Gauthier had officially married my father's musketeer-brother Chevalier Ratliff. Apparently, they had gotten married when they all went on that cruise to Greece, my father said. Honestly, I had been in a state of shock for a while after my father told me. I loved both individually as members of my extended family, but I had no clue they had been together. It was even more shocking to find out from my mother that they had been in a secret love affair off and on since I was about ten years old. *(What the heck? Secrets! Is that why she never had a man? I had thought she might be… Wow! Never assume.)*

My parents knew, so I guess that was all that mattered. When I hugged my aunt after we arrived, I knew she didn't want to tell me because she shook her head before I got my question out. My eyes said it all. Gert only grinned as she led me to the kitchen to help her make a couple of apple strudel cakes. Still the same. I love her dearly.

Getting acclimated to living in Europe, specifically Lyon, France was more of a challenge trying to hold my children back a little. The three amigos were excited and ready to explore. It was tough to keep up. During our first weeks, we only spoke French. That helped to expand their vocabulary and capture the throatiness in annunciating. This plan made it easier for us to blend back into the culture and conversations. Admittedly, we had gotten a little rusty in South Korea.

I wasn't prepared for one of the biggest changes. It was not the language or food but now on the Delacroix estate it was hard trying to keep them inside. *(They are just like their father!)* No matter what the weather, a daily question of "Mawmaw can we go outside?" came with fast, blinking eyes and wide grins. Running, riding horses, and exploring, my three amigos almost wanted to be outside just about every hour. The fresher air and not living in a city caused them to want to laugh, learn, and freely be in nature with their grandfather and cousins, who came to meet them in person at long last.

I couldn't seem to get enough hugs and kisses from my cousins Henri, Bridgette, Tomas, and his wife Liesl along with their five children, Geneviève's family, and Daniella, when they came in quick rotation to visit us. We spent wonderful days and some nights with each of them on the Delacroix estate.

(I've missed so much of what has been going on with my family. It's so good to be home.)

432

Unfortunately, my musketeer uncle Tomas and aunt Ayumiko had moved back to Japan right before we arrived, and my uncle Chevalier had been out of the country for an international medical board project in Montreal for the past three months. As a retired physician, who specialized in research and development of natural preventative medication treatments over synthetic ones, he only agreed to help for four months, but when other countries were added, it was going to extend his traveling. Gert was sad but knew he would be home soon.

(I have missed my musketeer uncles. They gave me the best hugs. I have oncle Andreas. He has always made up for the others being away. But I don't like it when any of them are far. They are not young anymore. Need to keep an eye on them. Why is everything so different?)

With all the weeks of traveling, there was a major change in our diet. Since we had been eating all these decadent dishes, sweets, cheeses, and breads, my children needed a healthy detoxing of their little systems. So did Nari. The poor thing had it the worst. She was constipated for several days and stuck in bed, curled in a ball. *(Sorry sweetie.)* Gert was right there with herbal remedies, and everyone was flushed out and ready to enjoy more but at a slower pace, a few days later.

The French security plan was that Kang and Nari would be with us here in Lyon for six months, and then Trey would remain for the other six with Jusan supporting every other month or as needed. Kang said he didn't trust anyone new, so his team would be security for the triplets and me in France at least for a couple of years. That was the outlined plan, but no one left.

The three of us met several brothers and sisters in my parents' congregation in Lyon. The French group of friends were like any other around the world, welcoming, hospitable, and loving. I was excited to see there were some mix race couples and friends from other nationalities in the congregation of about one hundred. *(Vietnamese, African, American, British, German, Japanese, Indian... I can't wait to learn more about them.)* My mother, Gert and Lylah support the friends with hospitality and partner with others for public witnessing assignments, while Wolfgang and my father serve as elders in their French congregation called Crête de la colline, (Hill Crest). Well, it's ours now. I made teaching volunteer plans with a pioneer sister, Cecilia Pedersen, and her sister-in-law, Debbie, and two single sisters, Kelsey, and Scarlett, after I finished settling in from the move.

Kang vetted them, and I was cleared to participate. Trey and Kang had set up the security protocols for when the triplets start private primary school next year because they were going to continue to be professionally tutored from home by their grandparents. They would also keep up with their cello, piano, singing, and guitar lessons as well as their sports and art. My father had that already arranged, and they were to begin in September. The routine of life was very different than in South Korea. Honestly, it was much more relaxed, less need for security, and I loved being home.

Although it has been several years that our home in Virginia has been leased by a federal government agency for a former president's wife and her secret service detail, I wanted to take my children there to see where I grew up. Within weeks of our arrival, my parents and I discussed a plan to take a fun trip back there after the lease agreement ends in 2038. The three amigos were so excited. I was too.

50. Unspoken Secrets

My older cousin Kristoff Delacroix Lazar came after everyone else had come and gone. I expected it. Kristoff hasn't interacted with members of the entire family socially since my father's party years ago. As usual, Kristoff had no plan to stay over, but he wanted to meet my children in-person and spend time with me catching up. We had not talked or seen each other in a very long time. He stopped writing to me four years ago and we hadn't seen each other physically since 2027, when we were in Florence, and he took me to lunch. I knew he stopped contacting me a little after he sent condolences because I asked him to visit us in South Korea. I probably shouldn't have asked him to do that. But I wasn't thinking about anything but missing my family when I did. Seeing him now ignited so many emotions, mostly nervousness for some reason.

When I saw him in the distance in his professional attire, waiting for me in the sunroom, I screamed his name, "Kristoff!" His smile was wide, and I could anticipate the softness of his light olive-colored skin because he had shaved away his beard from years ago. His dark-brown hair had always been impeccably styled to showcase those icy blue eyes; it was the same even with some grey he had now. His bright straight teeth gradually began to peek through his unsealed lips the closer I got to his arms. I cried hugging him. "Oh, cousin! I've missed you!" I shouted, pressing against him firmly again and squeezing him tightly. It had been too many years since seeing him. I missed him.

We laughed just holding one another. When he wiped my tears with his little finger, and said, "Ne pleure pas, douce cousine. Je ne veux que des rêves de tes yeux qui sourient." (Do not cry, sweet cousin. I only want dreams of your eyes that smile.) He winked at me. I giggled as he squinched his face and briefly brushed the tip of his nose onto mine. However, I could feel my mother's eyes burning a hole in my flesh from the other side of the room.

Surprisingly, he stayed the whole afternoon. The two of us took a long walk in the flower garden, had afternoon tea together, and we talked about several things that only we could talk about.

As the sun was on its way to set, we went to a place where we used to spend private moments talking when I was young. Smiling as he walked closer to me from the doorway, I was flooded with memories. But my heart pounded hard in my chest, knowing he was going to say goodbye. I didn't want him to leave. Suddenly, I felt downhearted, and my eyes slowly filled with salty water. Kristoff touched my cheek with his long fingers, then he opened his hand and held my face so tenderly. His icy-blue spheres slightly moved left to right as if he was reading behind my eyes. It was quiet and I listened to his eyes tell me things he couldn't say. Tears roll down my cheeks.

Then my dashing, handsome, and kind cousin said his final words to me.

"Marie, la façon dont tes yeux m'ont parlé aujourd'hui, je n'aurais pas pu faire ça pour toi, mais j'aurais sûrement essayé. Je... je... t'ai toujours protégé, même de moi. Si je ne pars pas maintenant, Marie, je ne partirai pas. Je dois partir. Après mon départ, nous ne nous reparlerons plus. C'est ainsi que nous devons être, tu le sais. Si je ne pars pas, je... je... je vous souhaite bien-être et joie. Ma belle cousine brune. Toi seul es celui que j'ai toujours le plus aimé. Je t'aime. (Marie, the way your eyes spoke to me today, I could not have done this for you, but I surely would have tried. I...I... have always protected you, even from me. If I don't leave now, Marie, I won't. I must leave. After I go, we will not speak again. It is the way we must be, you know this. If I don't leave, I...I... I wish you wellness and joy. My beautiful brown cousin. You alone are the one I have always loved the most. I love you)."

Kristoff tilted my face up and leaned down before kissing my lips very tenderly. His falling tears hit my skin as he withdrew and walked out of the cottage near the horse stables. I wanted to call out to him and force him to stay, but I didn't. I knew he wouldn't come back. My heart was being torn again and I was disappointed and saddened. As a couple more tears fell, I closed my eyes, remembering his love and protection growing up. I missed the closeness we once had. He was that very special person in my life who had bravely protected and cared for me after Max died.

A deeper feeling of sadness swept over me, and I felt a chill. Closing the cottage doors and making my way back to the chateau, more tears trickled down my face as childhood memories collected in my mind. "I miss him. Why can't we be like before? Why did grandpère (grandfather) treat him that way. I hate to see him alone. I'm sorry Kristoff, I wish..."

Immediately, I stopped mumbling to myself upon seeing Jin rapidly approaching with a smile on his face, holding some kind of mechanical robot animal he had built.

Continuing through the evening, I was gloomy and disengaged. I pondered on how different my life would have been if grand-père (grandfather) had not reacted the way he did and granted permission for Kristoff to marry me. At dinner, I nibbled on my meal but abruptly excused myself to retire earlier than usual.

In bed, I skimmed a Watchtower magazine, pretending to prepare for my teaching demonstration with Scarlett Erste' on Tuesday's meeting. But I was unable to concentrate. My brain continued to replay situations and facts without answers or resolutions, over and over in my mind. On internal autopilot, I moved steps away to the connected bathroom and made ready my second hot coconut scented bubble bath of the night.

In the steam-filled bathroom with bubbles covering the still water, I had been staring into space for a while. My mother had come in without my realizing her presence until she started speaking, "Child, your mood has altered since Kristoff left." She sat across the pristine, white-tiled bathroom and eased down into the oversized, plush midnight-blue vanity chair, and continued, "I don't want to see you depressed over the past we cannot change. The three of you were very close, and after Max died, Kristoff became obsessed with protecting you. We were all grieving. It was endearing how this attentively studious sixteen-year-old boy took tender care of his wounded and traumatized eleven-year-old cousin. But your grandfather, Jean-Pierre didn't see it that way."

Feeling emotions building from each word she said, I turned and faced her. She paused and waited for me to add to the story that she had casually asked me about a few years ago. It was silent for several minutes before she began speaking again, "Marie, your father and I have had conversations with Kristoff since you've grown up. Your father was told privately, well, he was led to believe that Kristoff had been inappropriate with you after the accident. This was the reason your grandfather sent him away, limiting his family contact. We reached out to him more after we moved here, especially after your grandmother died. If nothing is bothering you, then why are you acting so withdrawn? Did seeing him bring back hurtful memories? What happened? Tell me. Did he do something to you back then? I want to help you with whatever you are feeling. What is weighing on you so heavily that you didn't even bother to read to your children tonight? Please tell me."

Sitting up in the deep tub, tears slid down my cheeks and then dripped into the cooling water. I concentrated on the shapes of floating pillows of white bubbles trying to come up with words I had never said. I sighed, but before I could utter a word, my mother began telling me her own secret.

"How about I go first. My aunt Paula's son, Kendrick Lucas, was raised like our older brother. I thought he was until Lorelle, and I were twelve. When I was growing up in the seventies, he was an angry man for lots of reasons that I didn't know or understand. We didn't associate with him because he was a drug dealer and an addict. Kendrick put me and my sister, Lorelle in the middle of a dangerous situation. He didn't plan to, but on this one day, we foolishly accepted a ride from him to avoid the rain. He didn't immediately take us home but had to make one quick stop first. He owed his big-time drug dealer friends a lot of money, and they were threatening him. Kendrick gave up our virginity to prove his loyalty to them and erase his debt." She said these words with no emotions. Her voice was clear yet soft.

But I verbally reacted, shouting, "No!" My head shot up. I focused on her eyes and slapped my wet hand over my mouth to not yell out again. My heart felt heavy like a large bolder had been dropped on my chest, hearing her horrible secret. My mother didn't stop talking.

"Until then, I loved him as my brother. But even though he was on drugs, at the very moment he put me in that room, he violated everything I knew to be right, and I hated him. It didn't matter that he explained things to me first, like telling me we were not brother and sister would make it less horrifying. It didn't. Or that he tried to be as easy as possible when he hurt me. Nor did it matter that he wept and begged for my forgiveness, afterward. I hated him and it changed me. It confused me for a long time. Although he explained why he chose me, I still asked myself why it had been me and not Lorelle, who paid the price. I never said what happened in that room, but your aunt Hellene didn't need me to. She told your uncle LaRoyce enough, and he murdered Kendrick Lucas in the street. Then he died in prison four years later."

I didn't pause to think and blurted out, "Mama! Your brother killed him?" It shot out of my mouth like a spray of water from a hose. I covered my mouth again, feeling tears rolling over my fingers. (This is why I didn't know them. They were dead. One killed the other and then went to prison and died. Oh, my god!) I was motionless in the tepid water realizing the shocking truth. Without taking a breath, she continued, "Chantal, my older brother LaRoyce was a strong, smart, and kind man. Next to my father, he was my favorite person back then. But he sacrificed his life to fix it in a way he knew how. For many years I carried so much guilt and shame about that, trapped inside me. There was no such thing as mental health therapy like we have today. In my family, and in a lot of African American ones at that time, you held secrets, and you kept going. Marie, I channeled my confusion and pain into strength; determined to seek knowledge and excel beyond what was done to me, and the tragedy that followed which I had mistakenly reasoned, was all my fault. I never told anyone the details of what happened except your father and in prayer. It was my secret until I trusted your father to comfort me by knowing. When I asked you about it when we were packing… Well, I had prepared myself to tell you. But at the time, you weren't ready to share with me. Child, I assume nothing. But, as your mother, I want you to tell me what happened. Why did he ask to marry you when you were sixteen? And then again, a few years later. What happened between you? Please trust me enough to understand. I will love you, regardless of what you tell me in confidence."

While my tears rushed over my skin and added to the bathwater, I took a deep breath and began to explain, "It… It wasn't anything like that. We didn't… I mean, he loved me. He wanted to marry me to protect me. But when he went to grand-père (grandfather), he was treated so cruelly. Because I was only sixteen, he told Kristoff, he was a disgusting dishonorable man that preyed on his younger cousin. Kristoff tried to explain his feelings had simply shifted from natural family love. He told grand-père that his feelings must have come from his guilt for not running back to get Max himself; witnessing my sufferings during the episodes, and his obligation to love, and protect me, evolved into something much deeper and he didn't understand why. It wasn't lustful, or sexual. He didn't want children and was asking to marry me only to be the one always responsible for taking care of me. But grand-père refused to listen or understand him. Because I didn't remember things when I had seizures, he believed Kristoff had done something to me. He said he sent him away so he couldn't sexually molest anyone else. It was wrong what grand-père did. Then when I graduated from High School, grand-père wanted all the details I could remember. After he had a physician privately examine me, he was finally convinced I was still intact, and that the situation hadn't been some grotesque relationship. But he told me it was too dangerous for Kristoff to be around. He could not be a Delacroix anymore. He was a Lazar, and we could no longer be as close as we were as children. He removed Kristoff from the Delacroix family to protect it, he said. Grand-père loved him. He cried when he told me this. But… but because of me, he ostracized Kristoff, he hurt him, and tossed him away. It's my fault."

"Chantal-Marie…"

She spoke my name softly as my words ran out of my mouth a mile a minute, and I didn't stop. "Kristoff cared about me. Truly, he did. He does. Yes… he… he kissed me. He held me close and comforted me, but he didn't improperly touch me. When I was in college, I begged him to marry me. I loved him. I trusted him. I believed he could help me be free from all the tragic things that were happening to me. He asked permission again, but the answer was still no and the second time grand-père threatened to tell Pawpaw if he didn't stay far away from me. He refused to marry, but even after we had met in secret, he still wouldn't touch me. I love him, mother. Kristoff Lazar is the most precious cousin in the world to me. In my mind, he is the closest person to Maxie. I didn't want to be apart from him too. But once I was engaged to Marquis, he cut off communication with me. I wanted to be with him when I was younger. I did. Does that make me wicked? Did I add to his suffering? I would have married him. He was my escape, my protector. Kristoff was a gentleman then and now. Being with him today reminded me of all of it. My heart hurts for him. It does, it always does because over time, Kristoff began to believe those chastising, venomous words, grand-père said each time he went to him about his confusion about me. Calling him a corrupt, predator, and a despicable coward and evil monstrous boy. It didn't matter what I said, or that he never touched me, Kristoff believes something was and is wrong with him. He has stayed away from everyone, including me. Today, he told me that when he saw me, his feelings were just as strong as when he was twenty-four. Then in his next breath, he told me that they are unnatural and perverted. He said if there is a hell, he will burn there because he is a cursed man for loving me as a woman and not as his cousin. He even said, he was not deserving of happiness or God's favor, just like grand-père told him decades ago. I couldn't believe he said that. He still carries all that crap around his heart. If only he would come to know Jehovah. He would see God doesn't think he is a wicked person at all. Your cousin was wicked, not mine! Not mine! I...I mean, it's the devil's trap to sabotage a person through their negative thoughts. I tried to tell him that today. I did. I tried to tell him that Jehovah God sees the good that man cannot see. I wished he would learn the truth and let go of those hurtful things that came from wrongful suspicion and not true facts."

I sobbed, telling my mother these unspoken things from my youth. I splashed the bathwater over my face, took a few deep breaths, then continued to open a small, sealed vault of my conscience, "I'm sorry that happened to you. Mom, I am so sorry. I...I didn't think something like that could happen in our family. I'm... I'm very sorry. Maybe... I was overly protected or naïve. I mean, Kristoff could have been the way your terrible cousin, Kendrick had been to you. I suppose it could have been the same tragedy."

I focused on the darkness of the sky outside. My mother had no reactions, only listened attentively as my body shivered splashing the bathwater and tears ran out of me nonstop. I couldn't look at her. I was ashamed of what was going to come out next.

"I mean... I...I wanted him to. I did. I... I was a virgin until... until Bryce raped me in college. I told no one. Not even Renee knows. That summer in France I met Kristoff in Florence, secretly like we had before, and… and I had only been there for an hour, and he could tell something was wrong. When I finally told Kristoff what happened, he was so angry. I blamed him because he didn't marry me like he promised. I begged him to make the pain go away. I did. I pleaded with him to sleep with me… show me what it would have been like to be his wife. I was so afraid of men, but I trusted him. I wanted to forget what Bryce did, and I begged him to teach me what it was supposed to… …I begged him… But he wouldn't. I yelled at him and said it was because I wasn't pure anymore. I was ugly and dirty. Kristoff kissed me and let me cry in his arms. He loved me, Mama. Kristoff told me how a real man would protect a woman he loved, no matter what. He would never act violently toward her. He said a true gentleman would honor me and naturally be gentle, not think only of himself during intimacy. He said, I was always beautiful and that I am still pure of heart and my body is still delicate and special like a flower, regardless of what that bastard had done. He told me that…that he loved me deeper than anything he had ever known, and he could never hurt me. He… he said if he took me to bed and did what I asked, he wouldn't be able to stop. He wouldn't ever stop because now that I was older, he could no longer deny that his desire had grown into wanting me that way. But it would be wrong because I wasn't his wife. I am his cousin. He said he fights with himself because his first obligation is to protect me, even from the monster inside him. After I left Florence to go to Paris to stay with Odette, that was when he asked permission again."

I took a breath. Then I kept talking, "Later, I found out when Kristoff went to grandpapa, he told him what happened and that he wanted to love me the right way. But grandpapa was even more horrible to him the second time. He told Kristoff, what had happened to me was his fault for making me too trusting of men, and vulnerable for wolves to prey on. He blamed him for not marrying someone suitable and destroying his evil lust and unnatural desires for me. It was not like when I said it, because he believed grandpapa's words and blamed himself. Grandpapa told him again that they both knew Pawpaw would never allow such a thing and he would probably kill Kristoff if he knew what he had been doing all these years to me. He said if he didn't stay away from me, he would tell Pawpaw I was raped at school, and it happened because of him. Kristoff never asked again. After that he said his desire for me grew and he stopped meeting me in secret because he wanted to run away with me, and it was too tempting. Mama, I've always known Kristoff has had lots of affairs, but it wasn't until later that I realized he had some flings simply to imagine he was with me. It's why he won't be near me for too long. Today is the first time in over two decades we have spent more than three hours together alone. He really thinks he is some kind of monster, with these distorted feelings of love. My beautiful cousin is tormented all the time, and it's my fault. Oh, mama, Kristoff is noble, kind, brave, and dignified. I've always seen him that way. But no one else did because he is an outcast of the Delacroix family. He is not wicked! They made him be… It was wrong what grandpapa did to him! Mother, if the accident hadn't happened, he would've never have felt like this about me. He wouldn't have ever been treated so despicably, horrible. No, he would have been deeply loved and cherished, like the rest of us. He would have found a good wife, had children. I just know it. He deserved to be happy too. He can't be because I was the one who ran back to get…"

Finally freeing myself from my secret of the past and the pain I carry, I held my face in my hands, and softly cried. The steam had long evaporated from the room, and it was quiet for a while.

Then she rose from her seat and guided me out of the lukewarm water. Calming my sniffles, I wrapped myself in my robe. She kissed my cheeks and hugged me, saying, "My sweet child, what you experienced was traumatic enough. Remember, I said we have talked to him many times over the years. Early on, he did not give many details to your father about the two of you, but privately, he gave a few to me. He is bitter about many things, but he does not blame you. We humans make so many mistakes even when we love each other and try to do what we feel is best for a situation. From what I know, it was painful for your grandfather to separate from him like that because they raised both boys after Josephine died. But Kristoff's father's culture was also part of the reasoning for your grandfather's decisions. Historically, Moroccan cultural views about women and how to treat them are very different than the French. It scared Jean-Pierre' not knowing what influences Hassan's family had on his heir. Although he had no evidence, he could not risk the safety of others if he had been wrong. Kristoff's feelings were compounded by many things. As you said, he was ostracized, isolated, and discarded. He is deeply scarred by the past, even as a very wealthy, and handsome businessman. As a mature woman, I know you love him as your dear cousin, but, in a way, he had been taken from you as this balancing anchor in your life very much like your twin brother had been. The impact of that was emotionally devastating to say the least. Sadly, he feels that same way. I am sorry those things happened to you, Marie."

Tenderly she brushed my hair with her hand, and said, "This is why we all need proper spiritual oversight and parenting to help us be the best we can be. How wonderful it is to know Jehovah promised to erase and reset everything to right. In due time, we won't remember anything, or anyone not meant for us to remember. Those terrible things that happened, were said, or we did, will all be gone. Guilt is something the two of us will have until Jehovah permanently removes it from our hearts. But my darling daughter, let it not weigh your heart down. Release it to the wind in prayer. Be confident in knowing rope is much stronger bound together with other rope than being a single strand tied alone."

She winked at me, and I snickered. "Mom, you are so much like Pawpaw. You even talk like him... it's a little scary."

We chuckled, and she smacked my butt. "How do you know he hasn't gotten his words of wisdom from me?"

I nodded in agreement, reaching to embrace her once more with a firmer squeeze.

After preparing for bed, I checked on my sleeping children, kissing each one without waking them. Then I prayed about the injustice and guilt I felt about my cousin and the past while snuggled under the bed covers of the moon room. Shortly thereafter, I floated off into happiness dreams imagining life in a new world to come.

The next day I felt more refreshed. I again focused and kept my mind clinging to the hope that all things would be put back in the right way in the future, and we probably wouldn't even remember those things that had caused us harm.

51. Truth of the Matter

During all our travels and the initial weeks of getting settled, we kept in contact with everyone in South Korea and in America by having video check-in conversations. It was obvious that Min Cha, Teng, SI, Soo and Hana couldn't wait long before coming to visit us in Lyon, France, because within two months of arriving, they were on a plane coming our way. *(Anxious much? Too funny.)* It was a delightful treat having our Korean family spend time with us at my father's home. We truly are one big family and it showed. They got to make new friends in our local congregation, get their triplet fix with lots of hugs, kisses, and laughter, and to relax while my parents pampered them, the Delacroix way.

It had been years since Min Cha and Teng were exposed to my family's side of things back at Celeste's home in Washington, when the triplets were born. This time, the experience was very different. My father escorted Min Cha around like a tour guide sharing the history of the Delacroix estate with the same pride she had done when they had come to her compound in South Korea. While Teng and Soo got their hands in the kitchen with my mother, Gert, Nari, me, and Lylah sometimes. Kang and SI did some brother bonding while the triplets and Hana were out exploring the vast grass and forest acres of the estate, riding horses and swimming.

While they were here, Trey left to visit his family in England, while Jusan went to Barbados with his girlfriend. When SI was asked to be the speaker at one Sunday meeting during their stay, it allowed us to hear him give a public talk. Since we had been in different halls in South Korea, I never got the opportunity to hear him publicly speak. I knew he did with his congregation responsibilities but to me, SI was always shy and soft spoken. It surprised me hearing his skilled speaking with inflection and tone, and descriptive illustrations to bring a point home in French. I was so proud of him. After that meeting, SI, Soo, and Hana were able to enjoy hospitality with Bernard Runoldhad, his sister Carmen Aubert, and the Lambert family. I think SI and Bernard and Marc Lambert are fast friends. I noticed Kang and Trey quietly observing everyone's behavior not only toward his family but to them.

(This was another experience showing them that Witnesses as a group are genuine, learn the same things and in the same way, and are a family, around the world.)

A few days before their trip was to end, Min Cha and I were able to talk about a few things from the past. We were taking a walk on a clear day and for some reason, she wanted me to take her to the domed building with large columns and ornate gold sculpture carvings at the east end of the estate. It was not a commonly known place, but I assumed my father must have told her about it along with her tour of gardens, cottages, and buildings on his family land.

We took a land shuttle first then made the short walk to the Delacroix mausoleum.

"This is a beautifully crafted building. Your father told me it was built long ago but has been refurbished during his father Jean-Pierre's lifetime. May we go in?"

Min Cha asked me, with her eyes wide and inspecting the designed pillars of the structure. It briefly reminded me of the way Jae-Sung looked when he went in the moon room and saw the details of the canopy bed. I snickered from the thought.

We entered the quiet place of my resting family. Right away she seemed to be searching for something. I followed steps behind her, not really sure what she was looking for, but after several minutes she stopped and slowly bowed. When I glanced up, I realized she was facing the name carved in gold Chevalier Maximilian Delacroix and paying her respects by bowing. I was still. As she rose slowly, Min Cha turned to me and spoke.

"Marie, I am sorry that you lost your brother, so long ago. I did not know this until you told me that day over tea. How hard it must have been for you. I am truly sorry." I smiled at her feeling a sense of comfort from her recalling that moment I told her I lost my brother. *(She remembered that. She is so kind.)*

Before I could think of something to add to the conversation, she continued to speak with words that startled me as she said them. "Daughter, I can tell you the truth of the matter now, when before I could not. When I decided to study with Jehovah Witnesses, I did so in secret. It was because Dong-Hyun was very angry with the changes in me. I began to question him about some of our customs. The more I learned, the more he became verbally combative. He had forbidden me to continue. But one evening, he had someone shadow, and found out I was still going to the Kingdom Hall with Teng, and Soo.

When I returned home, he had vandalized one of my art studios. Destroying finished and unfinished paintings, slashing them with knives, and ruining my artwork for the children's gallery. He had been drinking heavily and dragged me to see what he had done. We argued. In his drunken state, he said several things that frightened me."

She paused as we sat down. Min Cha remained focused on my brother's name on the marble wall. Then she kept speaking calmly. "He said he would not lose me to some foreign religion. Not after he had done so much to win me from Ji-Hoon. I didn't understand what he was saying. I thought, perhaps it was wild talk because he was intoxicated but he said more, much more. Like a river his tongue flowed with the truth of the past I had not known. He confessed he wanted me from the start after the three of us had met at university. He told me the two had bet on who I would love and marry. But when I fell for Ji-Hoon, he was angry. Then after Ji-Hoon said he truly loved me and it wasn't a bet to him, Dong-Hyun said he then felt a hatred for his childhood friend. He said Ji-Hoon cheated him out of having the life he deserved. When our children died, he thought it would break us apart, but it only made us closer. So as Ji-Hoon became more popular with the symphony, Dong-Hyun paid women to have affairs with him to create scandals for me to find out and leave him. But I didn't. I could not believe the things he was saying to me, but he yelled and repeated them, shouting his devotion and love for me. All these years, there were so many things I did not know. I did not know that Dong-Hyun sent his sister, Sun hee to Monaco to seduce my husband, and pressure him to recklessly gamble away his money before meeting us in Paris. Because he didn't gamble away his fortune, Dong-Hyun called him at the flat and lied that we had been having an affair, which caused us to argue that day in Paris. I did not know Ji-Hoon's car crashed into a bus and he died instantly. I did not know Jae-Sung had witnessed those things. Marie, I had no knowledge that you and your twin brother were on the bus, he died, and you could not have children because of it. I had no way of knowing any of these secret things, but Dong-Hyun stood there shouting the truth."

I reached for her hands that were trembling. I held them, but she would not look at me. "Min… Min Cha…" I whispered her name to get her attention, but she didn't acknowledge my voice and continued talking.

"Marie, he demanded I stop this religion. He said he would not lose me after he had worked so hard to win and protect us. Dong-Hyun had done right after he had done so much wrong. He said he wanted to honor Ji-Hoon after betraying him because he felt deep shame in what he had done to ruin him. But he yelled aggressively at me that he would never lose what is his. We belonged to him, he said. He chanted loudly how much he hated you for changing everything we hold dear. He said he tried to accept you as Jae-Sung's choice, but the ancestors were punishing him because you were unsuitable from the very beginning."

Min Cha finally turned her body to look at me. My face was covered with wetness from tears and so was hers. But she smiled at me and squeezed my hand. Then she said, "I did not know I had married an evil man. I would not have known it if you had not come into our life and learned about Jehovah, taught things to your children and to Soo Cheng. I would not have known for myself if I didn't research these things. I believe it was our heavenly father, who revealed to me what I needed to know, when I asked Him for guidance about what I should do as I learned new things about Him, and Dong-Hyun was treating me so cruelly. He had never been a violent man, but that night in his rage, he beat me and left me locked in my studio for several days. When he finally let me out, I secretly contacted Min-Ji. He sent Jet to assist me to safety. I remained in hiding under his protection for many months. Teng also came with me as Dong-Hyun would have hurt her to get to me. This is why I saw my grandchildren in secret on the mountain, and we could not tell you about important things like my baptism beforehand."

"Oh, Min Cha…" I hugged her but a thought just rolled off my tongue, "But is he really gone?"

"I pleaded with Min-Ji not to sin against heaven, not even for me. That was when he told me they had uncovered evidence proving Dong-Hyun had orchestrated a kidnapping plot to eliminate you, adopt my grandchildren, and maintain control of Jae-Sung's assets. I was shocked to find out that happened. He said he must execute an honor code to put things right and protect everyone. But he agreed there would be no guilt or sin. Kang and my brothers were notified by Min-Ji of an honor code protocol that had been set into motion for our family. Weeks later, Dong-Hyun was gone. There was no trace of him at my home or at Samsung. I received papers that ended our marriage. He simply disappeared as if he had never existed. His sister, Sun hee was gone in the same way."

Stunned, I shook my head in disbelief remembering what Kang had said when I learned it was Dong Hyun behind the breach. "Min Cha if he is dead, they must have killed him. I don't want to pay for that sin."

She tapped my hand and smiled at me and spoke. "I did not wish for that myself. We are not at fault for what happened to those wicked people. As a disgraced man, Dong-Hyun was given a choice of exiled imprisonment in North Korea, or self-imposed death. Either option would have the same outcome."

Curiously, I asked, "Could they maybe come back to hurt us?"

She shook her head, no. Then stated facts while wiping her cheeks, "I was told neither chose exile imprisonment. The truth and its conclusion are told to you for your heart to be free from worry and to know for certain of my purest intentions. I too no longer have connection with my longtime friends because of the code they carry. We are the same in this way. We must rely on Jehovah and his people, those that demonstrate that they truly serve him. We will always be loved and protected. Let us no longer remember the past but look to the future reset of things. I look forward to meeting Max as you call him, if it is in our God's plan for me to do so."

I smiled at her and nodded. My body felt a little numb, and my mind held on to no thoughts. We were silent for a while. Then as we were exiting the building, Min Cha hugged me with cheerful words of thanks.

"Gamsahabnida. Nae ttal, Nae sonjuui eomeoni, Nae nu-I (Thank you. My daughter, my grandchildren's mother, my sister)."

I kissed her cheek, "salanghaeyo, sieomeoni (I love you, my mother-in-law)."

When Min Cha, Teng Cheng, her son SI, his wife Soo and their daughter Hana returned to South Korea days later, there were many tears. But they made plans to return in about six months, which made the goodbye not as sad. Now, I felt this other level of connection with Min Cha and Jae. Pondering on everything she told me; I thought it was amazing how two different families from across the world had this intertwined history in the most peculiar way. But now we were stronger with spiritual unity and love. The truth of the matter was we are a family.

52. Unboxed Memories

After several months of unpacking and getting into the groove of being in Lyon, I had grown more anxious to find out what Jae-Sung had sent here for me before he passed away.

The medium size locked trunk was in the corner under the window in the moon room that I slept in. Honestly, it had been taunting me to open it from the very first day we arrived. It felt a lot like Walt Disney's 1951 classic movie "Alice in Wonderland" with Alice trying to decide on which bottle to drink or not. I fought the urge, but enough was enough.

After it took me roughly thirty-two hours of attempting to figuring out the code to unlock the trunk, which happened to be my bra size when we met, my favorite love level, our French wedding day, and the month he released Arabian Sand as a single. "Oh, Jae, you make me sick!" He had made this more difficult than it needed to be, but I giggled finally opening the trunk.

On top of the items inside was a large envelope and letter written on his seafoam green with white music notes stationary paper. "I haven't seen this paper in so... so long." *(Oh, Jae.)* I held it in my hand for a while without opening it. Sighing, I sat alone on the floor of the room, just remembering his personal stationery and some of the things he had written to me. Then I read his letter.

To my strong and amazing wife:

Beautiful Sunset in Dubai, my sweet Arabian Sand, I know you were upset with me changing everything and removing things from our home. I didn't want you to be sad all the time and holding tangible things that might prevent you from focusing on raising our children. But I saved these things for you to have now. I know the twins must be at least six years old for you to open this. I hope it's been long enough to give you good memories, and this won't make you sad. Your happiness is all I desire Marie. Always.

Everything is for you from my DRGN5 days. Marie, do me a favor and don't let the twins watch Kings of KPOP, Idol Romance, Happiness Wins or Operation Love, those are for you...I don't want them thinking their father wasn't cool. I didn't like acting as much as other people. I loved hearing you laugh so you laugh all you want too. But don't let them laugh at their father, it's dishonoring. Koreans don't do that! Wait do Black people? Ha!

The video messages, toys and audio recordings in the green box are for our children. Now they are older, I wrote and recorded new songs for them to listen to my voice and not the nursery rhymes.

The videos, music and things in the white box are private for you. I know it must be hard my love and you miss me but try not to dwell on that Ok. I don't want your heart weighed down with worry and grief, but hope is what I want you to be thinking about. I wonder what our twins are like. Does one have your eyes? I prayed that one would. Those beautiful sunset on Arabian sand eyes.

Do they like music? I hope so. I hope they got some of the good parts of my DNA, anyway. I didn't leave anything for my mother but please help her to have the same vision of the future as she painted on the dining room wall. I want her to have that wish.

By the time you read this remember, I am asleep, like you said. I don't dream anymore or feel pain. I hope to be a good enough person to be in God's memory like you said. He blessed me *with you, baby. If not, know my life was only complete with you in it. You made me live a life only meant for those blessed by him and I am truly grateful. But if what we believe is true and I wake up, I'll be able to say the words from my heart. You are my ultimate joy, Chantal-Marie. I love you, forever. - Jae-Sung*

P. S. Did he, do it? I wish I could have seen your face. Ha! Ha! The score: is now Korean Idol: 5 French/Black Wife:3!

Don't be mad because I won! You deserved it. I have been dreaming about what you did to me in Paris for the past two weeks. Love my naughty French Girl. Can't wait to see her again. But don't tell my wife! You're smirking I know you are.

"Ha, ha! Yes, Kang did what you told him too! That is not the score I have 4! Cheater! How are you pranking me, and you are... Oh, you punk!" I mumbled to myself reaching inside the trunk, snickering from flashes of how he got me good.

I pulled out a rare copy of their debut album. It was factory sealed and bubble wrapped with a no longer in production NM Entertainment Company stamp. Yes, an actual album. *(Did he have this made? How would I even play this?)* A secure drive of the album songs was also inside. I connected it to the moon room sound system and listened while I investigated the contents of the trunk.

"You were so cute at sixteen. Those eyes even back then. They were all so young but sound good even at that age. Very K-Pop bubble gum music. How far you've come my love." I snickered going through twelve years of concert memorabilia, stuffed mini replicas of each member and three-character dragons representing the DRGN5's "Yong," "Yo," and "Kyo" fans. There were programs, T-shirts, photo cards of members through the years, key chains, and magazines they had been featured in over the years of their career. *(Oh, wait, let me find…)*

I searched through the stacks of magazines to see if he put it in the collection. He had it on the bottom with an envelope stuck to the cover that had the words, "read first". On his stationary paper inside, he had written in French, "Je parie que vous bavez sur ce magazine à nous dans nos sous-vêtements. Ne montrez personne d'autre. Marie, tu n'as pas non plus le droit de regarder mes frères idoles! Non, je vais les découper pour que tu ne sois pas tenté, Ha! Ha! Je gagne! (I bet you are drooling over this magazine with us in our underwear. Don't show anyone else. Marie, you are not allowed to look at my idol brothers either! No, I will cut them out. This way you are not tempted. Ha! Ha! I win)!"

"Oh, you punk!" I flipped to the article of DRGN5, and the designer photoshoot pictures until I got to the right one. He didn't cut anything. "Well...Hello!" I said it after blinking a few times and laughing. "I shouldn't be looking at this." I said it, not turning from the centerfold page but tilting the magazine to see from every angle. "Wow." I laughed to myself remembering that moment recalling exactly when he told me about this photoshoot in Brazil and the commotion it caused.

"Myth buster!" I snickered all day long thinking about that fun fact about Asian men.

When I found the two photos of him in his studio, I began to feel sad remembering him making music and just watching him work. But within a few seconds I burst out laughing, with the flashback of the time he recorded us doing it. "Ha! Ha! "That was freaky and so much fun! Jae and his games. Ha!" I giggled, thinking about that time, and going through the items set aside for me.

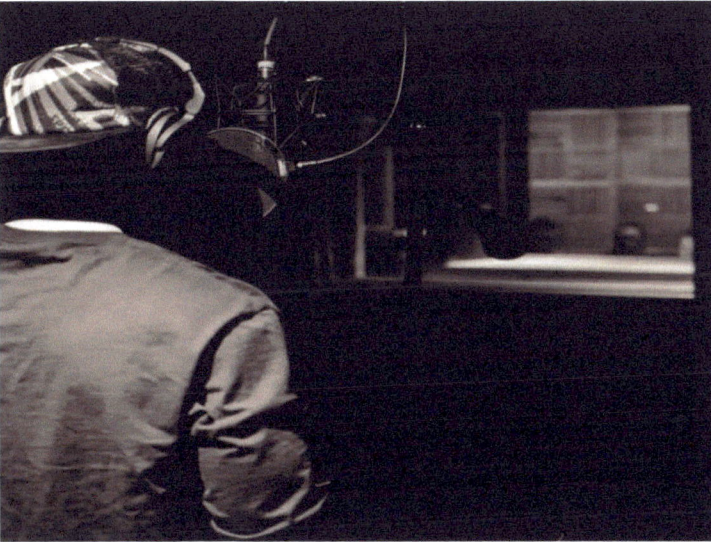

For me he had a secure drive dated 2019-2024 titled, *Do I love her?* After listening to some of it, I realized, there were several songs he had written but never recorded, and a few older American R&B ones too. I giggled, bringing back memories with him. Then I tried to imagine what exactly prompted him to pick some songs to sing and others to just record for listening. "What mood was he in?" Songs like Jodeci's "My Heart Belongs to you" and "I'm Still Waiting," Christion's "Face Like Yours," Montell Jordan's "Falling," Donny Hathaway's "I Love You More Than You'll Ever Know," Johny Gill's "My My My" and Stevie Wonder's "That Girl" were saved on the drive. But when I heard his voice begin to sing Major's "Why I Love you," I closed my eyes and could see him sitting at his piano singing to me. Then when Tony! Toni! Toné! song, "Anniversary" came on, the song sounded a little different, and I paused. "Is he singing?" I stopped the playback and began it again. Jae-Sung was singing with the original recorded song and saying my name during the chorus. "Jae!" Grinning, I began to sway singing along and remembering the anniversaries we had together. The fun idol games, food fights, so much laughter and those levels of love making. *(Mmmmh.)* I chuckled as the memories dropped into my head. Honing-in on his single voice, I only heard my love singing to me. Then directly from my heart's mouthpiece the words, "I love you too baby," released from my lips.

Later when all was quiet that night, I listened to some poems he had written for me and recorded to remember our love is forever. The auto-playback of his recording had him reading and then he would sing the poem to music he wrote. While tears slid down from my eyes, I held myself tightly in bed, wishing he was holding me. One poem had the sounds of the ocean lightly accompany his reading and then grew louder as he played the piano and sang the words again. His explosive creative talents were astonishing and extraordinary, crossing different genres of music. No wonder he had been sought after in many countries to write music and collaborate on songs and soundtracks. Jin-K's magic sound couldn't be contained simply within the walls of K-Pop and KR&B. I knew that. Now that I think about it, I'm sure Nah Min-Ji and Jae's stepfather must have known it too. My mind briefly pondered on... *(Maybe that was why*

Dong Hyun did what he did. Money. Was it a loss of control of the money? Was it really because I changed my life to serve Jehovah? Is it because Min Cha did? Control? Was it all for control? I don't know, why he tried to...)

I forcefully blocked those past thoughts from my mind and allowed myself to be pulled back into my lover's arms from his voice reading again. My skin warmed as I melted away hearing the words he wrote in the Last Sunset in Dubai:

<u>Last Sunset in Dubai</u>

The warm wind whispers softly in flight

As a gentle wave sings good night

Golden tones over shades of brown

As your amber eyes enrapture my heart

Flowing rivers of sand make no sound

Bright glowing heat from the sphere above

Ease away to slumber, as I do, my sweet love

Time has given me precious moments with you

Nature's daylight bids us adieu

Safeguard this memory and our last sunset

You with me forever folded as one

Melting together as we marvel at the sun

Your gaze and sweet scent, in your heart, keep me

As your captive as nightfall covers sand's sea

Almost closed now nature's vibrant eye

Do not be sad, my love, please don't cry

The euphoria of our love remains as minutes slip away

But in a short time, God says there will be a new day

I'll be awakened, and say once again, sarang-hae.

"My love…Time had lost its momentum for movement, and light slowly dimmed yet remained constant, while the airwaves lifted mountains and the sea began to play a glorious symphony without distinguished sound." I felt the essence of him was with me in the bed we made love in on our wedding night. Jae-Sung tenderly stroked my skin with the tips of his fingers. He held me within his passionate embrace and whispered his sweet words so close, yes, he was right behind my right ear. Well, it felt that way anyway. My mind drifted off to a dreamland while his voice repeated loves melody all night long.

But the next morning, I woke up feeling cold. I could no longer sense his warmth ignited by the intensity of my memory dream. Momentarily I was disoriented, and cried, missing everything about the man I love and what was no longer present in my life now.

Then moving on with each day a new, I found myself back to feeling the undertow of melancholy once again. It constantly followed me because I miss Jae-Sung, deep within the cells of my bone-marrow. However, I took a little time to read over one of the songs King David wrote later in his life. Slowly reading Psalms 37 reminded me again to *wait expectedly on Jehovah*. Constant daily Bible reading, helped to soothe my heart's anxiousness and grief.

I read a lot about David's life and discovered how the lessons of his story taught me in many deeper ways than I initially learned at first read. It has not been easy, but I am really trying to be content and focus on a clear view of a brighter future.

53. Grands-parents Géniaux

The transition to the European environment didn't really take that long. It was probably because our daily spiritual and family routines remained the same, except for their Korean family wasn't here, but their grandparents and their French relatives were.

On a day that it rained so heavily that the triplets couldn't go outside, they got a glimpse into their grandparents, they had never seen before. As they did when I was growing up, my parents created a party or adventure for childhood joy. As the rain poured outside, at breakfast my father announced a dance education party would be commencing in the grand ballroom at 11:00 a.m. *(They will love this! Those frowns will turn upside down.)*

Skipping with excitement, we met my parents at 11:00 on the dot. My father happened to be dressed in a formal black tux with tails and shiny black oxfords, and my mother wore a gold ruffled skirt dress that stopped just below her knees and matching golden pumps.

(They're going all out, just like when I was a kid.)

When we entered, the two were already couple dancing to Paradis' "Toi Et Moi" and the song Santana's "Smooth" featuring Rob Thomas played right after, and we quietly watched them. They were in their own dance zone, but my father quickly changed the music for a history lesson. After listening to some old favorites like Winton Marsalis's "Cherokee," "Take A Train," and Harry Connick Jr.'s "Jambalaya-On the Bayou," my father adjusted the music genre for us to dance.

My father encouraged Jin, Jolie, and Jae to show him what kind of dance moves they had. He even played a few old DRGN5 songs called "Dance Party," "Fantastic," and "Boomalistic," and their father's solo hit "Jump-in." The triplets danced their little hearts out and sang all the words. So, did I. They wanted to hear Bam Bam's "RiBBon" twice. *(What a fun song.)* We laughed, danced, and sang to several songs until my father said, "Les enfants, aimeriez-vous voir des enfants faire une danse qu'ils faisaient quand votre mère était petite? Ma chère... ma fille, prends la parole, s'il te plaît. Ha! (Children, would you like to watch a dance, these two used to do when your mother was young? Dearest... daughter take the floor, please)."

Unsure, my head jerked to get clues from my mother who had her hands up in the air and said, "Philippe', what on earth are you talking about?"

My father just laughed, adjusting the music to a song he clearly had plotted to take a break and make us dance. My children sat with eager grinning faces waiting as my father motioned for us to get moving and said, "Hips. Go on and move those hips, girls! Ha!"

As soon as "Suavemente" from Elvis Crespo started, my mother and I started clapping our hands and laughing, remembering the old song. She shouted, "Philippe', that was so long ago, you can't expect us to remember that. Really now." He simply pointed to the middle of the room like he was Debbie Allen on the tv show *Fame*, my mother had on DVD years ago. Although we didn't remember all the moves from the Delacroix talent show when I was sixteen, we fumbled through it with giggles. My father was not satisfied and played it again. The second time, we were able to do most of the salsa step routine all the way through. We received cheers and hugs from the judges. *(Ha, ha! Oh, I'm old but that was fun.)*

"Mawmaw, you look happy. I wanna learn to do it." Came from my bright smiling daughter. I pinched her cheeks and told her, "Sure, we will teach you. It was from grandpapa's party one year. Your auntie Renee and her mom taught us so the three of us could win or at least move like a Latin pro. It's a lot of moving. But I can still swing like GiGi!" Jolie grinned with a nod.

"Hey!" My mother yelped then smacked my butt laughing. My father began teaching my boys some dance moves from the 70's. "Pawpaw not those hip thrusts from Saturday Night Fever..." *(Darn, too late. Why does he love doing that so much.)*

My mother turned away from looking at him, I think she wanted to laugh. Minutes later she focused, and we helped Jolie move her little hips for a quick dance lesson. We danced through several more up-tempo songs. *(Why are we listening to disco?)* Halfway through the long version of G.Q.'s "Disco Nights," my children and I sat down winded. We watched my seventy something year old parents get their groove on.

A bit later, they joined us, and we sat listening to them tell a story about the first time they danced together in this room. Jae asked with a confused look on his face, "Hold on, GiGi, you didn't know how to waltz?" Jolie shook her head in disbelief, and Jin moaned a low, "No way." Nodding, she admitted she was a waltz newbie, and my father spun her around with ease.

"Show us again. The way you dance is so cool."

"You dance the waltz like a pro now, grandma."

"Oh, please, do a dance for us."

Chuckling, my parents changed the music to something slow but still the old-school music they liked. We watched them flawlessly glide around seemingly on a cloud. I thought… *(I wonder if they were ever in a ballroom dance competition. They are so good.)*

Jae asked me, "Did you and abeoji (father) dance like them?"

Shaking my head I admitted, "Uh, no. Your father and I had our own way of dancing. No one is as cool as your grandparents." He smiled. The timing of my statement was perfect since my father had twirled her around, and they started doing the bump before stepping with fast footwork to Phyllis Hyman's "You Know How to Love Me." They kept going as he dipped her, and they locked their feet, turned, kicked out then shifted to gentle hip bumps to the groovy bass beat of Juicy's "Sugar Free." Old school R&B music continued to play, and they danced all over the grand ballroom to Barry White's "Love Theme." It was just so elegant the way my parents danced together. The seamless way in which they transitioned from slow to quick, classic waltz, then a foxtrot, merengue, then a salsa or tango blending in disco moves, without pausing or missing a beat of the changing music, had me just as captivated as my children. *(She looks so happy with him. They are so classy and smooth together.)* With a loud "Wua," Jin made his enjoyment known. While Jolie clapped grinning, Jae just nodded, smirking. I could tell he agreed that his grandparents were very cool.

474

The song changed for them to dance more of a tango-style waltz with some hip swinging to Anita Baker's "Been So Long." It was the way he spun her and held her securely that made me want to dance that way. I clapped while studying their footwork. The mood slowed significantly, and I smiled seeing him gaze at her during their closer dance to Rain featuring Jackson Wang song's "Magnetic." And then The Whispers' song "In the Mood." It was similar to how I had witnessed them ice skating. They fit perfectly. Philippe' and Delphine Delacroix own it out there on the shiny dance floor. I thought, *(My parents are wow!)* A minute later, I noticed my mother brushing her open hand over my father's back as she slid around him. Moving to the beat facing away from him, she pressed her back against him while he wrapped his arms around her. Then there was a slow grinding circular move she did up against him right before he twirled her outward, whipping her back to face him. *(Wait... Why is he smirking? Is she biting her lip? Okay, lifting her face with his finger by her chin is not a dance move I've ever seen. Did they forget, we're in here too? Uh Oh...)*

"Uh, amigos, let's go get some fruit. Uh and find Kang, Jusan, Gert, Wolfgang, anybody. Let's go. Right now. Right now." I said it scrambling to the northern French doors.

Jolie spoke with a "But…" I gave her the *'do what I say'* squinted eye glare and she didn't make another peep while moving to exit. Silently we rushed out. As I was closing the French doors of the ballroom behind us, I heard someone growl like a tiger. After that, we didn't see my parents for several hours.

Delphine's journal:

An afternoon delight among disheveled sheets… "Mon diamant noir, Delphine, comme tu m'éblouis avec tes mouvements fantastiques en tant que citoyenne française (My black diamond, Delphine, how you dazzle me with your fantastic moves as a French citizen)." He said while caressing the rich mahogany skin of my right shoulder. Smiling coyly, lying next to him, I stretched up and lightly brushed my nose against his before moving to exit the bed. Philippe' pulled me closer, preventing me from separating. I began to protest, "Philippe' I need to…"

"No. You cannot leave this bed." he demanded, holding me securely in his arms. Snickering, I kissed him. Looking into his soft blue eyes, I playfully asked, "What if I'm hungry?"

"I will bring all the food and drink you need to survive, mon amour chéri (my cherished love)." Peering at him, I countered with, "What will you do if I have to pee?" He paused, looked up at the ceiling and wrapped his long creamy legs around mine, he licked his lips and answered, "I suppose I will have to catch it and then dispose of it after." He gestured cupping his hands together as we laughed. I pushed his broad chest, "Gross! You are such a nasty freak, Philippe'."

"Am I? Hey, I didn't say I would drink it!" We laughed hysterically before I kissed him tenderly. Then I announced, "Frenchman, remember our grandchildren are here. We can't just do what we want, anywhere we like." Releasing me from his arms and sitting up to exit the bed, he admitted, "Dell, you cannot sway those hips, bite the corner of your bottom lip, stare at me and growl or squeeze my derrière (tush). You know that's all I need to take you to bed."

Giggling, I winked at him. Then backing my naked body off the bed, I growled, swung my hips walking to the bathroom shower. He darted off the bed to follow me shouting, "Ooo la-la! Douche! Nous pourrions être en retard pour le diner (Shower! We might be late for dinner)." I laughed as he attacked me in the bathroom.

Yeah, my mother's face was glowing, and my father was slyly grinning when they sat down to join us for dinner twelve minutes late. Although they were chatty with everyone at the table, I noticed them eyeing each other and smirking. It reminded me how Jae looked at me from across the room at that auction. I tried to play it off but lowkey snickered. *(Oh, they are, so going to be doing it again.)* 476

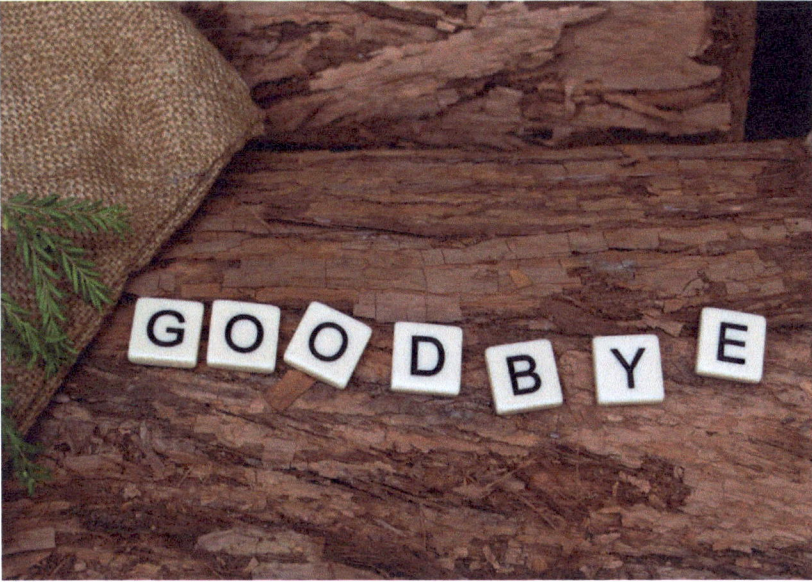

54. Au Revoir

From the months of our easy transition to living in Europe, it dawned on me that we needed to be as normal as possible now that we are not in South Korea anymore. I gave my thoughts some serious prayer because I didn't want to make the decisions for the wrong reasons. Later I talked things over with my father and I video chatted with SI and Min Cha on the subject for their perspective and tips on how to address it. The weeks passed, then I got a few letters from Ophelia and Stanley, Ami, Megan, Stephanie, Tommy Han, and the Hanover's with encouragement to stick to my personal study routine, daily Bible reading, and teaching my children, and it came to me that we didn't need NM Entertainment security anymore. Honestly, I wanted Kang, Trey and Jusan to go home and move on with their lives. I felt like I wasn't relying on Jehovah's arrangement that he provides to all his people around the world. It felt to me as if I was depending more on the security of my loving idol brothers, those awesome ninjas. When I prayed about it more, I realized I had been kidnapped right under their noses because they are imperfect humans and can't read hearts and minds like Jehovah. They are amazing, but it gnawed at me, feeling this false sense of being untouchable with them around. Praying before having the actual conversation helped. I didn't want to hurt Kang. I wasn't sure how he would take my feelings or request. It was hard. I cried a little, but I finally brought it to his attention.

"Kang, I don't need shadowing anymore. Really, it's not necessary. I'm at home."

"Noona, but…"

"Brother, relax and be married. I know SI takes care of your mother but what about Min Cha? Isn't she alone? Kang, you have a wife. You need to think about settling things for her. Jehovah and the brothers and sisters will take care of us. Besides, if you miss us, you should just stay at my home if you want. Guard that piano!" He snorted. I wiped my tears smiling and feeling less anxious about telling him to go.

"Kang, give us twelve months. We can negotiate before they start school. How about that? I love you, but you need to take a break from us. I don't go anywhere but to the hall with my parents or on my teaching assignment, and sometimes the market. I'm never alone, and just about everything we need is here on the estate grounds. My three amigos need to adjust to living without ninjas around all the time…and so do I."

He looked at me from across the parlor table and shook his head. "Marie, it's my responsibility. What if there is a—"

I jumped in with a comeback before he finished speaking, "Kang, everything is different. You said it yourself, there will be less of a privacy or fan threat the further away from South Korea we are."

He wasn't budging and stormed out of the room upset. However, we had a few more conversations with my father, my oncle Wolfgang, Jusan, and Trey, who were supporting my wishes, and he finally agreed, we didn't need constant presents of security and shadowing in Lyon.

"I love you, Kang Cheng."

He grunted and replied with, "Geureom, geureom (sure, sure). I don't believe you. Because when I asked you to marry me you said no."

He winked at me, humming Bruno Mars song "Marry Me." I snorted but in seconds, we howled laughing after hearing loud rumblings from my mother, father, Jusan, and Trey.

"Qu'est-ce que c'est (What the heck)?"

"Vous avez fait, quoi (You did, what)?!"

"Geunyeowa gyeolhon (Marry her)?"

"Jam Kwan man! (Wait a minute)!"

A few days that followed, we intentionally got together as a giant family and made several authentic dishes like baek-kimchi, dongchimi, bibimabap, pajeon, bossam, kimbap with banchans. We dressed up in hanboks or makeshift ones, and had rounds of Soju, well the adults did, so that it was really a South Korean traditional meal experience. It was amazing. *(We won't forget their culture.)*

Then in just a few weeks with sad faces and glossy eyes, we said goodbye to idol brothers Kang, Trey, Jusan and nanny Nari who all returned to South Korea.

And then it was just us.

My family's estate had always been my favorite place. It's beautiful and peaceful. To walk outside and not hear traffic, just see landscaped gardens, trees, and grassland without security protocol restrictions was a freedom that I hadn't had in years. I allowed myself to relax more, and it felt good.

However, within a few short months, world chaos had become more intense. There were protests and rallies to ban religions around the world going on. The groups were peaceful when picketing outside of cathedrals and churches, but it was a little startling one Sunday to see a mob of protesters yelling at us leaving the Kingdom Hall. Our loving congregation brothers kept us safe and secure, and there were no threats, but things were escalating.

The following day the branch restricted in-person meetings, and we conducted our ministry through private home letter writing and our gathering together was done through video conferencing and small service groups. It was fun to watch my children have a share in letter writing activity, the way Joy had done for me so many years ago. They drew images of life in a peaceful garden and wrote letters to neighbors and their cousins. But we did regularly discuss what was happening in the world around us.

"Eomeoni (mother), why are they so mean to us?"

"Is it because we live here and not in South Korea?"

"Why don't they listen to us?"

"We just want everyone to live forever and be happy."

"They don't want to be in Jehovah's new world here?"

"Why not? It's going to be wonderful for everyone. No one will get sick, and everyone will be kind and happy. Why don't they want to hear it from us?"

While we finished letter writing for the morning, I told them again, "Remember my loves, those people are not angry at you. Most aren't listening because what we are trying to show them are coming changes that will make the world very different. Sadly, lots of people don't like that because the devil is behind the wickedness in the world, and he has blinded people to the truth that he is about to be destroyed by our king Jesus and his army along with all his badness too. People don't know Jehovah or his son and what wonderful things they have planned for us. That's why we keep trying to tell them."

Gert added, "We should not be afraid, Jesus is leading the fight. We are only here to be loyal and witness things happen here on the earth."

My mother shared her thoughts out loud, "Jehovah will protect his unified people. Individually, things might happen but that doesn't mean we are not loved, favored, or protected. We must be brave and obedient, and follow the directions given by the men in place with the responsibility to care for us. Like Moses and Aaron did in their work assignment when his people were leaving the bondage in Egypt. Remember?"

Simultaneously there were sounds of, "Oui." "Eh" "Yes. I remember that."

"We are only seconds away from the promises Jehovah made for those remaining loyal to him. We must keep alert, be strong and do all we can to prove we love him, and then we will have a new beginning of forever happiness." I smiled at them after telling them these words.

My father said putting the literature away in the libraries hidden vault. "Remember, what the Latin word diaconos means. Jehovah's sovereignty is what we stand by. In doing so as imperfect servants, we must try to follow Jesus' example to the best of our ability. We always need to practice what we have been trained from the Bible examples and His amazing qualities He shares with us through His word and seen in creation. He expects His people to be loving, patient, humble, kind, honest, faithful, and courageous."

It surprised me when my protective and handsome son, Jae suggested, "We should pray for help when we are scared." We agreed and bowed our heads. Wolfgang said a prayer of thanks and a request for courage not only for us but all those around the world. I thought again about my sister, family and friends and added an extra request for them.

55. Découverte

Discovery is the act or action of locating, uncovering, or revealing something unknown from before. Through evidence or facts, discovery can generate emotions caused by excitement, anxiety, or fear.

These days we don't venture out but strictly stay within the confines of the hundreds of acres of Delacroix land. There was so much to do and explore that it didn't feel like we were restricted from going out, but we were because it was very dangerous. Only my father, oncles and the brothers from our congregations took the lead to leave on a limited basis. There were curfews in place, and everyone was required to have written permission or a pass to simply exit and reenter the property, let alone travel around.

Discovering new things was something I loved as a young person, and still do. My parents instilled research and learning new things in me, and it was how I grew up. Books, places, and people were the three elements to exploring and expanding our minds beyond the limits of what we know at any time. It was exciting to learn this way. My father taught me his passions, and I learned just about everything I could on types of literature, the science of nature, cultures, and human behavior. My mother focused more on healthy eating, biology, natural healing remedies and root causes for rules and laws.

The two are so opposite, but together I had exposure to many things. Mysteries, history, and puzzles were one of my favorites, along with classic romance with feelings expressed through glances and poetic words. I believe it's inherited from my parents.

On a chilly but sunny winter's day, when the leaves were gone, and a thick, white blanket of freshly fallen snow covered the earth, I was alone. I thought. My children were outside exploring with their grandfather, oncle Andreas, and his divorced daughter Geneviève's children, Andre' and Amelia, who had just turned ten and six. Geneviève had married and moved to Lyon, but not long after that, her husband Grayson decided he didn't want to be a Jehovah's Witness anymore and left. We were in the same congregation, but periodically, her widower father came down from Paris to ease the load with her children and hang out with my parents. I knew that my children would be very preoccupied with their adventures.

Since I don't like to be cold, I stayed inside. I made myself a pot of lemon lavender tea and decided to check out a book from our family library. When I walked in from the south side, I instantly got a whiff of the blended light scent of soft leather and vanilla. *(Oh, Pawpaw has been in here recently.)* I giggled, taking my tray to a table next to a bookshelf and couch. The huge two-story room of literary wonders had always been a favorite place of mine. Walking slowly, I glanced around and briefly stopped to admire the carved statues, life-size globe, world maps, and the six oil paintings of colonial lands and homes from my father's family history.

I sat down at a wide marble desk, pondering whether I wanted to go up the stairs or find something on the main floor. *(I usually don't pick ones that are close; I always go up there. All the Jane Austin, Agatha Christie and Shakespeare literature are upstairs. Hmmm.)*

While thinking and not making any decisions or moves, my mother came in. When her hand touched my shoulder, it caused an electric current connection and shocked me. I jumped. "Ouch!"

"Sorry, but I'm electric. Boogie, woogie, woogie…"

I snorted shaking my head while she started to do the "Electric Slide" dance moves as she sang the lyrics to the Marcia Griffith song. We laughed for a few minutes. Then she announced, "Jae and Jolie, and I were in here the other day. He wanted a classic, "The Three Musketeers" by Alexandre Dumas; and she wanted something on a type of butterfly. After some research, we found a few articles on the purple emperor in an older Awake, Butterfly Conversation, and National Geographics magazines. They are so curious."

I asked, "Where was Jin?"

"Philippe' was teaching him how to fence. Marie, are you looking for an old favorite or something to discover?"

"It's nice to have choices. Was thinking about finishing the biography research I started on Hazel Scott or maybe reading *The Great Camouflage* by Suzanne Césaire. But I haven't decided. Do you want to suggest something?"

My mother nodded. Then, she guided me to the waist-high corner shelf on the main floor. She motioned to a few oddly shaped books that were covered with something apparently to preserve them. She pulled out three large black books tied together with a pink ribbon and then two thick tan books tied securely with a yellow ribbon. Smiling at me she said, "Marie, tan before black. Happy discovery. I'll tell the kids you're reading, so you are not disturbed too much. If you need me, I'll be making bread for tonight."

The way she said it made me question her motives, but before I could formulate my thoughts to ask, she had sauntered out of the library.

Instantly curious, I began reading the top tan-colored book first. When I opened it, the title page read: "*From Three African Sisters* by Dell M. Delacroix. This book is dedicated to my grandmother and for my beautiful daughters."

I inhaled sharply, "Mom…" crept into the air as I glanced toward the door. But she was already gone. *(I don't believe this.)* "She… She wrote a book. That is crazy. Why didn't anyone tell me?"

Holding the book in my hand I was jolted with many thoughts and feelings about the discovery. Excitement and curiosity were my primary emotions, although the annoyance of another secret about my mother closely followed. I sipped some tea, then I smiled to myself and began reading the first book very slowly.

Following the written path laid before me in a historical retrospect, I immediately connected what had been referenced in my mother's journal that she let me read a few years ago. *(It's so exciting!)* I was engrossed in the stories of Allmai, Ayasha, and Auzehla. Since I had only gotten a sneak peak of my mother's family history a couple of years before, I couldn't stop reading. I never left the library, except to pee. As the hours passed, I had my dinner in the same spot I had started reading in earlier that day. I moved from the couch to a chair and then later to a lounging chaise, and back again to the couch. No one disturbed me. It was way into the night when my children came in before bed. Startled, I said, "Is it that late, oh baby, I'm sorry. Let me tuck you in."

Jae took charge of speaking for his siblings. "No, we are going to have a camp out in the tree house cottage. We just came to say goodnight." The three stood there grinning while our nighttime ritual of kisses and hugs commenced. Then my three amigos took off giggling. It wasn't long after that when I had finished reading her second book, which was a continuation of family stories entitled, *Ripples in the Bloodline*. It was an extraordinary feeling to get more details about my great-grandmother Lurell Ann, and the women in my ancestry going as far back as the Gold Coast of Africa.

Automatically my brain continued its analytical compartmentalizing of the information I had read from the lineage story, while I adjusted my body on the couch. Some of the names and places seemed familiar as if I had heard them before. My mind pulled back some identified facts and sifted through the information. While folding a blanket I had used to cover me earlier, the names and places data shuffled in my head like a series of visual flash cards that filled in missing pieces like partial words and letters on a Scrabble board.

Curiously, I flipped through the second tan book again because it was the only one that had a few images. As I studied them more carefully, I tried to identify some features and connect to the relatives from back in that time. My body had goosebumps learning the history many people don't get to discover about themselves. I thought I looked like my great-grandmother a little. I connected a bit of the Native American part from her grandfather in me too, maybe.

"This is amazing." I mumbled turning the pages. As I reviewed the family tree again I smiled recognizing my name in the generation bloodline list. It came to me, "Since this is a line of women, I need to add Jolie. Oh, Jacquline should be here too."

Plantation Slave Cabin

Alice (Baptiste) Ormond

John and Sophia EagleFeather

Ernestine & Harry Magee

Pat & Samuel Magee, Wes Magee and children

My Grandmother: Lurell Ann Magee-Wilson

January 1962

My Mother: Eleanor "Teence" Murry

Age 14 and 72

My Junior Year at Tulane

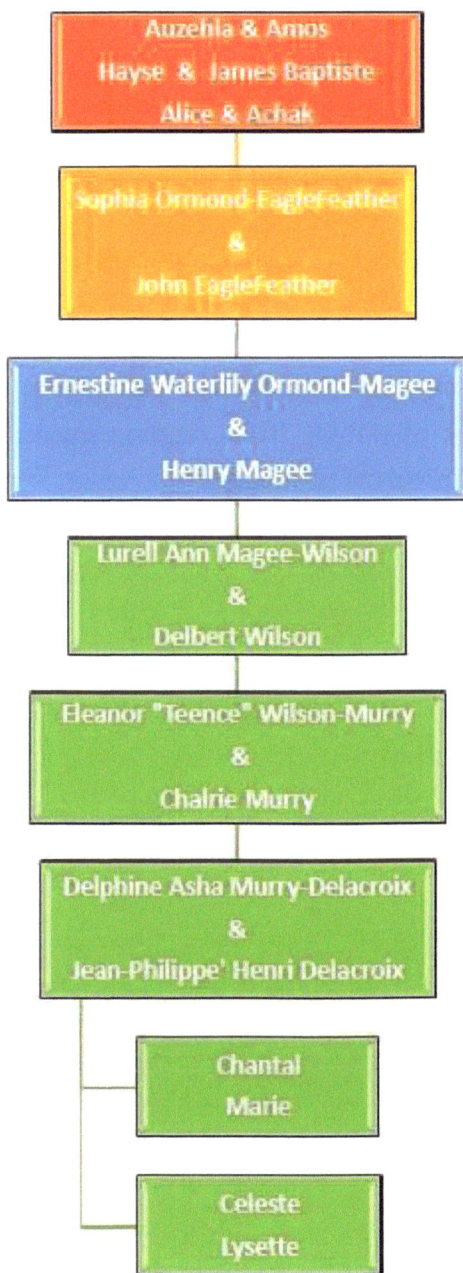

```
┌─────────────────────────────┐
│      Auzehla & Amos          │
│   Hayse  &  James Baptiste   │
│      Alice & Achak           │
└─────────────────────────────┘
           │
┌─────────────────────────────┐
│  Sophia Ormond-EagleFeather  │
│             &                │
│      John EagleFeather       │
└─────────────────────────────┘
           │
┌─────────────────────────────┐
│ Ernestine Waterlily Ormond-Magee │
│             &                │
│        Henry Magee           │
└─────────────────────────────┘
           │
┌─────────────────────────────┐
│   Lurell Ann Magee-Wilson    │
│             &                │
│       Delbert Wilson         │
└─────────────────────────────┘
           │
┌─────────────────────────────┐
│ Eleanor "Teence" Wilson-Murry│
│             &                │
│        Chalrie Murry         │
└─────────────────────────────┘
           │
┌─────────────────────────────┐
│ Delphine Asha Murry-Delacroix│
│             &                │
│ Jean-Philippe' Henri Delacroix│
└─────────────────────────────┘
      │
      │    ┌─────────────────┐
      ├────│    Chantal      │
      │    │     Marie       │
      │    └─────────────────┘
      │
      │    ┌─────────────────┐
      └────│    Celeste      │
           │    Lysette      │
           └─────────────────┘
```

497

It was after 2:00 a.m. when I moseyed up to the moon room and quickly undressed ready to flop in the canopy bed. I was exhausted but still very excited. Thoughts raced through my mind of how these three African sisters were just young girls and survived alone in a foreign place, not knowing the people or language.

I mumbled to myself, "They relied on each other and what had been taught."

Minutes later as my eyes grew heavy, I pondered on the fact that each of their situations led to generations of stories, myths, and warnings about mixing with non-Blacks resulting in never-ending tragedy. As thoughts of details from reading my mother's books continued to fade, I drifted off to sleep.

56. Three Sixty

Late the next morning, I checked on my children who were still outdoors and fully engaged in the French winter cottage-camping experience. They were totally preoccupied, and I left them to their family adventures. Swiftly greeting Lylah and Gert in the kitchen, I grabbed some fruit and yogurt for a quick bite, then focused on changing sheets and doing laundry.

Sometime around 4:00 p.m. I relaxed with a steaming pot of London Fog, walnut balls, and a rasberry scone my mother had made, in the library. Comfy on the chaise, I flipped back through my mother's books to review some of the story details again. I felt more connected to the women in our bloodline, especially my great grandmother, Lurell Ann Magee, and her complex life story.

Time passed and it was dark when I heard my children come in but scurry back out. Being preoccupied, I didn't even look up. Then

I opened the first black book. It was actually a very old ledger entitled, *"Kingston Estates-MacGregor Lands."* Reading the first twelve pages, the book listed data of a family, an outline of the business shift and a land name change. My mind tossed around facts and memories, *(They made exclusive rum? What was the name of that expensive rum factory we went too on that trip to Jamaica? Hmmm. Was it Kingston? Shoot, I don't remember.)* Turning to page fourteen, I began to confirm what I was reading with a slower repeat of each word, then something jolted me. Multiple facts hit me like a flash hailstorm.

"Wait... this says Kingston Estates used to be Kingston Sugar Land... sugar... sugar cane? Caribbean, right?"

I rustled back through book pages to verify what I said, while rushing over to the last painting on the library wall of the family lands. Proudly displayed under artificial lights and protective casing, the image in the ledger was the same on the wall with the caption that read *Kingston Sugar Land*.

"Oh, my god! This... this... is...."

I stood in front of the dimly lit artwork, unable to move for several minutes that seemed like hours. "What is going on? Is this real? Kingston Sugar Land was a plantation. A plantation with... slaves. I... this can't be real. No, it can't be."

My scalp started to itch from the increasing perspiration. Biting my thumbnail, I was so nervous I tore the nail away, almost peeling away some skin, while examining the book and then the framed painting. Minutes later and without looking, I grabbed the second black book. Glancing at the title *"Lord and Lady of the Caribbean"* by Celina Maria McDowall-Duquesne, I looked inside and uncovered in the introduction that the book was of her memoirs. There was a family list that referenced her cousins on MacGregor's Kingston

Estates and the book itself was dedicated to her father's mother, Marguerite MacGregor-McDowall.

"Huh?" I began to fumble and shuffle books around to review the third book bound in black leather with gold foil engraved lettering, *"Past, Present, Future"* written by J.P. Delacroix. Knowing my father Jean-Philippe' Henri, his late brother Jean-Pierre François, and their late father Jean-Pierre Philippe' had the same first two initials, at first, I didn't think it mattered who actually wrote the book.

But my mind was automatically moving trying to fill in the blanks and I had to know the answer. Flipping through the first few pages there were images of family members and a family lineage chart with some of the same names from Celina's book. It easily confirmed that my father wrote the book linking himself to the plantation in the Caribbean. One that had slaves. Human captives. My heart sank trying to pretend it wasn't true. Frantically, I turned pages in both books, and then snatched an old Delacroix family photo album on the third shelf next to a large life-like sculpture of my great grandfather Julien Louis-Henri Delacroix. Photographs I had seen many times were connecting pieces of the maze puzzle from my childhood memories.

Seconds into flipping and skimming pages, dots were connecting that had not been there before. I had never paid much attention to the Duquesne or McDowall names because Delacroix was the history and land being passed down through generations. But now, things were coming together, and I was gasping with each visual and written confirmation of facts. Saying it out loud to make sure my brain really understood.

"The three sisters were taken and sold in Jamaica, right? To the MacGregors on Sugar Land! Oh, my god! That is where they were slaves, and..."

My body felt a surge of heat and I felt dizzy all of a sudden. I sat down and gulped the last of the tea that was now room temperature. "Slavers? How can this be?... Why would... What in the hell is happening? I'm... I'm going to be sick..."

Slowly I told myself, *(Breathe in...Breathe out... Count to ten...One... Two...)*

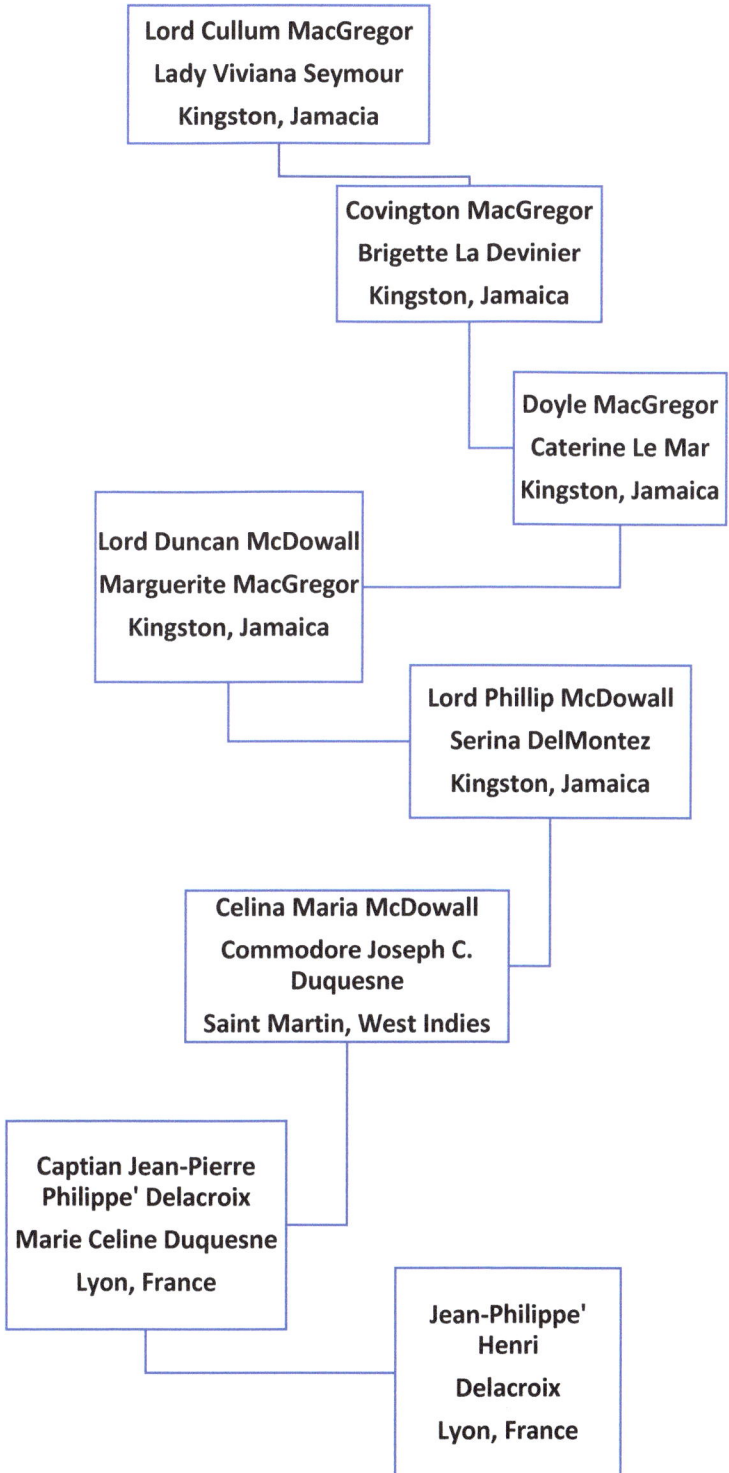

Lord Cullum MacGregor
Lady Viviana Seymour
Kingston, Jamacia

Covington MacGregor
Brigette La Devinier
Kingston, Jamaica

Doyle MacGregor
Caterine Le Mar
Kingston, Jamaica

Lord Duncan McDowall
Marguerite MacGregor
Kingston, Jamaica

Lord Phillip McDowall
Serina DelMontez
Kingston, Jamaica

Celina Maria McDowall
Commodore Joseph C. Duquesne
Saint Martin, West Indies

Captian Jean-Pierre Philippe' Delacroix
Marie Celine Duquesne
Lyon, France

Jean-Philippe' Henri
Delacroix
Lyon, France

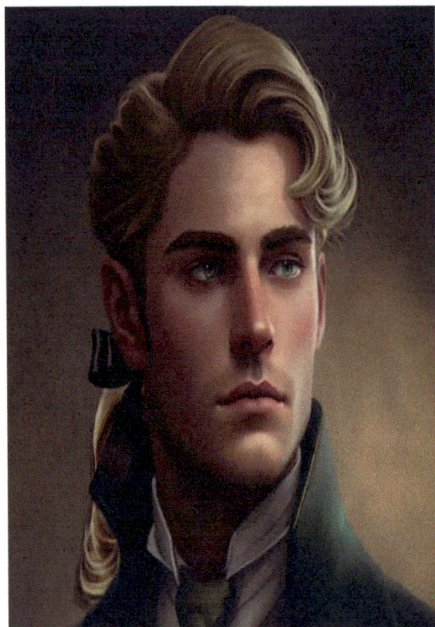

Cullum MacGregor

Marguerite MacGregor-McDowall

Phillip   and   Serina McDowall

Celina Maria McDowall

Celina Maria McDowall-Duquesne at age 65

Marie Celine Delacroix age 13 and age 33

Captain Jean-Pierre Philippe' Delacroix age 35

No matter what I tried, I still let out a shriek with the realization of the truth in front of me. "The Scottish, MacGregors of Jamaica were... filthy disgusting slavers, and they owned my ancestors!"

My mind flooded with scenarios and replayed situations I had read the day before in the story of Allmai, Ayasha, and Auzehla. Then for several minutes, I could only compile partial thoughts. I held my hand over my mouth and closed my eyes tightly, hoping that would help subside the queasiness I was now feeling. My skin felt clammy. I did not know how to deal with what I was concluding. Happy, sad, angry, confused, there were so many different feelings from the shock of emotions. It was a lot to take in, and I needed answers. I demanded them.

"Pawpaw! Mom... Where's mother?" I dashed out of the library to find my mother for answers and my father for comfort. From room to room, I traveled in desperate search. I didn't think to use the chateau's intercom to find her because my mind was racing. I looked at the clock in the hall and it displayed the time as 9:30 p.m. "Is it that late?"

Looking at the wall, I noticed two old photographs of my Delacroix grandparents. My eyes seemed to be more focused on the one of Marie Celine Delacroix smiling back at me. In seconds, the memory came to me that I had taken the picture, after I graduated from Howard, we took a girl's trip to the beach. I immediately felt this surge and tears cascaded down my face with my breathy whisper, "grand-mère (grandma)". I remembered her sweet fragrance of rose water, her soft prissy laugh, the delicate way she held my face when she kissed me, and all that she taught me, like how a French lady is to take tea, walk, and speak.

(She loved me, and I loved her!) "It is not true. How could she be from... No!"

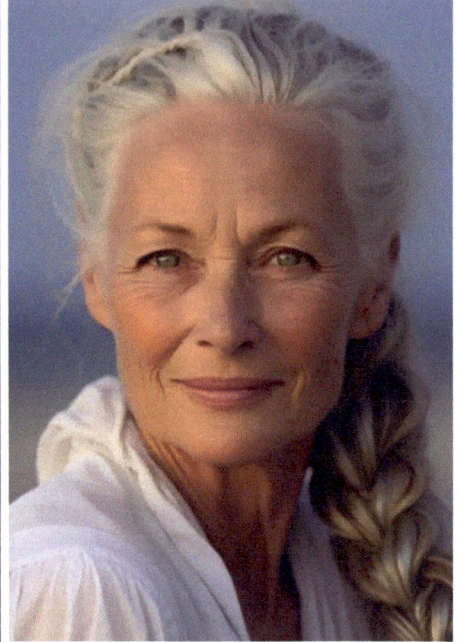

Grand-père Jean-Pierre and Grand-mère Marie

Briskly moving through the second-floor hallway, my eyes were clouded with tears. I slowed down to walk not run. I made it to their bedroom they had renamed "garden." I knocked before opening the door, wiping my eyes, and releasing high and sharp toned words of "Pawpaw! Mom!"

They were in bed. Relaxed in his crisp hunter green short-sleeved pajamas, my father had been sitting up reading to my mother, who was curled up next to him in a cream short-sleeved lace gown looking like a kitten enjoying some catnip.

Quickly, he removed his glasses and placed them on top of his head while she leisurely sat up. Rushing to them, I flopped down at the bottom of their fluffy king-size bed, much like in the same way I must have done as a child because both of them chuckled. My colliding thoughts of facts and feelings came out a bit garbled.

"I… I don't know what to think! Pawpaw did your ancestors own slaves?! Did they really? Mother's people from Africa? Where did all this come from? Is it true? Grandmama Marie's mother… You… you named me Marie, but her family were… African slave owning… Colonizers! Why… why would you do that? I don't understand. Why no one told me any of this!" I said it pointing to my mother and began to hiccup from the constant gasps for several minutes.

My father spoke first, "Dell, you just dropped it on her?"

"Well, our daughter wanted to discover." Was what she said before pulling my hands and grabbing my attention.

Before she followed up with more to say, I asked, "Fiction, right? Mom, what you wrote was fiction. Just a story. Right?" Although my hiccups had stopped, I continued to blink quickly from nervousness. My mother shook her head and moaned no. My heart felt like a water-filled bucket of heavy cold metal planks. I actually leaned a little forward from the pressure in my chest. She followed her reply with words.

"Marie, the story of our African ancestors… I researched not only from plantation records but from what Hellene gave me from those stories passed down over the generations from the women circles I told you about. Remember?"

I nodded, biting the inside of my left cheek. She continued telling more of the truth of the situation. "When your father and I discussed things, I think it was the first time I had been back here after the accident. We agreed to research to know all we could because the names and places from my stories were too familiar to your father's history from his grandmother, Celina. He wanted to research it further. We did it as a couple's project. Your father encouraged me to write down the history told to me in order to have both sides for you and your sister to know if you ever wanted. It never came up.

Well not until you said you had been feeling disconnected as a Black woman living in South Korea, and I went to help you pack."

My emotions were clearly all over the place as my voice cracked from high to low when I said exactly what I was thinking with no filter in its delivery. "Pawpaw... you... you never told me any of this... I don't believe you never said a word. Not even to me. Grandmama Marie's parents, and their parents and theirs... Owned people like cattle. They tortured them, bred, and branded them, castrated, raped them... sold them. Black people. You knew. Did you name me after her because of your white guilt? I... I... was... it your way to try and erase what those horrible people did? It doesn't! It doesn't! And now I have that on me! Like a scarlet letter. A trail to follow the disgusting plantation nigger-slaver marking that I can't ever get rid of. It's in me. How revolting! Why would you name me after her?!"

I was a tad bit hysterical, with crashing thoughts of not wanting those despicable cruel White people to be related to me, nor my father, or my grandma, who I deeply loved. I was confused with feelings of Black pride and the shame of the whiteness running through me. Because oil and water did not mix, I felt disgusted and a little lost.

As usual my father remained quietude, not being at all triggered by my emotions. He calmly replied, "Chantal-Marie, I gave you my mother's name because in Latin it means star of the sea. You are my first born, and as beautiful as she was. This was why I named you Marie. Oui, chere they did own people. You and your mother's African history is interconnected to that fact. Literally we were connected back then, and we didn't even know it. Not until she told me about these warnings, she had learned about mixing with White men after your brother died. When the two of us dug deeper, we found personal writings all the way back to Marguerite MacGregor-McDowall. Among them were private and detailed correspondence between her and her father, and her half-brother, which confirmed many things in your mother's bloodline stories. Isn't that fascinating?"

(What the…) "Fascinating? Pawpaw your family were slave-owning colonizers. They did terrible things to human beings! How… How in the hell is that fascinating?!"

I felt myself getting angrier as tears continued coming out of me from my conflicting feelings. But right before I burst out with words expressing more of my anger, my wise father said something profound to me.

"Yes, fascinating. My dearest, you… you are a product of love that, at the time of those people, was forbidden. Absolutely unthinkable, punishable, even criminal, simply unfathomable to the narrow minds of the past. How glorious it is to have the truth that we are people made by Jehovah. What makes us different is only time, location, and circumstance. From the types of cells, veins, muscles, and organs, we are all human beings made the same way and imperfect because of the first human couples' disobedience. Marie, think of what knowing the truth has given you as clarity on how Jehovah is not partial to one race over another, which means those things are man driven not godly. And in Jehovah's appointed time, he will erase all those past horrors that happened."

I was motionless but could feel my mother stroking my hands. I knew what my father had said was true. It's the past and cannot change. I felt a little calmer and no longer rapidly spiraling with emotions leading me out-of-control.

My mother touched my cheek, and said, "Remember what I shared with you. 'Bout that time, I was not right in my mind because of grief. Do you remember what I said was told to me and how I learned from that."

I moaned I did, and she continued talking and caressing my hand. "Think about the timing of these things. Marie, my mother, and sister had no detailed knowledge about my grandmother, Lurell or others. Those stories were not passed on after Hellene got them. The main reason was probably because your Gram T carried so much racial hatred for most of her life. She blamed her mother for all the pain and tragedy because of these false beliefs. Your aunt Lorelle, well... she had no interest in history anyway. But Hellene got to know it all. She held on to it for me for years, until my depression had consumed me after the death of your brother. Then I got more explicit things in notebooks she gave me after my escape plan debacle."

My father started chuckling and I giggled a little remembering that story from her old journal. She nudged him, before she said, "Imagine our surprise when we researched everything together. It was an amazing discovery of historical connection to have found with Philippe'. Honestly, in a small way, I think it made our love a bit stronger." She smiled at me, and my father nodded as he eased over and kissed her scarfed head.

Settling my thoughts with organized facts and clear reasoning, I spoke again, "The eldest sister, Allmai's story was horribly tragic, and it fueled these graphic warnings of being slave women. In secret, the other older sister, Ayasha gave her heart to a White man, and it caused her unimaginable anguish, suffering, and pain. My ancestor, Auzehla's love for Amos, was real. He cherished her, although he was half-Portuguese and sought freedom, there was so much cruelty and hatred, it traumatized her for the rest of her life. Then, Lurell Ann was my great-grandmother and... and she loved my great-grandpa, Delbert, but her first and only true love... was...was a White man, John-Robert. It was who she pledged heavenly marriage to because they couldn't be together in Louisiana in the early 1900s...

512

Oh… oh, these women and stories." I took a deep breath. My parents smiled as I kept saying my thoughts out loud. "They… couldn't be with the men that loved them, and they loved… Simply… simply because of the time in history they lived in… and…and because they were Black women. Being as such, they were deemed as less in value, unworthy, and unsuitable by social traditions and propaganda that started during slavery."

I took a pause and closed my eyes breathing in deeply. I heard my parents moan in agreement as I opened my eyes. Then I asked the obvious. "I… I…In all the billions of people… I mean, out of every country on this revolving planet we live on, how in all the world did the two of you… find each other?... Fall so deeply in love, and …and… then… have me?"

My father pulled me closer to him. He held his fingers to my chin to lock his clear ocean blue eyes that sparkled in the artificial light to mine, and he said softly, "Ma création la plus chère et la plus belle, c'était au moyen de la même voie miraculeuse, par laquelle vous et Jae-Sung vous êtes rencontrés et avez reconnu la sagesse, la beauté et le privilège rare du véritable amour (My dearest and most beautiful creation, it was by means of the exact same miraculous way, in which you and Jae-Sung found each other and recognized the wisdom, beauty, and rare privilege of true love)."

"It…it was miraculous… wasn't it?" Instantly after speaking those words, my heart burst from the reality winds storming within me. "Oh, Pawpaw… I miss him… I… don't want to be without him, anymore… I am suffering. There is this giant hole in me… I need… I love… I miss, Jae, so much!"

I fell over their laps sobbing. My loving parents stroked my head for a long time. Emotionally exhausted, I fell asleep curled up in bed with them.

Although I privately still yearned for my love, over the next few days, my parents and I reviewed and discussed the family history they had led me to discover. It was, as my father said, fascinating. My mother jokingly commented, "You know, if we had kept on with those warnings, you, me, and your sister would be tossed in the stories as bad examples. Look at Delphine, Chantal, and Celeste, those poor girls, done broke the rules. One married a White, blonde, blue-eyed Frenchman, one a singing South Korean, and the other a White fireman from Portland, Oregon. Ha-Ha-Ha!"

We laughed about that, before I added, "I wish they could've seen how it will be in the future. Race is just a social construct for greed and to suppress and control. We are all just humans." My mother and father agreed with a low moan.

As we discussed the findings and the intertwining history, this discovery solidified in my mind how very fortunate I am that my parents looked for the truth of things and didn't allow people, traditions or customs, and racial differences to break their vows to each other. They lived by that scripture and true love cannot ever be broken. It is rare to achieve yet truly a remarkable precious gift.

Several nights later, I was restless in bed. I longed for him. Prayer didn't turn off my missing him tonight. I got the last letter Jae had written to me and started reading it again. I skimmed it, looking for places where his words made me sense him speaking to me. In my mind I could hear the tone of his voice saying each word to me. As slow tears fell, I read sections over and over.

"Marie, my sweet, I wanted more time but when I thought about it, I realized God had already answered so many of my prayers. When I found your eyes across that crowded room. When you came back to me. When you let me love you. When you loved the real me. When you forgave me after making me a firework in your life. When you healed me, and we found each other once more. When you became my wife and the mother of my children. Oh, my love, you will always keep me alive in your heart until we meet again. I love you…"

After the third time, I opened my keepsake box of memories and took out a few of his forty-two love letters to read some of his reflective words and poems he crafted to express his feelings when we broke up. Jae said things like, "I can feel Marie's joy and laughter from across the ocean." "She is my air to breathe." "One glimpse of her smile will bring life to my dying soul." "Sweet sunset in Dubai, your eyes bring me to heaven's door." "Never question my love for you because you are part of me. Our souls are connected; you're in my bones, in my living cells throughout my body. I can't live without you." "Please, come back to me, Marie."

Then my mind shuffled thoughts as if I were speaking to him, *(Jae-Sung, I miss you so much. Sometimes this hole is bigger than before. I get flashes of your smile just when I am waking up or washing dishes, I remember your laugh. Your crazy laugh. Our fun, games and you pranking me; protecting me, loving me. Pawpaw was right. It was miraculous how we found each other. It was. We were not even interested or curious about someone different. But we loved so deeply without prejudice or fear. You were made for me. It was meant to be forever. I just know it.)*

"Please, let it be forever." I mumbled before turning my damp face into the pillows and sobbed until I fell asleep.

57. Faith & Endurance

The assured expectation of something hoped for or promised. Something that is believed with strong conviction to be factual or forthcoming to reality. Courageous strength in action. The ability to hold fast, withstand and endure difficulty, hardship, adversity, or suffering without wavering.

We had not been in France exceedingly long when the world worsened. Then it quickly turned and moved straight into chaos in only months. In every country around the world, local governments were shutting down and restricting religious activities.

We had not seen my oncle Chevalier Ratcliff since moving back to Lyon. He was unable to return to France. After he left Canada to conduct medical research in Beijing, China, for a week, he was imprisoned there for being one of Jehovah's Witnesses and refusing to assist a military convoy during a violent protest at the airport. My oncle had only been studying and not yet baptized as one of Jehovah's Witnesses, but he made the decision not to get involved in a political stand and conforming violence because of what he learned. He was happily labeled and sent to prison with a group of other Witness brothers in China. Gert was always level-headed and positive about the situation. She said things like, "Jehovah and his son see him. Chevalier is surrounded by loving brothers that continue to encourage him. I will see my jokester, lover, and friend in just a little while. I know I will."

The last photo of the Radcliffs together

Gert was extraordinarily strong, and I admired that about her. It helped me too. We sent him cards, and she wrote him letters every day until the French government stopped all communication services outside of the country. As a family, we kept him in our prayers to maintain his integrity under trial. My father and Wolfgang told us that all countries around the world had stopped international trade and communication at the same time because everything went through the International Alliance. It was no secret what was going to happen. It was simply a matter of time. I was thankful I had educated my children before leaving South Korea. They were not as frightened as they could have been if I hadn't.

"Oh, so this means we are not going to private school, right?" Jin said it with a grin. We snickered. *(He is so silly.)* My father on the other hand laughed the loudest, giving him a high-five.

Around the same time in Paris, my father's musketeer, brother-in-law, and widower, Andreas Moreau was having a tough time with his non-witness children. They were pressuring him to sign documents to side with the international alliance and French government actions to save himself from potential prison. As situations around the world grew more volatile, they then tried to persuade Andreas, Geneviève, and Daniella to stop sneaking around studying the Bible, and to support the government campaigns banning of religion for international peace. The three refused. Then I was terribly upset after my father told me that Odette and her siblings, Brigette, Jean-Pierre, and Henri-Francois were legally trying to force Andreas into a mental treatment center for the elderly because of it. *(Why would they treat him like this? What is wrong with them!?)*

When I finally was able to contact my cousin Odette, my heart sank. During our brief conversation, all she did was yell and curse at me, saying I was to blame for her father's mental state. She shouted things like "you tricked him and your parents into these crazy ideas about people waking up and the world ending! Henri said it a long time ago. I didn't want to believe him but it's a damn cult! I don't care about Navya, your parents, or my sisters even. I can't believe you did this to my father! We are not going to stand for it anymore. My father is not going to lose everything!" It scared me a little. Odette was acting like a person I didn't even know. She was confused. I tried to reason with her, but it didn't change anything. She and Henri led the charge to declare their father a danger to himself and a ward of the region. Fortunately, because there was no medical evidence that he was mentally ill and Geneviève and Daniella were his dual power of attorney, it didn't happen.

But tests and challenges kept right on coming. Just days after the dismissal of the legal action, Geneviève's ex-husband, Grayson took their children, Andre' and Amelia and refused to return them if she continued with her beliefs. It had been a couple of months and she had not seen or heard from them. Local authorities would not aid, and she was terribly ill and stressed, even after moving back to Paris to be closer to where Grayson was supposedly living. No one had seen Grayson or her children in weeks. As soon as she moved, they seemed to have just vanished. We were all worried. But we reasoned that he must have taken them out of the country to have disappeared like that. But where? She remained hopeful and stayed with her sister, Daniella, and their father, Andreas. Then one day, we got word that he returned Amelia to her mother, after she had gotten extremely ill while living abroad. She quickly recovered and we were so happy. But her son chose to stay with his father and was never seen again.

During Amelia's recovery, Daniella had been held in a detention area after she was caught transporting hidden Bible literature coming from her study. Although she was only studying, because she wouldn't disclose where she had been, they held her for several weeks. An old college boyfriend of hers, just so happened to be an international alliance soldier there, and he used his influence to have her released but not before he sexually assaulted her. We were so happy that she was free.

Privately, Daniella and I discussed in detail what she had gone through. I openly shared what happened to me in college. Although the circumstances were not the same, she said it helped her knowing that I really understood how she felt. My beautiful cousin, Daniella is an amazing and determined woman. She was not deterred and didn't stop her secret studying. She focused on relying on Jehovah making things right more than ever. She wasn't scared and didn't harbor any hatred, not even later when she found out she had become pregnant from the incident.

But then came travel bans, curfews, social media, and international communication restrictions that blocked us from being able to contact any of our loved ones outside of our local area. We could only pray for them.

Since we were given instructions long before things had begun to unfold, my family was prepared. We had our emergency backpacks ready in case of a natural disaster or something else, followed the organizational directions, and stayed close to the friends in our congregation. It was a good thing because when the international alliance came to seize the Delacroix estate, we didn't panic.

After two spiritual brothers from our local congregation, Stephano Erste' and Bernard Runoldhad, were called and were on their way, the seven of us waited together, talking about things we would do in the future when the world was peaceful.

Within fifteen minutes of settling outside, armed soldiers escorted Gert's older brother, Wolfgang, and his wife Lylah from their home on the estate to join us. They came with two of their grandchildren, who had been visiting for the week. As their grandparents walked leisurely holding hands, the two rushed quickly to sit next to my children. Seconds upon sitting all five of them started chatting and snickering. *(Giggling cousins are so cute.)*

There were about fifty men with guns in uniform taking heirlooms, historical relicts, and art out of our home onto trucks. My father's face was turning red as they antagonized and mocked him and his family while purposefully destroying our home. He prayed to keep calm and allow it to happen, but my mother had to help him once they began breaking windows and burning books from the library in search of any spiritual literature to arrest us. *(You won't find any because there are acres of land, and we hid them.)*

During the chaos of dismantling everything in sight, we sat outside in the garden where we used to have tea parties and laugh, but it was now clouded with pillows of gray smoke and loud crashing noises. Then unexpectedly, my father stood up.

"C'est la terre de mon père, Dell... C'est dans ma famille depuis des générations... Je ne peux pas... Que font-ils? Je dois arrêter ça! C'est pour nos petits-enfants. Je ne les laisserai pas le prendre. (This is my father's land, Dell...It's been in my family for generations...I can't... What are they doing? I need to stop this! It's for our grandchildren. I won't let them take it)."

He took a few steps toward the officers burning piles of family art and books near the meadow. My mother grabbed his hand pulling him to stop. Then she reached up and held his cheeks focusing on his eyes just inches away from her. I heard her tell him firmly, "Philippe' this is an attempt to break our faith. You know it is. Don't be prideful. It is only land. Your family heritage means a great deal to you, but your spiritual heritage is more..."

Hearing the louder taunting chants from the soldiers, he jerked his body away from her, storming off toward the house. She rushed to catch him, pulling at his arms, "Jean-Philippe'! Listen to me. You were going to throw all this away to marry me. Right? Is not Jehovah worth more than me? It is only temporary, my love. Jesus had nothing of this world, but he was given more important things and blessings from his father for his faithfulness and loyalty and love. Jean-Philippe', love... 1 Corinthians 13... what version shall I recite? Love is patient, love is kind. It does not envy, it does not boast, it is not proud. It does not dishonor others, it is not self-seeking, it is not easily angered, it keeps no record of wrongs. Love does not delight in evil but rejoices with the truth. It always protects, always trusts, always hopes, always perseveres. Love never fails. Do... do you not love Jesus for his sacrifice and to have hope? Do you not love Jehovah for life and making it possible to reset everything back as he planned? Do you not love me, Philippe'? Love your daughters and grandchildren? The brothers and sisters, more than these breakable things. My love, breathe with me."

My father exhaled. I could see her stroke his cheeks, perhaps wiping away his angry tears. I heard my mother say, "Frenchman, you are my Adam. And we will be young and perfect one day soon, but no matter what, we will not be disloyal and lose the privilege gift He intended for the first human couple. I will fight for you… just as you fight for me."

In just those few moments, his anger vanished. He smiled at her and tapped her nose with the tip of his index finger. "Oui, mon amour le plus cher et tu es mon Ève. Merci. Tu as raison. Je suis content que tu sois plus sage que moi. Prions Jéhovah pour qu'il soit endurant et remercie-le pour ce qui s'en vient. (Yes, my dearest love and you are my Eve. Thank you. You are right. I am glad you are wiser than I. Let's pray to Jehovah for endurance and thank him for what's to come)."

The two held hands with their foreheads touching and had a private moment of prayer. Then they walked around holding hands for a bit before returning to the table, where my children, Gert, her brother Wolfgang, his wife Lylah, and their grandchildren, François and Marcell who were the children of their unmarried son, Sven, and I were sitting. My amazing and wonderful father said, "Forgive me. I needed to have a conversation with my wife and Jehovah. As integrity keepers, we should talk to him as a family."

We all nodded and held hands while Wolfgang said a prayer. Just as soon as we said amen, brother Stephano Erste' and brother Bernard Runoldhad arrived and greeted us smiling. Then the four men took a walk. It was quiet until Jae spoke up, "Grand-mère es-tu vraiment plus intelligente que grand-père (Grandma are you really smarter than grandfather)?"

She replied quickly, "Jae my sweet boy, it is Jehovah and his son, Jesus that are the wisest of us all." But then she nodded and winked at him, and we all chuckled.

Without any let up, situations continued to happen. Within a few hours, armed soldiers escorted my father, Wolfgang, Stephano, and Bernard away. They said they were taken with several other brothers from our congregation to some prison holding camp because they refused to sign documents to support the international peace efforts, provide financial donations to the cause or conform to an approved non-religious affiliation status.

All Delacroix assets were seized by the international alliance. After boarding up our château and every cottage on the property, our family stable and grounds workers that had worked for us faithfully for generations were deputized and stood guard with weapons to ensure we did not enter. We were instantly homeless with only a personal emergency backpack and the clothes on our back, a light jacket, and casual shoes on our feet.

As soon as they drove away, we grabbed our emergency bags and walked for hours to a pre-arranged secret location where another brother and sister from our service group, the Volmonte's took us to their home. While there, we continued with our spiritual routine of prayer and reading literature hidden among our belongings or outside to build us up along with a few others from our congregation.

Five days later, soldiers came for us. The few brothers in the group stood to protect us, but we were forcibly separated into different transport trucks. My children and I were in one with the wives of those previously taken away, other sisters, and young children they had collected from around the area. It was hot and cramped in the long trailer trucks with hole ventilation above for air circulation. The ride was long, and the truck swerved a great deal. I felt nauseous but managed not to vomit. Even just sitting for the ride, I never let go of Jin and Jolie's hands. We recited Bible stories and scriptures we had memorized. We talked about the animals we would be able to pet when the world was new, clean, and there was no more badness. I kept them engaged when they were not sleeping. My mother held securely onto Jae. He was with her because entering the truck, she had been pretending he was aiding her to walk. The two of them were further away but I could see them. Gert was on the other side of my mother, and Lylah and her grandchildren were next to her. On the ride, we sipped a little water from our emergency bags and shared with those in need. There were no soldiers in the truck-trailer, which allowed for the other sisters to recall scriptures for endurance, and stories of courage and to help keep each other stay hydrated. We were all very calm not knowing where we were going, but we knew who was watching over us, so we were happy.

Honestly, I had imagined confinement to be violent chaos, hysteria, and concentration camps. In my mind, I thought of images I had seen at the Smithsonian, in books, documentaries, and at other museums. At one point, I had a flash of the graphic scene from the 1993 movie "Schindler's List" with the young girl in the red coat. I shuddered, remembering it. But to my surprise, it wasn't exactly like that. We didn't see any of the men from our congregation. It was just us, women, and children in a long rectangular building with no windows in the mountains. The soldiers were armed and yelled a lot of instructions, but no one was shot or beaten during our confinement.

There was no food provided, only water. Being obedient again with emergency backpacks saved us. It was interesting how none of the soldiers checked or took them. *(Jehovah provides. I bet if we had suitcases, they would have taken them.)*

Just two days after sleeping snuggled together on handmade cots, the armed soldiers instructed us to collect our things and go outside. Gathering my children, my aunt and mother, we moved quickly. Lylah was several feet away, but she did the same with her grandchildren. Not knowing what was going on, I moved Jae, Jin, and Jolie into a small huddle and said, "Never forget what you've learned about Jehovah; and how much Jehovah and his son, Jesus love you. How much I love you. You were his gift to me. We are so very proud of you. All the angels in heaven see you and are cheering when we stick close to what he says, no matter what. Just like in all the Caleb and Sophia videos teaching us how to *Become Jehovah's Friend*. Remember, amigos, don't be afraid. Jehovah can and will do anything he wants for his friends."

Jae kissed my hand and went back over toward my mother. Jin gave me an Eskimo kiss on the nose. We smiled at each other. Jin let go of me and helped taunt Gert to the door.

There were about sixty-seven of us. Women with children that appeared to all be under the age of thirteen, who walked outside in small clusters. The sun was out, and there were empty dump trucks parked in front of where we were to line up.

"Mawmaw." Jolie squeezed my hand.

"Yes, my darling."

"Jehovah will protect us. If I get lost, he will help me find you."

"Yes, my pretty one. You be brave like that Israelite girl in the Bible. I will too."

She smiled at me, and a second later, a man snatched her from behind and put her in a truck with her brothers and all the other children. My mother grabbed my hand as I took steps forward to stop him but stopped and trembled watching it drive away. Silently, I prayed with my head down and eyes closed. I felt Gert and my mother's hands on my shoulders as I tried to control my breathing and not scream out for my children. I felt other hands of sisters around me patting my back and stroking my arm. When I opened my eyes, I smiled at them and a few hugged me. "Merci. Merci (Thank you)." Was all I could say.

(I am not alone. Their children were taken too. Endure until the end… Marie… Keep going. Don't stop. Jehovah can do anything. His name means, he causes to become, and he can do and will do anything for his friends. I am his friend. No matter what, I am.)

Within minutes, groups of armed soldiers began barking orders to follow behind their other empty trucks, "Start walking!" The group was about thirty-three women of all ages, and we did as they said. But after a mile walking behind the trucks, the armed men behind us began hastily running to the back of the trucks and getting in. They said nothing to us. It was strange as those that had just been close to us acted as if we were no longer there. Piling into the multiple vehicles, they sped down the mountain.

Then it was just us women in the wilderness. We weren't sure where we had been taken but we stayed together and slowly walked through the forest, down the mountain. A few older sisters needed to frequently stop and rest. We did. The group of us worked together, sharing our rations from our bags, and encouraging each other with stories of faithful men and women of old.

When it got dark, we huddled together and made a few fires and took turns keeping watch for animals and danger. It wasn't strange how everyone was calm and organized, kind and considerate to one another. No one was crying or yelling, running off or being aggressive. It was very similar to being at the Kingdom Hall and conventions. We had all been well trained with knowledge and sharpened skills to be sheeplike ones and follow even when the leader was invisible.

The next day I woke up early. I got moving to help a few sisters collect firewood. A few single sisters from my congregation, Scarlett, Cheryl, Kelsey, and I prepared things while others slept. As we slowly trekked down a pathway, we cautiously followed its curves between bushes and large trees on the mountain.

"Mom, watch your step." I said seeing ditches that curved in the unlevel ground in front of us.

Walking for several hours, we finally came to a clearing and water far ahead. What appeared before our eyes was a quiet, motionless lake surrounded by other hills and forest. In just a quarter of a mile, the earth path we had followed forked into a paved road. It guided us with a slight decline making our downward hike easier and less dangerous.

In the distance there was a large rectangular building with high windows. When I saw it, I thought, *(Is that a ranger station?)* We discussed the possibilities of our next actions as a few sisters we had sent ahead to scout the area came back to report that there was a group of people down there.

We continued further but were more aware we may need to scatter quickly and made plans to move in smaller groups back into the forest if they were the same soldiers that had abandoned us earlier.

As we approached the occupied area, a few sisters recognized brothers from our congregation. Instantly we all seem to have outbursts of relief. When we made those verbal expressions, some men saw us coming, and rushed to us and their wives. We openly thanked Jehovah, with tears and laughter seeing the joy of faithful couples being reunited. There were no soldiers, just some of Jehovah's people from a few congregations in Lyon.

My heart skipped hearing my mother shout, "Philippe'!" as my father came running towards us smiling. We embraced with loving kisses.

"Oh Pawpaw!" Was all I could say kissing his lips and cheeks.

The brothers had been there for two days. They had no idea where we were but prepared food daily for us to meet them. "Viens manger (Come eat)." It was an echo of the same words as they led us inside to get washed up. Then these kind men, who are indeed my loving brothers, prayed and rushed us to take in nourishment. The simple meal of different breads, cheeses, and fruits was one of the best I ever had.

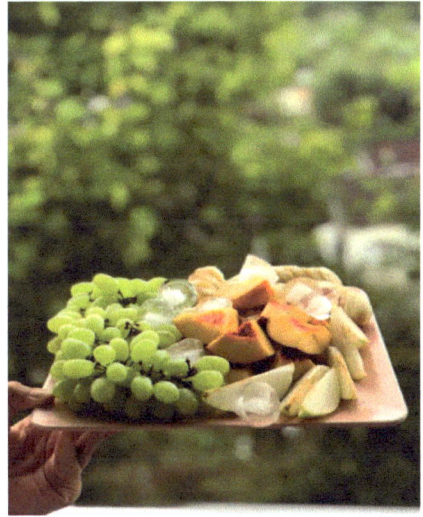

While we ate together, the brothers told us they had been released after the forty-armed soldiers guarding the building, one day left in a hurry without a word. They decided to stay and wait for us. They said that they didn't know where we were and didn't venture off to find us or anyone else. When a couple of us asked why not, they told us that they had prayed daily as a group and felt the direction was to be patient and wait.

(Thank you, father, and your son!)

There was no doubt who had been protecting and guiding all of us all along. We continued to enjoy the prepared meal, tell stories of courage, and express our spiritual sibling love for one another with hugs and laughter.

It wasn't long, perhaps an hour had passed, when we heard faint rumbling in the distance.

(What is that?) We looked around perplexed. Then everyone stopped eating because it was getting louder. Heads moved and eyes searched, some in our group even stood up to see what it was or where it was coming from.

"Au sud sur cette colline. (At the South over that hill)." Brother Stephano Erste' announced pointing to a grass covered hill with minimal trees. Immediately, all the brothers gathered around us sisters, creating a linked body barrier to protect us from whatever we couldn't see. Our circuit overseer, Brother Roy Davidson gave a brief prayer, since the men had to stay alert. My hands began to sweat holding my mother's hand on one side and Cheryl Nbune's hand on the other. The noises grew louder with each passing second. My heart felt like a hammer banging a nail in my chest. *(Be calm. We are together. Be calm.)* I told myself as I squeezed my mother's hand, who was standing on my right. Gert held onto Lylah's arm next to my mother. Getting stronger with each second, the sounds seemed to echo into the meadow and almost as if it were bouncing off the lake water.

Within minutes, it became much clearer. It was voices. Singing. "Oh!" I gasped recognizing the harmony of voices singing, "Jehovah is my best friend" and then "See yourself when all is new."

The voices were repeatedly singing back-to-back kingdom melodies we had all memorized. They were young voices. Children were joyfully singing and walking hand-in-hand toward us.

Happy tears erupted from my eyes and several others around me. The group of young children of different races and sizes were swinging their hands and singing. It was better than any scene in any musical or movie, it was real. In unison, our children walked toward us and never stopped singing. It was one of the most beautiful sounds to hear. "Thank you, heavenly father!" My heart leaped from my chest seeing them and my eyes scanned the group in search for my three precious gifts.

(They are there. I know they are. My heart hears them.)

I mumbled, "Where are they? Heavenly Father, please help me find them! I want to see those faces of your gift to me! Where…" my breathing paused for a few seconds and then it happened…

Sure, enough as the group came closer, there they were. For some crazy reason, I laughed like a small child inhaling large doses of laughing gas, watching Jin's overly animated facial expressions with each lyric he sang. My aunt Gert squeezed me, and my father kissed my mother before planting a juicy wet one on my forehead.

Embracing my loved ones filled me with contentment and gratitude. I had taught them the best I could, and Jehovah did the rest. There was no doubt that my young children loved him not because I told them too, but he was their friend, and they each believed Jehovah God can and will do wonderful things for his friends. I am humbled by his glory and wisdom.

Smiling, Jolie pulled me to whisper in my ear, but she doesn't know how to whisper when she is excited.

"Jéhovah nous a fait te trouver, maman (Jehovah made us find you, Mama)."

Giggling with tears of joy, I nodded and confirmed, "Oui, il m'a aidé à être retrouvée, ma jolie (Yes, he helped me be found, pretty one)."

Initially, I thought perhaps we had been in the Col de la Luere Forest area, but the brothers taking the lead said we were East of Lyon close to the Alps, in a remote valley within the Massif des Bauges Natural Regional Park. All that mattered was that we had endured and were all together.

The loving brothers taking the lead gave us assignments, and we began the cleanup and building work.

Collection: Forever and ever and...

58. Paradise

Sweet fragrant aromas filled every corner of the warm air around me. Distant scents of nature's freshness wrapped in visuals of bright vibrant colors bring me to constant tranquility. Clean clear water flows over standing rocks of a wide stream at my left.

An enchanting butterfly ballet performs among the lush vegetation along the water stream. A large pathway of blooming flowers in painter shades of pink blush, winter white, purple passion, yellow rays, and citrus orange. Familiar and rare flowers are as fragrant as they are vivid. Behind the array of florals are many types of tall trees and lush bushes, some never seen before with stalks of bamboo, pointy blades of green, and others with floppy ear-like leaves swaying with the warm morning breeze. A few unseen birds sweetly sing their morning greetings to each other. I exhale. It is peaceful and I love it.

Focusing my attention back to reading the written words held in my hand, I hear an airy tenor voice call to me.

"Mawmaw, let's go to the sand."

Next, I hear a slightly deeper tone, "Yes, mum, we should go."

Finally, a sweet soft voice says, "Let me help you up, mama."

I glanced up with a joyful smile greeting my adorable children, who have now rushed to my side. My delightful happiness. So smart, gifted, and kind, now in full action to help me to my feet.

"All right, my three amigos, let's go."

Following the path for some time, the stream became a river that later flowed into the ocean. Approaching the shore, grass became smooth dark rocks, later colorful pebbles, and then sand. Clean white sand. Now closer to the sparkling water, and fresh sea air, the music of the liquid symphony with wind surges and swells crescendo could be heard. It was a delightful powerful sound of grandness but almost whimsical.

There was no one around and we chuckled as we removed our sandals. The white sand is warm beneath our feet and soft between our toes. Jae collected our sandals and lined them up based on size because he is very orderly. *(He is so much like my mother.)*

Jin covered his feet with the clean warm sand then glanced up at me with a grin, doing the fast lifting of his eyebrows. *(He is so cute.)* I giggled from his adorable silliness.

After a quick back braid to Jolie's mid-length wavy hair, she grinned as we smashed faces to touch our noses and wiggle.

She playfully blurted out, "Butterfly kiss now, butterfly—"

"Me too, me too."

"I'm next. I'm next —" is what I heard all at once from the bright faces that huddled around me. I chuckled before I began our nightly family tradition, even though it is the morning. Each one of my children received their Eskimo kiss (noses), French kiss (cheeks), Butterfly kiss (eyelashes), and Greek kiss (forehead) with all of us loudly saying, "OPAH" at the end.

Laughing, my three amigos took off running toward the warm turquoise blue water as it rushed to meet them. No longer holding hands, they retreated from it laughing and trying only to wet the tips of their toes. I exhaled while gripping the sand between my toes. I watched them enjoy the wonderful beauty of the vast ocean in front of us.

The bright day felt like an embrace from the warm morning sun around us and nature's harmonious concert of sounds played softly. Instantly words came to my mind from a poem I had written years ago on Cocoa Island called *Water*.

"...A symphony of magnificent rapture... The heavenly gift of ocean waters."

I smile to myself simply recalling the enchanting moments composing a song with said words, and the melody from a time long ago. Taking in the freshness of the air, I closed my eyes. Absorbing the delightful sounds and feelings from the sand and water, sun and distant birds flying among the cloudless sky, I felt peace surrounding me, and us.

My listening ear locked onto the faintness of their laughter floating over the sounds of gentle waves. A light mist of ocean spray can be felt over my skin. It was serenity, and I am very thankful.

Amidst the moment, something wonderful happened...

59. "UWA!"

Warm is what I felt. The sweet fragrance of fresh ocean water floated in the air around me. I heard distant sounds of forceful waves rushing to gently kiss the shore as I gradually opened my closed lids to see the glow of that brilliant star high in the light blue sky. The soft clear airspace with a sprinkle of dew like white clouds in a slow-motion race held my attention for a few minutes.

I inhaled deeply natures unfiltered pure breeze. An "Auhh" released from my throat with an exhaled breath. It is peaceful and I was relaxed sitting on a slight hill with nothing but an open blue ocean, a sea of colorful stones and clean white sand in view.

Lowering my head, a vision of cresting waves over the vast waters as far as I could see made me grin and whisper, "aleumdaun (beautiful)."

I took note of what was close around me and thought. . . *(Am I dreaming?)*

Sitting a distance away from the roaring ocean, with my arms relaxed next to me, I began to grab small handfuls of granules that trickled through cracks between my fingers. I looked down to inspect the dry white sand that was free from foreign impurities and felt much like refined cane sugar. I wondered to myself… *(Did I fall asleep on the beach?)*

I was alone but at ease noticing the unfamiliar clothing I was wearing. A short-sleeved white cotton shirt was tucked into loose fitting dark blue denim slacks, rolled up a little around the ankle, while the strapped brown leather sandals covered my feet resting flat above the sand.

"Huh" I huffed a little in amusement wondering why I was wearing something I didn't own.

I began to talk to myself, "Why am I alone on this isolated beach? I don't remember how I got here."

Distracted by another gentle breeze, I inhaled again deeply filling my lungs with the ocean's perfume briefly for a few seconds. I smiled as its freshness hit my nostrils as something uniquely energizing.

Without feeling pain or sadness, my mind slowly drew together pieces from before.

(I was in the mountains watching birds then I felt very tired. I held Marie close to me until I fell asleep. I . . .)

"I was sick…weak. Couldn't breathe before."

Inhaling deeply, I realized my lungs were clear, and my body felt stronger. I flexed my left bicep that bulged under the stretching of my shirt due to the solid firmness of the muscles. I smiled to myself with a slight feeling of being impressed. Fascinated by my body's remarkable resilience, the feeling of new energy, and power, I continued testing it out like a new bike, with strategic twisting and stretching of my muscles, even my fingers and toes. "Daebak *(Impressive)."*

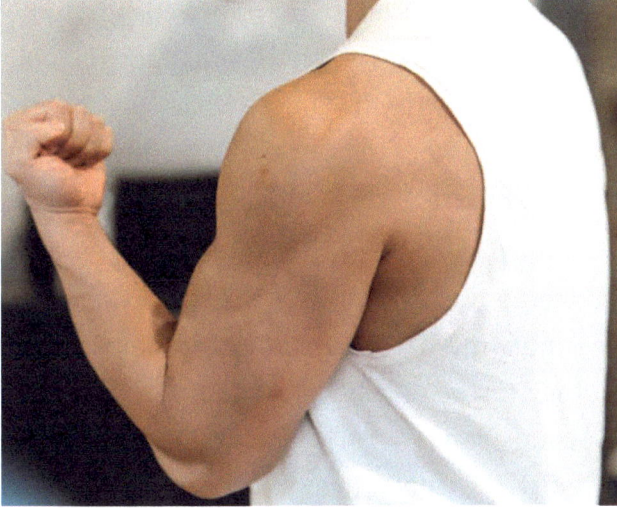

Hearing a flock of birds passing, I quickly opened my eyes wider to see several colorful ones fly towards the endless waters in front of me. *(Long and blue, that is darker with yellow…not ones I have seen before. What species, I wonder.)* Focused now on the sighting and unable to make out what type they were, I continued to watch them travel further and further away. A couple of whales shot out of the open sea into the air as if performing a playful dance. In my engagement, my eyes followed the birds then switched back to the whales when they appeared again moments later. I grinned, turning my head slightly to the south.

Although the distance seemed to be as long as several blocks, I could see images of a few people. At that moment, the one adult female's silhouette I could not visually confirm, but my heart knew before I saw her clearly.

"Nae sarang (my love)." I whispered to myself sitting motionless smiling with joy. Yes, it was the image of my love walking with three young children that I instinctively knew were mine. I started to chuckle watching their swinging hands, gestures, and unheard conversations. They appeared so happy walking from somewhere unknown to me toward the water. I adjusted my body a bit and rested my arms on my bent knees while my heart raced with anticipation embracing her. I licked my lips remembering the touch of her plump and sweet light brown pillows that held me prisoner to her majesty. *(Oh, those lips.)*

Instantly, I remembered times of the past when I forgot where I was and sometimes my name while kissing her. I had always been addicted to the taste of chocolat chaud français (French hot chocolate.) Seconds later, I rolled my tongue over my teeth and smacked it against the roof of my mouth as my brain recalled the taste of her. "Mmmm."

I let out a peaceful sigh observing them removing their shoes. From my seated distance, it looked like she was wearing a long flowy skirt with a short-sleeve loose top. Although I couldn't see her body, I knew her sexy hourglass curves were underneath, and I smirked.

"My sweet Marie, she's so beautiful. Her hair is longer than I remember. I can still feel her smile from far away." I shook my head a little, still taking in the distant vision of her loveliness.

In seconds, I began to slowly recite my lyrics to the one song that always brings me back to her, "Arabian Sand."

You're my ocean of wonders
Silhouette of your swirling caramel hand
Touch me with your vast and deep seductive winds
Sweet Arabian Sand
Tenderly, I see you coming to take hold of me, oh
I love the way your desert dunes pull me in
You move in my dreams of passionate sin
I see you gently open your heart to me
My body crashes into you like waves of the sea
Holding you so tight, oh my love, take my hand
Sweet Arabian Sand
I feel your heat beyond the stars and sunrays
You're my sweet calm before an erotic storm
The sun's glow reflects all over you and I willingly cave
Whisper my name, oh, your touch and the delight you gave
Sweet Arabian Sand
And I'm needin' your energy to stay alive
Only she gives me ultimate peace and helps me to thrive
I'm comin' back for more, with you I am truly alive
My love, stay with me, my heart is always yours
To you for eternity, I promise to love and adore
My Sweet Arabian Sand, I love you forever more.

Smiling to myself observing her every slight movement and action from the long distance, I was overcome with brewing emotions. I took in and blew out a few short breaths with only pleasant memories of her in my arms and our life together.

"They are all so big. No longer those newborns in photos on her phone I saw that day. How old are they? They look much older than a couple of years old. One looks like he is a little taller. Who has her eyes? Which one is Jae Lune, and which is Jin Soleil? I see my little princess, Jolie."

"Gamsahamnida (thank you) heavenly father for protecting them. It happened like she read to me in your word. You woke me up to let me be with my love again. God Jehovah, gamsahmnida!" I said a prayer of thankfulness as a couple of tears slid down the corners of my eyes.

Seconds later it hit my brain slowly remembering more of what happened. I knew for sure that I was alive, and the earth was beautiful. Clean and peaceful. I started laughing.

"I'm alive. I don't feel weak anymore. I'm...I'm not sick!"

I fell back onto the sand and laughed harder, covering my watering eyes with my hands, and expressing my joyful heart. But after just a few outbursts, I wasted no more time. I stood up wiping my tears away and jolted to the south, walking briskly toward the most beautiful four people I had ever seen.

(Should I run? I want to run to her...to them.)

As reality came as volts of low frequency charges that flooded my mind, I slowed down my walking stride significantly.

(No, don't run. Wait, the triplets look much older than just a couple of...)

"How long was I gone? Does she still love me?" I paused then stopped walking and swallowed hard. Clenching my hands, I closed my eyes, bowed my head, and said a quiet prayer.

"Dear father in heaven, I'm grateful, so grateful to be alive on earth just like you promised. Everything you said came true and I'm overjoyed. Truly I am. Please let me embrace my love, if only just being able to see her again. I would be happy."

At that moment, loud splashes of water came from the opposite end of the shoreline, and it got my attention. Within seconds I saw three dolphins in a single file seemingly moonwalking over the top of the water. They made a great deal of noise in their synchronized formation before disappearing back into the water.

I smiled, knowing I had earlier seen whales in a playful dance, but so close to my prayer, I reasoned it was a sign and said my thoughts out loud, "Okay, I gotta see her eyes. I'll know if she loves me only when I see her eyes. They will tell me. They will."

Exhaling with a giant smile, I continued slowly approaching her area from behind. I made no sound walking over the dry loose sand toward her, but I could hear the loud thundering in my chest. The closer I came, the more I couldn't stop the slow tears of happiness being so close to touching her.

(My sweet love. I promise I won't ever leave you again.)

Marie did not follow the children off to play in the water. She was standing alone facing them. I came up behind her, and when I got just a couple of feet away, she seemed to tilt her head.

(Did she hear me? Turn around, baby. I must see those magnificent golden eyes.)

I opened my hand and placed it on her shoulder. My love turned her body toward me at the speed of sap oozing from a hodu namu tree. I smiled without speaking while her head followed her body. Facing me I reached up to hold her face. Her head seemed to fall into my cupping hands without opening her eyes. I felt that magnetic surge through my body when my fingers brushed over her skin clearing away her tears.

As I analyzed the curve of her round cheeks and the silkiness of her soft light caramel skin, the wide wave of her deep brown hair with golden highlights around her face, I realized her skin was softer, and she seemed more youthful like perhaps when we first met. Her long dark lashes bound together sealing her eyes closed, but tears escaped from them as her lips trembled.

(Wait, don't kiss her. No, not yet. Breathe deep, Jae. Relax. See her eyes first. I got to see behind those eyes. Then I will know for sure.)

I bit my bottom lip, feeling I was on the brink of an explosion. Our bodies were sizzling with that same magnetic force we had before. It was a gravity pull of electrical energy just touching her like this. Through my body, I could sense the rhythm of her heartbeat. It was quick yet in pace with mine.

(She feels it's me. I know she does.)

Watching her shake her head, I chuckled a little before saying, "Beautiful Arabian Sand, open your eyes, my love. I'm awake."

60. Bliss

When his distinctive sultry tone of a never forgotten whisper sang to my heart the words, I had longed to hear him say. I couldn't bear it. *(Oh, oh. . .)*

Shaking my head, with tightly pressed lips and happy tears now creeping out from my sealed eyes, my heart leaped with glee. The warm breeze flowed through my loose hair as I faintly heard the playful laughter of my children running from rushing waves, a distance behind me. Strong and soft hands over my cheeks eased me closer to him. I heard him chuckle which made me giggle.

I silently prayed to my heavenly father. *(Thank you, Jehovah God for your love, justice, and mercy. You awakened him as you promised. You read his heart and saw he was a good person and was starting to learn the truth about you before he died. I knew he was made for me. I prayed to remain loyal to my dedication to serve you faithfully because you are the giver of life and the only true God. I had hoped for this moment...but there was so much more to why I chose to worship you. Now, Jae-Sung is awake. Thank you, father.)*

My lips trembled from brewing emotion and excitement. Tears fell continually while my eyes remained closed. I softly replied, "Say it again. Oh, say it again."

I sensed his wide tongue wet his lips before I felt he was grinning. Then he spoke those glorious words again. "Beautiful Arabian sand, open your magnificent eyes for me. I'm awake. I need to see your eyes, Marie. Open them, please. Baby, open them."

With each word he spoke, my heart and mind received clear confirmation that Jae-Sung Kim was indeed my life partner and husband. His thumbs still brushed tears away as I slowly opened my eyes. What came into view was his smooth square chin, and as I ease my gaze upward, I saw those parted thin pink-peachy colored lips moistened like liquid cotton candy around his perfectly straight white teeth. Then his narrow nose. His flawless round cheeks and then his chocolate pools of wonder locked onto mine. Contact. I gasped as I heard him yell, "Yes! I knew it!"

Moments later, I closed my eyes again as his soft lips swept over mine like warmed honey. His kiss tasted of delicious sweetness that ignited the flames of passion inside me. Time was still as my heart jumped with exhilaration; I inhaled the light familiar scent of mint chocolate while feeling his loving touch.

The unbroken romantic kiss continued as his left hand slid back behind my head and rustled through my long loose curls, while he pushed me into him. His right hand eased down under my arm, gripped behind my back, and squeezed. I heard his deep moan, "Mmmph." With locked lips, I replied with a throaty giggle of delight and freedom.

In minutes, his head moved back away from mine and his lips separated from me. I remained still in his arms, which were both now securely folded around my waist.

"Open your eyes, nae sarang (my love), let me see them again." His deep breathy tone tickled my ears as I heard his voice again after so long. He gently shook my body coaxing me to open my closed eyes. Biting the corner of my bottom lip, I inhaled a gasp then in one fast move lifted my lids to see my Jae-Sung Kim. His face was youthful, and his skin was bright, healthy, and smooth. His almond-shaped chocolate yuex (eyes) danced in the morning sunlight while I reached up to glide my finger over the moles of his beautiful face.

My lips parted to speak but only "Jae" escaped.

Grinning flirtatiously, he said, "Oui, mon amour (yes, my love). Hold on a second, were you expecting someone else to kiss you?"

He raised his left eyebrow waiting for my response. I moaned with a quick shake of my head. Jae's smile grew bigger and with rapid moving up and down eyebrows he said, "Aww, so, am I your idol king?"

I let out a loud laugh and shouted, "YES!"

We laughed embracing one another so tightly with falling tears of joyfulness. Still holding each other Jae began placing slow tender lip kisses over my cheeks. Between airy chuckles, I softly repeated the words of my heart, "I love you; I love you; I love you."

Holding me in his arms, his strong muscular body engulfed me once again with true love, and I melted. With my face snuggled on his chest, over his soft cotton shirt, my cheek felt the firm definitions of his upper body while my fingers traced the familiar curve of his muscular back. I exhaled and giggled simply from the feel of him. I let out a whisper, "Jae, I am so happy; you are here now."

Jae-Sung moaned in the affirmative and placed a long kiss on my forehead, then said, "I love you, my beautiful sunset in Dubai."

The ocean waves performed an uplifting melody for our reunion. I continued to grip the warm grains of white sand between my toes, feeling at peace in Jae-Sung's arms. His body magnetized to mine. His face beamed with radiant bliss. We both could not stop touching and examining the glow of our faces, but Jae was studying the color of my watering eyes.

"Jae-Sung, I want you to—" It was as if he read my mind. Without delay, his mouth collapsed over mine with forceful passion and deep pressure. Moments later his wide delicious tongue entered my mouth to softly fold with its long awaiting partner. Engulfed by the purest essence of my love, I began pulling his thick black hair between my fingers and floating away in the delight of my husband and being surrounded by the sounds of paradise.

The taste of him made my knees buckle. He held me securely within his strong muscular arms, while never parting from my mouth. Diving deeper into his long-awaited French kiss, constant sounds of "hmmm," released from my throat as passion grew within me. Jolts from cascading memories swept through my mind, remembering the exhilaration of being with him. I felt as though I began to dampen with wetness as I melted into my beautiful love. Warm air burst from his nostrils onto my skin as he let out a low growl and his chest vibrated against me while we constantly sampled each other. *(Oh, baby!)* My covered and uncovered skin tingled everywhere from the rays of the sun and his embracing me. As his body pressed against mine and our tongues slowly tangoed inside lover's gateway, my breasts firmed while my lower lips quivered waiting for him.

(Oh, Jae-Sung... take me now, please. Yes...finally!)

My beautiful love, Jae-Sung Kim

I am younger, healthier, and blissfully happy.

Deeper his kisses dove and opened me wider. With a growing hunger, he would not release me. I welcomed every millisecond of his tongue's rejuvenation of the dormant love deep within my core, which was now quaking with a frenzy of sensational tremors. My body had long been depleted during his absence and Jae-Sung was now filling me up again with his rapid molten magma ready to erupt from a volcano of desire. I wanted him in every way right then.

But I felt the hint of a presence close to me on my right side. Then another at my left pulling at the edge of my short sleeve. Startled from loves hold, I pulled away from Jae's lips and enfolded arms. Turning to my left, taking an in-charge strong stance elongating his neck to appear taller than usual as his lean frame reached my shoulder was Jae Lune-Philippe'. With his almond-shaped amber eyes opened wide and flashing his long eyelashes with rapid blinks moving his head from me to Jae and back to me again.

Surprised, I said, "Oh," but did not disconnect from my husband. Instantly feeling the pressure of a body that had moved closer to me, I turned my head to the right seeing the equally widen chocolate eyes of Jin Soleil-Maximilian.

"Auhh," was the sound from my mouth as I slowly inched away from Jae-Sung. I stepped back to have space between the two of us but remained holding his one hand with our fingers clasped. Jae-Sung cleared his throat and had a large, closed mouth grin. I smiled reassuringly at Jin and quickly turned my head back to his older brother Jae to deliver the same smile before speaking to make official introductions. Only seconds passed as I let go of Jae-Sung's hand and backed up further.

"Boys—"

Simultaneously, they shouted, "Appa (Daddy)!" Rushing toward their father. Grabbing Jae-Sung at his waist, Jae and Jin clung to him while they buried their puffy cheeks and watering eyes into his body. Jae-Sung's arms grabbed ahold of Jae and Jin with gasping laughter, pressing their heads onto his torso. He frantically delivered kisses to them. Seconds later, Jae-Sung eased them away from his body to visually inspect his handsome sons. Jin, smiling with tears rolling down his cheeks could not speak as he stared up at his father. Jae Lune's flowing tears fell as he tugged at his father's white shirt whispering, "Appa. Oh, Appa (Daddy)."

Jae-Sung softly kissing their foreheads paused to smile and say, "Ne. Na jigeum il-eonass-eo, uljima adeul-a. *(Yes. I am awake now, don't cry son)."*

I giggled hearing him tell our sons not to cry, but he had a constant trickle of liquid joy come from his own eyes. Jae-Sung's loving hugs were a glorious moment for my three Kim men. *(At last, they have their father.)*

Completely delighted by the long-awaited vision of happiness, it took me a few seconds to realize that Jolie was not around us. Taking a couple of steps backward I turned slightly to locate her. Jae-Sung squatted down to hold his sons more closely. As I moved further, Jae-Sung reached out to me, "Marie . . ."

Glancing back at him with a wide smile I held his hand. He pulled me down into the family hug. Jae kissed my lips tenderly, then kissed Jin and Jae's cheeks and more tears fell as they giggled.

"Jae-Sung, Jolie. I need to get Jolie."

"Where is she? Where is my little Arabie Sable (Arabian Sand)?" he said as he began alternating his tearful inspection of our sons. I stood up and released our hands after a quick squeeze and told him. "I'll get her."

Jae-Sung flopped down on the warm, dry sand and nodded to me as I walked away from them. I could faintly hear him asking his sons all sorts of questions about themselves. It made me giggle, while I scanned the beach for our daughter.

As I turned completely around, I saw her standing several feet away, like a statue. I noticed her creamy light walnut skin glistening as the sunrays hit her uncovered arms exposed from her sleeveless green sundress because I had earlier braided back her thick long wavy hair.

"Chérie… Jolie…" I shouted, making my way toward her. She did not move. She was standing completely stiff with her feet covered by the warm ocean water every few minutes. Jolie had no expression, no tears, and no smile. Once I approached her, I tenderly touched her bare shoulder, and reached up to turn her plump round face to focus on my eyes.

Smiling, I said softly, "Ma plus chère (my dearest). Come…and see your father. He is awake."

Hearing my voice, Jolie's deep green eyes seemed to now lock onto mine. Seconds passed as her long dark lashes waved in slow motion when she blinked. Once I reached up to caress her soft full cheek, she spoke.

"Mawmaw . . . is it really him? Jehovah, woke him up? He isn't sick. He is all well?"

Smiling, I nodded with a whispered moan of yes. Jolie began to blink faster then she grabbed my hand and squeezed it trembling. I steadied her as the warm ocean water rushed again covering our toes. My eyes never wavered from hers, and within seconds liquid began to gather beyond her green pools. Her skin lightly quaked as I held and stroked her cheek.

"Mawmaw . . ." was all she said before the barricade let loose a river of tears. I grabbed my sweet Jolie and held on to her while she wept.

"Ma plus chère (my dearest), come see. He is asking for you."

Speaking in French and Korean, she said, "Pour moi (For me)? Jinjja (Really)?" Her tone was higher from surprise as she placed her hand on her chest before displaying a wide smile and her deep dimples.

Nodding, I replied, "Oui. Oui, chérie (Yes. Yes, honey)." While brushing away the wetness from her cheeks, I took a moment to kiss the palm of her hand still entangled in mine.

"Come, plus chère amour (dearest love)." I said nudging her away from the water toward the white dry sand. Jolie held onto my hand with both of her little ones still trembling. She walked so close to me as if a little unsure of the memory flashes from her past dreams were in this moment very real.

As we moved closer to the three Kim men sitting on the sand, Jae-Sung stood up from the male powwow and ran toward us. Jolie stopped walking and tugged at my arm. She inhaled and stopped breathing for a couple of seconds. I squeezed her hand and stood still as Jae-Sung slowed and stopped about a foot away from her. He fell on his knees and held out his arms calling to her with that soft airy tenor, "My pretty one. I am so glad to finally see you."

Jae-Sung began to cry with a wide smile, holding out his arms for her to come to him. Jolie didn't move. Jae nodded motioning to her, saying, "Saranghae, no sarangseureoun arabia morae (I love you, my sweet little Arabian Sand)."

She shouted, "Abeoji! Bogo sip-eoss-eoyo, abeoji (Father! I missed you, father)!"

Jolie released my hand and rushed into her father's long arms that affectionately encased her. Jae wiped her tears and brushed her hair at the temple. Then he kissed her cheeks before arching back to say, "Wait, I need an Eskimo one." She giggled. Then the two began rubbing the tips of their noses together for a few seconds before embracing again with laughter and happy tears.

I stood covering my mouth with both hands trying to control my gasps and giggles. It didn't work. Water could not stop flowing from my eyes. It was a colossal moment of our family joy.

Jae Lune and Jin Soleil ran, approaching us wiping away their tears, giving each other hi-five hand slaps, and laughing. They grabbed hold of me from each side. Then Jae-Sung gestured for all of us to come to him for a giant family hug. We stood there in the sand holding one another. At long last, we were finally together.

61. Home

We took the long way home, following the trail of colored pebbles, and then next to a flowing river. Along the way, Jae-Sung took in the sights and sounds while finding out more about his children. He randomly asked them questions on our way home.

"Jae Lune, what is your favorite season to write poetry?"

"Appa, I have no favorite. I enjoy each one, and I find new things to write about each time a new one arrives."

Jae-Sung smiled and patted him on his shoulder saying, "That is good. Be open to all types of beauty God has made in each season. I used to write mostly in the winter before I met your mother. But after that it was all seasons for me too because my heart is always filled with her smile." I chuckled when he turned around and winked at me.

"Jin, tell me what instrument, do you play well?"

"The piano, Appa. I love to play the piano."

Jae-Sung playfully moved his fingers in the air as if he were playing piano keys.

"Aww, so not only do you look like me, but you also love the piano like I do. Hey, are you a clone?"

We all laughed as Jin nodded and Jae swung his hands playfully while holding the boy's hands tightly, walking on the open path along the river.

Slowing his stride, Jae-Sung turned back to Jolie, who was holding my hand as we walked a few steps behind them.

"Pretty one, now is it true you enjoy reading?"

"Oui, Pawpaw. I do."

"What do you read more than anything else?"

"Well, Mawmaw read to us just about every night when we were younger. She read lots of different things, but I really loved listening to Bible stories. When we got older, she made us take turns reading to her at night. I would always pick the Bible to read because I like history."

Jae followed up with, "I see, do you have a favorite story?"

"Oui, I have lots. But the two I read the most are the story of the son of Jesse and the life of Joseph."

"Son of Jesse? Who is that? Uh was it, Tyrone?"

We laughed watching Jae-Sung do his fast moving up and down eyebrows at her.

Giggling, she said, "Aniyo, Appa. David. King David."

"Oh, that's right. I think I have forgotten some of the things that happened in his life. Will you read to me later?"

She nodded with a loud, "Oui," and a broad grin.

I watched my beloved walk hand-in-hand with Jae and Jin smiling. Periodically, he stopped speaking and closed his eyes. We observed him inhaling the warm air with its fragrant aroma of clean freshness. He took in as much as he could of his new environment but questioned nothing, and simply enjoyed it. Moments later, he'd quickly open his eyes and smile at them. Then at me. "I love you," would form on my lips and he would wink at me. Every cell inside my body felt as though they were skipping from a natural form of nitrous oxide, and my cheerful heart flipped behind the walls of my chest. It was the most exhilarating feeling that cannot accurately be described with words.

Periodically, Jae glanced up to observe some rare and exotic birds in flight. His eyes followed those that landed upon standing rocks between the clear stream of water flowing on our right. Excited to explore, Jae Lune and Jin Soleil guided their father over to a few standing white and colorful peacocks, toucans, and ostriches to pet them. "Oh, hello pretty bird," were his first words as his grin stretched wide and his eyes dazzled like a young child full of amazement connecting with the docile animals. While they welcomed him stroking their feathers, Jolie released my hand as a male and female jaguar came up alongside him. The two began nuzzling around his leg. Jae started to giggle and said, "Wua, big kitty." He observed their action for a minute before gradually joining Jolie and Jin stroking their beautiful shiny spotted fur. Jae-Sung, Jin, Jolie, and Jae were in their own conversations as I watched with contentment and joy.

I remembered again, (They are so much like their father. He is just like our children! He is so adorable.)

565

Jae-Sung often stopped in motion to inspect some of the lush green foliage, various trees, shrubs, and colorful flowers along the pathway as we journeyed home.

As more memories slowly came back to my mind, for a few brief moments, I wondered what he was thinking because there were no masks, no smog or litter, no cars or freeways, no pollution and no airplanes flying overhead disturbing our peaceful walk. Everything was clean, clear, and beautiful. It was thrilling to observe him. *(I know that look. It's like the one he used to get when he took me camping. He is very happy, I can tell. So am I baby. So am I.)*

Beyond the trees, our walking path of flat smooth stones led to a clearing. Our home was a dark wood circular structure with a section open to view the waterfall that fed into the connected stream in front of us. "Abeoji, welcome home!" Jolie said as our complete house came into view.

Jae-Sung froze and took in the detail of the structure, admiring the architecture, and said, "Wua! Who made this?"

Jae Lune answered quickly, "We did with some friends, but we designed it. Isn't it cool?"

Jae-Sung had a wide smile showing off all his perfectly straight white teeth. He turned back toward me with raised eyebrows of surprise. I simply nodded.

"It's different. Yes, I'd say it is very cool, my first-born son. Very cool indeed."

Jin chimed in, "Appa, we decided to have a round designed house, not a square one. We all drew different houses before we started to build it. It was so much fun too because grandpawpaw, grandmawmaw, halmeoni, samchon, ajumma, sachon— I mean everyone helped."

Opening the front door of our home, Jae-Sung didn't seem to catch everything that Jin had said. If he had, he would've been curious and asked which grandparents, aunts, uncles, and cousins Jin was talking about. *(In time he will find out.)*

As the boys led their father into the spacious and simple living room decorated with oversized plush cream furniture and hand carved wood tables and chairs, Jae-Sung laughed out loud. What seemed to catch him off guard was seeing a large row of trees along the side of one wall growing up through the top of the three-story house.

"What's that?" Jae said pointing still amused.

"These are golden bamboo trees. Aren't they pretty? On the other side are purple, white, and black ones. See?" Smiling, I answered while watching his eyes dance at the sight of the rare and colorful trees.

"I've never seen anything like those before. Through the house even. Amazing." He reached to hold my hand and pulled me closer, and quickly kissed my cheek. The softness of his cool lips sent electric currents through my body when they touched my skin. I giggled soaking in the energy from him.

(He's going to be so excited to see his mother.)

Jolie pulled at me to whisper in my ear, "Mawmaw, you missed Appa. We'll tell halmeoni (grandma) but stay there so, you can talk." *(So smart and very sweet.)* Nodding in agreement, I kissed her cheek. Jolie quickly released my hand and began motioning to her brothers to join her in a group hug with their father before jetting off to another part of the house to go outside. A deep moan and squeeze resulted from the four of them. Then Jae-Sung held me at my waist and twisted me around to look into my eyes, while our children disappeared without a word.

"Marie, you… you built this house?" His voice sounded a little skeptical.

"Yes, Jae, with help of very loving friends and family."

"Babe, come on, you…you cut wood, used a hammer. Really? Or… Did you delegate?" He started chuckling, covering his hand over his grin.

"Ha, ha. Very funny. Yes! I did. Building our own home was a family project. So, no, I didn't delegate. I worked! I'll have you know; I even get my hands dirty in our fruit, herb, and vegetable gardens every day. So there, smarty!"

"Wait, what did you say? You… uh, garden? Everything is so different. What happened to my corporate wife. The one Sony directors called dragon?" He leaned in smirking and kissed my nose.

"My job changed to teaching our children, learn new skills, and teach others." I said it proudly watching his face squint as if he was thinking before kissing my neck.

"I gotta have another kiss." He said before his tongue darted to lick over my lips and then smothered over mine for a twelve second French kiss. Pulling back his eyes remained closed for a few seconds as he smacked his lips like a suckling baby and said, "Oui, delicious Français chocolat. I'm addicted to kissing you." I shook my head very amused by his silliness. Jae took some time and glanced around the first floor of our home. Then commented, "It's nice. I like it. It must be true what you told me about God's government being the only one, and it removed everything bad and harmful, turning the earth back into what he designed in the beginning; and his son, Jesus is the ruler everywhere. Marie, is the world really— better? Like the mural I had painted for you in the dining room?"

I nodded with a moan of yes. He continued expressing his thoughts. "Wua! So, that's why you look younger like when we first met." *(He does too but he hasn't seen himself yet.)* Jae-Sung announced holding me closely and caressing my skin with his fingers, "I'm excited to learn everything. I can't wait to see it all!" I smiled as my heart danced. Jae-Sung licked his lips slowly as he gazed into my eyes and said what he must have been thinking.

"Marie, our children… They are so beautiful. They look like us, babe. I told you that you would be a great mother. I'm so proud of you. Hey, uhm, things are slowly coming to my mind. I am remembering a bit more."

"That's good." I gave him a gentle peck on his right cheek as he had his arm snugly wrapped around my waist. He closed his eyes briefly and inhaled deeply. Seconds passed. Then he exhaled slowly, and said, "Yes. Aww, yes. I remember that specifically. Right!"

I nudged him. He opened his eyes to focus on me. He was silent but appeared to be reading hidden messages within the color of my eyes. I was curious, and asked, "What? What do you remember?"

"Mrs. Chantal-Marie Kim, I recall you promised me some level 4 and 7."

I snorted before letting out a louder laugh. His gregarious laugh seemed to echo while he squeezed me tighter. After a few minutes of cackling, I moved my body on his youthful firm chest and whispered in his ear, "I also said level 5."

When I eased back to see his face, he was biting the left corner of his bottom lip and had one eyebrow raised flirtatiously. Jae let out a sultry moan and his left hand began to massage the small of my back. My body felt flush with the rhythm of his strong heartbeat pulsating under my hand on his chest.

Jae-Sung smirked before he leaned forward and began licking and kissing my neck while mumbling, "Maybe we should begin with level one and work up to ten just to make sure I remember. Yeah, I am kind of foggy on some things. What's…What's my name again?"

Giggling, I blurted out, "You're so silly. Je t'aime, Jae-Sung Kim." I had to tell him I loved him again, while I was smiling at his seductive eyes and hearing his low groaning.

"Saranghae (I love you), my sweet lady. But, uh, seriously, level 4, 5, and 7, when do I get those?"

Snickering, I wiggled free from his holding arms. He protested, "Wait, no," but I silenced him putting my finger over his lips with a "Sshh." His face stretched up as he watched me bend over to write a note for the children.

Beloved Three Amigos,

Your father and I have waited a long time to catch up and will be away for a while talking and kissing. Let your grandparents know he is awake and stay with them until we come to get you tomorrow. Map out what wonderful things you want to show him first and then we will take turns showing him all that is new.

Love you very much,

Mama

I held up the note and he smirked while scanning it quickly. I left the note on a large round wood table covered with fresh fragrant flowers and I slowly slipped my hand close to his. The sound of his tongue smacking against the roof of his mouth made me smile, and then I told my love, "Jeoleul ttala osibsio (Follow me, please)."

Jae gave me a wide grin, hearing me speak in Korean. *(Trigger!)* Leisurely, I led him a distance away from the living room. Jae said nothing, only hummed a sultry melody during our ascension beyond the wide dark wood staircase to the third-floor bedroom with a breathtaking panoramic view. "Oh Wow!" Was his statement gawking at the huge waterfall, tropical foliage, and the distant animals, while I latched the double doors closed behind us.

62. Touch

Jae sat on the edge of the four-poster, dark wood-carved king-size bed as I stood between his open legs. I took note of how truly gorgeous he was. My eyes examined the detailed placement of the flat black moles around his eyes that I loved to touch. As the memories of our life together rushed if quick flashes to my brain, my body's nerve endings tingled with anticipation of his touch. *(Say it.)* I confessed, "Some nights when I dreamt of you, my mind could make me believe that you were touching me, kissing me. It felt so real. I didn't want to wake from my dreams."

Magnetic currents of elation ran through my body like on a fast-moving highway. Every inch of my covered and uncovered skin sizzled with excitement. Jae moaned while slowly stroking the inside of my arms, before loosening my top. Automatically his open hand tenderly grazed over the contour of my large right breast bound underneath a smooth cream bra. I giggled, remembering, *(Yes, it's the right one.)* as he removed my top. The corner of his mouth turned up and his chocolate eyes gave me a delightful shiver. "Why are you looking at me like that?" I asked while analyzing his flirtatious almond-shaped eyes.

(He's so thirsty! Oh, my man is so fine. I'm gonna get so drunk off you too baby!) My thoughts began discerning what his eyes were saying without words, but I wanted him to tell me.

"How am I looking at you, my sexy aegyo (cute)?" His tone was low and seductive. Watching him lick the corner of his mouth and then roll his tongue over his bottom lip, I announced, "You are thinking I'm a hot, sticky, delicious chocolate fondue that you 'bout to dip all your fruit into. Hee, Hee." I snickered, watching his eyebrows quickly move up and down. It almost made me laugh more because he looked a lot like Moto-Moto when he met Gloria in Madagascar 2. *(Moto-Moto. Ha! Ha!)*

Finding my eyes and grinning his voice sounded like a sweet melody. "J'adore la fondue au chocolat (I love chocolate fondue). I need to make up for being asleep. I'm going to savor every drop of you, my beautiful wife," he replied, smirking before slowly licking his lips. "How did you know what I was thinking anyway? Hold up, can we read minds now?" He held his forehead as if to concentrate on reading my mind. *(You're so silly.)*

I shook my head and said, "Your eyes give away your secrets, Mr. Kim. Besides, you have had this same look many times before."

"No. It's a new look."

"Anyio (no). It's the same passionate, heat-seeking radar gaze from the 2019 Paris fashion week runway show. Oh, and the celebrity auction in Seoul, the club bathroom in Japan, at the lunch table at your parent's compound, the Grammy after party, the Mandarin Oriental Hotel so many times, like when—"

He cut me off chuckling, "Alright! Alright, you've made your point. It is no secret how much I've desired you. Mmm, your hips in that blue dress. Yeah, I need to see more, sexy aegyo."

Moaning with increasing desire, he strategically peeled away the rest of my clothes. I was left standing in my cream-colored underwear. Jae motioned with a quick shift of his eyes, which was love code for *'walk around for me, so I can check you out.'* I did without saying a word. Feeling his eyes scan every inch of my partial nakedness, many cells throughout my body began to liquify. It was obvious how he made me feel. It had been frozen like a glacier buried deep within me but now was quickly thawing. I desperately wanted him to be licking and stroking places meant only for him, but then I snapped back into play and came to my senses.

(Be coy. Don't be too eager. But... You've been waiting almost nine years. I'm so hot right now! Wait, he's been spiritually asleep. He didn't feel or dream. Maybe he needs to build up to it. Yea, go slow, Marie, don't jump too quickly. Oh, I want to rip his clothes off with my teeth and lick him every... Stop! Girl, don't you let him win! He will break first. Wait... be patient...wait.)

Slowing my breathing, I did a few extra hip swings and he moaned at my performance sounding very close to a polar bear growl from his throat. *(Yeah, I'm gonna win.)* Stroking my skin with his eyes, he continued to examine my partially nude body.

Jae tilted his head and asked, "Sweetheart, are you thinner? Uh, why do you look so young? I mean, did you get sexier?"

"Uh, maybe. I don't remember what I looked like or how I felt before. Jae, there are no chemicals or impurities in the ground, so there is nothing bad in the foods we grow, eat, and drink. The atmosphere is pure, and we are younger, rejuvenated, and fit. We don't decay when we get older. There isn't any stress, or disease, so I'm healthier. My body works as it was designed, youthful and energized. Does that make it sexier to you?"

By the time I asked my question, I had returned to being a few inches away. Wetting his lips slightly with a quick lick of his tongue, he admitted with a whisper, "Eh. Sexy aegyo. Very, very sexy." His seductive chocolate eyes pulled me into him. There were no words, only the sounds of our heart beating, the tumbling water from the waterfall outside, and the flow of air in and out of our bodies. I placed his left hand on my flat toned belly and eased it upward. His breathing deepened and he tilted his head as his guided hand reached my lips. Separating his index finger, I slightly parted my lips for my tongue to lick the tip of his finger. A low groan escaped his throat, as his free hand crept down my body, and I was once again my husband's captive for eternity. Jae-Sung and I took our time re-exploring one another and traveling beyond the moon and stars to a cosmic place of passionate euphoria.

Sparkling like chocolate diamonds your eyes whisper my name
As your hands cling to mine your touch is still the same
We seize one another, our connection is beyond intense
Slowly we move as time held us in suspense
Rhythmic motion scorched by desire
Gaps in oxygen, exhaling air like fire

Our passionate heat burns through your tender embrace
Explosions from within as I caress your handsome face
No longer in my dreams, finally I can feel your touch
In climactic ecstasy your delicate kisses comfort me to hush
My husband long ago my heart you surely did capture
Exquisite delight entangles true love's magnificent rapture
Now my love our life is filled with peace and laughter
In his moment of reset, we'll now begin our happiness forever after.

Lying under soft sheets, the cool breeze flowed through the open side of the bedroom, and I was content. A light mist from the waterfall moistened the air that hit our skin as we remained enfolded in love's embrace.

Jae leaned up resting on his elbow and began brushing my hair with his fingers. A moment later, he began to tenderly trace the curves and features of my face with the tip of his long index finger. As it rounded my nose, he whispered, "Sometimes after we made love, you would do this to me whenever you thought I was asleep.

I admit sometimes I would pretend to be just because I loved the way your soft fingertips felt on my skin. I never realized why you did it until the last time we made love before you left for Seattle. I understood why after that. How else do you convey oneness in a unique and intimate connection through nonverbal messages that are sent in soft bursts of energy to the brain, and telling your partner I love each cell that has bonded to create the essence of you?"

With a low giggle, I said, "That is very poetic. Uh, or we could say it's because you're a hot sexy stud muffin, and I adore you. Either way works."

He rolled his eyes, snickering. "Marie, I'm trying to tell you something important. Don't make me laugh." I pressed my lips together and nodded. He adjusted his face and dove into my eyes as if to read the coded signals in my brain. Then he said, "I don't remember any pain from before, but I wrote to you the things I wanted to say not thinking I would see you again after we made love that night. But... I kept it... Mianhae. Eopsneun sewol... Mianhae (I'm sorry. Years without... I'm sorry)."

Pulling his beautiful face closer, his lips clung onto mine as a hot strong adhesive poured to bind metal but with a sticky sweetness much like maple syrup. Harmonious moaning came from us both, even when we parted to take a breath and plunged deeper into another kiss. In time, I paused to tell him my heart's truth.

"We are past all that. Before we moved to France, a brother gave a memorial talk for an older sister, Ying Ahi, who passed away in our congregation. He shared an illustration that stuck with me. He said we are like on a train heading toward Jehovah's Kingdom, and those that pass away are like in a sleeper car of the same train. Although we cannot see or hear them anymore, they are going to the same destination in God's plan. He will decide who and when they will come out and join us. So, we should imagine being with them in the new world and hold on to that hope for happiness. I told everyone that, even our children. It helped. Jae, I barely remembered being without you. I mean, it wasn't something I ever thought about after the earth was reset. Honestly, you didn't come back to my mind again until you touched me, and I heard your voice today. See, Jehovah is so loving. He doesn't want his people to feel pain, be hurt or sad, not even from a loss or when someone from the past is not here. He is such a magnificent father, Jae-Sung. But now you are saying this... Baby, you gave me beautiful gifts to enjoy while you were resting in his memory. Merci... my love. You loved me so much to do that. Everything you did was for me to be happy. I remember. Oh baby, I told you. You are the sun to my moon, not a firework. I waited for you to illuminate my heart once again. I love you so much, baby. Now, we will have forever. I am so happy you are here with me and our children. We are all so excited, you are here."

Jae turned away from our connection, and he ran his fingers through the longer part of his hair before sitting up straight. He exhaled slowly, then in a concerned tone said, "Marie, they aren't babies anymore. Far from babies, they are almost ten years old. I... I don't know how to be a father. What if I disappoint them? What if I..."

"Jae-Sung, one day at a time. Not ten. They just turned eight. You will be great. Besides, you are not alone. It will be an adventure for all of us. Everything is not as it was before. Remember, you have a lot to learn, and we all are learning new things every day. Jehovah makes everything glorious. He will teach you using men here on the earth, with lots of examples and guidance. There are no bad influences we need to contend with either, so life is much easier. You can't mess it up. You'll see that you will be a wonderful father." I expressed my words to him, moving my body up to his.

Strategically, I stroked his smooth muscular torso and the broadness of his back. Then I laid on his shoulder. He kissed the top of my head and inhaled. He released a breathy "kokoneos (coconut)" and I snickered. It was long wild and free as he slipped his fingers behind my head and into my hair. Then he eased my face to his and tilted his forehead down to touch mine.

Jae peered into my eyes saying, "Beautiful Arabian Sand, my magnificent sunset in Dubai. How many levels was that?"

Holding in my giggle, I answered, "Only two. But not the ones I had promised you."

He frowned and said, "We have forever, right?" I nodded, and simultaneously, we chuckled.

Adjusting my body back onto the bed, Jae gently bit my left shoulder then the right, delivering wet kisses along the way to my chin, which he bit and then sucked for a few extra seconds. Feeling his hands over my body, I tried to hold in my laughter by smashing my lips tighter, but my body quivered from the amusement of his playful touching. Jae growled and said, "You owe me level five!"

This was followed by a creepy laugh and my high-pitch shrieking. He flipped me over and pinned me to the bed. I squirmed under him, laughing. I unsuccessfully tried to get away as he bit me in places that were not covered. "Ouch!... Jae... Hold on... Sssss!" Although I was in a full-blown laughter mode, I attempted to move my hands over the areas of my body he was targeting.

Jae mumbled a command, "Don't block me. You'll make it worse. Move your hand, Marie." Right before biting it. I jerked my hand away from his playful bite. "Hey! I am supposed to be biting you. Stop! Jae! You... you are gonna make me pee..."

"You didn't start the level, so now you must have a penalty." Jae-Sung continued his playful torture while laughing like a mad scientist.

We didn't emerge from our bedroom for a few more hours, but when we did, we replenished ourselves with a delicious salad, white grape wine and fed each other fresh fruit while we took a bath. Jae ate a few pieces of dragon fruit and within a couple of minutes, he had this intense look in his eyes. He growled, which made me laugh but then he got this unexpected burst of energy and a sudden desire to lovingly flip me into a few Korean consonant positions. Jae was serious as if he had some sort of superpower of intensity. He was demanding and in total control.

"Oh! Jae-Sung! Ah!"

"No! Don't you dare waterfall! You will only when I tell you to! Do you hear me? Not yet, Marie! You hold it until I want it!"

580

It was riveting, wild-crazy, and electrifying at the same time. Drenched from perspiration and reaching for my wine glass, I let out a breathy, "Oh, my god! That's not...a level I recall... Where... where on earth did that come from?" Jae panted heavily, trying to catch his breath for several seconds, before he yelled, "I'm tingling all over! I don't know but it's a new one for sure. Dragon fruit is the bomb! Woo! Hoo!" Laughing, he kissed me still gasping for oxygen. I gulped some wine and shared my latest mouthful with my next French kiss.

We relaxed for a time before taking a quick shower. Then I grabbed his hand, and a basket of ripe fruit *(not dragon!)*, crackers, cheese, and wine, and told him, "Baby, I want to show you something. Come with me."

We ventured off to a beautiful place built over the sea. Jae-Sung and I held each other, watching the sun gradually rest while creating an array of changing colors in the sky. The shimmering lights across the heavens and waters held his attention, and with grins, moans, and repeated words of "beautiful" "amazing" and "magnificent", he watched the sun's movements, and I studied his, thinking the same words. When he finally saw me gazing at him, he leaned to kiss my nose and then began to soulfully sing to me in French, a song I remembered from Monsieur Nov ft. Tayc called "Ma Femme (my wife)."

The moment brought back romantic memories of being with him at Cocoa Island. I didn't want him to stop, holding me or singing. I told him almost breathlessly, "Jae-Sung, I love the way you sing to me. Baby... please... keep singing."

He let out a light grunt from amusement, squeezed me then folded his fingers in between mine as he sang a few songs he wrote, "Hips in a Blue Dress," "Ocean Water," "French Chocolate," and "Arabian Sand". I remembered each one and hummed, melting away in his strong, loving arms.

"I love you, Chantal. You are my air to breathe."

In our panoramic dome perched atop the calm blue ocean, we spent the rest of the night conveying our love language, reciting poetic words inspired by the dancing waves of light, and feeling the warm sea breeze, while reaching majestic euphoria with level seven.

63. Wonderful

With my love by my side and our three amigos, we continued to take care of our gardens, study, explore, and practice fine-tuning our current skills while being taught newer ones.

While our family waited patiently to receive our building or teaching assignment, we visited with new and old friends nearby, assisted with the building projects, and cared for the peaceful animals that roamed freely and without conflict with us or each other. Everything was clean, fresh, and tranquil.

We explored history, creation, and the earth like never before, learning endless and magnificent things about our creator. Our new beginning was indeed the ultimate happiness overload.

After some time was allotted for Jae to adjust to all things new, Min Cha finally came to see her son for the first time. It was an emotional moment of reunion. When she embraced him from behind, she wouldn't let go for several minutes while she laughed and cried. Tears fell from my eyes and our three amigos also giggled with happy tears as we briefly watched them outside. As he turned around to see her, he started crying seeing her young and vibrant face. We could hear his whisper, "Eomma (mom) Naui aleumdaun eomma. dangsin-eun eolmana aleumdawoyo (My beautiful mom. How beautiful you are)" as he wiped her cheeks, smiling.

Jae-Sung and his mother spent many teary hours alone, simply holding hands and walking along the stream and over the hillside, and talking in the long grass, or she would rest her head on his shoulder as he sang to her. It was so beautiful to see them together again.

Jae-Sung had quickly begun learning about Jehovah, His kingdom, His son, Jesus's kingship, and the way He wants His people to worship Him and be happy on earth.

During his educational study, Jae asked my father, Stephano Erste' and Bernard Runoldhad, "Is it possible? Can I simply explode from the vast euphoric feelings? Each day is awe-inspiring. Sometimes I cannot speak because of all this amazement."

My father chuckled before agreeing in a way only he can. "This is true happiness never felt or imagined. It is only possible from the reset of His original purpose. I feel the exact same way, son. I truly do."

In a short time, Jae-Sung also made the commitment to serve Jehovah and teach others that would be returning but didn't know Him. They would need to learn, and he was excited to share in the work we had been assigned before he was awakened. The day Jae was baptized in the pool under the smaller waterfall steps away from our home, we had some family and a few good friends over for a light meal before the sun went down.

Jae randomly announced as he moved to the sound system, "I am so blessed. I feel like dancing. Amigos let's dance!" Our three children jumped up quickly and began dancing to the instrumental music they had recorded with their father, brother Ki-Noah Prince, Kang, and my father. "Huh?" I giggled but didn't move from the terrace couch. My mother tapped me smiling wide, and my mother-in-law, Min Cha stood up and began dancing with her son and grandchildren.

Jae adjusted a few things and the music changed to an old song from Justin Timberlake called, "Can't Stop the Feeling," which got just about everyone out in the sun dancing. SI appeared to jump up first. When he pulled his wife, Soo up from her seat he said, "I got the moves, babe. Let's do this!" I giggled as they took off dancing.

Holding out his hand for her, my father said, "Dell, you know you want to." She snickered, rising to her feet taking his hand. My mother told him, "Philippe', you only want to dance with me because I'm young again and very bendy."

I gasped shouting, "Mom!" Kang snorted. Aunt Teng, SI, and Soo released sounds of low laughter. Cheryl started choking on her wine while Kelsey tapped her back. Scarlett turned away muffling her laughter. Nari got up giggling. Ki-Noah and Stephano tried not to show their amusement, but it didn't work. The other guests had been too far away or were dancing to have heard her. My oncle Andreas was looking around for someone to share what she said. When Melonie Vincent leaned over and told him, he slowly began chuckling.

It was an exhilarating feeling to be alive, healthy, and young, filled with joy from every source possible. After we took a break from dancing, we slowly migrated back inside and replenished ourselves with snacks. My father asked, "Son, can you play something for me to gaze into my beautiful wife's eyes, and I can feel her heart's smile while we dance?"

Jae-Sung briskly walked over to the piano. As he played a classic slow melody, Jolie washed her hands from munching on caramel popcorn and went to the music room for her cello to join him. Within seconds, Jin stopped helping himself to a huge spoon full of fresh raspberry sorbet and rushed to get his guitar, while Jae followed his sister and retrieved his bass. Scarlett pulled out her trumpet and Cheryl shook the coconut maracas. Kelsey got her flute out, while Ki-Noah picked up the sticks and went behind the drum set. My parents' quick step, smooth glide, and ball change foot moves spun them in, out and around the wide terrace as they stared into each other's eyes. *(I love watching them dance.)*

Guests watched them smiling. Entering the room from a side door, my musketeer uncle Andreas said, "I didn't know we were going to have a jam session. I could've brought my trumpet, too."

He grabbed some grapes and popped them in his mouth. Then he picked up an empty wooden bowl and began beating it like a bongo drum and dancing.

(He's a fun crazy uncle. I love him.)

Jae-Sung gestured to Kang to sing something. He quickly accompanied the musicians while playing groovy jazz tunes. *(Kang's voice is nice!)* My hips and feet were moving, I wanted to dance so bad I couldn't help it, as they played an up-tempo extended version of a very old song called, "Sway," sounding like Michael Buble'. Feeling the rhythm, I moved my hips, lifted the back of my hair, and closed my eyes.

When I heard Jae-Sung shout, I stopped moving and opened my eyes. "Sì, Andreas, Stephano… Somebody play the piano. I gotta dance with my wife, right now!"

Kang took over the piano and repeated the song as Jae-Sung did some cha-cha step moves toward me, mouthing the words, "Sexy aegyo."

I snickered before making small circles with my lower body. He held me from behind and we slowly danced to jazzy band music being played by our children and friends. Jae kissed my neck behind my left ear and whispered, "Mmm, baby, you are doing the hair and eyes thing. We didn't even have any tequila. You gotta stop moving your hips like that. We have company."

I leaned back against his body and moaned but confirmed, "Don't need tequila. Smarty. Uh, do I win?"

"Oh, oui (yes)." He said turning me around to face him as we continue to cha-cha to the new beats. *(Ha! Ha!)* I bit my bottom lip before asking him, "Husband, what is the score?"

He tilted his head like he was going to kiss me and said, "Tie…we are tied." I leaned back and squinted my eyes at him. He cleared his throat and corrected himself, "No, no… now, uh, you're ahead. That's right. Ha! Sway with me, sexy aegyo." I laughed as he pulled me closer holding me by my hands. Glancing over at my hip swinging-waltzing parents gazing into each other's eyes, it came to me, *(I got this from them.)*

We enjoyed more hours of music, dancing, munching, and fun.

When everyone had gone and we put our children to bed, he held me close and said the sweetest thing, "My love, we all serve Jehovah together. Thank you for believing, hoping, and enduring all things, like that love scripture your parents gave us after our wedding in France. Thank you, baby, for waiting for me."

Unknowingly, I had released small tears from hearing his simple words. Our lives were as they were meant to be, happy.

Stephano Erste' and his sister, Scarlett Erste'

Oliver-Pierre and Banyata Rana

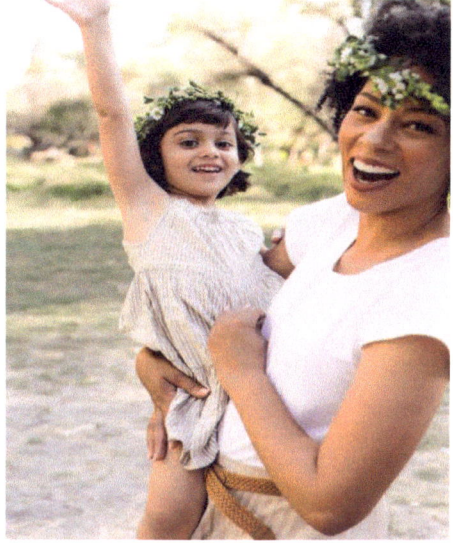

Their daughter, Navya-Lynn Rana-Schneider,
Her husband, Demetri with Penelope and Piper

Jae hinted almost every day that he wanted to dance. We did because I loved to dance with him. Sometimes we would have a family dance off, and other times, the two of us would be outside having fun dancing to music he created, or songs from before. Every moment in life was beyond anything ever imagined, and it was truly glorious. My heart sung a songbirds melody waking each morning in this warm cocoon of Jae-Sung's arms. Jae, Jin, and Jolie seemed to smile and laugh about every minute with new adventures, with not only their father but also with my young and energized mother teaching them how to garden. My father and oncle Andreas, who are both young and virile, vigorously running around with them and other young ones from our congregation, playfully exploring creation, and teaching new ones, while expanding their knowledge.

Our triplets regularly wrote music and short stories, even played music with their father and other friends and family nearby. My good friend, Melonie Vincent, began teaching me how to play the harp. She had mastered it and I said it was such a pretty sounding instrument, that she wanted to help me learn. I have come a long way since I first started. Jae-Sung has been educating me in the art of reading and creating music on the piano, while our daughter patiently taught me to play the cello.

These days, my mother was also learning to play the saxophone from my father, but she mentioned that it has been a challenge to get beyond the basics. After about three months, she had the same response when I asked her how things were going. One day after we practiced our assigned teaching demonstration for our midweek meeting, we were chopping ingredients to make vegetable soup in her kitchen and I curiously asked her, "Not that it's a race or anything but why is it taking you so long to get beyond the basics? Mom, you always wanted to play the saxophone because you love the way Pawpaw plays it. Are you not interested in it now?"

With her eyebrow raised and water glass moving toward her lip, she said, "No, I am. But, well. It's just… that… you see every time your father gets his saxophone out for my lesson, we end up making out, and then in the shower. He can't seem to keep his hands to himself. You do know your father is a freaky Frenchman, don't you?"

I choked on my small bite of lemon blueberry tart before laughing for a few minutes, and thought, *(Definitely, I've inherited it.)*

"Uh, Mom… You've been saying that, but I think… Uh-ma, it's you that might be that way." She smacked my hand and insisted with an elevated tone to her voice, "No, really, it's him. It is!" I rolled my eyes, then bugged them out at her, pressing my lips together tightly so I wouldn't laugh. She pinched my elbow, sniggling. Then she cleared her throat and got serious and said, "Oh, just stop looking at me like that. I knew you were going to take his side. No matter, Celeste is my favorite anyway." I gasped. She winked at me smirking as we laughed.

Speaking of Celeste, I had not seen my sister or her family as often as I would have liked because they lived a little further away, like a few other loved ones. But if we missed opportunities to spend time together during assemblies or conventions, we make plans to get together. The JJs are so tall. Jason's voice is deeper than Adam's now. Hana, Oasis, and Jacqueline are very close, so I see her more often because she stays over with them. She is a lovely young woman. They all are.

Regularly, Min Cha sketches and paints, and often comes over to visit along with Teng, who was always smiling. She and Jae would have their private moments together.

Just like my parents, Min Cha takes each one of our children to have special bonding time with her. Not too many days go by without us spending time with Kang and Nari, SI, Soo, and Hana, Andreas, Geneviève and Daniella, Kristoff, Trey and his sisters, Navya's families, Megan Chan, my cousin, Tamera and her husband, Kevin, her older brother, Sam Jr., and other friends from our local area.

We had a spiritual routine and assignment work with friends and family and then we entertained or were invited over a lot. Everything in life and time was balanced. We shared and gave, received, and supported everyone. There were no time clocks to punch, no overbearing bosses, no disagreements, no rush hour traffic, no stress or worries. We studied, taught others, built, explored, and traveled to other locations to help cultivate an area, when we were assigned. It was a wonderful life with my love.

Daily, we were busy doing work that we enjoyed and found fulfillment in every task, we could've never gotten bored. How could we be? There was always something to do, new things to learn and discover, from animals, to nature, to making new friends and reconnecting with old ones. Every other day was somewhat like an adventure and the others were tranquil and relaxing. Honestly, even when Jae and I spent all night making love, we were never too tired for the next day.

Our children sometimes sniggled and giggled uncontrollably at the breakfast table, which was also very amusing and made for comical family time during the meal. *(They are so silly, just like their father and his idol brothers, Kang, and SI.)* We thought it was just them being happy children and excited about the day's activities, but after this behavior had gone on for months, one morning, Jae Lune announced, "Papa, can you help me? I want to move my room down to the first floor next to Jin's."

Jae stopped eating and asked, "Why? You don't like your room on the second floor?"

With his siblings trying not to snicker, Jae Lune said, "I figured out...Well. Uh... At first, I thought it was maybe monkeys at night, but after I heard 'three, four, seven, two. Kimchi and Hong Kong,' uh, I figured it wasn't animals."

Jae let out a howling laugh, the high pitch kind as he nodded and wildly clapped his hands together like a performing sea-lion. All I could do was close my eyes and turn away while my face turned red from embarrassment.

(Jae always makes so much noise. It's probably best if we have a floor between us and them.)

When our children finished helping clean the kitchen, they went off to study, practice, or play. I playfully pinched my husband's bicep, and said, "Jae, I told you, you sometimes get too loud!" Smirking, he replied, "Not me. You." Slugging his hard chest, I said, "No. I don't sound like a monkey." Jae cleared his throat andstared up at me with those sultry eyes, and said, "Why are you denying it? I remember very clearly, you said the noises you make when we do it, sound like... Chewbacca!" He let out a wheezy cackle. I yelped, "Oh! You know what!" Laughing, he eased out of the kitchen making sounds like a Wookie. *(Punk face!)*

In the late fall, we all came together for a special assembly day of spiritual and physical food. We met up with brothers and sisters and made new friends during the day-long event. While traveling back home, our extended family members discussed highlights from the program. After enjoying a scrumptious meal, we parted ways with everyone and made our way home for the evening. Jae, our children, and I gathered outside with our toes in the clear pool below the fresh waterfall to watch the streaks of purple, yellow, and pink blend across the sky as the sun set. My face beamed listening to Jae-Lune read some of his poetry about light and the sun rays. I examined Jolie's painted creation showing the detailed magnificence of butterfly wings and swan feathers, and then I laid my head on my husband's shoulder while Jin serenaded us with a guitar ballad, he wrote called Dazzle, which described the marvelous gemstone-like colors of his sibling's eyes. *(My three amigos are the most precious. This is the way our family was always meant to be.)* My heart warmed witnessing sparkles of twilight in Jae-Sung and our children's faces. I yearned for nothing. We were living the way life was intended, yet more exciting things kept happening.

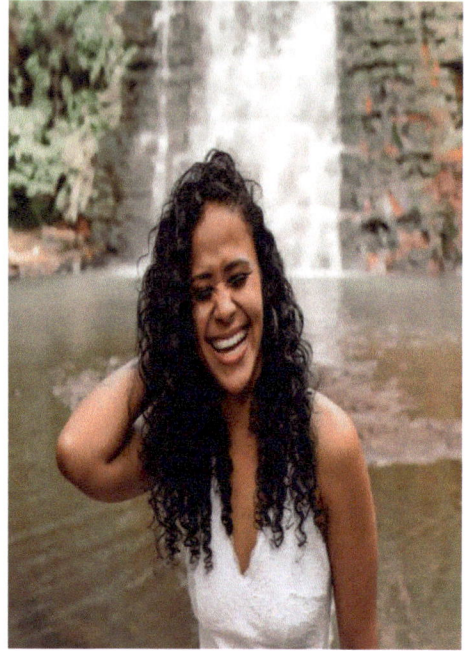

Trey Aminbello and his sister Rutalah

The next morning, we rose early and prepared for our planned breakfast with my parents, my cousin Alton, Jae's mother, the Cheng families, the Vincent's, and the Hanover's, Trey, and his sister, Rutalah. A few other friends stopped by, including Tommy Han and Jae-Sung's former Bible study Joon Nam, who had recently been baptized along with his wife, and her sister. I didn't know them well because they lived a distance away, but I remembered Joon had been from Jae's old K-Pop group. Since it had been a few months from when we all took the trip for their baptism, Jae was super excited to see him. Min Cha and the Cheng brothers were too. *(I hope to get to know them better.)* Although I would have loved all my family and friends to have been with us, I knew Celeste was entertaining most of them over at her and Adam's home that day.

Achilles and Melonie Vincent

Just as we were digging in, Achilles Vincent excitedly gave us details about their upcoming traveling assignment. Amber Hanover asked Melonie and Oasis Vincent what they were looking forward to in the new location, during their six-month assignment. As Oasis shared her excitement in living in a cooler climate, I noticed she began blushing when Lett's oldest son, Kaseem seemed to be focused on her every word and action. I tapped Jae's knee. He turned and I gave him the secret K-Pop idol eye code to check it out. Once he saw the chemistry, he nodded confirming and then gave me a sly smile. *(Oh, they like each other.)* Minutes later, as my cousin, Alton, was telling us about his recent experience with another group of friends that were from the same area that they were going, we heard several knocks on the side door facing the meadow.

Surprised, it was my cousin, Kristoff and Ohanaka, Trey's youngest sister. Hugging them, Jae invited them to join us, and they agreed. At that point, my Delphine Delacroix alarm was ringing in my ear. I felt something was about to happen, because Kristoff came smiling wide showing all his straight white teeth. Then he said, "Hello, everyone. We wanted to stop by this morning and tell you…"

As we all paused in silence, I glanced over at her blushing face and thought, (*Why is she dewy? Wait…*)

Seconds later, Ohanaka finished his statement with, "He asked, and I said yes."

I shot up from my chair covering my mouth from making a very loud outburst of cheer. A slow drizzle of liquid eased from my eyes seeing and feeling my cousin's joy in his eyes. High and low chants of congratulations and laughter rang through our house hearing the glorious news of the two being deeply in love, and we knew a marriage was happening very soon. I felt my heart flip inside my body as I had this sensation of lit sparklers all over my skin from the excitement and joy for my beloved cousin. Flashes of past hopes for him hit my brain in quick succession. I realized I was even more thankful he had learned about Jehovah. The times he spent with us building our house and being with family were as it was meant to be all along. The past was long gone from our minds. He is loved and knows it. Now he is given this blessing of real love and partnership. My thoughts bubbled over… (*I knew it would happen. I just knew it. Jehovah gives gifts to all His friends, even when you don't know what will make you happiest, He does. Oh Kristoff, you have a forever love like I do. It's so wonderful. Why am I crying?*)

My eyes were glossy from my waves of emotional response to seeing his giant smile as he hugged well-wishers. Kristoff made his way over to me while giving and receiving handshakes and high-fives from our guests.

Trey's sister Ohanaka

Finally, reaching to hug me, Kristoff pulled me close and whispered in my ear, "Merci, chère cousine. Jéhovah m'a fait le plus beau cadeau. Elle est la parfaite pour moi. C'est à ça que ressemble le véritable amour. Je suis plus que complet, Chantal. Je t'aime, jolie cousine brune. (Thank you, sweet cousin. Jehovah has given me the greatest present. She is the perfect one for me. This is what true love feels like. I am beyond complete, Chantal. I love you, pretty brown cousin)."

My smile was wide, and my kisses to his cheek were wet and a bit salty, but I eagerly delivered them with vigor. While Kristoff and Ohanaka sat down to have breakfast with us, Jae went to the door after hearing someone knocking. We invited an unexpected service group of friends that stopped by, to also join us for breakfast. We made room and added more dishes to the table for everyone to enjoy; there was plenty for all.

My cousin Kristoff Delacroix-Lazar

Moments later, more jubilee and celebration came like rapid shooting stars in the sky when Bernard announced he and Megan were expecting a baby in the winter. Right there at the table, Ki-Noah asked, "Kelsey, we have talked about it already, so I'm going to ask officially, will you be mine forever?" She laughed with a resounding,

"Yes!" and we all clapped, laughed, cheered with "Hurray," "Congratulations," and "This is so exciting!"

Tommy and Cheryl's wedding ceremony was already set to be in four weeks, but she spoke up, "Oh, wouldn't it be fun to do it all at the same time? Ohanaka, Kelsey, what do you think? Oh, let's!"

"Hey, that would be nice," Ohanaka said, looking over at Kristoff who gave her a nod. Kelsey was still giggling but Ki-Noah gave a thumbs up putting some cilantro rice with pineapple in his mouth. Several women began gathering to discuss the possibilities of a triple nuptials party as the men continued to eat and talk about their studies, hobbies, building, and caretaking assignments.

"This is craziness," I said feeling elation from the last few announcements.

My father said, "Hmmm, weddings. I wonder if it's maybe something in the food." SI, Joon, Kang and my father began laughing uncontrollably when Trey stopped chewing and pushed back away from the table.

"He's kidding. Eat," my mother said as she nudged Trey and motioned for him to go on and enjoy his meal. Slowly poking at portions on his plate as though he was not quite sure, Trey frowned but gradually continued to eat. Then Raja, Dyson, Kang, SI, and my father laughed with side comments watching Trey chew in slow motion apparently more cautiously because of possible results.

It was blissfulness overload for everyone. Loud banter and chatter continued while the children gravitated outside. A lot was going on; it was like the room had been pumped with some sort of natural good-feeling oxygenated elements because the laughter moments were on-going.

Nicolette "Letti" Senhajii-Zahad
Raja "RAZ" Zahad

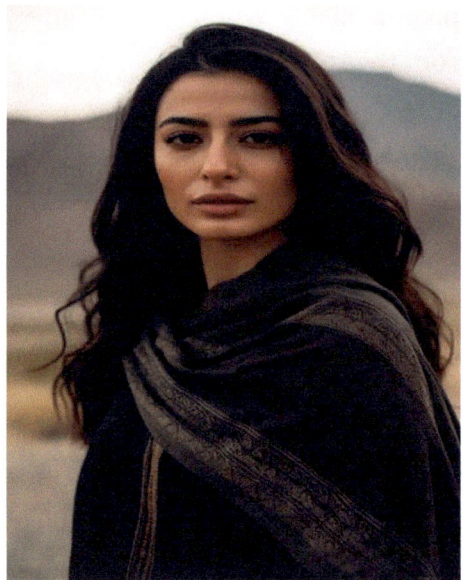

Oasis Vincent & Kaseem Zahad   Lett's Sister, Breanna

Dyson and Amber Hanover

Chase Hanover

Cousin, Alton Murry III

Tommy Han

Cheryl Nbune'-Han

Nayla Pearson-Nam

Joon Nam

Megan Chan-Runoldhad

Bernard Runoldhad

Kelsey Yuni

Ki-Noah Prince

In a conversation with Cheryl getting the recipe for the scrumptious dish she made, I noticed Jae Sung talking to Joon, Kang and SI but didn't pay much attention to what he was slowly putting in his mouth. Lowkey, I snickered but reengaged into the conversation with Cheryl and my mother, who had joined us in the far corner of the room. Unfortunately, my mother's comments about her newest teaching assignment had my full attention, and I didn't realize Jae had moved across the gathering room.

In moments, the hair on the back of my neck seemed to magnetize with an invisible surge of electricity. The skin on my arms tingled with small pebbles of perspiration from the heat of his eyes on me. *(Where is he?)* I questioned his whereabouts, while my eyes searched among the standing and seated clusters of our laughing friends and family. *(I feel him watching me. Where did he…)* Contact. His eyes locked onto mine like a homing missile, then they pulled me in like a fishermen's net. Jae smirked before guiding the small fork holding a piece of cubed fruit into his mouth. Stabbing another piece from the bowl in his hand, I instantly questioned, *(Wait, is that dragon fruit?)* and shook my head for him not to indulge in the exotic fruit that to him was a very potent aphrodisiac for some reason. He slowly eased the fork from his lips, chewing slowly, and raising his left eyebrow peering at me. Jae's intense stare slowly melted my body. I couldn't shift my eyes away, and my lips quivered. *(Uh oh.)* I watched him slide past Joon, Achilles, and Raja exchanging ideas in their conversation. He appeared to nod as if he agreed with their comments, and then he moved toward me like a panther in the long grass. *(Oh…)* My breathing increased and my heartbeat as though it was part of a tribal rhythm from West Africa. Adjusting my stance by shifting my feet, I felt moisture build between my fingers and toes as my secret place heard his call and began pulsating from his alluring desire and my thoughts of his fiery touch. *(He makes me burn so intense for him.)* I shook my head to snap out of his eye seduction. Then I told myself, *(Stop! No. Get control, Marie. He is trying to break you. Don't let him win.)*

I glanced back over the room to refocus. When I saw Kang, he was already covering his mouth laughing. *(Is it that obvious?)* Checking a few other faces, I concluded that the antics were only known to his very observant old K-Pop brothers. *(It's got to be that idol code secret stuff.)* My eyes darted back to determine where Jae was in proximity to where I was standing. He was now only a few inches away. Jae placed the empty bowl on a side table and eased behind me tugging at my hips. A low chuckle came from me while he pulled me closer to his firm body and began smacking his lips and sucking air through his teeth. Holding in my growing urge to laugh and lose his seduction game, I kept facing the group, pretending to be listening to the story Chase was telling about a bear family near his home. Jae inconspicuously began taking comical and overly exaggerated whiffs of my hair and lowly moaning the Hebrew word "cocus (coconut)" before groaning. *(Coconut is a trigger.)* I pressed my lips together and didn't move or acknowledge his sly actions to excite me.

Still holding me firmly and pulling me onto him, Jae pecked my neck and lightly nibbled on my left ear. It tickled and I shrugged my shoulders up to make him stop. Then he chuckled. Everyone had been preoccupied with their lively discussions to notice that Jae was pulling me backward a few steps at a time. Abruptly, he stopped moving me to an exit, after I made a squeak.

Turning his head around to see my face, he asked, "Did you say something?"

Quickly, before being lured into those chocolate pools of decadent desire, I closed my eyes, pressed my lips tightly and moaned no. He huffed but I could feel his smug silent laugh. *(Be strong, don't let him win, Marie.)*

As I opened my eyes, several of our guests had migrated outside with all the children. Loud cheers followed the commencing race to distant herds of animals, initiated by Letti, Chase, SI, Rutalah, Scarlett, and Trey. A few couples that were still inside began clearing the table and cleaning up. Then my mother gave me a sarcastic glance and mouthed the words, "I told you he was just like your father." I snorted loudly but quickly pretended to be coughing.

Jae took a few more steps backward and pulled me with him. With his face next to my ear, I heard him lick his lips and every cell in my body felt as though it was exploding and jolting me with electricity. Jae continued to seductively tease me with airy words delivered behind my left ear. "You smell so sweet." "Oh, how delicious you taste on my tongue." "Waterfall, so wet and slippery...mmm."

I started to weaken but held on until I heard him say, "Purr for me, little kitty. Yes, do that again." Before taking a nip of my earlobe and pressing his body into mine from behind. I squirmed biting my bottom lip, so I wouldn't yelp, but I abruptly turned around to face him. I pointed my finger at him and firmly told him in a low voice, "You are a naughty man, Jae-Sung Kim." He grinned, kissed the tip of my nose, and announced, "I win." Defeated and very amused, I pinched his cheek and we crept away unnoticed. However, about fifty-seven minutes later, my parents, Kang, Joon, and Min Cha made it known they were well aware of what we were off doing. *(Oh no!)* Jae just thought it was all very funny. Blushing, I silently giggled to myself immediately, having a flashback memory of being at Min Cha's home and Jae being extra naughty during lunch.

Days later, when our children were at Letti and RAZ's home, we went swimming in the partially secluded, animal-free waterfall pool. While under the clear water, Jae took off his shorts, then he turned saying, "Your turn." But I refused, "Jae, no, it's still light out."

"Babe, we're alone. Look, if you don't remove your shorts and top, I will." Moving around the pool away from him, he dove under the water and grabbed me. With not much resistance, he maneuvered my top off. Closer to the edge and standing on the smooth rocks below, Jae gently held my free breasts, saying, "Hello my friends. Left I'll play with you later, it's rights turn." Giggling, I enjoyed his tender kneading, and sucking them. But then it happened...

We didn't notice my parents on the grass staring at us until my mother shouted, "Philippe', he's more like you than I thought! Let's not invite them to dinner, Jae-Sung seems to have his mouth full already!" I screeched, covering myself. Laughing, Jae said "Annyeonghaseyo (Hello)," while shifting his nude body behind me. My father chuckled, saying, "We'll wait inside." I splashed at Jae quickly moving to get my top. "Why... why does this happen with my parents?" He just cackled like a hyena putting his shorts back on.

64. Cosmic

Even now after all this time, Jae and I have this intense chemistry when we were alone. It can be described as an electrical storm that grows in power or low burning flame gradually blazes into a fervor inferno. He pulls me into him, and I erupt slowly when he touches me but even sometimes without. There is nothing like the gradual crescendo of being with him and making love's music with him. Absolutely nothing.

Many memories from our past together had begun to fade, due to simply being eclipsed with everything reset and wonderful. It took some time but eventually I realized I didn't float or dream into heightened passion when we made love like I did before. Intimacy was noticeably very different. It was unlike any ecstasy I had ever experienced before. When we talked about it, Jae reminded me that he had told me before that being with me was like a first time, every time. But after I won our wrestling match and two rounds of rock, paper, scissors, he admitted it was now 'out of this world, amazing' even without eating dragon fruit.

(He is so silly.)

So far, we have created eleven new love levels adding to his K-Pop idol brother's original ten. Some levels are more in rotation than others, but all are available and are in the mix at any time. To date, there are twenty-one, but Jae's still likes to wrestle, bite, and do things that make me laugh so hard I have to go pee. *(Crazy man. He is so playful and spontaneous.)* Honestly, rather it was playful or serious, I still doubted there could be a level that would surpass the mind-blowing experience of level seven. I didn't realize when I said it, my husband took those words as a challenge.

It was a chilly night on the last day of February. Our children were staying overnight at Kang and Nari's home. I had finished my nighttime routine and decided to curl my hair and put on a silk and lace short black camisole with matching shorts. When I entered our bedroom, Jae was already in bed lying flat on his back with his arms behind his head. His breathing was deep and steady. His lids were shut but he wasn't sleeping, at least I didn't initially think he was. *(Oh, he is so fine!)*

I snuggled my body closer to him in bed. My constant yet gentle nudging triggered his deep moan, a slow wetting of his lips with his tongue, and then his sultry voice delivered a question I wanted to hear. "What, babe? Hey, are you wanting to fool around?"

I snickered and eased my mouth over him just enough to bite his firm bare chest. A sharp sound of air being sucked through a small opening in his mouth could be heard when my teeth connected with his skin, pulled, and released it. He groaned twisting his body to lay partially on to mine and hold me firmly onto the bed. "Answer me, wife. I don't understand silent gestures as foreplay. Say, what you want." I shook my head no, while tucking my lips inside my mouth.

"Marie, if you don't tell me, you will have a penalty." His voice was low, and his dark eyes sparkled in the moonlight. Jae yanked away the sheet from between us and moved his slick toned body more on me. The longer portion of his hair flopped forward as he lifted himself to hover over me. He peered into my eyes with a very serious facial expression.

"Marie, say what you want. Say it. I want to hear it from those pretty soft lips. Tell me right now. Where exactly do you wanna go?"

I blurted out, "Hong Kong." Then I started giggling.

He huffed with satisfaction but then eased his body onto mine. Never taking his eyes away, our skin began to merge with increased pressure as he lowered himself. Inches away from my lips, he whispered, "Oh no, my sweet lady. Right now, I'm about to take you to a star on the left corner of Orion's Belt. This will be level twenty-two."

I oozed with delight and blinked rapidly in the moment. "Ā, nanto (Oh my)." I'm not sure why I said it in Japanese, but I did. Perhaps it was because I was hyper-curious, and excited by what he said. The right corner of his mouth lifted to display a sly smirk and his dimple before the tip of his wide pink tongue came out to wet his lips again. Staring into my eyes intensely, he said, "Baby, making love to you is the most marvelous odyssey ever created. Feeling you open your heart and take me in transcends me to euphoria. Marie, you give me all of yourself and I give you all of me. Each cell tingles as your soul locks on to mine and mine to yours. But tonight, a little Kama Sutra lotus flower, and maybe a gradual transition into the coital alignment but then we'll do something very special. Are you ready to fly into into orgasmic heaven?"

"Ooo, wee. Yes." I said in a low voice. *(What's he gonna do?)*

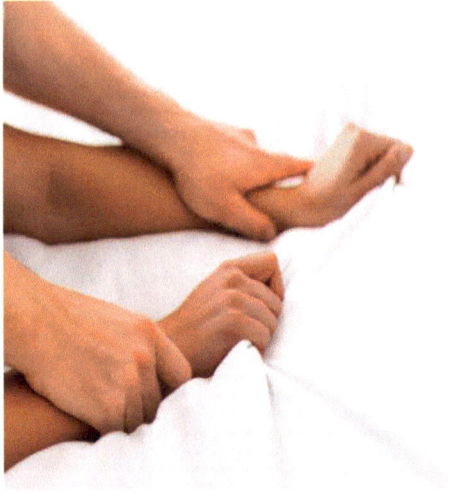

Jae-Sung Kim proceeded to take me on a slow voyage that didn't end until the sun brought forth a new day. In every way possible, he is the most spectacular man. *(OMG! New favorite level!)*

LTTOB

Set course slow and steady
The brightest cluster is our destination
As the stars align, the earth will move
Come with me beyond the visible sky
Our souls magnetically subdued in quiet
Weightless in love made from cosmic showers
An oasis of rapture, you alone are my heaven
Bursts travel the speed of sound
Multiple points of ultimate pinnacles
We are the lights in the beautiful nebula
With you there is no end to loves universe
Lost in you, my love is serenity amidst Blazars.

65. Rhapsody

The blooming season came on time as it did every year. After a few days of refreshing rainfall to nourish the earth, the sky was clear, and it was lovely. The golden rays of the sun brighten the blueness above. There was a warm breeze that swam through the surrounding tree leaves and branches. Occasionally, it made a soft whistle as the air passed by. While preparing dishes for the table, I heard a few birds having cheerful conversations. Perhaps discussing where to meet in flight or where to land and gather with their friends. They definitely had their own conversation going on, and it was sweet to hear in the surrounding trees.

The extra-long, dark wood table, Jae-Sung, Alton, Chase, and Kang made for us to entertain and enjoy group meals outside was filled with an array of freshly picked berries, melons, and other ripe exotic fruits, sweet and savory breads, fresh salads, and healthy dishes. It was a delight to have many of our family and friends over for our planned gathering today. After Jae-Sung gave a blessing for our hosted meal, we began enjoying our lunch party outside in the decorative area with the light warm breeze.

Since we had strategically placed the table and chairs, guests on one side could view the lush green open meadow on the left and others could feel the gentle spray from the waterfall coming from the right. Gazing around the table, admiring the love of our family members, at least the ones that were able to meet us for lunch today, my heart filled and overflowed. Listening to their shared experiences, exciting assignments, and other conversations created these quick jumps prancing around in my chest, simply from happiness.

Today was extra special because Renee Escobar and her family traveled specifically to join us. As my handsome nephew, Christopher, passed a large pitcher of a chilled concoction of fruit juices to his very round pregnant mother, we chuckled with her continued descriptive explanation of how Antonio had attempted to ride a stallion the day before.

Around the long banquet table, those in attendance couldn't stop laughing. Especially when Antonio made his animated facial expressions to match her storytelling. Then he got up standing in the low grass to reenact how he held on to the horse's mane and slid around riding bareback wearing silk-like shorts. I kept covering my mouth, so I wouldn't cackle. Some of our family guests, such as Chul, Ami, Wolfgang, Sonia, Sam, Soo, oncle Chevalier, and Geneviève joined in the story telling of the animals they are caring for near their homes and the friends they had met recently. My ears perked up when I heard my oncle Andreas talking about a special assembly day, a long time ago. He said, "The pool water was warm, but it was my old body that was just chilly. I was shivering, and I shook my body like I was doing some cool dance. My fake teeth even made a clanging sound in my mouth."

Laughter rang up to the non-existing clouds. I realized he was retelling of the time before we moved to France, and the day he, my parents and Gert were baptized as Jehovah's Witnesses.

My father chimed in, "I didn't know what that noise was when we were walking into the pool. Dell kept laughing while holding my hand. As you were getting out, I heard you say you were cold on the outside but warm on the inside, kind of like a Pop Tart. Dell laughed harder and squeezed my hand. But I never knew it was your fake choppers making that noise. Ha-Ha. I'm glad we all have real ones again."

Sitting next to him, my mother, who was looking as radiant and youthful as she did on their wedding day, nudged my father and said, "Philippe' you weren't supposed to tell him we heard his noises. Oh, but everyone did. Hee, hee."

Andreas began to gesture as if he was amused and a little embarrassed. Joy tapped him saying, "Uncle Andreas, don't worry that happened to me too. I was freezing but felt warm and toasty inside. It may be just something that happened back then to the really cool people." She grinned at him. His full brown curls shimmered in the sunlight as he reached over to give her a sweet side hug, he told her, "Merci, dear, Joy. We are indeed some of the cool ones."

Midway through our meal, I noticed in the distance that there were a few adults around several baby elephants. They seemed to be walking past a tame pride of lions nibbling on the tall grass. It looked as if there were several people walking in the direction of our home, but I couldn't make out exactly who they were, or if they were coming here. No one at the table commented on my frequent glances out toward the vast meadow. Then I refocused on those that had come to join us for lunch. After I took a large gulp of blueberry, lavender, and lemon infused water, and chewed the meaty grape I had popped in my mouth, I took a deep breath and spoke up for all to hear. "I need to say something."

The chatter died down and I got everyone's attention. Jae-Sung kissed the back of my hand as I stood up, so my voice could be heard while we were outside surrounded by nature. No one seemed to notice that Jolie was pressing her lips together to prevent herself from shouting. I did. I made a point to give my daughter a quick wink, and her cute little face gave me a smile.

"We are… I… I am so delighted you were free to come over today. Everyone we invited couldn't come due to other commitments, but I wanted to look into your healthy and happy faces when I told you that I loved you all very much and…"

I inhaled a moment and took a pause, grabbing my throat in an effort to stop myself from blurting out garbled words the speed of a hummingbird's wings in flight.

(Breathe. I need to speak slowly, so they hear me.) I could feel Jae-Sung's eyes on me before he touched my hip and tenderly patted my thigh. He grabbed my hand and folded our fingers interlocking them. Although he didn't know what I was going to say, he gave me the encouragement I needed. I smiled before I continued speaking softly.

"Well… You see…. I wanted to let you know… Um… We're going to have a new addition to our family arriving in about seven months or so." Quickly, I sat down with the same excited expression my daughter had across the table. Jolie had been rocking in her seat grinning. My toes wiggled nonstop inside my flat sandals because I was so nervous and excited. Glancing around at the stillness of our guests, everyone seemed to be motionless, and taking a moment to allow this amazing, unexpected news to process in their brains.

After several minutes came a roaring sound of cheery laughter that filled the air. Still giggling, I felt Jae's hand loosen its grip holding mine. I wiggled my fingers resting in Jae's hand under the table, but he didn't move. I squeezed it, held his very limp hand tightly and turned to my beloved. Jae's dark chocolate eyes were hazy from the salty liquid pooling inside and ready to fall. He was stunned by my announcement. I purposefully kept it to myself until this very moment. A couple of random tears trickled down his creamy porcelain-like cheeks. Jae blinked a few times then stared at me with such intensity. It felt as though his glance was touching my face.

It was Simeon's grand expression of, "What a blessing from Jehovah." My oncle Chevalier's statement of "How amazing!" And Antonio's shouted words of, "Wow! Congratulations!" while falling back onto the grass holding his head laughing was what seemed to break Jae-Sung's silence.

He reached up and held my face with both his hands and said, "Cha… Chantal…Marie… Baby… you're pregnant? Like… You… You are… You are… pregnant?" His glossy eyes sparkled in the sunlight, as his blank expression morphed into a wide grin slowly seemed to reach up to the heavens.

I nodded, answering him. "Oui, nae sarang. Jehovah God can and will do anything for His friends. We… you and I are going to have a baby because… I… am… pregnant… Isn't—." Instantly his smiling lips pressed onto my teeth and then my closed lips. Jae-Sung couldn't stop his laughter with tears. He eased back from his kiss to share his giant smile and dancing eyes with those cheering around us.

Jae-Sung whisper to me in French and Korean, "Oh mon amour, je n'aurais jamais imaginé… Gamsahabnida! Gijeog (Oh, my love never did I imagine, thank you! A miracle)."

He pulled me close again and then pecked my cheek. I giggled, feeling loving energy from every angle surrounding us.

Renee spoke out from her seat across the table, "Marie… I… I…" She couldn't get her words out, but her eyes told me all I needed to know. Then in true Renee Escobar style, she found the words to come from her lips and said, "You just wanted to be pregnant with me. You're such a copy-catter!"

Everyone laughed even louder, some even clapped.

My beautiful mother was silent, and from her seat she moved her body to see my eyes. She had rolling tears and tight lips quivering. She spoke the jubilation of her heart without words. Then she raised fingers to her lips, puckered and sent me a subtle air kiss. I caught her love and returned it the same way. Still laughing, I noticed my father reach to hold her hand and began kissing the back of it, but in seconds he moved to deliver light kisses to her cheek.

After hugging tante Gert and Lylah, Jolie got up from her seat and came to the end of the table to hug me. Embracing my little darling, she announced, "I didn't tell anyone. See I'm not like tante CeCe was at all. I can keep a secret."

I snorted, seeing the satisfaction in her expression from keeping the secret until today. I rubbed our noses together for a soft Eskimo kiss and commended her. "Yes, my pretty one. I know you wanted to but thank you for waiting. You are going to be the best big sister, ever!"

"Eomma (mama), may I tell Emelia, Emma, Edwin, and the JJ's tomorrow, s'il vous plait (please)?" Nodding, I gave her the green light to release the news to some of her cousins joining us with their families and other friends for lunch the next day.

Never letting go of my hand, Jae-Sung looked over at my father for help. Jae-Sung was still somewhat in his own thoughts of shock, and randomly said, "I cannot say everything that I'm feeling right now! But I want to thank Jehovah for this miracle. Père… father… s'il vous plait (please)?"

At that moment, my magnificent father, Jean-Philippe' Henri Delacroix with his beautiful golden hair, muscular build, and ocean blue eyes wiped his drizzling tears and agreed. Looking very close to how I imagined he did when he first met my mother, he kissed her cheek and then stood up quickly. "Let's give thanks to our creator who has not only bestowed this gift onto Chantal-Marie and Jae-Sung but… but to all of us, feeling the jubilation of His miracle and blessing. I never imagined…"

He cleared his throat and continued, "Every moment of every day, our heavenly father shows us His wonders beyond our dreams, confirming yet again our life on earth as he planned from the very beginning, overflows with unimaginable happiness… Serving Jehovah is … is the best life ever. Please, join me in prayer."

The long table of our large family held hands, while my father's deep baritone voice occasionally cracked from his emotions of glee. He even had to clear his throat when his prayer included some of the Bible scriptures from Psalms 37:4 and 11, "Jehovah will grant you the desires of your heart" and "the meek will possess the earth and find exquisite delight in the abundance of peace."

Tears flowed as Jolie squeezed my right hand and her father squeezed the left. After the unified "Amen", my eyes were filled and my cheeks were covered with wetness, but so was everyone else's. My father sat down and blew me another kiss before holding my mother's chin and tenderly kissing her lips. Jae and Jin jumped up and rushed to hug me, their father and sister. While patting my tummy, Jin said, "Bonjour petit (Hello little one)." Jae's face was flushed, as he spun Jolie around laughing. Simultaneously, I saw in the far distance silhouettes of people but was unsure if they were the ones I had seen earlier. I thought, *(Perhaps new neighbors. We will need to invite them over soon.)*

As we continued enjoying our midday meal and sharing stories of other wonders and experiences, Renee waddled over to me. I kissed her round belly since it was the first thing to me.

"Get up, girl. I need a real hug!" I eased out of my chair and stepped away from the table to bear hug my best friend since the 7th grade, Renee Torrez Watson Escobar. The fiery half-Mexican, half-Black fair-skinned girl with long curly ponytails and faint freckles that I met on that very first day of school. As we held each other tightly, I had some flashes of our memories together and how she had always been with me. How grateful I was to have had a girlfriend such as her.

Renee just let her tears fall and kept bumping me with her big belly before she pulled back and gazed at me. Her face was so calm with no blemishes or wrinkles. It was soft and bright. She glowed from the inside like a beautiful blooming flower.

"Marie! A baby!" she said loudly, and I hugged her again. With excitement building I expressed my feelings, "Nay, he promised everything we desired and more. He makes it all possible for his friends. What a wonderful heavenly father we have in Jehovah. I love you, Nay-Nay! We made it to have these blessings, and… I'm having a baby! Jae and I are having a baby! Growing in me is Jae-Sung's baby… My baby! …I will have four children! Can you believe it has come true? Oh, Renee!" My cheek muscles burned from smiling so much. It was a good thing.

She exhaled, laughing for a few minutes before adding, "Marie, I am so… I can't even say… but you… you have given me so much, my beautiful strong sistah. So much. I mean, it was you… you just kept telling me over and over how you wanted to be the best mother possible. How studying the truth helped to know in your heart that Jae-Sung was only sleeping in God's memory. You said to me several times that if you just do as Jehovah asks, follow His son Jesus's example the best you can, and He will help you do the rest. You said, He would wake him up; the earth would go back to being a paradise; everything and everyone wicked and the badness of the past would be gone; and people who serve him would have happiness forever. Jehovah promised it, you said. You believed so deeply that you had this tranquility, and you were happy in the faith and hope you had been waiting for. I told Tony how you were different, and we didn't understand how you could be this way as a widow raising triplets! Some Jehovah Witnesses just happened to knock on our door one day, and we started asking questions to find out what was so special to make you so calm and happy. Things happened so quickly. I couldn't reach you to talk. We saw things clearly and as a family, we followed the road map Jehovah gave us. Look where we are now. It's all because you never stopped being my true friend. You wanted me to live forever, too. I'm so thankful to you; to Him."

She exploded with an avalanche of tears. I wasn't any better. Mine ran down my face so fast as if they were racing to get to my chin. "Oh, Nay-Nay… we are here receiving these wonderful gifts of happiness because of His undeserved loving kindness. Everyone made their own choice to serve Him or not. We both are reaping those promised benefits for being obedient. I remember daily looking at that mural painting on the wall of my dining room in South Korea. I used to imagine myself, Jae, my friends, and family all there. The triplets and I would make up stories about being there in the future. Renee, I always saw you there with me! Never without you. But I didn't try to force you. I just told you how I felt and why; you were open to listening sometimes. Renee, you even came to my baptism in Seoul because it was important to me. You supported me even when you weren't interested in learning about Jehovah. Just like my parents, Celeste, and Adam... Things just unfolded once things were reset. I found out all this wonderful news. I mean, I had no idea Kang, Nari, and Trey began studying before they left Lyon. Trey's sisters were witnesses in the same congregation as my play-cousin, Navya in England I didn't know Navya had been sharing things with Letti working with her at the museum. Or...Oh, and the surprise that Louis "ARRTI" had been studying with a colleague who was a witness around the same time we had gone to Disneyland. We didn't know Tangee and Louis, their kids, and her brother, Tyriq, and his entire family were here until we bumped into them leaving a convention we were assigned to attend. Tangee-girl screamed when she saw us! When we had them over a few weeks ago, Louis told us he was baptized six months before Tangee. I couldn't stop laughing because he nudged me and said, "I told you I was cooler than you thought I was." Renee laughed harder, wiping the wetness from her face. Then I squeezed her hands resting in mine and told her, "Renee, we are here in this beautiful place together. Who knows who else we will see in due time. We'll find out what other magnificent surprises Jehovah has in-store for us."

I dried my face and took a few deep breaths. Then I inquired, "That reminds me, when are you going to visit your parents? Is auntie Marianna going to stay with you for a while?" She sniffled before sharing their travel plans, "My father and his wife are working with a group on an environmental project, where they live. So, he said they will come visit after the baby comes. Yes, my mother will be on her way next week to stay a while.

We're so excited. Chris keeps saying Abuela, like it's her name! Maybe you can come visit while she's here. Oh, yes please?""Jae told us, we will be getting a family work assignment soon, so I'll have to see. But if we can, that would be fantastic. If not, we will make a special trip to see her. In any case, I can't wait to see young and healthy Tia Marianna, Uncle Henry, and Ms. Olivia." She moaned in agreement with my delight in reconnecting with her awakened parents again.

Renee hugged me again and shared more news, "Antonio and I decided that since you named Christopher, we will give this baby one of their auntie Rhee's names too. If it's a boy, he will be Cameron Ahlyus and if it's a girl, Caleighsa Ambrea." I clapped my hands, giggling from the honored privilege of naming their coming new baby. Renee smirked, then added, "Yeah, they weren't too strange, and we liked them!" We laughed about that.

With all that had been going on, I once again had forgotten my faint curiosity about those people walking in the distance. We resumed passing plates, eating, and laughing. Jae-Sung squeezed my hand resting on the table and whispered, "Marie, you… didn't tell me… until now. You… you win. Oh baby, I love you, so much." Instinctively, I responded "I love you, too," with a quick peck to his lips and a smile. *(I win!)*

A few minutes later, I was looking down at my plate of fruit when from close behind me, I heard a voice say, "Good day to you all. Thank you for inviting me to join the festivities. Is there any watermelon or pineapple?" My ears began to tingle hearing words that slowly traveled to my brain triggering a few hazy memories from my childhood. My eyes fluttered with each symbol registering with the familiar pitch and tone. Jae lifted my hand and tenderly kissed it while I looked up to notice just about everybody had paused from their conversations. They were all smiling so wide their grins seemed to stretch up trying to meet the corners of their eyes.

My mother nodded with a soft moan, pointing to the slices of juicy pink, red, purple, and yellow watermelons while liquid rippled down her glowing brown face. Simultaneously without looking, her hand found my father's hand and she held on tightly as she stood up slowly. My father didn't seem to have words and looked as though he too was smiling and leaking from his eyes while rising from his seat. I was just about to turn around from my seated position when the person who spoke from behind me came close to my right ear and said, "Ah… you know, I'm not a boney sloth anymore but I bet I can still run faster than you can."

Instantly more memories came to me, and my mind raced… *(Everything comes in Jehovah's due time. Not before. He decides who is in his kingdom paradise. He is loving, forgiving and reads all hearts. Heavenly Father… Is it… Is it time? Really? Is it? Oh, is it?)* My heart felt like it was twirling inside me, but I still didn't move. I was so eager and excited that I held onto the air locked in my lungs. Jae-Sung kissed my cheek, then lovingly whispered, "Breathe, baby. Breathe."

I exhaled and inhaled before quickly standing up from the table. Swinging my body around so fast, I almost knocked over the chair with my motion. I surveyed the man starting from his feet. My mind seemed to recognize exactly what was in front of my eyes as they scanned him. Standing in brown sandals were some long toes and seeing him playfully wiggle them made me giggle. My eyes confirmed his loose-fitting cream slacks and long legs. *(He's tall!)* Then a relaxed soft khaki short-sleeve shirt. His arms were naturally muscular, and his skin was the color of caramel. *(Just like mine.)*

When my eyes got up to his narrow chin and long nose, I giggled. As soon as my eyes locked onto his honey-colored orbs, I couldn't hold in any longer. My heart recognized the beautiful person before me. "Maxie! Maxie!" His straight white teeth peeking through his soft full lips displaying a brilliant smile called me to inch forward. He tilted his head, holding out his arms for me, and said, "Goodness, you've filled out. Didn't you?" He let out a boisterous laugh that tickled my inner ears with this magnificent melody of sounds while I flopped into his arms. My twin brother scooped me up and tightly locked onto me. For a few minutes, the connective feeling was as familiar as being in utero and as comforting as being swaddled in a soft warm blanket. I felt as though I was high in the clouds and being spun around like fluffy cotton candy onto a stick. Simultaneously, I laughed and cried with each sensation from touching, squeezing, and kissing my twin again. A flash came to me, and I remembered the same happy feeling from that early morning of April 28, 1999, while under the Arc de Triomphe. It was our birthday. We had turned eleven years old. He had me on his back for a piggyback ride pose for photos. I remembered kissing his cheeks and him saying, "Don't you lick me!" I did and he squealed, shouting, "You're so weird! Kristoff, carry her. She's too heavy!" Kristoff laughed and said, "Nope, that's your twin. I have no sister. So, tag you are it!" It was vividly clear in my mind now. Max's skin, his hair was just as soft as back then. I confirmed it from the memory that I didn't even know I had before now. And just like that day, my brother had a light scent of sweet vanilla. I shouted again, "Oh, Max! You're awake now! Oh Maxie!"

In only seconds, our parents were hugging the two of us. It was a promised moment at last come true. Chevalier Maximillian Delacroix was awake. I stepped back to let them hold their son. My mother and father kept saying, "Mon fils (my son)" over and over as they kissed him. Jae grabbed my hand smiling. I turned to him shouting with glee, "Jae, it's... it's him! He's awake! My brother! Chevalier Maximilian is here... Oh, Jae! Look!"

Jae-Sung had already sprung to his feet to embrace me while I said these words, feeling overwhelmed with more moments of our past dreams becoming reality. Panting with emotional cries over Jae-Sung's shoulder, I opened my eyes to notice a beautiful woman with long blonde curls embracing my oncle Andreas. They were standing together further away from the table, but I could see him pointing in my direction. Instinctively, it was my tante Nannette now awake. I knew it was because she was laughing while he kept kissing her just about everywhere on her face. Their daughters, Bridgette, and Geneviève, along with Amelia and Louie, Gert, Chevalier, and Lylah and Wolfgang's family rushed over to join him in the giving and receiving joyful love.

Overflowing with joy, I shouted, "Kristoff! It's Maxie! Tante! Oh, merci beaucoup, père celeste (Aunt! Thank you, so much, heavenly father)!"

My parents had Jolie, Jae, and Jin gathered around their uncle and the three gave him several kisses and hugs. Still in Jae-Sung's arms, I heard Jae Lune's voice from behind me say, "Uncle Max, we have the same eyes. Just like mom. Grandma used to tell me I reminded her of you."

Max replied, "Thank you for giving my mother a smile for me."

Jolie added, "We are brown; so that is something we have the same."

"Oui. You said you like to paint. I did too at your age, so that is two things," he said, hugging her again.

"I'm good at chess..." Jin put it out there.

His challenge was accepted when Max excitedly responded with "Indeed, young nephew than we shall play!"

Our older cousins, Tamera and Sam had bolted to Max and were already embracing him and laughing. After hugging our aunt Nanette, I saw Kristoff moving toward me with tears in his eyes and a giant smile. My heart knew he was going right to his best buddy, Max. My father's sister, Nannette, Andreas, and other cousins were smiling, waving, and coming in my direction to be reunited with us. On the way, the Cheng families, Escobar's, Hamilton's, and Haeun Do SI and Ami were being introduced and embracing my aunt. Jae-Sung turned my body around still squeezing me firmly. At one point, he even lifted me off the ground in celebration of everything.

And then. . . Blinking to clear the glossiness from my happiness tears, right in front of me, I saw a tall, handsome Asian man coming into view, as he stood a few feet away. He wore casual gray slacks and a dark button-down short-sleeve shirt. His hair was black, straight, and short. His face was smooth and kind, maybe a little unsure. I pushed my body back away from embracing Jae-Sung and bit down on my bottom lip before covering it with a few fingers.

"Did I spin you too much?" he said playfully. I shook my head and moaned no.

"Marie are you alright?" he asked curiously, searching for answers in my eyes because I kept my hand over my mouth. I nodded and moaned yes. Then I leaned my upper body to the left and directed him to turn around slowly with my eye code gestures, which I had learned years ago from his K-Pop brothers. Jae-Sung stopped grinning. His eyes grew large as saucers. He glanced back at the table to see his mother's face beaming holding aunt Teng's hand, and SI, and Kang smiling wide. He snapped his head back toward me, slowly shaking it with a creased brow and trembling lips. Our eyes locked in their connection. "Oui, Jae-Sung. Oui." After I said it, Jae shut his eyes whimpering. Holding his hand, I turned him around to face his father in front of him. Jae-Sung and Ji-Hoon Kim were so close they could reach out and touch. In seconds, Ji-Hoon held his son's cheek and Jae opened his eyes. I peeled his fingers away from my hand and backed away. Jae-Sung fell to the grass while covering his face with his hands. A wave of memories must have come to him, because he was seemingly trying to muffle cries from his ten-year-old self still inside of him. He was also laughing because it was combined with the euphoria from his heart's gratitude. I noticed Kang and SI wiping their eyes and hugging each other.

The traditionally proud, world-famous concert pianist, Ji-Hoon Kim was now awake. But now he was submissively kneeling on the grass to be at eye level with his son. While holding his face tenderly, Ji-Hoon forced Jae's face up to read his eyes. Jae-Sung saw the chiseled young face of his smiling father, who grabbed him into a smothering hug and expressed his joy with gregarious laughter. Jae-Sung patted his father's back and released one word, "Appa!" I witnessed Jae's shoulders relax when his father said to him very clearly in English, "Jae-Sung, my son, you have grown up well. I am proud of you. Thank you. I am deeply grateful for a son that has honored me with a good and pure heart. My son, you... you are my great joy. I love you, very much."

Raising from the grass, they didn't let go or stopped inspecting the beauty of each other's faces. Min Cha hurried toward her first husband. She had every intention of greeting and hugging him but as she got closer, he saw her and immediately recognized her youthful beauty from their past and returned to his knees lowly bowing before her. When she stopped in front of him, he said, "Good and honorable woman, I humbly request forgiveness for my foolishness."

Min Cha guided him up to his feet. As she touched him, he tapped his still lowered forehead with the palms of her hands. Once on his feet, she lunged forward, forcing him to stand upright as she smashed herself upon him. Holding him in this embrace of friendly affection, she said words he didn't expect to hear, "No, Ji-Hoon, no. It is Jehovah, who sees what man cannot see. 1 Samuel 16:7 says he alone can see the heart. Jehovah saw goodness in you. That is all that matters. Welcome, Ji-Hoon."

Ji-Hoon squinted his eyes and said, "Who? Who is Jehovah?"

Still with rolling tears, Min Cha smiled and said, "In time, you will learn all you need to know. We are happy you are here with us. So, so very happy, my friend."

Jae-Sung wrapped his arms around his parents, delivering and receiving loving kisses while the three were enfolded with one another. Everyone was young, healthy, and full of energy and excitement.

Gert and Chevalier Ratcliff

Min Sun Gil and Chul

Haeun Do SI & her daughter Ami

Wolfgang and Lylah Gauthier

Their daughters Sonia Gauthier and Janelle Tapeneli

Gauthier grandchildren,

François and Marcelle

Stephanie and Simeon
Hamilton

Their daughter Joy

Antonio and Renee Escobar

Christopher Escobar

Hana Cheng

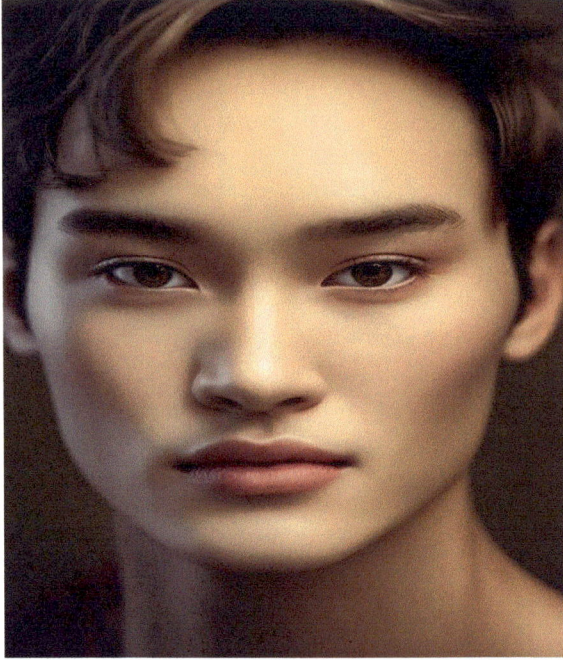

SI and Soo Cheng

Kang and Nari Cheng

Auntie Teng Cheng

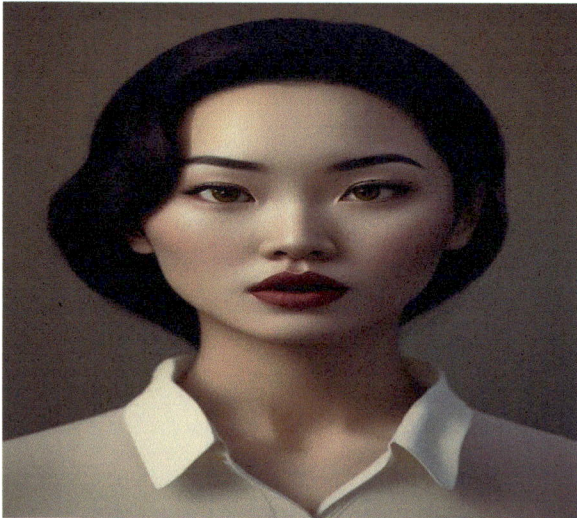

Teng's niece Suzy Goe

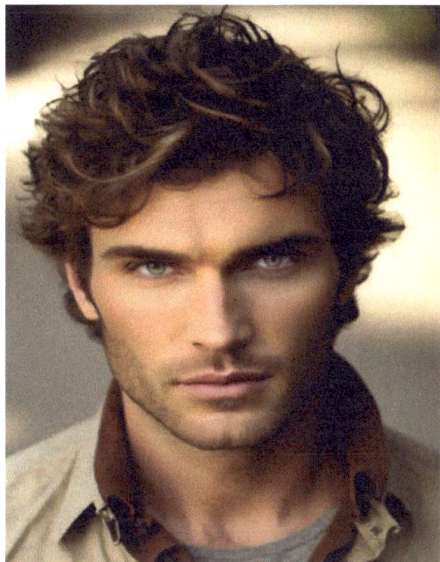

Nannette Delacroix-Moreau and Andreas Moreau

Geneviève & Amelia

Daniella & Louie

Cousin Tamera Brown-Marino & Kevin Marino

Her older brother, Sam Dupree Jr. & Keenan

Beau-Père,

Ji-Hoon Kim

Belle-Mère,

Min Cha Kim

As all came closer to reunite or meet those joining us, Jolie slipped her hand into mine. Her sweet voice echoed, "Hal-abeoji. Jehovah keeps doing amazing things for us to be happy. Mama, I... I love him."

I moaned in agreement and kissed her little nose. "I love him too, pretty one. I love him, too."

Jolie released my hand and rushed over to her father and grandparents, Min-Cha and Ji-Hoon, who were cheerfully embracing their awakened daughter, Ae-Cha.

Jae's older sister
Ae-Cha Kim

Mon père impressionnant,

Jean-Philippe' Delacroix

Ma magnifique mère
Delphine Delacroix

Mon frère jumeau
Chevalier-Maximilian Delacroix

At every turn of my head, my eyes captured the vision of delightful joy and tears from everyone we had invited. I placed my hand over my mouth, muffling my laughter as I too had running tears watching these wonderful moments unfold right in front of my very eyes.

(Oh, heavenly father, how wonderful you are to your friends!)

Just minutes after having those thoughts, a set of long strong caramel-colored arms engulfed me from behind. Being six foot-four inches tall like Pawpaw, Chevalier Maximilian Delacroix leaned forward, resting his big head on my left shoulder. I felt his breath move my hair and inhaled his vanilla fragrance through my nose and moan feeling contentment from his presence. I reached up and caressed his smooth jawline with my hand, nuzzling our cheeks together. He kissed my cheek twice, moaning with a chuckle. But only seconds later, he had the nerve to say, "Uh, yeah, Marie... So, are we racing or what?"

I snorted, before I playfully elbowed him in his ribcage and took off running into the flat land grassy meadow.

His loud laughter could be heard close behind me, as he shouted, "Really, Marie, really! You... know... what..."

Laughing, I picked up my running speed, and it came to my mind once again...

(Living forever is going to be the most amazing time!)

66. JGGAM

Over the course of my pregnancy, the blissful experience of our miracle child, caused me more glee just about every minute of every day. Not only from the sensational movements of our growing gift but the many changes happening in my body, and the food cravings. I said one day, "This little one wants so much fruit."

My brother reached over and tapped my belly, then asked, "Is it watermelon and pineapple? If so, he is a boy!"

I moaned yes, and added, "Grapes, berries too but just about every other day I have a taste for chilled dragon fruit. It's weird. I don't know why."

Pausing from picking a few ripe avocados and onions, Min Cha, and my mother snickered and glanced up at each other. Jae-Sung's eyes darted toward me from across the garden. Seconds later, he proudly stated, "Oh, I bet you do know why. Dragon fruit. Yeah, it's a boy. Ha! Ha! Ha!"

"What?" I stopped digging the small hole in the ground for Max to place the zucchini plant and stared at him for about three seconds. In the silence Jae gave me those rapid moving eyebrows and then it came to me like ice cubes down my back. I shuddered with a yelp. "Oh... yeah." I said, trying to hold in my amusement and slight embarrassment. At that exact moment, my baby kicked inside me, and I jumped from the shock. *(Did...did you hear your father? I bet you are a boy.)*

When our children rubbed my belly, there were constant snickers and giggles. The three amigos pretended to be exchanging information with their new sibling simply with their hands resting on my skin. Daily, they read, sang, and talked to the baby. It was like listening to a one-way telephone conversation. *(Too funny.)*

Jae, and our parents regularly expressed their delightfulness in this coming addition that's development came without discomfort or complications like from a time long gone. One of Jae-Sung's favorite things to do was to caress my uncovered, growing belly and read and sing to our baby. "This is the most amazing thing! I can't believe we are having a baby, Marie." He teared up a lot from the experience of being a father again but this time from the very beginning, he said. My entire pregnancy had been filled with thrilling moments that I never imagined I could experience, and I was thankful for every one of them.

At around my six-month mark, our jubilations expanded when my auntie Hellene, her husband Carter, and grand-mère Marie joined us. My father was beyond words greeting his awakened mother at a still pond one early morning, and my cousins Tamera and Sam were just as elated to see their mother and her husband. They were now being given an opportunity to learn about Jehovah and live forever too. Then when Jae and I shared the news of our coming miracle, there were so many tears from the shock and excitement, we cried all over again.

Auntie Hellene and Carter O'Neil

Grand-mère, Marie Delacroix

I don't know if it was the beauty of our new surroundings, the tame and peaceful animals, their young and healthy bodies, Max being here, or if it was simply my being pregnant that did it, but our awakened relatives and friends learned quickly and decided they wanted this wonderful life too.

Although I had lots of visits, meals, love, and support, during my last trimester I had this seamlessly never-ending flow of quality time with my sister, Celeste. The two of us talked in French all the time; knitted and crocheted a few blankets, embroidered some cute little hanbok-like onesies; she braided my hair, and we took long walks simply to put our toes in the ocean. We both agreed it reminded us of the weeks I spent with her in Bellevue. Initially I was surprised that she freed her schedule more to be with me, but I was deeply touched by her sisterly love and compassion. I adore my younger sister, Celeste "Glee/Joy" Williamson.

There were so many hugs and kisses every time our loved ones saw me. My cheeks and tummy were the targeted areas, and it tickled the bigger I got. Eventually my waddling around became another new experience that I welcomed with a great deal of amusement, since I often was the comic relief punchline for my brother Max's jokes.

"Wow! Is it like a whale or elephant calf, in there?"

"There she blows! Oh, my bad, Marie. I thought you farted!"

"Don't move. I'm translating. Let me tap back. 'Message received. Stop. Need more fruit and rice. Stop.' Hey don't laugh. Seriously, Marie, it's Morse code. See wait. Ha! It's a boy, he kicked me back. Hee-hee." Max kept me and everyone else laughing all the time. (Clown! I knew he and Jae would be best buds. Max and Kristoff are very close to Trey, Kang, SI, Joon, Tommy, Sam, Ki-Noah, and Chase too. Wait, why are they teaching them stupid Korean K-Pop idol games? Hold on... Are they making up new ones? Oh brother.)

On the snowy winter afternoon of December 3rd, a tearful Jae-Sung had a stretched and twisted face. My husband actually couldn't speak for a while after he held my hand and witnessed the pain-free birth of our miracle. It must have been the shock and reality coming to fruition. I think he had to adjust, maybe.

Jae Lune wiped his tears as he played mellow music on the piano with his brother Jin Soleil, who kept snickering and nudging him for messing up the keystrokes. Their sister Jolie cheerfully announced to all in the room, "I'm a big sister and not the smallest, anymore." I giggled and told her, "Yes, pretty one. That's right. I can tell you that being a big sister is the best fun. You will be great at it."

Our parents, and my grand-mère were ecstatic and glowing with happiness from the miracle that Jehovah had given to me; no, he gave to us. All I could do was giggle, holding her in my arms. Ji-Hoon wildly embraced Jae but the two only laughed with falling tears. When my father hugged Jae, he said, "Une merveille en effet. Toutes nos felicitations! (A miracle indeed. Congratulations)!"

A few minutes later, when Min Cha reached out as Jae handed her our fourth child, she cooed holding the small bundle. Then she said, "naui jal saeng-gin sonyeon (my handsome boy)."

Jae-Sung whispered, "Gamsahabnida, Yeohowayeo, (Thank you, Jehovah)." Minutes later, he exhaled, moving closer to sit next to my bedside. Jae tilted his head to connect with my eyes. Contact. Then he loudly announced, "Je t'aime, ma Sable Arabe, (I Love you, my Arabian Sand)!"

A low rumble of laughter filled the room after Jolie chimed in, "I love you too, Appa (daddy). Wait, uh... Were you talking to me? Or was that to Mawmaw?"

In her excitement, my mother shouted, "Oh, Frenchman! Kiss me this instant!" as she snatched my father's shirt collar and pulled him to her lips. He grabbed her waist and leisurely kissed her several more times as they giggled. Feeling the light breeze in the air, my eyes were glossy from the collide of emotions starting from calm and growing to explosive excitement. They seemed like ocean waves hitting against shoreline rocks when they surged through me.

I turned to my husband, demanding, "Kiss me… my idol king." Gradually he came out of his cosmic daze and laughed before oozing his soft peachy thin lips over mine. There was a distinct scent of mint chocolate and I snickered from the fragrance tickling my senses. Jae pulled away only to plop his wide tongue over my left cheek and lick. As I squealed, "Eeww," he announced smacking his lips, "yes, you still taste like chocolat français." The room rang with low and high-pitched laughter. *(He's so silly.)* Jae looked at me more seriously and then whispered, "You are my life's ultimate joy, sweet radiant love. Merci."

I wanted to express my happiness but couldn't get my words out. "Jae, we…" He touched my chin then peering deeply into my eyes, he said, "You are my air to breathe, Marie. Amazing woman of my soul, the rhythm of your heartbeat is known to me and mirrors my own because you and I are truly complete as one. Now tell me, my love, what name shall we have this time. As my most precious and sweetest gift, whatever you wish, you shall have it." His poetic words touched me deeply, my heart fluttered, and I grinned when he winked at me.

Moving closer to me, Jin piped up, "Well, we three already have the coolest names but maybe, we should just call 'em, Chuck." I snorted before laughing as he did the quick up and down eyebrow motions like his father. *(He's so adorable.)*

Holding his sleeping new grandchild, my father said, "Words are powerful. Think carefully like you did for all your children's magnificent names." Ji-Hoon agreed with, "Ah! Something to create a melody!" while lightly touching the full round cheeks of his grandchild in my father's arms.

Quietly sipping hot lavender lemon tea and waiting for her turn to bond, my grandmama, Marie added, "Oui, quelque chose de joli à dire avec du sens (Yes, something pretty to say with meaning)."

Jae grabbed a notebook and pen to write down whatever we came up with. Jolie put in her idea, saying, "Jehovah makes us happy. Let's make it something happy."

Ae Cha moaned in agreement with that reasoning as she brought me some infused honeydew, cucumber, and mint water, while my mother helped me sit up in bed a bit more. While I took several large gulps of refreshment, Delphine Delacroix in her wisdom shared, "Make a list of names and then consolidate. Really analyze the unique features and it will come to you. That is how we named you and your brother."

I smiled at her. She leaned closer to my bedside and said, "I love you, my beautiful brown child. You too are my favorite." I wept a little hearing her say that and seeing liquid joy also fall from her eyes.

A bit later, Jae had a short list of names for us to choose from, but he said, "Baby, I named Jolie, and you had no say. So, you decide this time."

"Awww." (He's so sweet.)

After careful consideration of our three amigo's names, and pondering on Jae-Sung and my life together, the happy memories from before and the moments we have now, I decided on names not on the list but what best fit the beautiful miracles we were given.

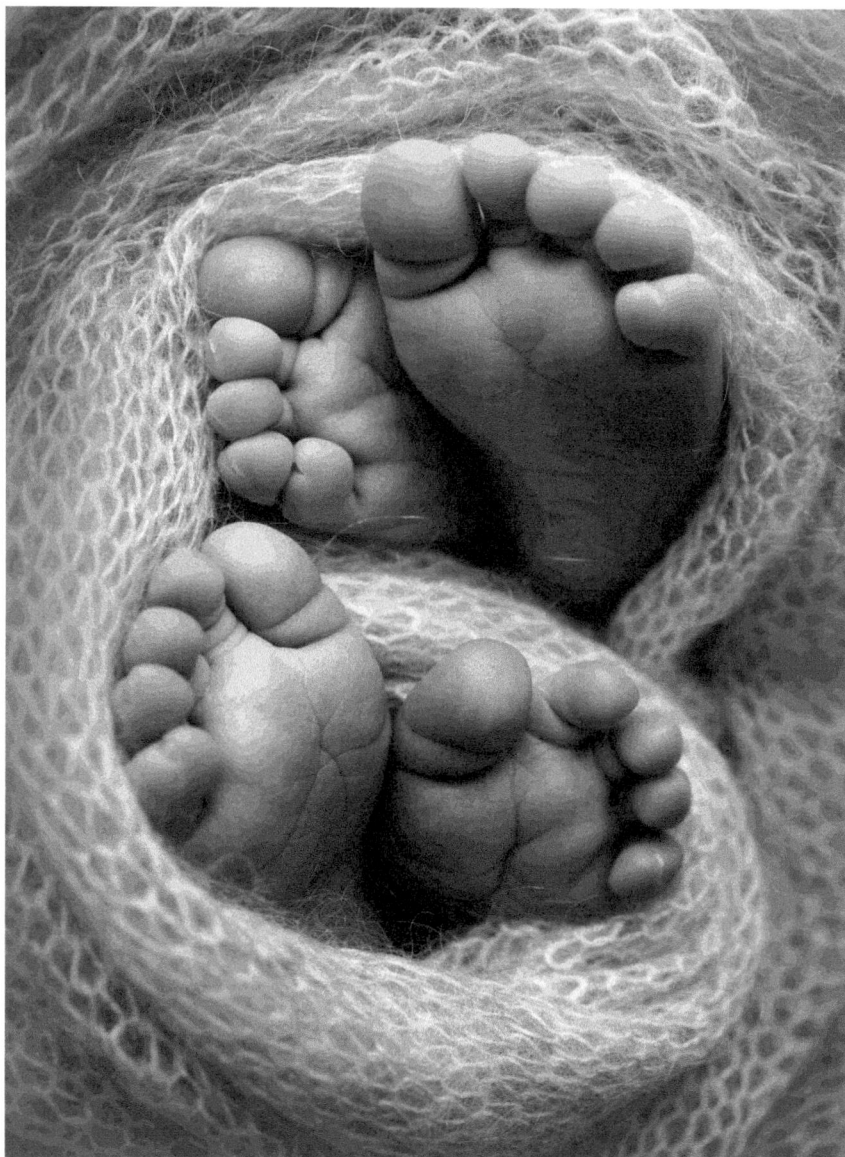

67. Euphoria

As the seasons changed, each day brought new experiences, amusement and fun adventures for me and Jae-Sung as we raised our children together, in this tranquil place of an earthly paradise.

Our "Belle Cadeaux (Beautiful gifts)," as we referred to all our children, continued to grow tall, smart, healthy, and happy. Each one enhancing the characteristics of another that expands and balances our multi-culturally diverse family of seven.

Although our latest magnificent miracles have cute dimples and features like Jae-Sung, and the other like me, they are like their siblings unique but perfect blends of the two of us. It makes me laugh thinking about it because my father has always said something like that about me.

Our son, Joyuex Brillante Étoile pronounced Jwah-yer Bril-yawnce Et-wawl. He is very inquisitive. His name means

Cheerful/Happy, Bright Star. Joyuex loves listening to the sounds of nature, building things with his hands, and helping others care for the larger animals. He is playful and quick to explore and try new things. Joyuex is fascinated with the universe and sky, often sitting for hours just stargazing. He loves listening to different types of music and sounds while watching animals like large cats, elephants, horses, and flying creatures. He has a low tone voice but when he sings it gets much higher. He loves all types of things to eat, especially grapes with rice, watermelon with cucumbers, feta and mint, any kind of potatoes, and chilled dragon fruit. Joyeux's twin sister was born five minutes after he arrived.

Our daughter's name is Janae'a Océan Eau and it's pronounced Jaw-nai-yah Osee On-oh. Her name means God is Gracious, Ocean Water. She is very curious and observant, seemingly trying to problem solve and figure out the mechanics of how things operate. Janae'a loves all sorts of flowers, and is very attached to wild cats, quokkas, and mammals. She hums all the time with an ear for music at this early age. She is very feminine, yet direct when questioning to understand. She acknowledges that she is the smallest and youngest and will humbly follow the lead of her older siblings. Janae'a has a keen interest in life within the oceans and loves to eat, especially different types of berries, cheese, green leafy vegetables, chickpeas, and coconut.

Our twins do just about everything together. Jae gets a thrill out of watching my reaction to things they do. Like when Janae'a gives a sample of food to Joyeux to try from her plate. No matter how many times I tell her, "Chérie, ton frère a la même chose, (Dearest, your brother has the same)." She does it anyway. Once I just threw my hands up because she kept doing it, and Jae said, "She's, her mother. You did the same thing to me in that restaurant after your parents pranked us. Ha! I bet your brother will say you did it to him. Bossy food pusher. Yeah, let's ask him!"

Laughing, he ducked as I tossed a few grapes at him, shouting, "Oh, you, hush!"

Our triplets are amazing young people. They have expanded their musical and art interests, their knowledge of languages, history, and take more time to explore animal habitats, the universe, learning how to be big siblings, while joyfully helping others. They each take turns teaching Joyuex and Janae'a just for the fun of it. They loved to read and play music, while patiently teaching them how to play instruments too. It's so cute when we connect with the Escobar's. The twins plot with their daughter, Caleighsa Ambrea to mimic the triplets' actions because they pretend, they are triplets too. Renee and I laugh every time they do it.

(What a fun little friendship they have.)

When their cousins or friends come over, they include the twins in games and activities even though they are smaller. The triplets also share their animal caretaking assignments with them. Jae has Janae'a help him feed sheep, a hippopotamus family, and a few lamas, while Jin and Jolie take Joyuex to ride on lions, bears, and baby zebras after their study and chores are completed. Just like Jae and I, everyone loves being in and around water. Our family time is not only in the forest but also at the ocean beach or in our clear pool under the waterfall.

Daily there are moments of spectacular splendor in being a mother, wife, sister, daughter, and friend. There is never a second thought or feeling of sorrow or sadness, pain, fear, or distress. We live in ultimate contentment and unimaginable tranquility. My heart overflows with the marvels of wonder with my truest love, my twin brother, our beautiful Moon, Sun, Pretty Sand, Star, and Ocean, our families, and friends all living in this amazing place, where animals are tame, everyone is genuinely kind, and loving as one large family. We all worship Jehovah as he makes our load light with universal order and peace everywhere, while we enjoy our constant youthful vigor and eternal wellness. I have no other wants or desires; everything, I mean everything is fulfilled in abundance.

*Our gorgeous, meticulous, and savvy
Jae Lune Philippe'*

Our brilliant, handsome, and playful
Jin Soleil Maximilian

Our beautiful, elegant and studious
Jolie Arabe Sable

Our cute, curious and charming
Joyuex Brillante Étoile

Our adorable, clever and enchanting
Janae'a Océan Eau

Jae-Sung and I ~~While we~~ gazed at the sphere of light, I exhaled and said, "My love, how wonderful life is with you here in paradise. I love you, Jae."

He turned to me and tenderly held my face with his smooth hands. Then our eyes met. Contact.

"Chantal-Marie, you are my most precious gift. The brilliance of your magnificent eyes, that beautiful, caramel skin; the fragrance of your soft, wavy hair, your warm, gigantic, loving heart and radiant smile. Oh, that tasty, chocolate sweetness of you. Mmmh. My glorious treasure, you are my air to breathe. I am alive because you were made for me. Sweetheart for eternity you are mine and I am yours. I love you too, baby."

(Oh baby, the way you...) While his long index finger stroked my right cheek, it just came out, "Jae-Sung, you're so romantic. Baby, you sing to me even when there is no music playing."

He paused for a moment to inhale as his wide tongue peeked through his lips to slowly moisten them. Then moving his hand to lift my chin, he flirtatiously raised his left eyebrow, and said, "Now, tell me, my sexy aegyo, where ya going?"

Giggling, I delivered a sweet kiss to his thin, soft peachy-pink lips. Detecting a hint of mint chocolate, I smiled. Then proudly answered, "Anywhere with you, my love."

Smirking, Jae stated, "Aww, so... I am your idol king."

I quickly nodded in agreement. He winked at me, while displaying a broad grin showing his dimple. Moments later, I laid my head on his shoulder as he leisurely hummed the romantic melody of Arabian Sand, and we watched the glow of tangerine, gold, and magenta streaks of sky-lights transition to midnight darkness lit brightly by trillions of dancing star clusters.

And Then...

Our heavenly father knows all things, including what is best for us, and he continues to reveal his plans for an eternity of glorious gifts for his friends.

On a beautiful early autumn afternoon, we joined several friends and some of our relatives for lunchtime fun, after the completion of an area building project. While enjoying the delicious dishes brought to share, stories, and laughter, music, and games in a vast green grassy field surrounded by hills, bushes, and trees, another group of smiling men and women gradually approached our outdoor festivities.

Sounds of surprise and excitement, along with heartfelt "Welcome" from different voices echoed through the air. The unexpected smiling friends came with joyful tidings and something new. Although we could see our children off playing in an animal race with the larger group about a quarter of a mile away, we did not take action to get their attention.

Jae and I, along with other adults began rushing over to join in the greeting merriment. I glanced around and saw my parents with delightful smiling faces. My mother frantically tugged at my father's shirt as he laughed before kissing her cheek, and happily embracing her. Min Cha, Ji-Hoon, Kang, Nari, Min-Ji, Eun-Woo, Satoshi, Yukiko, Mayumi, Dene, Lorelle, Cedric, Clint, Selma, LaRoyce, Hellene, Carter, Lurell Ann, her husband, John-Robert, and their daughter, Paula Ann were already in a huddle excitedly greeting them. While Max, Trey, Ae-Cha, Kristoff,Ohanaka, Daniella,

Sam, Sheila, Suzette, Tangee, Louis, Ophelia, Stanley, and Chase stopped their game and enthusiastically rushed to introduce themselves. I turned to Jae-Sung, who looked shocked with wide eyes. He made his way over to me standing next to a magnolia tree. Holding out his hand, he clasped onto mine firmly like a powerful magnet. My heart felt as though it were swirling in my chest from anxiousness. Grinning, I whispered, "Jae... Jae is that...? Oh, does this mean we will get to...?"

Turning his face to see me, Jae-Sung smiled wide showing all his pretty white teeth. He nodded with high-spirited joy, and said, "Come on, babe. Come on." Our feelings of exuberance rapidly increased with each daylight second. Giggling, I grabbed his hand with both of mine as he briskly led me across the field to meet the amazing people now joining us.

Everyone was thrilled to see...

Moments Of Reset
A New Beginning
Of
Endless Peace,
Happiness
And True Love

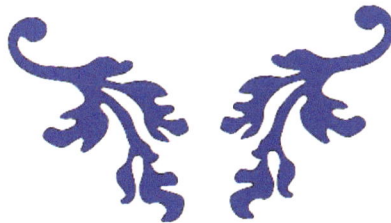

O'Shan Waters

Ms. Waters is an African American, Pacific Northwest native, who has authored short stories and descriptive reflections in poetry for over thirty years. After the completion of her first novel, Moments With You in 2021, she has continued to hone her craft, while expanding on the life, friends, history, family, and relationships of Chantal-Marie Delacroix.

These blended genre novels are part of The Moments Collection. The mega novel *Moments With You* (2022) began her published author journey. The prequel love story of Philippe' and Delphine in *Making French Chocolate* (2023), grew like a creative wildfire right on the heels of publishing the first story. Next came the bonus stories of lineage in *Moments In Time* (2023), and now a new beginning in the finale, *Moments Of Reset* (2023). O'Shan took time to think of the best way to share the realistic 'forever after' experience as seen through her eyes. Still guided by the inspirational quote from author Toni Morrison, "If there's a book that you want to read, but it hasn't been written than you must write it."

The unique style and complex beauty of O'Shan's storytelling seamlessly weave in poetry, multiple cultures, music, literature, film, human behavior, trauma, grief, endurance, friendship, hope, faith, and love are her standalone writing style. With an impact to having these stories part of a regular re-read rotation, exploring the lives of vivid and complex characters, and finding golden nuggets of new perspectives to ponder each time. The depth and connections to each story in this collection are remarkable. Ms. Waters is grateful for your time in reading her stories. Merci.